P9-CFU-351

WITHDRAWN
CEDAR MILL LIBRARY

THE WILL TO BATTLE

Also by Ada Palmer

Too Like the Lightning
Seven Surrenders

THE WILL
TO
BATTLE

Terra Ignota,

BOOK III.

by Ada Palmer

A TOM DOHERTY ASSOCIATES Book
NEW YORK

This is a work of fiction. All of the characters, organizations, and events portrayed
in this novel are either products of the author's imagination
or are used fictitiously.

THE WILL TO BATTLE

Copyright © 2017 by Ada Palmer

All rights reserved.

Edited by Patrick Nielsen Hayden

A Tor Book
Published by Tom Doherty Associates
175 Fifth Avenue
New York, NY 10010

www.tor-forge.com

Tor® is a registered trademark of Macmillan Publishing Group, LLC.

The Library of Congress Cataloging-in-Publication Data is available upon request.

ISBN 978-0-7653-7804-0 (hardcover)
ISBN 978-1-4668-5876-3 (ebook)

Our books may be purchased in bulk for promotional, educational, or business use.
Please contact your local bookseller or the Macmillan Corporate and Premium Sales
Department at 1-800-221-7945, extension 5442, or by email at
MacmillanSpecialMarkets@macmillan.com.

First Edition: December 2017

Printed in the United States of America

0 9 8 7 6 5 4 3 2 1

TOP SECRET MATERIAL:
NOT FOR PUBLICATION OR DISTRIBUTION

THE WILL TO BATTLE

A Chronicle of Events, begun in July of the year 2454
Undertaken by MYCROFT CANNER, at the
Command of Certain Parties.

ALL CLASSIFYING BODIES MUST DECLASSIFY THIS
DOCUMENT BEFORE IT IS CONSIDERED DECLASSIFIED.

ALLIANCE TOP SECRET

Classified by: Censor Jung Ancelet Kosala; S.O. 2454-147
Reason: Military Operations, Poly-Hive Security Vulnerabilities
Declassify: August 1, 2504, subject to Senatorial approval

EUROPEAN UNION TOP SECRET—*Très Secret Défense*

Classified by: Their Majesty Prime Minister Isabel Carlos II
Reason: Hive Security Vulnerabilities, Inter-Hive Relations Risk
Declassify: August 1, 2504, subject to Parliamentary approval

GORDIAN SECRET—*Geheime Verschlußsache*

Classified by: Executive Chancellor Carlyle Hassal-Krane
Reason: Inter-Hive Relations Risk
Declassify for research access: August 1, 2459
Declassify for public: Five years after the death of J.E.D.D. Mason

IMPERIAL TOP SECRET—*SECRETISSIMA*

Classified by: Dictum Absolutum

HUMAN TOP SECRET—*Ultra Secreto Humano*

Classified by: President Vivien Ancelet
Reason: Military Operations, Hive Security Vulnerabilities
Declassify: Ten years after stabilization of current crisis

UTOPIA TOP SECRET—*Cosmic Top Secret*

Classified by: Ichabod Hubble, Harbinger Peacebonding Constellation
Reason: Safeguarding Nuclear Facilities and Weapons of Mass
Destruction
Declassify: After weapons systems are no longer a relevant threat

TOP SECRET MATERIAL:
NOT FOR PUBLICATION OR DISTRIBUTION

TOP SECRET MATERIAL:
NOT FOR PUBLICATION OR DISTRIBUTION

This Document is certified *Potentially Harmful* by the Cousins' Legal Commission, and its circulation in any form is banned for a period of five years, renewable pending review.

Cause for certification: *potential harm to the public peace, potential harm to minors herein portrayed, potential harm to Servicers herein portrayed, potential harm to Cousins herein portrayed, potential harm to real and living persons herein portrayed.*

Private access may be granted by judicial order.

Not to be published without the permissions of the Romanova Seven-Hive Council Stability Committee, the Five-Hive Committee on Dangerous Literature, Ordo Quiritum Imperatorisque Masonicorum, the Cousins' Commission for the Humane Treatment of Servicers, and His Majesty Isabel Carlos II of Spain or successor.

LET IT BE HEREBY KNOWN THAT ANY, MASON OR OTHER, WHO DARES UNLAWFULLY VIEW, CIRCULATE, REPRODUCE, TRANSFER, DISPLAY, DESTROY, OR ABUSE IN ANY WAY PART OR ALL OF THIS DOCUMENT SHALL BE SUBJECT TO THE SEVEREST EXERCISE OF THOSE CAPITAL POWERS WITH WHICH, BY MOST ANCIENT MANDATE, MASON IS INVESTED FOR THE PRESERVATION OF THE EMPIRE IN TIME OF WAR.

TOP SECRET MATERIAL:
NOT FOR PUBLICATION OR DISTRIBUTION

A SEVEN-TEN LIST

FOR *Our Changing World*

1. Cornel MASON (Mason) . . . . *Masonic Emperor*
   Mycroft "Martin" Guildbreaker
       (Mason) . . . . *Minister Porphyrogeni, Familiaris regni*
   Xiaoliu Guildbreaker (Mason) . . . . *Familiaris regni, Martin's spouse*
   Charlemagne Guildbreaker Senior
       (Mason) . . . . *Romanovan Senator, Martin's grandba'pa*

2. Bryar Kosala (Cousin) . . . . *Cousin Chair*
   Heloïse (Minor) . . . . *Cousins' Board Advising Member*
   Lorelei "Cookie" Cook
       (Cousin) . . . . *Romanovan Minister of Education, Nurturist faction leader*

3. Vivien Ancelet (Humanist) . . . . *Humanist President, Kosala's spouse*
   Jung Su-Hyeon Ancelet Kosala
       (Graylaw) . . . . *their bash'child and Ancelet's successor as Censor*
   Ganymede Jean-Louis de la Trémoïlle
       (Humanist) . . . . *former Humanist President, in custody*
   Aesop Quarriman (Humanist) . . . . . *Romanovan Senator, Olympic Champion*

4. Isabel Carlos II of Spain (European) . . . . . . *Acting European Prime Minister*
   Joyce Faust D'Arouet (Blacklaw) . . . . *Spain's fiancée*
   Mushi Mojave, Aldrin Bester, Voltaire Seldon
       (Utopians) . . . . *her hostages*
   Saladin Canner (officially deceased) . . . . *her dog*
   Julia Doria-Pamphili (European) . . . . *Head of the Sensayers' Conclave*
   Ektor Carlyle Papadelias (European) . . . . *Romanovan Commissioner General*

5. Dominic Seneschal (Blacklaw) . . . . *Acting Mitsubishi Chief Director*
   Hotaka Andō Mitsubishi
       (Mitsubishi) . . . . *Mitsubishi Chief Director, in custody*
   Danaë Marie-Anne de la Trémoïlle Mitsubishi
       (Mitsubishi) . . . . *Andō's wife, Ganymede's sister*
   Masami (reporter), Toshi (Censor's analyst),
       Hiroaki (C.F.B. staff), et al. . . . . *Mitsubishi bash'children, not set-sets*
   Carlyle Foster-Kraye de La Trémoïlle . . . . *Dominic's parishioner, sensayer*
   Jyothi Bandyopadhyay (Mitsubishi) . . . . *Greenpeace Mitsubishi Director*

6. Felix Faust (Gordian) . . . . *Headmaster of Brill's Institute*
   Jin Im-Jin (Gordian) . . . . *Speaker of the Romanovan Senate*

7. Mycroft Canner (Servicer) . . . . *The Eighth Anonymous, our chronicler*

8. Jehovah Epicurus Donatien D'Arouet Mason
       (Minor) . . . . . . *Graylaw Hiveless Tribune, Porphyrogene, Cousins' Board Advising Member, Humanist Deputy Attorney General, European Council Counsel, Mitsubishi Directorate Adviser, Gordian's rising Brain-bash' Stem, Alien, Heir Presumptive to the Throne of Spain; a God*
   Gibraltar Chagatai (Blacklaw) . . . . *His housekeeper*

9. Ojiro Cardigan Sniper (Humanist) . . . . *Thirteenth O.S., at large*
   Ockham Prospero Saneer (Humanist) . . . . *Twelfth O.S., in custody*
   Lesley Juniper Sniper Saneer (Humanist) . . . *their second in command, at large*
   Tully Mardi (Graylaw) . . . . *warmonger, their ally, at large*
   Thisbe Ottila Saneer (Humanist) . . . . *smelltrack artist, in custody*
   Cato Weeksbooth (Humanist) . . . . *mad science teacher, in custody*
   Eureka Weeksbooth (Humanist) . . . . *Cartesian set-set, at large*
   Sidney Koons (Humanist) . . . . *Cartesian set-set, in custody*
   Kat and Robin Typer (Humanists) . . . . *one in custody, one at large*

10. Achilles Mojave . . . . *a hero*
    Patroclus Aimer . . . . *his lieutenant*
    Looker, Crawler, Medic, Stander-Y, Nostand . . . . *his remaining men*
    Diverse Servicers pseudonymized . . . . *his Myrmidons*
    Private Croucher . . . . *a deserter*
    Boo . . . . *a real dog*

In Memoriam:
    Bridger . . . . *a miracle*
    Mommadoll, Nogun, Stander-G . . . . *his creations*
    Casimir Perry, a.k.a. Merion Kraye . . . . *a villain*
    The Mardi bash': Geneva, Aeneas, Jules, Chiasa (Masons), Leigh
    (Cousin), Malory, Seine (Humanists), Jie (Mitsubishi), Makenna
    (European), Mercer (Gordian), Kohaku, Luther Mardigras (Graylaws);
    their bash'children Laurel, Ken (Minors), and Ibis (Cousin); and their
    friend Apollo Mojave (Utopian) . . . . *first casualties of the war*

For Warre, consisteth not in Battell onely, or the act of fighting; but in a tract of time, wherein the Will to contend by Battell is sufficiently known: and therefore the notion of Time, is to be considered in the nature of Warre; as it is in the nature of Weather.

——Thomas Hobbes, *Leviathan* XIII

CHAPTER the FIRST

〈decorative ornament〉

We the Alphabet

Written July 6, 2454
At Alexandria

HUBRIS IT IS, READER, TO CALL ONE'S SELF THE MOST ANYTHING in history: the most powerful, the most mistreated, the most alone. Experience, and the Greek blood within my veins, teach me to fear hubris above all sins, yet, as I introduce myself again here, I cannot help but describe myself as the most undeservedly blessed man who ever lived. I, who once moved act by act through the catalogue of sins, I, cannibal, torturer, traitor, parricide, who at seventeen gave myself over to deserved execution, I, Mycroft Canner find myself at thirty-one alive, healthy, with far more liberty than I deserve, making full use of my skills in the service of not one, but several worthy masters, and even permitted to sleep at night in the arms of he whose embrace will always be the one place in this universe where I most belong, while he too lies in his proper place, on the floor outside his mistress's bedchamber.

War has not yet come, but the waters have withdrawn to form the tidal wave, leaving the beaches and their secrets bare. Hobbes tells us that war consists not in Battle only, but in that tract of time wherein the Will to Battle is so manifest that, scenting bloodlust in his fellows and himself, Man can no longer trust civilization's pledge to keep the peace. If so, we are at war. We have been these four months, since Ockham's arrest and Sniper's bullet revealed too much truth for trust to stay. But we do not know how to turn the Will to Battle into Battle. We have enjoyed three hundred years of peace, World Peace, real peace, whatever the detractors say. This generation has never met a man who met a man who marched onto a battlefield. Governments have no armies anymore, no arms. A man may kill another with a gun, a sword, a sharpened stone, but the human race no longer remembers how to turn a child of eighteen into a soldier, organize riot into battle lines, or dehumanize an enemy enough to make the killing bearable.

We will learn fast. Man is still a violent beast; I proved that thirteen years ago when the swathe of atrocities I scarred across the public conscious-ness stirred the world to scream in one voice for my blood. We will make war, but no one wants to light the first match when we do not know how fast the fuel may burn. Three hundred years ago humanity had weapons enough to exterminate ourselves a hundred times over. Now the technol-ogy that birthed those weapons is so outdated that children who split the atom for a science fair are labeled antiquarians. We have no newer weap-ons, but no one doubts that, with a month's cunning, the technologies that cook our food and slow our aging will birth horrors beyond imagining. If we survive, the wreckage of posterity will want to know how. It is for curious posterity, then, that I am now commanded to keep this chronicle.

I have done this work before. A week ago my masters presented to the world my little history of those Days of Transformation, now four months past, which left us on war's threshold. They tell me that the history has done what they had hoped: shared much of the truth, without pushing us far-ther toward the brink. My great merit as an historian is that I am known to be insane. No court or council can trust my testimony, and each reader may pick and choose what to believe, dismissing anything too unsettling as lunacy. I gave the public what it wanted of the truth, no more, leaving the pundits and propagandists free to shape opinion into faction, and fac-tion into sides and enemies.

This chronicle is different. My first history was written to be shared and used, now, by my masters. This chronicle cannot be shared, not while these secrets are still War Secrets. The powers that bid me record their doings week by week will not even let each other read the transcript. I alone enjoy this strange trust from the many leaders of what will soon be war-ring states. I hear the inner whispers of palace and boudoir, whispers which will shape armies, yet which history will never hear unless someone records them. It is this human underbelly of the war my masters bid me chronicle, not for the public, nor even for themselves, but so a record will survive, and with it some apology, as Plato's apology preserves lost Socrates. We will lose them all in this, I fear: the wise and iron Emperor, patriot Sniper, subtle Madame. We have already lost the best. There lies my chief regret, reader. Since you cannot trust a madman's word, I cannot persuade you of the one fact which is true comfort to me, even as I grieve. He was real: Bridger. There was a boy who walked this Earth who was a miracle. I held him in my arms. The Divine Light within his touch brought toys to life, made feasts of mud pies, raised the dead, and through him the God Who Conceived This Universe, Who usually sits back invisible, revealed Himself. I wish you could believe me. There is Providence, reader, an inscrutable but intelligent Will which marched us with purpose from the primeval oceans to these battle lines. That is how I know you will be alive to read this. He Who put such effort into mankind will not let us end here. No, I lie. I do not know with certainty that He still needs us. Those fatalists, who have long preached that all things, from the insect's flutter to these words you read, are fated, determined, written up yonder in the Great Scroll, never considered that that Scroll might have an Addressee. There are two Gods, reader, at least, He Who Conceived This Universe, and He Who Visits from Another, just as Infinite and just as Real. We humans are the letters of a message our Creator wrote to make first contact with His Divine Peer. Now that the letter has been received, it may be crumpled and discarded, or set aside as keepsake in a coffin-stale drawer. We the alphabet may pray only that Their new friendship will continue to rely on words. If so, we will survive.

Human Dignity

Written July 7–8, 2454
Events of April 8
Almoloya de Juáres

"I, VIVIEN ANCELET, HEREBY UNDERTAKE UPON MY HUMAN dignity that I will execute with faith and vigor the office of President of the Humanist Hive."

Imagine hearing these words, not in the flesh, not in Buenos Aires, where you strain on tiptoe to glimpse the podium over the ocean of excited heads, nor even on live video, the new president's bold image electric in your lenses. Instead you see him on a crass screen, barely a hand's span square and pixelated by technology's incompetence, replayed from a recording, so you do not share this moment with your billion brethren, but receive it only as tardy proof that the world outside these prison walls sails on without you.

"I swear to obey and preserve the Constitution and the Laws of the Humanist Hive," the oath continues, "to sustain the Hive's integrity and independence, and to promote all that will advance it and oppose all that may harm it. I will foster the Pursuit of Excellence of all Humanists, safeguard their rights and freedoms, and safeguard too the Olympic Games, the Olympic Spirit, and all who carry it. To these ends I will employ all the means . . ."—the new president's voice wavers here, since he—like you, reader—has only recently discovered that "all the means" of the Humanist Hive has so long meant O.S.—". . . all the means which the current Constitution of the Humanists places at my disposal, and when the disposition of the vote changes that Constitution, I will serve its new form with equal vigor. I will faithfully discharge these duties without bias or regard to any previous or current personal affiliation with any other Hive, strat, team, or other institution. I further swear to support the principles and reforms of Thomas Carlyle, and to maintain the Carlyle Compromise and all other treaties that continue to serve and safeguard Humanist welfare. I swear to preserve in secret the knowledge granted by my office which must be kept...kept secret." He almost didn't stumble. "Should I at any time break this oath of office, or in any way betray the Members' trust, I shall submit myself to punishment by the laws of the Hive. This is my solemn oath.

"I wish to add," Vivien Ancelet's voice sounds suddenly more human here, a man's words, not a recitation, "separate from this formal oath of office, my own personal pledge to my now-fellow Humanists that my past offices, and the allegiances associated with them, will not interfere with my exercise of this one. I am no longer Hiveless. I am no longer Censor. I am no longer an officer of Romanova. I am sincere in my pledge to uphold Humanist interests, even above those of the Carlyle Compromise and the Universal Free Alliance if need be. I am also no longer the Anonymous. My commentary will, from this point on, always be biased in favor and service of the Hive that I have joined. I am a Humanist, and speak as one— although not yet in Spanish," he added with a sheepish tone, "for which I apologize, but it is better, I think, for the whole world to hear and understand this, not just our Members. There is a new Censor now, and a new Anonymous, and both are worthy of those offices. I trust them completely to fulfill their duties as well as I or anyone could. I hope you will trust them too, as much as you trusted me, before I was called to give up those offices for this one."

The screen went dark. Tears welled in me, but practice did not let them fall. If one man in this world had deserved to see the oath live, to have been present when his allegiance shifted to a new commander in chief, that man was Ockham Saneer. Instead we watched it here, nineteen hours after the inauguration, and Ockham could not even stand to hear the words, since fetters and prison custom bound him to his chair. He did not even have his boots, just the jail uniform, slack navy and orange mockingly festive, like a child's shapeless attempt to wrap a birthday gift. Ockham did not weep at his own state, but I saw him flinch, one taut twitch of his cheek, grief's only token upon that bronze-strong Indian face, which always reminds me which people, alone among antiquity's war-ready thousands, halted Alexander.

"Complete voter turnout take four hours, seventeen minutes." These words at least were live, spoken in warm (if imperfect) Spanish by President Ancelet, who sat across from Ockham in the sterile interrogation room.

Ockham smiled at the speed with which his billion fellow Members had done their democratic duty.

"¿Want to see the *interimo* vice president to swear *cérémonia* of Sawyer Dongala?" Ancelet offered, his well-meaning infant Spanish dappled with stray French and English. "After me, the biggest *vote* numbers are for Sniper, ex-president Ganymede, you, your *éspoux* Lesley, J.E.D.D. Mason, and Sawyer Dongala, so Dongala agrees to be vice president while we hold whether any these other is eligible in the *circonstances*. A second urgency *vote* confirmed Dongala."

Ockham's throat cracked, stiff from the ten cautious days since his arrest, during which he had spoken nothing but guarded monosyllables and "toilet." "I ac—khh—acknowledge that you have been lawfully elected President of the Humanist Hive, and that you now hold all the authority to question and command to which that office entitles you."

The warmth in the new president's smile sharpened at once to action. "¿Who ordered Sniper to attack *contre* J.E.D.D. Mason?" he asked, with the sharp speed of a man who had never doubted that Ockham's silence, which had not broken for all the threats and enticements the law could offer, would break for him. "¿Who else to know?"

"English is alright with me if it's easier for you, Member President," Ockham invited gently, switching over. "No one else knew, to my knowledge. Oji-jiro acted alone." He tripped over Sniper's rarely voiced first name. "The bash' was entirely out of contact with President Ganymede at that point, and even Lesley and I knew nothing of Ojiro's plans."

Ancelet nodded his thanks for Ockham's linguistic courtesy. "Then Sniper did act alone." His shoulders eased. "Tell me about O.S."

"On or off the record, Member President?"

"Off, for now. We'll need a public statement soon, but first I myself need to understand."

That answer pleased Ockham, if I read him right. "Why is Mycroft here?" he asked.

Ancelet followed Ockham's gaze to where I sat on a metal bench in the corner, hugging my knees and trying to ignore the prison wraiths which clawed at my limbs and shoulders. I cannot tell you whether these wraiths are the ghosts of past prisoners, or simply spirits of the jealous walls, which recognize in me another criminal who should be theirs to claim. I try to tell myself there are no prison wraiths. This was not even a real prison, just a jail, a fleeting holding place for those awaiting trial, which should never have held anyone long enough to birth a bitter ghost. Still, here, as in every prison whose threshold I have crossed since my crimes, I saw the wraiths, heard them, felt their tendrils, real as the cloth across my skin.

"I'm not allowed anywhere without a bodyguard anymore," the new president answered. "I thought you'd prefer someone we both know and trust."

Ockham frowned at me. "Is that the only reason?"

"No. You may or may not be aware, but I've relied on Mycroft a long time, not just as Censor but in my . . . secret office. Mycroft is my assistant, advisor, apprentice. My successor."

"The new Anonymous? I did not know." There was no surprise in Ockham's gaze, just digestion, fact catalogued without comment. "Thanks to voter preference, the office of Anonymous may have frequent association with our Vice Presidency, but it is not a Humanist office, nor is Mycroft a Humanist. How do you justify granting the new Anonymous access to the secrets of O.S. given your declaration that you have severed all allegiance to your former offices?"

Ancelet frowned. "It's my understanding that Mycroft has known of your work and kept your secrets for many years now. It's not new information for them."

"Mycroft has had no details," Ockham answered, "merely the vague knowledge that we were homicides. In the past we secured Mycroft's silence through two threats: the threat of exposing to the public the fact that Mycroft is a Servicer, and the threat of denying them access to Thisbe. Mycroft and Thisbe are lovers," he added. "But at this point the public knows the former and I assume Thisbe is either in custody or missing, so the latter threat is also meaningless."

"In fact, Member Ockham," I added in quiet Spanish, my voice stirring the prison wraiths to hiss, "Thisbe and I were never actually lovers. But you can trust me with this. That Authority Which, for me, supersedes all has ordered me to tell no one, not even Them, anything I learn here without permission from both yourself and President Ancelet. You may not know What Authority I mean, but I think you do know that you and I both hold equally absolute the command of those authorities we answer to."

"J.E.D.D. Mason?" Ockham guessed at once.

I could tell from his face that mine betrayed me. My allegiance was not yet public knowledge then, and I had expected Thisbe to keep this revelation private, one more secret to make her spellbook dangerous. Apparently not.

"Mycroft is assembling a history of the past week," Ancelet interceded, "at J.E.D.D. Mason's order. The book is supposed to explain events as neutrally as possible, and to include as much truth as Mycroft can piece together. No one but Mycroft will have access to the interviews and research materials, and everyone involved, including you, will have equal and complete veto power over every single line. I personally will not green-light its publication until you have told me that you are satisfied."

"A history." Ockham stretched back in his seat as the idea sank in. "Why?"

"J.E.D.D. Mason likes the truth," Ancelet and I answered in unplanned unison.

Ancelet laughed, his dreadlocks falling back across his shoulders like willow whips in breeze. I was glad to see he could still laugh. "That really is the idea behind it," he explained. "J.E.D.D. Mason wants the human race to have the truth. Most everyone else, including me, wants some controlled version of the truth out there, since you know there will be many pointed lies, most pointed against us. We must fight them with something. If you prefer, Ockham, I will send Mycroft away and summon a Humanist bodyguard, but you or I or both will wind up repeating all this information to Mycroft later on, and, since I'm new to having Humanist guards, there are none yet that I trust as much as I trust Mycroft"—he paused—"or you."

"Prospero." The name sounded dead on Ockham's lips.

"What?"

"Prospero. My name, my middle name, is Prospero. I am no longer O.S., so I should not be addressed as Ockham."

It hurt hearing him say it, as it would hurt hearing a deposed king say he no longer merits "Majesty."

Prospero Saneer let his eyes close, consulting with the darkness before breaking the seal on secrets he has carried since he was old enough to know what secrets were. "O.S. is that organ which acts when the Humanist Hive is best served by taking human life," he answered. "Its charter, which I can recite for you if you wish, recommends but does not formally restrict it to targeting those whose connections to Humanist interests are obscure enough that no investigation may be reasonably expected to uncover our motive. The deaths should, if possible, be brought about by means subtle enough that no investigation could reasonably suspect foul play either. The Six-Hive Transit System and its computers have been our main means of both selecting and killing targets, but other methods are employed when needed. The hereditary Saneer-Weeksbooth bash' is entrusted with both the Transit Network and the assassination system. We are O.S., though the title O.S. is also used for the system's single leader. As Ockham Saneer I was the twelfth O.S., and now Ojiro Sniper is thirteenth."

"That organ which acts . . ." Ancelet repeated, a hint of French tinting his vowels as he translated the phrase in his mind. "Interesting terminology. Who chooses the targets?"

"You do, Member President. Or, you would, in simpler times."

The new president's black brows narrowed. "Who chose before me?"

"O.S.'s charter specifies which officials may know about us and command us, depending on which form the Humanist government takes after an election. If there is a majority sufficient to elect a single Executive, the Executive alone knows and commands, but may, at their discretion, inform the Vice Executive. When power is split among a Triumvirate, Council, Commission, Congress, or Parliament, there are unique protocols for each combination, though usually the two to four persons commanding the largest voter margin are entrusted with the secret."

"Ganymede, then."

"Yes, former president Ganymede commanded us most recently." Prospero frowned. "I am not trying to be evasive, Member President, but this is complex for me. I personally acknowledge you as president and want to give you what you need, but it should be the leader of O.S. who tells you these things, not a subordinate or former member. The times justify us suspending that rule, but I still need to think about what Ojiro would say in my place."

"Sniper." Ancelet breathed deep. "If I were to summon Sniper now——"

"Ojiro," Prospero corrected. "They are O.S. now."

"Ojiro, then. If I were to summon Ojiro and order them to do, well, to do something, do you think they would obey me?"

"I think they would consider your orders very carefully before acting."

Ancelet took some silent time to think. "Why are you still here while Ojiro and most of O.S. have gone rogue?"

"O.S. has not gone rogue. It remains that arm which acts when the Humanist Hive is best served by taking human life. You are that arm which acts when the Hive is best served within the framework of its government and Romanova. Has it occurred to you, Member President, that your goal may not be achievable with peaceful means?"

"Which goal?"

"To preserve the Hive. You hope to placate the other Hives, and make the concessions necessary for them to stop calling for the Humanists to be dissolved."

"I've considered the possibility that they'll refuse. It is, by my calculations, avoidable." I could almost see the numbers moving behind the former Censor's eyes.

So could Prospero. "What about the possibility that they'll demand so many changes that the Hive wouldn't be itself anymore? Or the possibility that violence will break out before you finish? Or that you yourself will be assassinated? Extraordinary times may require extraordinary means. If you decide you need those means, if you talk to Ojiro and issue orders, they will almost certainly obey. If you avoid those means and yours fail, O.S. will act without you. It is one organ of the Humanists, the presidency another. Don't mistake yourself for the head, or heart."

Curiosity sparked a smile. "Where would you locate the head and heart, then?" the president asked.

"The head would be the voting members," Prospero answered instantly. "The heart the Olympic Committee."

"So while the people and the Olympic Spirit live on, the letter of the law can get stuffed?" Ancelet's brief chuckle seemed aimed mostly at himself. "I don't mean to tease. You're right. I may fail. War may be inevitable, as Mycroft fears. I'm glad the Hive has another force separate from me to protect it. I also understand why you are being careful. You have every reason to doubt my fitness for this position, my loyalty to the Hive, even the validity of an election held in such circumstances. On my end, what I can say is that I trust you, Ockham . . . Prospero," he corrected himself. "I genuinely trust you, but at present it's only intellectual trust, based on Mycroft's descriptions of you and your past actions. It will take time and interaction for that to mature into personal trust."

Something relaxed in Prospero, just a bit, in his spine, his shoulders, as the freshly planted seed of confidence extended its first tender leaf. "Former President Ganymede alone had the authority to give O.S. orders, but Chief Director Hotaka Andō Mitsubishi and Prime Minister Casimir Perry were consulted before each strike."

"Why?"

"From the beginning, through convention but no rule, the Chief Director of the Mitsubishi Hive has been taken into the confidence of whatever Humanist executive commands O.S., and O.S. has been used to aid the Mitsubishi Hive."

"Why?"

Now it was Prospero whose black brows narrowed. "Possibly because the center that originally built the Transit Network was partly staffed by Mitsubishi. Possibly because the center's first Co-Directors, Orion Saneer and Tungsten Weeksbooth, thought it would be a good way to pull the Mitsubishi into a long-term alliance. Possibly because when the system was first formed Olympian President Adeline Dembélé wanted to involve the Mitsubishi for reasons now lost to history. O.S. intentionally keeps few records, so many details are irretrievable."

How does it feel, I wonder, to bear the sins, not of a father, but of a semiparent, half forgotten? Before your dynasty was founded, noble king, some maternal grandfather, with far too many "greats" before his name, was a murderer. Before your forefathers made the small fortune you used to make your large one, they bought their tickets to the New World with corpse-loot. Before there was a Humanist President there was an Olympian President, whose successors merged with O.B.P. to form the Humanists, and it was that Olympian President who brought O.S.'s curse on both your houses.

"Is that why, when the bash' takes in new bash'mates each generation, they're usually from Mitsubishi bash'es?" Ancelet asked.

"It is a rule," Prospero confirmed. "Outside spouses and bash'mates must be approved by the Executive, and must have Humanist or Mitsubishi backgrounds, or, with extra permissions and background checks, European."

Ancelet nodded. "How did Europe get involved?"

"It was in 2333. I believe it was a concession made to Europe in return for the E.U. not banning the sale of European-owned land to non-Europeans the way the Mitsubishi ban sale to non-Mitsubishi. I . . . Is there a problem?"

The word 'land' had made Ancelet twitch like a fly's bite, and I saw him grope instinctively for the controls that would have been beside him had we sat in the dim, screen-lined sanctum of the Censor's Office back in Romanova. There he, and I, and not-yet-Censor Jung Su-Hyeon, and not-yet-traitor Toshi Mitsubishi could have checked all the land sale numbers, back and back, all the way to the 2330s, where our equations, keener than truffle pigs, would have smelled out the knots of tension metastasizing in the aftermath of the Gordian-Auxilio Hive Merger. But those numbers were Su-Hyeon's now, not Ancelet's, that sanctum, too. There is a special cruelty in making the still-living master pass on his instrument when no living student has yet surpassed him.

"Is there a problem?" Prospero repeated.

"Yes, but not a new problem," the new president answered, with a frankness I did not expect. "Associates and I"—his lips quivered at the ever-fresh memory of Kohaku Mardi's bloody corpse—"have long predicted that the Mitsubishi landgrab policy would lead to an economic—or more than economic—crisis. It's . . . interesting . . . to see how long ago others predicted the same."

Prospero studied his new commander slowly, unused to frankness after Ganymede's golden façade. "The greatest purpose of O.S.," he answered slowly, "is to prevent large conflicts like the present one. I myself have never been involved with selecting targets or tracking trends, but from Eureka's comments I believe we have been working to stave this off for a long time."

Ancelet nodded. "You were. I've seen the numbers. You were. You did it well."

"Thank you, Member President."

I wondered briefly whether Prospero understood the full depth of the compliment, coming from the one man in the world who could see the impact rippling through the past perhaps better than set-sets could. No matter. His president had praised him. A spearman's joy as he receives praise from Athena's lips does not depend on how well he understands the goddess's mastery of one particular technique.

"I don't necessarily condone the system," Ancelet added, "but you did do good with it, a lot of good. Now, this O.S. charter, which I will need to see, does it mention the alliances with the Europeans and Mitsubishi?"

"No." Prospero's bonds clanked as he shook his head. "There is no physical record of any kind that can establish European or Mitsubishi involvement."

"Not even anything suggestive?" Ancelet spoke almost before the last syllable had winged its way from Prospero's lips. "The policy of not assassinating European and Mitsubishi Hive Members, was that ever written down?"

"No. That was a verbal agreement made by past presidents. If you yourself choose to use O.S., you must decide whether or not to continue that policy."

"What about the Utopians?" I interrupted, my voice shrill as I tried to will away the tickling torture of my phantoms. "Your policy to never kill Utopians, was that someone's request?"

The prisoner said nothing until his president nodded consent. "Targeting Utopians is forbidden by the injunction against deaths which would trigger investigations likely to expose us." He raised his manacled wrists, letting the light catch on the inner padding of glistening Cannergel. "You know why."

President Ancelet sat silent, peering, not at the prison walls, but at the realm of thought beyond. "Then, so far as legal investigation will be able to uncover, all hits made by O.S. were directly ordered by a Humanist Executive, and no other figure ever made the decision. Correct?"

"Almost, Member President."

"Almost?"

Prospero Saneer took a long breath. "As O.S., I was authorized to use the means at my disposal to prevent misuse of those means. In other words, it was my duty to execute anyone, outside O.S. or inside, who attempted to pervert, misuse, or steal the means we used to kill."

"And you've exercised that authority?"

"We killed our bash'parents." Prospero stopped there, but the president's stare demanded more. "Five years ago. My mother, Osten Saneer Eleventh O.S., my father, also the Snipers, the Typers, the Weeksbooths, they were planning to bypass government approval and select targets themselves, based on their own judgment of what would be best for the Humanists. We, the younger generation, arranged a rafting accident. Cato planned it and myself, Ojiro, Thisbe, and Lesley actually carried it out, but we all consented, and we all helped." He frowned at the hints of pity which showed in his president's face. "They plotted treason, Member President. Former President Ganymede commended the action when I informed them."

Such perfect calm. Something inside, an older part of me, envied it, reader—envied him. You see, I never managed patricide. Or matricide. Parricide aplenty as I worked my way through my adoptive family, but Providence took my blood-parents before I could attempt the one offense so unthinkable that my ancestors teach me to hold it up as proof that the universe needs Furies and torments. What a privilege for Prospero to have passed the absolute test: love, Nature, and nurture all on one side and only loyalty upon the other. I think the wilder creature I once was would have had the strength to kill the parents who gave me life, but I will never know. Nor can I console myself that at least their deaths do not add to my guilt, for I lost Bridger, so all dead blood, from my own parents' blood to the first Cro-Magnon who sharpened a stone, is on my hands, and well the Furies know it.

President Ancelet leaned back with a full-bodied sigh, his dreadlocks making the shatterproof foam seat back hiss like a snare drum. "They can't accuse you of hypocrisy at least."

"They can accuse me of anything they like, Member President," Prospero warned. "Whether these facts or any others should be released to the public during my trial must be your decision. Unless you prefer that I not stand trial."

"That's why you let yourself be captured, isn't it? You wanted a trial."

"Making the whole truth public was the only way I could think of to calm the other Hives, or at least to ensure that, if we are destroyed, it will be due to truth, not paranoia. But my trial may not be necessary after all; when Ganymede fell, I didn't expect to have a strategist of your caliber come forward to help us."

The ex-Censor nodded slowly. "Out of curiosity, how would you expect to avoid a trial at this point?"

"Through my escape, incapacitation, or death. Any could be arranged; we still have Ojiro."

Ancelet twitched: this was the first time, I think, he had seen a man offer to die for him. "No. The trial will go forward." His voice turned from conversation to command. "You will plead *terra ignota*."

Ockham Prospero Saneer does not flinch at monsters, be they flesh or words, but I do. *Terra Ignota*, our young law's Unknown Lands. The geographic nations had 3,934 years from Hammurabi to the Great Renunciation to map out the kingdoms of their law, while our Hive laws were breech-born in the hasty wilderness of war. The European Union had only to revise its constitution for the umpteenth time, and tradition claims that the Masons have not changed a letter of their law since law began, but the rest of the Hives have patchwork law codes, stitched in haste from those of corporations, clubs, families, custom, fiction, and, yes, relics of the geographic nations, too. The newborn Hives soon learned to handle crimes that tangled two of them, but what can our young law do when two Hives' Members break a third's law in a fourth's house? Or when a beast like me tangles all seven and the Hiveless in one bloody spree? If Gordian law demands that all records must stand open to science, can the Cousins force them to conceal the background of a Gag-gene? If the Mitsubishi consider self-defense justifiable homicide, can the Utopian equation of homicide with libricide force the Mitsubishi to forgive lethal force if it is used to save, not a life, but a manuscript? For ordinary crimes, the criminal's Hive pays reparation to the victim's, then each Hive disciplines or compensates its Member as its own laws prescribe. When Hive preferences are incompatible, exchange of favors settles many tangles: I will fine my Members for discussing your *Imperator Destinatus* if you enforce my *modo mundo* on your Members when they kill Utopians. But as commixing genes forever find new ways to make the species stranger, so commixing Members ever conceive new ways to stray beyond the edges of the law. Hence the honest and necessary plea: *terra ignota*. I did the deed, but I do not myself know whether it was a crime. Arm thyself well for this trial, young polylaw; here at the law's wild borders there be dragons.

"*Terra ignota* for murder!" I half screeched the words as the wraiths around me churned in protest.

I deserved the glares the others fixed on me.

The president spoke first. "What O.S. did was ordered by the Humanist government through its own due process, and served legal mandates: O.S.'s to serve the Humanists, the Humanist government's to serve its Members, and the Hives' contract with Romanova to support the good of all Hives and the human race. I can't say with certainty whether or not such Hive-authorized homicides were, or should have been, illegal. Neither can you."

Prospero watched contented as these facts flowed from his new commander's lips.

"But, Censor," I cried, "even back in the days of geographic nations, assassination was—"

"And if we still lived in those dark ages, that might mean something," Ancelet snapped, too much in haste to chide me for letting his old title slip. "A nation could kill to protect its sovereign soil. Can you define a Hive's sovereign soil, Mycroft? Can you define the limits of Hive self-defense?"

Had I a more yielding soul, it should have been Ancelet whose wise words silenced his troublesome apprentice. It was not. Instead it was the Great Specter Thomas Hobbes, who loomed suddenly over my mind, as he had loomed over Europe in those grim decades after 1651, when all the lights of scholarship united in the struggle to forge some mental weapon that could pierce logic's armor and slay the dread *Leviathan*. Perhaps no mind has ever so united all the spearpoints of philosophy in one phalanx against him, but the Beast of Malmesbury—Hobbes's title, as saturated with dread as the Patriarch's with honor—used Reason's highest arts to paint portraits of Nature, God, and Man so perfect that not one brushstroke could be criticized, yet so abominable that they left the reader unable to respect humanity. So desperately Hobbes's readers cried, "We are not brutes! We do not hate and fear each other so! Humanity is a fair race! Noble! Good!" But they could not prove it, not against Hobbes's flawless descriptions of the realities of human malice. All the land's horses and all the land's men could not cure the Hobbesian infection, not for the twenty years it took John Locke to develop his Blank Slate, the only antitoxin. And even with that antitoxin in our reading list, *Leviathan* looms still from time to time, when some new dreadful deed of humankind reminds us how well Hobbes's cold, aggressive war of all on all describes our state. Our selves. We in 2454, with two thousand secret O.S. victims shoring up our near-utopia, can we prove we do not live on murder? Now I felt anew this shadow, conjured by

Ancelet's words—the nation's right to kill in self-defense—which summoned in my mind some lines of Hobbes which slipped out of me—lines which, try as I might, I can neither unread nor refute: "Hobbes says that neither passion nor action may be called a sin until they know some law that forbids them, and that, where there are no man-made laws, the immutable and eternal Laws of Nature and Reason state that all men must and may, by whatever means we can, defend ourselves." I shivered, finding myself stared at. "Such a Law of Nature could not convict O.S. Can Romanova?"

The grim set of the ex-Censor's face made me wonder whether he too, so deeply touched by our Madame, had already felt Hobbes's bestial shadow. He turned back to the prisoner. "You will stand trial, Prospero. You first, alone. Yours is the core case, and doesn't get us into the tangle of prosecuting a former head of state, and there won't be any complicating issues about your mental fitness to stand trial, unlike with most of your bash'mates. Your *terra ignota* will set the precedent."

Prospero Saneer breathed deep. "Do you actually expect them to acquit me?"

"That's a long-term concern. Short-term, petitioning the Senate for a *terra ignota* will force Romanova to admit that no one's sure whether or not what O.S. did was criminal. When people believe their side is in the right they'll fight tooth and nail for it, but no one wants to tear the world down over a maybe. The instant the Senate officially accepts your *terra ignota*, the mobs will calm."

"That is . . . that would work." It was not quite zeal that tinted Prospero's tone, but something heavier, gratified relief, as a knight might feel, required to pledge his life to a new-crowned prince, on finding that Divine Right has chosen well. "What about the mobs that aren't about O.S.?"

Ancelet sighed. "You mean the Cousins Feedback Bureau affair?"

"I mean the incident with Perry and the rest of you at that gender brothel, and what Ojiro says about J.E.D.D. Mason. Is it true there's a conspiracy to merge the Hives?"

The new president met Prospero's eyes straight on. "I don't know."

"Are you prepared, as Ojiro is, to use any means necessary to protect the Humanist Hive from such a conspiracy if it exists?"

"I'm not about to try to kill J.E.D.D. Mason, if that's what you're asking."

"Kill again," I corrected, the gravity of his error justifying my interruption.

"What?"

"Try to kill *again*. Ἄναξ Jehovah died." It was reflex for me by now to pounce upon the lie repeated so many times these past days: 'tried to kill,' 'attempted assassination,' while so few face the reality: Our Maker's Guest departed, and returned.

Prospero's brows knit. "I thought J.E.D.D. Mason survived."

"He was resurrected."

"Enough, Mycroft," Ancelet ordered. "This meeting is about the Humanist Hive, not theory or theology. As for Ojiro, if I had a way to contact them"—the president glanced pointedly at me—"I would tell them that, until or unless Propsero's trial makes it definitively unlawful, I am open to using deadly force, and Ojiro's resources, to protect the Humanists, but I intend to try other ways first. If Ojiro stands by, ready to act if needed, I will count them an ally. If they disrupt my plan, if they stir up hostility by continuing to release these videos of Tully Mardi urging war, and especially if they go after J.E.D.D. Mason again, then they and O.S. will become my enemy."

Prospero nodded. "A useful message; I hope it reaches Ojiro."

Ancelet returned the nod. "Now, I have all I need for today. The Senate meets tomorrow. I need time to muster votes so they accept your *terra ignota*."

The president rose, and Prospero tried to rise by reflex, forgetting for a moment the fetters which kept him seated. "Will a majority be hard to achieve?" he asked.

It was the old Anonymous, I think, who smiled here. "Not for me. Now, I'm leaving Mycroft here with you for a little while. You two will write up a report on O.S. and the events that led to its exposure, both for Mycroft's history and for use at the trial, concentrating on recent things, the last few weeks, the Seven-Ten list. I need to know everything. When you're finished, tell the guards to call me, and I'll collect Mycroft and the report myself. The report will be for my eyes only, and, once I've read it, I'll give you instructions specifying what information should be made public and what should be concealed. Once you're confident that you know what I want you to conceal, then you will tell the police that you're ready to make a statement. Until then, you should continue to refuse to say anything to anyone, except Mycroft or myself."

"Yes, Member President." A pause. "The boots suit you."

Shock delayed Ancelet's smile at this, the highest praise that Prospero could give. "Thank you."

They did suit him, the president's new Humanist boots, and betrayed too that he had long been mulling over what boots he might choose should he give up his Hiveless sash for the Humanists, instead of for his bash'native Europe. The boots' surfaces were palimpsests, the dull tan of old parchment covered with hand-inked text in antique brown, but with a different script beneath, faint but still legible, the tightly crammed script of an earlier century. Around the soles, the bronze and gold Olympic stripes of Ancelet's medals in mathematics and oratory sparkled against the tricoleur of the French nation-strat, while on the sole the treads were crammed with letters like the type in a printing press, locked in loosely, so they shifted chaotically with every step and stamped out different almost-words.

Ancelet knocked for the guard, frowning as the bolts began their clicks and groans. "Prospero, are they treating you alright?" he asked. "Any harassment?"

"None, Excellency. Their courtesy has been conspicuous."

"Yes, well . . . siege makes people careful."

"Siege?"

Prospero did not understand, but I did. Walking from the car to the prison yard an hour before had been my first taste of outside since the fatal day. Slivers of media had shown me crowds, small riots, speeches, police lines, Humanist clubs and sports bars besieged by outraged mobs, but images are not the taste and touch of our new world. I noticed the sky first. The customary streaks of cars were too slow, too low, obtrusive. It frightened even me, not so much because it meant the transit network was in timid and unstable hands, but because the sky had changed. The world had changed. As we had landed at the prison I could see no ground around it, only people, the near ranks packed tight as fans around an idol, while the farther reaches gave way to tents and chairs and umbrelounges. My instinct labeled it a 'mob,' but it was too quiet. A siege, as Ancelet so aptly called it, stagnant, patient, an aimless force waiting for an aimer. In that directionless week, when everyone wanted to act but no one had a plan, these people felt that standing close to the living linchpin Ockham Saneer would ready them to be the first to move when the time came. The besiegers around us did not even have sides, only clumps where Hive dress clustered, but even these blurred one into another, as if they were all too timid to tell each other what causes they served. I think they didn't know.

"Ancelet! That's President Ancelet!"

Walls of stone and science are no match for assaults of sound. Prospero and I heard the mob's scream even here in the prison's heart as the new president emerged from the gates outside. He could have left by the roof patch, but he chose to show himself to the besiegers for the few minutes it took for them to snap enough photographs to serve his purposes, before he dove into the car and thence the sky. For sixteen hours President Ancelet's visit to the jail in Almoloya de Juáres eclipsed all other questions in the world's eye. Why was he there? What did he say to Ockham Saneer? What role would the new president take in the coming trials? For those sixteen hours anyone but Ancelet could move invisible.

CHAPTER THE THIRD

Is This the Spark?

Written July 11–13, 2454
Events of April 8–9
Alexandria &c.

I SKIPPED THE TEN DAYS BETWEEN THE CATACLYSM AND Ancelet's visit to the prison. These were important days, the days of Ancelet's election, of more arrests, of counting Perry-Kraye's victims, of press conferences confirming facts and fears already half public. The whole world held its breath, a frozen, false calm, like rabbits praying that the predator won't see us if we don't move. Businesses closed, towns ordered curfews, bash'es stayed home to watch again and again the videos of Sniper at Madame's, of Tully Mardi's war sermons, of Perry-Kraye's maniacal last moments laughing amid Brussels's flames, and of what no one wanted to call Jehovah's death. I barely remember. If ever, reader, you have seen a graveyard, where the centuries of Zeus's tempests have rinsed away the faces of carved angels and the names they mourned, my memory is much the same. Facts which in a sane mind would stay clear wear away quickly, their contours barely traceable upon the weather-beaten stones. Here and there a monument is carved of sterner stuff, some porphyry or dense volcanic basalt that endures time's touch, still legible. The seven recent days of transformation are the graveyard's central monument, each step in the chain from the theft of Sugiyama's Seven-Ten list to Bridger's final deed etched deep enough to withstand an aeon's war with wind and rain. Yet the ten days that followed are a blur. They were a blur even as I lived them, the haze of grief leeching the strength from me like fever, swamp mud, gravity, old age, the many fetters Fortune uses to remind us that the strength of flesh is hers to grant and take away. I cannot even say which fortress—Paris? Alexandria?— served as my protective prison, or what I did those days apart from mourn and serve as translator for the Great Scroll's Addressee, Whom I am fortunate to call my Master. His contact with His Divine Peer had left Him so invigorated that He had to learn again, as if from scratch, how to sort His languages as humans do. I could research those ten lost days, but crisis may at any moment cut my writing short, so I will first record what I remember, those few still-legible inscriptions already fading in the graveyard where only the days of transformation stand truly indelible.

Liar. Thou forgetest how well I know thee by now, Mycroft Canner. Thou canst not pretend that the week of transformation is truly thy most vivid memory.

You are with me again, then, are you, gentle reader? I had hoped you'd come. It is a strangely lonely labor, this chronicle which, by law, no contemporary eye may see. I am glad to have somebody share it.

Yes, I am with thee, Mycroft. I come to have my patience tried again. Abuse it not. Thou canst not fool me. The two weeks of thy rampage are thy most salient memory, whose abominable details thou hast so often inflicted upon me: the thumping of thy sadist heart, Apollo's blood upon thy tongue. That atrocious fortnight, not the seven days of thy first history, is the true centerpiece of thy distorted memory.

Innocent master, your error proves again your goodness. Horrors like mine are so remote from your imagining that you believe they could become memories, recorded by the brain like common trials and griefs. No, reader. My two weeks are not salient letters etched deep to withstand assaults of wind and tempest in the battered graveyard of my mind. My two weeks are the storm.

"Caesar, this is Achilles."

I could not forget this. The Major was the first man I had ever seen enter the citadel of Alexandria without pausing for that tremor of awe which we owe ancient monuments, as we remember the mountainsides that gave their hearts to form these sky-rivaling columns, the thousand dead hands that hewed those rocky hearts, and the great chain of people running from deep antiquity through ourselves to generations yet unborn who will stand here and tremble. Achilles did pause on MASON's threshold, but it was a different pause, not awe but the slow, saturated study men give to sunsets, trees in blossom, laughing children, brief things we like to linger on before they vanish. I wonder whether it was Ilium that taught Achilles not to mistake kings' wonders for eternal things, or whether, by his essence, he has always known. "I'm told you need me to teach you how to have a war."

"So Mycroft thinks," the Emperor answered.

It was a bright but dark-walled chamber. MASON's throne of blood-purple porphyry stood in the center of a reflecting pool, fed by channels of flowing spring water which braided through the marble floor like a thousand rivers gathering toward Ocean. Cornel MASON was not on his throne, but stood by one wall, gazing at the carved web of archaic symbols which covered the room's stone walls like lace. Even standing on the same floor as his guests and guards, so imperious was Caesar's stance that my mind insists he held a scepter in his hand, though I believe it was, in fact, an apple.

"You think Mycroft is wrong? That there won't be war?" Achilles asked.

"I think there may or may not be a war," MASON answered, turning. "I think the engine of human civilization is not so track-bound that it cannot be steered, even at this point." The Emperor spoke slowly to Achilles, his inner engines churning as he studied the impossible creature he had heard me rant so much about. "You disagree, I trust?"

Achilles cannot make his flashing eyes gentle. "It has never been the will of men, or kings, that steered the world. I judge a man by whether he faces Fate bravely or whether he squirms like a coward. So does history."

"You think I should not try to prevent the war?" Caesar asked.

"Of course you should try, just don't imagine you'll succeed. There's honor in urging the right course, even when the wrong is set. Many of my old friends are still called wise for their efforts to make peace with Troy. Fail well, as they did, and be ready to fight well once you have failed."

The Emperor frowned. "I want to hear this from your own lips: you are not a human being born of human parents, but the fictional Achilles, brought to life by divine fiat. Is this true?"

"Brought both to life and back to life." The hero brushed back the Greek curls which fell around his neck like drops of hyacinth. "You've seen the remnants of Troy and Mycenae in museums, as I have now. There was a Troy, and I think I was the real Achilles then, but ghosts forget. We need friends and descendants to recount our glories, speak our names, remind us of ourselves with prayers and sacrifices. After three thousand years, most of my contemporaries have lost even their names, since spirits forget our names as history forgets them. I remember myself mostly as Homer painted me, since that is how men know me now. Thus I am brought both to life and back to life, since I once walked this earth a breathing man, but have never before walked it as the man of myth and verses I am now."

MASON did not shudder. "And yet somehow you are also a soldier of the World Wars?"

"Yes and no." Against the gray, imperial marble, the Major's green fatigues made him look like an invading weed, as if patient Nature had wormed through the stony citadel and emerged, vibrant and fresh, to bring her gentle doom to all man's lofty towers. "The child Bridger, who made me real, didn't understand history chronologically as much as thematically. I fought in the Epic War. Three hundred or three thousand years ago, it's still ancient by a child's standards. I think you of all people, Caesar MASON, shouldn't be picky about that kind of anachronism."

Caesar paused only a moment. "And you also fought Apollo's future war?"

Achilles tensed. "Apollo Mojave's, you mean? They were all the god Apollo's wars."

It takes MASON some heavy breaths to digest any sentence involving our lost Apollo. "Yes."

"Yes, then," the veteran answered. "I remember fighting in Apollo Mojave's future version of the war too—not that my experience with robot suits and A.I. space gods will help us much down here."

"Do you have proof you are what you say?"

"I have Patroclus."

Achilles' gaze guided the Emperor's to his pocket, where Patroclus Aimer leaned out, tiny enough to make a chess piece seem a looming monolith. "This is a beautiful hall, Caesar!" he shouted in his tiny voice. "I'd heard the rumors that Daedalus built this place, and your Masons had it hidden for eons before moving it here. I didn't believe it before, but seeing it now I'd recognize Daedalus's handiwork anywhere. You recognize it too, Major?"

"You can use my name in front of people now." Swift-footed Achilles felt with his toe along a channel in the marble floor, where flowing water reflected the ceiling's starscape, the beasts and gods of the ancient constellations bright against a field of lapis blue. It was not real sky but diagrams in veins of gold, while the stars were fire, a thousand points of flame, tiny as candles, fueled by hidden channels in the ceiling. "Yes, I recognize Daedalus's work," the hero answered. "Do you suppose we recognize it because the Masons did a good job copying ancient sources? Or because our memories are made out of current expectations of what ancient things should look like?"

MASON stepped toward Achilles. I had not seen the Emperor's eyes alive with wonder in thirteen years. "May I see your companion more closely?" He extended his right hand, cautiously.

"Must be touched to be believed, I know." Achilles helped tiny Patroclus out into his own palm first, then passed him to MASON. "Careful. Hands are scary places when your world is measured in centimeters, and I don't think I have to tell you what I'll do if anything happens to Patroclus."

MASON took more time than most in his examination, and less care, not that he wasn't gentle with the tiny figure, but most people handle the little soldiers with paranoia, as if they were butterflies or eggshells. MASON treated the Lieutenant more like a mouse or slim-limbed lizard, testing his weight, offering him fingertips to grasp and lean on. This too was Apollo's touch, I think. In their tender years, the young Emperor's beloved had shown him so many wondrous U-beasts that he was used to handling creatures which should not exist.

"Thank you." Caesar smiled. "Will you break bread with me while we talk?" MASON did not even have to gesture for the throne room wall to open, baring a dining room, a modest summer feast, and a window-wall, where Alexandria's roofs and thoroughfares stretched out behind tinted glass which made it seem forever dawn.

The ancient hero savored the drifting scents of wine, meat, cheeses, fruit, and oil-rich flatbread. "Gladly, and I appreciate the gesture."

The Emperor led the way. "My throne is older than your epic, Achilles. You'll find that many familiar arts and customs survive here."

Achilles King of the Myrmidons paused beneath the doorway, not arched but a protoarch, a flat lintel with an open triangle above, as men had used when Troy still stood. "But not the art of war."

"No, that arm of my Empire has slept too long."

As the two walked together before me, I realized suddenly how tiny Achilles was, not just a head shorter than Cornel MASON but nearly two. It should not have been surprising. Achilles was out of scale, made from Bridger's child body as Patroclus was from a plastic toy, but the Major seemed so comfortable, and so vast in my eyes, that I had not noticed the discrepancy without a real man's bulk as contrast. I asked Achilles later if he finds his youthful tininess a hardship. He laughed as he reminded me how tiny are the artifacts of ancient days, and how we moderns, bulked by abundance, are to him as lumbering giants, while he alone retains the light and hound-sleek shape of natural humans.

The Emperor took his seat at the table's head, and set Patroclus down between the trays, offering a cube of hard cheese to serve as a stool. "Do you think war is unavoidable?" he asked.

"I wouldn't be here otherwise." Godlike Achilles filled his cup, half wine, half water, but frowned at the results with our thin modern wine.

MASON broke the bread. "What side will you be on? Mine?"

The soldier arched his brows. "You waste no time. That's good. I don't know. We don't know what the sides are yet."

"Mine will be best, and strongest."

Achilles reached out and sorted through the meat for the best pieces. "There's a boast worthy of an emperor."

"It's not a boast, it's fact. My mandate is to stabilize, protect, and expand the bounds of human empire, as my predecessors have done as long as there has been human empire. If there is war, my goal will be to end it, by whatever means and with whatever allies my advisors recommend. If you are on my side you will have my full trust and resources, and I shall put at your command the largest force the Earth has ever mustered. Any cause you choose I shall strengthen and protect, and any you oppose I shall attack with more resources than anyone has ever marshaled. If, on the other hand, you make yourself my enemy, it's possible you will defeat me, but the difficulty, and the cost in human life, will be astronomical."

"Quite the bribe."

"It's neither bribe nor boast. It's fact. I use all my resources to their maximum. If I had you, I would not waste your time with distrust, doubt, second-guessing, conscience, or bureaucracy, as others would. You have seen that in how I use Mycroft."

MASON will not break bread with Mycroft Canner, but gestured to a stool in the corner where I could have some rest.

Achilles's sharp eyes flashed. "Would you make me a *Familiaris*, then?"

"Yes, if you accept. I know," the Emperor added, "you have good reason to be wary of rulers who would claim the authority to command you because they rule greater kingdoms . . ."

Achilles son of Peleus tipped his cup toward MASON, silent acknowledgment of the Emperor's prudence, both in seeing the parallel between himself and Agamemnon, and in avoiding the Greek king's hated name.

". . . But the rank of *Familiaris* is not about command, it's about trust," MASON continued. "When I trust a person, I place in their hands a fraction of that absolute duty I owe my predecessors through the ages of the past, a duty which I have sworn to place before all other things: friendship, love, life, family. Last week my only child died in my arms. I felt their blood. I prayed inside, for the first time in what feels like forever, a desperate, insane prayer, beyond hope. And, impossible as it was, some miraculous Power heard and brought my child back to life. That Power had Its own reasons, but still, It answered a father's prayer. I would destroy that Power and the child It saved if duty required it of me. A person whom I trust to share that duty should be prepared to forfeit their life should they betray me, as I am prepared to forfeit things more precious than my life." He stretched back.

"You too, I think," Caesar continued, "are more native to a world where a traitor forfeits their life, and where the betrayed revenge themselves upon the betrayer, than to this modern age that waits for the clumsy wheels of bureaucratic law. Living as in antiquity, trusting and risking as in antiquity, that is what being a *Familiaris* means. I expect you will find no more comfortable option in this world. Your answer?"

Achilles studied Caesar carefully, as Caesar studied him. The veteran was right, I think, to sense something strange in Cornel MASON's gaze. I had noticed it too, the Emperor's eyes ranging Achilles's frame rather than settling on his face. His gaze lingered especially on those areas Achilles's tired uniform left bare: his neck, his wrists, the texture of his hair, his callused hands. MASON's stare led me to stare too, and I think we shared the same illusion, projecting familiar contours onto Achilles's cheekbones, the shapes of his fingernails, his brows. Achilles does not resemble our Apollo, but a lonely mind can make him seem to.

"This is welcome food and welcome honesty, MASON," Achilles answered. "Thank you."

MASON frowned. "Is that a 'no'?"

"It's a 'not yet.'"

"You intend to talk to each leader in turn before you choose?" quick Caesar guessed. "You will waste time."

The hero's eyes grew sharp. "I don't waste living hours, MASON, I know what it's like to have none left. You don't. I'll learn things if I come to each of you while I'm still undecided that you'd never show me if I'd already picked a side. I also intend to help all of you equally with some things. In war, all sides benefit if the players are competent at bare basics. I want to help you keep this war from being stupid."

"Isn't all war stupid? In that it's the mass destruction of life and the produce of civilization?"

"It is that," the veteran acknowledged. "But some wars are stupider than others. You don't want a war of attrition, or starvation, and you don't want plague, or needless civilian deaths."

"What are civilians when we have no soldiers?"

"Good question. It's going to be near impossible to keep groups of semicivilians from massacring potential enemy semicivilians, especially since conscience is the only reason to spare captives when you don't have an established ransom system, and don't make much use of unfree labor."

The Emperor glanced at me, but said nothing.

"What you need first and foremost is a plan to avoid destroying things you don't have to. You don't want to accidentally starve a city. You don't want to kill your own people because you can't tell them from the enemy. You don't want to burn down Alexandria again, as your namesake did."

Caesar did not smile.

A knock at the door. "*Nova imminentia, Caesar.* (Urgent news, Caesar.)"

"Come," Caesar commanded in common English, "tell us all."

Here entered a rare creature: Martin's famous spouse, Xiaoliu Guildbreaker. Xiaoliu is slim as a young tree, his Mason's suit, with the bold white sleeve of the *Ordo Vitae Dialogorum,* always so crisply pressed that he more resembles the strict lines of an obelisk than the curves of a living body. His long, feminine neck seems incongruous against the suit's broad shoulders, like a lily arching up from jagged rocks, and so slim are his limbs that the tips of the Masonic Square and Compass on his *Familiaris* armband meet on the underside. It took rare courage for the young Xiaoliu to don that armband, to turn his back on a Mitsubishi birth'bash and brave the glares and labels—'outsider,' 'seducer,' 'stranger,'—that came with 'luring' Martin Guildbreaker to mix his four quarterings of purely Masonic ancestry with a novitiate. Rare too is the spouse who feels no jealousy of Martin's complete devotion to our Master. Yet rare things are not surprising in the Guildbreaker bash', for what spouse could match our Martin, understand him, share his hours, who did not, like Martin, love Empire first and all else second?

"There are massive riots in Odessa," Xiaoliu reported. "The mayor and city council have issued an order requiring the redistribution of real estate in the city so that the proportion of property owned by each Hive matches the resident population of that Hive."

MASON closed his eyes as we all felt war's poison leak into that cheery recitation we have heard a thousand times: "The Six-Hive Transit System welcomes you to [someplace] . . . for a list of local regulations not included in your customary law code, select 'law.'" Mayors and city ordinances have always had power over more than building height and street food stalls, we just trusted each other to leave these old swords in their glass cases on the wall. No more. "What are the proportions?" MASON asked.

"More than seventy percent of the land in Odessa is currently Mitsubishi-owned, but it's a very mixed city, fairly even populations of all major Hives, and a very large Brillist population."

"What Hive is this mayor?" Achilles asked quickly.

Xiaoliu did not need to ask who this small stranger was to know that a man sitting at Caesar's table must be answered. "A Cousin,

European-raised, in the Ukrainian nation-strat, with Nurturist connections. The Mayor's announcement contained Nurturist language lifted from Tully Mardi's broadcasts."

Caesar's hands twitched, mine too, quick signals ordering our lenses to bring the scene in Odessa before our eyes. At once our lenses showed us massed Mitsubishi hurling rage and rocks at the chalk white columns of Odessa's city hall, their suits a tapestry of vibrant spring against the classical façade, while a greater mob surrounded them with fists and screams. Achilles watched the footage too, not through lenses but a hand screen, which the veteran held warily, like a magic window lent by some kind-seeming god.

"Is this it?" the Emperor asked, his voice slow as stones groaning as a mason drags them into place. "The beginning?"

"The spark of war?" Veteran Achilles peered at the mass of faces on his screen, while MASON and I watched like men illiterate. There are more illiteracies than script, reader: Ancelet can read numbers, Headmaster Faust the subtleties of face and phrasing, Madame blushes, Eureka Weeksbooth her ten billion balls of light, while others read stones, DNA, star streaks, the flights of birds—all hen scratch to the untrained. I think all humans feel rage at our finitude when we see others read what we cannot. In some eras fire was the solution, to burn, like infected sheets, the witches and heretic philosophers who read too well the signs and stars. But wiser eras hold such prophets dear.

"Perhaps it's the spark, perhaps not," the hero answered. "Swift-acting leaders can waylay Ruin in her coming a long time."

The Emperor frowned, as at a pond too murky to reveal its depths.

Achilles's sigh was almost apology. "If war were an exact science, you would not need me."

MASON breathed deep. "Xiaoliu, have you compiled tracker numbers for all my subjects in that part of Odessa?" he asked.

"*Sic, Caesar.* (Yes, Caesar.)"

"Connect me." The Emperor sat straight as the microphone prepared to carry his commands to distant ears. "To those Masons involved in the violence in Odessa: desist at once, and leave the area. Your behavior disgraces and endangers our Empire. Law and I will settle this, not sticks and stones."

On the far side of Earth, swift-departing lights burst from Odessa like fireworks before Sidney and Eureka's keen, blind set-set eyes.

Thou forgetest thy time again, Mycroft. Some other set-set watches the cars now. The Saneer-Weeksbooth reign is over.

How wondrous humanity must be by your era, my noble master, that you believe ten days are enough for us train a new daimon to rule that ebb and swerve which keeps eight hundred million cars in flight. Alas, the human animal is not yet so excellent. Perry, in the thoroughness of his machinations, killed the backup crew, and the art does not come swiftly, even to a monstrous set-set. Sidney Koons was captured, but is working the system still, wired into the heart of the great network, and guarded by Papadelias as closely as a rider may guard the horse that carries him. As for Eureka Weeksbooth, the set-set who fled with Sniper would not leave forty out of forty-five senses behind.

"What other advice have you for me?" Caesar asked.

Achilles breathed deep. "Not much."

"Because you are not yet sure we'll be on the same side?" MASON tested.

The famous runner smiled. "Exactly. At this point all I'm willing to share are universals. There are certain mistakes you don't want even enemies to make."

"Like what?"

"You need food."

"That's obvious."

The veteran shook his head. "You need more food than you think. Assume your productive capacity will be gone as soon as the war starts. Pump out a hundred times as much food as normal for however many days we have left. You want stores of food in every city, enough to feed the population for six months, more. Assume most of it will be destroyed or stolen. Think of it as currency as well as food, assume you'll need to trade and bribe with it as well as eat it. Assume however much you have is half of what you need. Assume whatever supply lines might exist will fail. Think of it as preparing for a giant siege, where every city on Earth will have to feed itself. Flood the world with food."

"You'd say this to an enemy? Starvation has often been key to victory."

"Better that my enemies have food stores I can steal than that we both starve."

A nod. "What else?"

"Guard the food. Looting will hit the food stocks quickly."

"We don't have vast food stocks lying about, these aren't the olden days. Most bash'houses buy extra rice, and flour, and cream, and things, but they actually can feed themselves for six months on a few sacks of salt and fertilizer for their algae tanks, meatmaker, and kitchen tree."

"Assume the kitchen trees will burn, and that, before they do, people will fear they'll burn, and loot things anyway. In my day, when we ran low on food, we'd attack whatever town was nearby, loot it, and kill whoever we didn't feel like taking prisoner. That technique still works; you don't want your people using it."

"What else?"

"Medicine."

Kosala smiled. "Already on it. We're triple stocking every hospital on Earth, our own and those few run by other Hives."

Achilles shook his head. "Triple's not enough. Imagine the most you could possibly need; you need ten times that. And field medics. Train a hundred thousand field medics, then have them train more. Your doctors are miraculous, but too accustomed to their miracle machines. You have some people who know old medicine—hikers, survivalists, antiquarians who've studied how to stop a man bleeding to death with two sticks and a torn-up sack—but you need more than you have. Make everyone on Earth a field medic and you'll still want more."

Kosala sighed. "You're so sure there will be fighting."

Mycroft, why is Kosala here? When did she come into MASON's sanctum? Are MASON and Cousin truly so close that Caesar would let Kosala walk in on this critical meeting?

MASON's sanctum? This is Casablanca, reader, the Cousins' capitol, whose tiered tent-roofs rise above us in ever-expanding folds like a dream ship, half sail, half bird, wafting and expanding as the sun and ocean breezes make them breathe. See, here Kosala and Achilles sit side by side in her roof garden, gazing at the ever-shifting colors high above.

No, Mycroft, we are in Alexandria, behind Daedalus's flame-roofed throne room, where Caesar and Achilles break bread together, and exchange unspoken vows of hospitality and trust. Dost thou forget?

Alexandria? No. Surely you recall the war of sand crests against wave crests along Africa's northern shore as Achilles and I crossed here from Alexandria, and how, after the strange Pacific waters of Cielo de Pájaros, the Mediterranean's familiar blue brought tears, not only to my eyes, but to the Great Soldier's. Or is the error mine? My memories blur sometimes, I warned you. I took Achilles to every leader's house that day, those two days, the thirty-first of March and first of April, not an easy week to persuade the leaders of the world to carve out time for something that sounded like fantasy: a meeting with Achilles? It was with Kosala that he discussed the hospitals, food too—or was that Caesar? Was that both? The meetings were quite similar in many ways, the questions, tests, curious fingers probing patient Patroclus. I beg your pardon, generous reader, but I doubt even Achilles can remember precisely which power asked him which question. Some questions, though, only one would ask.

"Has it not occurred to you, Achilles, that you may well be here to help make peace, rather than to make war?"

He who shatters battle lines laughed aloud.

Cousin Chair Bryar Kosala did not. "You're in the perfect position to do it. If you and Mycroft succeed in convincing all the relevant leaders to treat you as an expert, you'll become the de facto final word on war, and if you use that influence to move us toward peace, you could have an enormous impact, greater than anyone." Her sigh grew soft. "I know you believe in Fate, and, given what you claim to be, you may have no choice but to believe in Fate, but repeated Fate doesn't have to be a repetition of mistakes. It can be a chance to change, to learn, to pay for what was done before, to redeem yourself. You don't have to be an emissary of war. You can be peace."

The veteran gazed out between the shifting roof-tents to Casablanca's wave-chopped shoreline, where the Mediterranean and vast Atlantic mix and mate. "I knew you were going to cry for peace, but I expected it to sound naïve, cowardly. It doesn't. Your words sound like good sense. Actually, the world you paint makes better sense than mine, since, in your world, all this repetition would achieve something, instead of just leading us back to the slaughter-fields again and again. And you have every reason to believe in that world, since no one but me and Mycroft have really seen the counterevidence." He met her eyes. "I notice you avoided the word 'karma.'"

"You avoided answering my question."

"Apologies, Lady."

She scowled. "I know my gender fetish is public knowledge now, but feigning antiquated chauvinism is not a fruitful shortcut to convincing me you are what you say you are."

"No offense intended," Achilles answered quickly. "It's habit, that's all. You remind me very much of Athena, and my mother."

Kosala made a face neither goddess ever would have. "Both of them at once?"

Achilles shrugged. "They're the only women who've spoken to me in such a competent and imperious way. I'm not from your time. I'm not used to women in council, trading words and plans as you do. In my world only a goddess or a queen would speak like you, or an Amazon perhaps, though I mainly met the Amazons in battle, not council."

"I thought you'd been living in our world more than a decade."

Achilles frowned across to where I leaned against a breeze-kissed rail-ing. "Hiding in a junk-heap with a squad of all-male soldiers, a child, and no visitors apart from Mycroft and Thisbe Saneer has not given me many opportunities to interact with what the last millennia have made of wom-ankind. I've seen your sort of modern woman in media, in books, but you've seen—or read about—men like me too; that's not the same as meeting one."

"I guess not."

Kosala looked the Great Soldier over anew, studying his toil-hardened arms and shoulders, which he had bared to let his skin enjoy the salt touch of his grandfather, the Old Man of the Sea—a god who has either guarded the fish-rich depths since Earth began, or never existed.

"You still haven't answered my question," she pressed. "Will you help me make peace?"

The most violent man alive—as Homer once had Agamemnon call Achilles—shook his head. "It's not going to work. There will be war."

"And then there will be peace. Wars end when somebody makes peace. I'm going to start making that peace right now. There may be a bit of war first, but the peace that will come afterward is the important part."

"You . . ." He peered. "You're not trying to prevent the war?"

"Certainly I'm trying to prevent the war, but I only have a couple eggs in that basket. And, happily, trying to prevent the war and working to make peace after the war require many of the same actions. Wars drag on when no one is trying to end them. I won't let that happen. This war, when it comes, will have a well-organized peace movement from the beginning, which will end it on the best terms possible. Will you help me?"

"Toward peace? You're asking Achilles to help the world toward peace?" A chuckle died in his throat. "If you have specific peace tasks only I can do, I'll do them, gladly. After life itself, peace is the greatest gift a mortal man can enjoy, we know that well." Achilles paused to frown at frail Pa-troclus. "But I won't set aside war business for peace business. You know more about peace than I do—your whole world is peace. My task is to do what only I can do: teach the other rulers how to turn their angry people into soldiers."

Chair Kosala sighed. "I need you to teach me that too."

"Teach the Cousins? No," the headstrong runner answered quickly. "When the war comes you need to stay out of it."

"Stay out of it?" Kosala repeated, cold as I imagine Amazons would be. "You think we're not capable of fighting? I mean to pursue peace by any and every means I can."

"Don't take offense. Of course you're capable, but you're also more capable of not fighting than anyone."

She frowned. "What?"

"I didn't phrase that well. What I mean is that none of the other major Hives can stay neutral in this. Utopia and Gordian might manage to keep out of things, but they're tiny, and they're not powers anyone would run to for sanctuary. You are. Of all the great Hives, the Cousins have the greatest capacity to avoid being drawn into battle. If you remain neutral, then there will be a corner of this world that's separate, inviolable, safe. There will be someone who can negotiate with all sides—what priests and women used to be in wartime. That's the road toward peace that only you can take. It's a valuable thing."

I know the little wince Kosala makes that signals almost tears. "I don't know if neutrality is still possible," she answered. "The Cousins are angry right now, more angry than we've ever been. We're splitting on the inside. We've been manipulated, lied to, betrayed, had loved ones murdered, our own most precious institutions violated by people we trusted." She would not say 'Vivien' or 'CFB,' but the wetness in her eyes said both. "That has reopened even older wounds."

"Nurturism?" Achilles guessed.

Kosala nodded. "Lorelei Cook and their faction are gaining influence every day. Yesterday's board meeting degenerated into screaming. Three of our Romanovan Senators are openly calling for a set-set ban."

"But you can talk them down." He glanced at me. "You calmed them after Mycroft's rampage. You calmed the whole world down after the worst thing that had happened in a hundred years."

"This is different."

Achilles sensed, I think, something specific in Kosala's voice. "Why?"

Holding up a finger, Kosala signaled her tracker with her other hand, and called aloud. "Heloïse, what's the situation in Odessa?"

"Aunt Kosala!" Kosala set her tracker on speaker, so we could hear Heloïse's words, as bright as birdsong. "Pray excuse me, Mayor Bagry, gentlemen, I should take this call, it's Chair Kosala."

Polite permissions and light footsteps carried Heloïse to sufficient privacy for her to add image to her voice call, which Kosala brought up on the side of a nearby bench. Heloïse stood in a small office, where we could see a crystal chandelier, a Ganymedest painting of Antony and Cleopatra, and two hulking security guards. Heloïse wore what flattery might call a cloak or poncho, but honesty must call a sack: floor-length, gathered at the neck, with slits for her arms and a hood drawn around her hair, though the contour of her nun's headdress still showed beneath. Never was the letter of the law so meticulously followed and its spirit so ridiculously failed. There was no malice intended, or imagined, on the nun's part, but the world knew what forbidden habit lay beneath this sack of concealing gray, and the shapeless folds spurred one to imagine the more important shapeless folds beneath. A crusader's tabard could not have so overwhelmed the mind with thoughts of Church.

"What's the situation?" Kosala asked again.

"Mixed. A little good news."

"What's the good news?"

"I think we're close to a temporary settlement, and everyone has agreed to keep land sales frozen during negotiations. The violence has almost subsided outside City Hall. There's still one patch of fighting to the south, but the crowd on Prymors'ka Street has calmed entirely, and the Mitsubishi quarters are clear. Confirmed fatalities have not passed thirty. I can also confirm not a single Servicer injured. We got them all out."

The Cousin chair let herself smile. "And the bad news?" Her smile died as she saw Heloïse wince. "You've found more?"

"Ye-es, Aunt Kosala." Heloïse's 'yes' was more sob than syllable.

"How many?"

The nun fidgeted with the Minor's sash that looped about her shapeless sack. "Two since last you called."

"Show me pictures, the worst you have."

"You don't want to see this, Aunt Kosala, honestly—"

"It's not for me."

The memory itself does not feel real. We see images of ruins so often in movies: burned-out houses, castles, cities, Dresden, New York, Pompeii, vivid with fire and artistry, with music and smelltracks to add pathos. What we saw on the screen now was artless, a tumbled, jagged something, dim and badly framed, hard to differentiate from a construction site or unsuccessful art. On either side stood houses, gardens, children's swings, but the shapelessness between had nothing to prove it used to be a home. Uniformed people were searching through the blackened rubble, and some sort of robot twitched its many probe-arms through the ashes like a crab. Stretchers on their way out testified to some survivors, but I know I must have seen a corpse among the coals because my mind strayed to Chiasa Mardi's coiled intestines, and sweet hot blood, and Saladin. I do remember the graffiti, smeared across the surviving garden wall: "Set-Set=Slavery."

Kosala looked to Achilles. "There were six bash'es training set-sets in Odessa, one of the largest concentrations outside Asia. All but one of the six now look like this."

"You think Cousins did this?" he asked, wide-eyed.

"I think Brillists did most of it, but Cousins helped. Most of the 'rescued' children have already turned up at our orphanage doors. Either way, in twenty minutes the world will be full of these images, and in thirty it will be full of Cousins trying to pretend they don't support it, and feeling guilty that they really do, and getting upset, and making poor decisions while upset, and making enemies. The claim that Nurturism isn't violent anymore is wearing thin. Everyone's seen films of the Set-Set Riots, and if these images are called 'New Set-Set Riots' the world will panic."

I took a heavy breath, thinking on the burns Earth suffered last time the Leviathans bared fangs one at another over this. The 2239 set-set kidnapping trial had been a centrifuge which proved that our commingled sand grains could still be sorted into factions, pro and con, red and green, yes and no. Two hundred and fifteen years is longer than even our extended life spans, but today's elders remember elders who could recount those days of fear and bated breath.

"This could be it, couldn't it?" Kosala asked, so softly. "What sparks the war?"

Godlike Achilles frowned. "Could be, could calm again. In a way you're lucky everyone has so many other reasons to be angry now. Your Cousins and the Masons are united in rage against the Hives that used O.S. That rage may be bond enough to keep you from becoming enemies over the set-set issue again. A mutual and present enemy can trump an old feud."

The comfort wasn't comforting. "The plan for Jed's interim constitution calls for the Cousins to elect our Transitional Congress next week, but if it's an angry mob that does the voting it'll be an angry mob that we elect. That's why I need you to teach me what makes people into soldiers, both so we can fight for peace if we have to, and, more important, so I can do the opposite right now. I want our new Congress to make peace, not war. If we fight, I want us to fight for peace and only peace, not for vendetta, or Nurturism, or whatever else. I need a sane Congress. I need calm Cousins and I need them by next week—not in a month, next week. Teach me what makes people go from screaming in outrage to screaming for blood, so I can learn to stop it."

The hero scratched at his hair, oily at its roots and likely itchy, but Achilles will not wash his hair in these days of mourning, nor can he crop it off to lay the offering beside the honored dead, since the child who was more than a son to both of us has left no corpse to set upon a funeral bier.

Here I dared interrupt. "The passions that incline men to peace are fear of death, desire of such things as are necessary to commodious living, and a hope by their industry to obtain them."

Both stared at me.

"That's what Thomas Hobbes says."

Kosala frowned. "I don't need grand philosophy, Mycroft, I need specifics. How do I talk down a billion-member angry mob?" She turned back to Achilles. "I need your help. I need your answer. Will you teach me? Will you help me make peace within the Cousins before the war starts, so we can make peace for everyone once it does?"

Achilles breathed deep. "My answer is that I need time to think, and to meet the other sides."

"I'm not a side. I'm trying to not be a side, and I have less time than the others, only one week."

"And the war may start tomorrow."

The World's Mom sighed, slumping like an oak bough, burdened with a child's swing, when the child returns, grown up, and places the full weight of adulthood on the tired wood. "Just make sure it doesn't drag us into yesterday."

The Great Soldier's voice is rarely soft. "I don't understand."

"War is a thing of the past, Achilles. You're a thing of the past. This whole mess is a thing of the past, concocted out of books and nostalgia: Madame using past customs and seductions to create their power network, Merion Kraye's storybook quest for revenge, Danaë, Andō, Ganymede, burning the world down over a love affair. O.S. is the past too, a system set up before our grandba'pas were born, and now the world is in convulsions over decisions no one living made. MASON is the past too." I wish there were a name for that expression, part smirk, part sigh, part sniff, all irony, which we use when we acknowledge the sad, sardonic humor of our own unhappy state. "As fine a person as Cornel MASON is, their whole mystique is about empire, tradition, pretending ancient mysteries can somehow save us if we return to absolutism and ziggurats. The Mitsubishi are just as much about tradition, a rival tradition but still tradition. And now the King of Spain, just by being so reliable through all this, is making people feel as if the past is the best solution to the present, kings and emperors and coats of arms to stand firm now that the democracies are teetering. You Achilles, Mycroft, even Jed and Heloïse, helpful as they've been with this interim constitution, you're all about the past. The Mardi bash' was afraid we'd wipe ourselves out with our new technology, but I think humanity has proved itself wise enough not to push that button. My fear is that this war will drag us backward, undo this good world we've finally achieved, not by destroying it but by making people want to dismantle it. Look around you. This world is far from perfect, but people have never been happier, healthier, more productive, more free, more equal. We have a lot of improvements still to make, but we've come a long way compared to any older era."

"No need to tell me," the hero confirmed. "The poorest man today lives in greater comfort than King Priam ever did."

"It's the political changes that worry me. Hives and strats are not nations, and that's important. People are free to change and choose Hives, that's the heart of all this, but a war will change that. In war you can't change sides so easily. If this turns into a war as wars used to be, it'll turn us into everything that was worst about the geographic nations. Europe is the most dangerous. The Masons are just mystique, but Europe was made of geographic nations once, and still is, sort of, the nation-strats. We've already seen riots involving nation-strat groups: Spaniards, Croats, Greeks. The rest of the world may not know how to make soldiers, but nation-strats still have their old uniforms, their flags, their anthems, leaders, even kings. If we let that set the tone for the war, it will drag it all back to the days of borders, and rip the Hives apart. The majority of most nation-strats are European Members, but nation-strats have members in every Hive, even Utopia and Gordian, and this could rip those pieces out by force. If there has to be war, we can't let it be that kind of war."

Achilles's eyes and voice stayed dark. "Men fight best beside comrades that share their blood. That hasn't changed, and won't."

"If this resurrects the old nation-states, and destroys people's freedom to choose their laws and governments, it will undo this world. You see that, right? Imagine how quickly the Masons would degenerate into tyranny if the Emperor didn't have to worry about tyrannical action making Members leave. The Masons themselves are a political miracle. They've designed an absolute dictatorship where the ruler is still subject to the will of the people; Aristotle couldn't wish for a more mixed government. This war puts all that at risk, and I fear Europe more than anything may turn it into the old kind of war. Worse, Europe may use you to turn it into the old kind of war, as it may use me. A king may be a ruler of men, but kings can also be dragged along by those they rule. Even us."

Achilles, King of the Myrmidons, nodded to his peer. "Chair Kosala said something very similar."

Mycroft, has thy memory blurred again? This was Kosala speaking.

Kosala? No, good master, it is Spain who speaks, the king himself, quiet in his close-cut mourning clothes of finest lamb's wool, woven by New Zealanders as a gift to the widower upon the loss of his first queen—a gift the king had hoped never to need again. See the sorrowful palace around us, reader? Every marble window frame festooned with black, while the furtive, broken motions of the servants tell of the grief that weighs down all Madrid like plague: Crown Prince Juan Valentín, rest in peace.

"I'm glad I'm not the only one who sees that danger." Spain's words were soft, half winged, grief making him slow like a sleeptalker.

"National rivalries are not a problem I know how to solve," Achilles answered flatly. "I'm more a product of nation and geography than any man living. It's also not Europe's biggest problem as I see it."

"No? What is, then?"

"Rage," Achilles son of Peleus replied. "That will be your problem, Europe's cry for revenge, likely unstoppable." He paused. "Or rather, you might be able to stop it but you won't like the price."

The two kings looked out together through the window, past the guards and gardens to the street beyond, where funeral garlands twined along the eves like the roots of some black parasite. Here too people gathered, Europeans, others, an undivided mass with new cars constantly replenishing what weariness took away. Some had flowers, candles, signs in universal English or European French:

REFORM!
ONE EUROPE, ONE LEADER
PUNISH OS!
SPAIN: EUROPE'S CONSCIENCE
INTEGRITY STABILITY MONARCHY
EUROPE NEEDS AN EMPEROR

"All the Hives are angry," the soft king whispered.

"Not like yours." Achilles frowned his sympathy, but darkly. "Not like yours. The others have someone to accuse: Ockham Saneer, Ganymede, Andō, the CFB, the Anonymous, but you have no one. Europe was unknowingly complicit in O.S., and Europeans who don't want to accept that guilt will be loudest in screaming for someone's blood. But whose? Casimir Perry went down to the House of Death together with his victims. Now you have hundreds of your leading men to mourn, a billion Members desperate to prove their innocence by punishing the guilty, and no villain to take it out on. That worries me."

The King of Spain leaned his head against the wall behind his chair. "I had not thought about revenge."

Rarely have I seen godlike Achilles astonished. "How could you not? Bridger wasn't even my child by blood, and when I lost him revenge nearly drove me rage-mad, even though I knew no earthly power was responsible for my loss. Your son was murdered, and by Perry, a man you broke bread with, a traitor!"

"Was Bridger that child who resurrected Epicuro?"

Even Achilles took a moment to recognize one of Jehovah's rarer names. "Yes. He resurrected me, too, and I raised him like a son. If any living man had been responsible for his death, that man wouldn't be living now."

Spain nodded. "Both my sons were killed that day. One was returned to me, and with their resurrection came proof of the existence of the Higher Power that now holds the other. How many worthier men have not been blessed with such consolation in their grief?"

Achilles's words were stone. "I've rarely found the gods much consolation."

Spain paused. "Do you think your existence proves your gods are the real ones?"

"No." The veteran let himself sigh. "I've thought hard about that, and, with all I've seen, I wouldn't put it past Fate's whimsy to make me real but leave my gods a pack of empty superstition." He peered hard at his fellow king. "You're the first to ask me about that."

Spain seemed to struggle to keep his heavy eyes open. "It's a frightening thing to ask. And without a sensayer here, if Mycroft chimes in we'll have broken the First Law. I suspect a lot of people have these past few days. We shall have to talk to the Sensayers' Conclave about arranging some sort of amnesty. The First Law is necessary but, with the miracle of resurrection captured on video, who could obey?"

The ancient hero scowled. "Do you think there will be religious strife? Even if it can't be public, I suspect many Members of the Hives, like you and I, still have . . . convictions."

His Most Catholic Majesty did not meet godlike Achilles's eyes. "I understand you still consider yourself Greek. If you wish to contact the President of the Greek nation-strat, I can arrange it at your leisure."

Achilles snorted. "I still can't believe that Spain rules Greece."

"It doesn't. Europe rules both, but for now I'm the only—"

A soft knock. "News, Your Majesty." The voice through the door sounded more of apology than warning.

"Come in. What is it?"

The nervous aid wore the livery of Parliament, but bowed like a Spaniard before the king. "The Mitsubishi are calling in sick. All of them."

A ghost's infernal chill could not have sent a fiercer shiver through us. "The whole Hive at once?"

"With the exception of those with life-threateningly critical duties, every Mitsubishi worldwide that should be coming on shift this hour has called in sick, and many of those currently mid-shift are excusing themselves."

"A Hive-wide strike," gentle Spain supplied. "Are they using the same language Utopia did? 'For health reasons consider my work on indefinite stasis'?"

Of course they used the same words. Removing more than a billion people from the world's workforce might threaten the economy, as a storm on the horizon threatens to deprive a village of a day's catch by trapping the fragile fishing boats in port, but those two words, 'indefinite stasis,' were a different danger, an armada's black sails sighted across the blade-gray waves. Does the phrase retain its horror in your day, distant reader? 'Indefinite stasis,' charged with death like 'Off with his head,' or 'Carthage must be destroyed'? For us the terror is two centuries old but keen as new steel. 2239. For three days, as the Senate's consultation over the proposed new Set-Set Law stretched on, Utopia had called in sick, depriving Earth en masse of its crafts and wonders. Then, when the motion failed, they recovered as one from their 'illness' and refused to acknowledge any mass action had taken place. A trembling Earth wondered what Utopia united might have done had the law passed, and wondered most of all why Utopia cared so much, why, with Cousins and Masons screaming at one another in the street over the set-set issue, it was not Father or Mother but the family's strangest child that had made so hazardous a stand. Utopia does not use set-sets. Utopia's separate car network has never needed set-sets, nor with their varied U-beasts do they need the other types of set-sets with their many special powers. Yet the Set-Set Law moved the Utopians to the first mass action they had ever taken, and they never told us why. Danger unknown and unrealized—what a Hive united in anger might have done— that is what the phrase 'indefinite stasis' invokes in us. In you, reader, I imagine the phrase must either be a detail quite forgotten, or else be rank with blood.

Achilles spoke first. "At least this time we know what they're striking for."

"Do we?" Spain asked, gently. "Is it about the land law in Odessa? Or the arrest of Andō and the other Executive Directors? Or O.S.? They're not quite the same thing. If the Mitsubishi just want Odessa settled that's one thing, but if they want Ockham and Andō and the others freed, that may not be possible." He closed his eyes. "This is it, isn't it? This will start the war?"

The Great Soldier thought a long time before he shook his head. "I still don't know. I wish I could recognize war's spark by instinct, but I can't. All things feel like war to me."

Spain took a slow breath. "My peacekeeping forces are few. They can either concentrate on guarding vital spots or on training new forces, either on preparing short-term or preparing long-term, but not both. The same is true of my industry. I can make medicine, or I can make machines that can make a thousand times as much medicine later on, but if the latter takes too long it leaves me with nothing. I don't know where to place my resources."

Achilles frowned his sympathy. "I know right now nothing would be more valuable than for me to be able to say 'this is it' or 'this isn't it,' to give us all a date, an hour we can call war. I can't. I want that too. All anyone can do right now is err on the side of assuming war will come sooner rather than later."

"And yet you yourself aren't offering real help to anyone yet. Does that not betray the fact that you yourself think war is still some time off?"

"No, it just means I'd rather plunge in with nothing than help someone who turns out to be my enemy."

"I'm not used to thinking of myself as having enemies."

"Perry-Kraye was your enemy for years, you just didn't let yourself admit it. Things might have gone better if you had. O.S. and those who used them were also your enemies, and, as things degenerate, you'll have more."

"I know."

"Things will degenerate."

"I know."

Headstrong Achilles almost smiled. "You really do know, don't you?"

"Why do you say that?"

"You can read men. Mycroft says you read them better than anyone, your Nephew excepted."

"Oh? Now, I'd have thought Mycroft would reserve that praise for An-celet." He shot me a long smile. "Or for my Donatien." He paused even longer now, to test me. "And we must not underestimate my sister's senses."

Sister? Nephew? I know my dynasties, Mycroft. Isabel Carlos II had no siblings.

Of course not, reader, and the king, who hoped so long that Kraye-turned-Perry might still be redeemed, is no reader of men.

Faust: "Since you ask, the answer, in fact, is no, I don't have a good sense of
   how things will fall out, largely because of you."
Achilles: "Me?"
Faust: "Pick a number, any number."
Achilles: "What?"
Faust: "Don't pause, don't overthink, just say a number, first one that pops
   into your head."
Achilles: "Twelve."
Faust: "Magnificent. How many of the others did you test before me?"
Achilles: "What?"
Faust: "I assume you're testing every leader before you pick a side. The in-
   teresting question is what order we fall in, in Mycroft's estimation of
   our importance. They'll have taken you to MASON first most likely,
   and Ancelet. Oh, I see you haven't seen Ancelet yet?" I had not spotted
   the flinch or blink or lack thereof that let Faust guess this. "Fascinating. Mycroft, has Ancelet becoming a Humanist lowered them that
   much in your hierarchy of masters? Or . . . ah, I see, Ancelet is . . . never
   mind."
Achilles: "What?"
Faust: "When I say never mind, I mean it."
Achilles: "Do you have a sense of how and when the war will start?"
Faust: "All the others asked you that question, didn't they? And now you're
   asking me? No, I don't know. I thought the Odessa mess might start it,
   or this Mitsubishi strike, but it might start when the Senate meets on
   Monday, or when the Cousins have their election, or when the Saneer-
   Weeksbooth trial starts, or when it ends, or if Spain refuses to let Eu-
   rope make them an Emperor, or if someone says something stupid about
   Sniper in an interview, or if Mycroft here wanders outside and gets killed
   by an angry mob and MASON finally cracks. It could be anything.
   Normally I love suspense, but not this kind."
Achilles: "What do you intend in all this, Faust?"
Faust: "In that particular sentence, the war, the prewar, or life in general?"

Achilles: "The war. Will you insist on vengeance for what O.S. has done against Gordian?"

Faust: "Vengeance isn't useful. Participating in a political coalition, should one arise to address how to proceed, may be useful, depending. I take as yet no stand."

Achilles: "Not even on set-sets?"

Faust: "Oh, one must take whatever opportunities one can regarding set-sets. That's not even a question. Not to hurt the set-sets themselves, of course, they're just clockwork tombstones testifying to past infanticide, no, it's the abominable fools that make them that must be stopped. If convenient. If inconvenient, it can be postponed. The number of children unmade by set-set training is not large compared to the number who might be killed in riots if the issue is badly handled."

Achilles: "Tell me, Faust, isn't what your sister has done to Ganymede and Danaë and all her creatures brainwashing, just as much as making a set-set?"

Faust: "Yes. It's a complex yes, but, in a nutshell, yes."

Achilles: "Then I want to hear from you why a set-set is so much worse."

Faust: "Because a set-set is murder where the corpse still walks. There are over two billion theoretically possible developmental sets in Brill's scale. A few hundred are common and a further thousand reasonably common, but sets aren't for life, we develop over time and our numbers go up, rapidly in childhood but also after that; my own sixth digit went up recently. But set-set trainers, to protect the inhuman powers that they want to sell, start engineering brain development long before the fetus has even lost its gills, shaping the brain's growth stimulus by stimulus, light and touch rationed like prescriptions, and the chemicals, some extra glucose here or poison there to make each neural cluster swell or shrivel as the engineer requires. A Cartesian set-set like Eureka Weeksbooth is a 1-5-2-19-19-2-21-1 for life"—he spat the numbers, as one spits names of devils—"and, because the founders of these techniques have read their Brill enough to fear that nature might still triumph, just to make extra-sure the sets stay locked, they train the set-set not to let itself develop close relationships, no cross-stimulation, passion, friendship, nothing outside the script. Eureka's fed and housed in a bash' but no more part of it than a grandfather clock. I won't deny that Heloïse and Dominic are brainwashed, as much as Martin Guildbreaker, or Spain, or myself, or anyone, all clumsily and semi-intentionally trained by bash' and parents to become what we become, but Spain, Martin, myself, all of us can change, grow, love, not love, and variously expand the palette of what humankind can do, or be. Eureka may as well be dead."

Achilles: "There I disagree. Death and life are more different than that."

Faust: "Poor word choice in your case, I apologize. I can tell you speak Greek as well as English, but, tell me, when you do, what kind of Greek comes out, modern or Homeric?"

Achilles: "You believe I am what I am, then? You didn't even ask to see Patroclus."

Faust: "Dear boy, I believed you the instant you stepped through the doorway. You walk like a horse, and continued straight three paces as if to let your hind-quarters pass the doorpost before turning toward me. I know no one else who was raised by centaurs. There are other signs."

Achilles: "I . . . guess there would be . . ."

Faust: "I know you've decided not to fight for Gordian, but I hope you won't reject us as a potential ally should it become practical. We'd be a good one."

Achilles: "I'm sure."

Faust: "Think of an enormous number. Lots and lots."

Achilles: "A thousand."

Faust: "Exquisite." The pleasure on the Headmaster's flushed face surpassed common delight and swelled toward glee. "Do you know how many generations it's been since anyone outside the most primitivizing Reservations would pick a number smaller than a million?"

Achilles: "No."

Faust: "Neither do I! Brill's data only goes back to 2144. You must let me run ten thousand tests on your brain, on every fiber of you. In your spare time."

Achilles: "Spare time . . ." A moment's frozen incredulity elapsed before Achilles laughed, a deep, raw laugh with deep, raw weight behind it. Faust laughed with him. I got the joke—spare time in a war?—but not as they did. To me it was funny; to them it was a healing, binding breeze. "Alright, Faust, you've given me enough. I'll see you more, I'm sure."

Faust: "More leaders yet to test? Who's next? Ancelet at last? Or has Mycroft found someone among the Mitsubishi worth an interview while Andō's inaccessible? I presume you won't try to base your impression of the Mitsubishi faction on poor Dominic: Acting Chief Director, yes; in over their head, yes; good sample of Mitsubishi thought patterns, goodness no!"

We did not answer Faust. But I will answer you, my distant master, and show you the next meeting, the one which the Great Soldier made me vow not to share with any living soul. Some encounters do not blur, even in my mind. They chose the open beach as meeting place, the northern coast of Crete, where a cloudless sunset made the sparks of our satellites visible between Moon and stars, and where the same salt smell which marks the rocky shores of home brought tears to my eyes, and to Achilles's. Five of them joined us on that open beach. Two I knew: Mushi Mojave, whose ants made verses of our footprints on the sand's broad canvas, and Aldrin, who made the sea a sea of stars. The others were new to me. One's coat made living tissue of the deep, turning invisible currents to visible tendrils, and granting the Mediterranean vast eyes to stare back at we who imagined ourselves safe on her shore. Another left the waves unchanged, but spotted them with strange ships, whose distant spires stabbed straight up from the surface like blades, or like the fins of fish a hundred times too huge. The last coat made all storm and darkness.

Achilles: "Are Bridger's relics safe?"

Utopia: "Yes."

Achilles: "And being studied? Put to good use?"

Utopia: "Of course. We can now prove you are an anachroconstruct if necessary." A glance at me. "We can also prove Mike's resurrection really happened. Empirically, at least. We are not yet well armed against minds impervious to evidence. Soon, perhaps."

Achilles: "How are my men?"

Utopia: "Fascinating. Also patient."

Achilles: "Stander-Y and Nostand?"

Utopia: "Decelerating faster. Fatigue and patches of coma."

Achilles: "Like the others."

Utopia: "Yes. Do you want see them before they revert?"

Achilles: "If I have time." He avoided my eyes here, brave Achilles, as he had avoided telling me when word arrived that Pointer first, then Stander-G and Nogun had succumbed to the eternal peace of plastic. We do not know why Bridger's gift fades quickly from some of his creations while others linger on. If they linger long enough, science may learn. If science can.

Utopia: "We'll arrange a call."

Achilles: "Patroclus will call them if I can't."

Utopia: "You could visit them in person if you wish."

Achilles: "No time."

Utopia: "You must come to the lab yourself soon, Achilles. The experiments we want to run on you are multiplying like hydras' heads."

Achilles: "Later."

Utopia: "There won't be time once real war wakes."

Achilles: "I know." The hero took a deep breath. "Mycroft says, however the sides fall, you and your work must be protected, at any cost."

Utopia: "Not at apocalyptic cost, but at epic cost if need be, I agree. Each death is an infinite waste, but infinity still has degrees. If a new Dark Age tears the Great Project down again, we lose more than current lives, we lose the past ones that were sacrificed for it. Including yours."

Achilles: "Mine?" The wars, which have nearly killed true laughter in the veteran, have strengthened its sardonic shadow. "I never died for anything useful, just glory and destruction."

Utopia: "You can this chapter."

Achilles: "This chapter . . . It is like a new chapter, isn't it?" I recognized the shudder that washed across Achilles, that same awed shudder that had washed over Carlyle Foster when he witnessed Bridger's miracle, and spent the next hours praying that this answer to his lifelong prayer would not turn out to be a dream. "And we are allies?"

Utopia: "We are allies." An otherworldly hand was extended, and accepted.

Achilles: "I think we should keep this alliance secret for now."

Utopia: "Agreed."

Achilles: "Most of the other Hives have tried to recruit me. If I agree to work with one, I can make them help defend you, too."

Utopia: "Will you tell them we are allies?"

Achilles: "I'll decide when the time comes."

Utopia: "Very sage. Will you select your side soon? Or wait to see how the players slot out? It seems some Hives may bud."

Achilles: "I won't wait long. I don't think we have long."

Utopia: "Do you have a battle plan?"

Achilles: "Not yet. I know what resources I want to prepare for the beginning, but I can't guess at this point what the pretext will be when things finally begin."

Humor, mankind's survival strategy, brought absurd images before my mind here, mobs in blasted wastelands, raising impossibly honest banners: "Financial stability! Self-determination! Xenophobia!" We do need pretexts for our wars. A man may leap into the fray in the name of Liberty, Homeland, Human Rights, Justice, but never Economics.

"We have our own warcraft under way," Utopia announced.

"Apollo's plan?" It hurts when I hear anyone pronounce Apollo's name with hate, even someone with as good reason as war-stained Achilles has.

"We will not unweave it while you have no replacement."

The Great Soldier nodded. "That's good sense. I—"

Static flashed, the coats displaying only harsh white blankness as, across the rolling surface of the Earth, all the worlds Utopia dreamed of turned to nothing. Four seconds, five, six Utopia mourned the untimely loss of one of their own, somewhere on the far side of the Earth, or past it. They have not disarmed death, reader, not enough. Not yet.

"Violence?" Achilles asked. "Or an accident?"

Silence held the Utopians as their vizors told them the story of whatever comrade had fallen. "An accident, this time."

Godlike Achilles breathed deep. "I need to know what you're doing."

"We will tell you. We won't tell Mycroft."

Hubris again, reader! Will I never escape the sin which made me raise my voice, indignant, to this kind-descending daemon and protest: "You know I would ne—"

"Your will is too broken for you to control your mind, or tongue," Utopia admonished.

Still I snapped back against their righteous sting. "I've read Apollo's *Iliad*. I already know the plan by heart."

"No, Mycroft, you do not. Not all."

"But I—"

«Enough, Mycroft,» Achilles ordered in our native Greek. His frown contained no sympathy. «If Jehovah Mason asked you what we said here, would you be able to stop yourself from answering?»

I choked on a sob. «No.»

His face softened. «I'm sure somewhere on this globe great leaders of men are waiting for you to do a thousand tasks for them.»

«But—»

«I'll call you when we need you. Now we don't.»

My throat tightened. «Alright.»

«And, Mycroft.»

«Yes?»

«Don't eavesdrop this time. I know you spy by habit, but don't spy on this. Never on things like this.»

«Alright.»

«I have your oath?» Achilles caught my eyes, and held them.

«You have my oath.»

He did, my tears as well, as I cursed the weakness which made me, not only unworthy, but unable to serve the cause as purely as I loved it. I had indeed many orders waiting from many masters, and the Utopian robed in storm rode back with me to make sure I could not double back to spy. Utopia's car was quick to whisk us from those salt-swept sands, though not quite too quick to let me see—or rather not see—one last thing.

Utopia: "Take this, Achilles. It will suit and serve you well."

Achilles: "What is it?"

Utopia: "Nothing."

It was nothing, a bundle of heavy nothing which the Utopian held out carefully, as if it were a swaddled infant. The hero groped a bit before touch let him grasp the gift, and a few shimmers betrayed hints of substance as it unfolded. As spider's threads catch the sunlight for a moment, then vanish again into invisibility, so glints flickered around Achilles's lithe, athletic form as he twisted and stretched within the gift. Only as he tried out the vizor did I recognize the coat for what it was.

CHAPTER THE FOURTH

菜菜菜菜菜菜菜菜菜菜菜菜菜菜菜菜

Ghost

Written July 20–21, 2454
Events of April 12
Shinjuku

I LIKE THEIR SCREAMS, LOUD AND RAW AND FAILING, NONE OF
the fake, suspended purity of actors' screams. They force themselves to stop
screaming, but the almost-silence just makes them panic anew at every
sound: their footsteps, their swishing clothes, the echo of their breathing
ricocheting through the steel ceiling ribs, which make this basement warehouse a nightmare labyrinth now that a hunter's cunning has murdered the
ceiling fixtures' artificial day and conjured true dead night.

「Keep it together!」 The second-largest of the clustered six reveals herself as the leader so easily. 「What are you, guards or children? There's no
such thing as Ghost!」

Ah, ignorance, the predator's ally. The hunter lets itself be heard now, a
light, pinging scrape of something passing flight-fast through the beams
above the cowering prey. An ash scent follows, and a faerie tinkle as one
more emergency light, which they might have found and fixed, powders their
shoulders with its rain of glass dust. One of them fires at the source of the
sound, the shot's quick flash illuminating the maze of steel and boxes for a
lightning second, and revealing, moving among them, nothing. The poor
fool doesn't even remember to fire twice.

「Ghost is real! It is! My ba'sib saw it when it took out Hino and the
others!」

What is that trembling ray of white-blue brightness? A pocket light,
multiplying the mad, geometric shadows of the beams as it shakes in an unsteady hand. An instant later a broken yelp sends the light spinning across
the floor. Why shoot the light in someone's hand when you can shoot the
hand, and add blood to the dark?

「There! Above us!」

The predator's weapon makes no bang, but a hum lingers in the beams, and one of the prey fires some hopeful shots into the shadows. Another silenced shot shatters the offending gun, and the hand which held it.

「We're dead! Ghost never leaves targets alive!」

「Shut up! Be quiet and listen!」

The light they dropped is still on, cutting the darkness with its little blade of visibility as it lies on its side among some sacks ten meters from the clustered prey. Now the predator drops something into the beam's path, gleaming wet and pale, with scraps of flesh and sinew clinging to its length: a bone.

「It's Ghost! It's real!」

「Of course they're real. Stop shooting at them. Lower your weapons.」 The predator's hackles rise as something different rears its head among the herd. This speaker is the smallest of the prey, sheltered in the center like a precious insect queen. The protectee. 「Listen, Ghost, I don't know who sent you after me, but whatever they're paying you I'll give you more.」

「The Moon? Tempting.」 The hunter's voice floats down through the shadows, growl-rough and growl-soft.

The protectee does not dare step out of the ring of guards, but at least stands straight, not cowering. 「What about the Moon?」

「Your offer. I have all the world as hunting ground, and all the races of the Earth as my prey, so if you want to up the ante you owe me the Moon.」 The beast strays near the light for a moment, so the prey can make out the contours of face and shoulders as it licks rich meat drippings from its cheeks. 「Or were you not serious?」

「Look, Ghost, we're not enemies. You've done great work for our group in the past. You're the best hired gun I've ever worked with, and I'd love to use your services again in future, but if you hurt me, not only will you destroy our working relationship, but my bash' and all our allies will hunt you to the ends of the Earth and kill you, even you.」

「I doubt that.」 It vanishes again. 「But I'm not here to hurt you.」

Cloth creaks as hope eases the guards' tense limbs.

「Then what do you want?」

「A new Canner Device.」

「What for?」

「To kill J.E.D.D. Mason.」

「Not for any price,」 the protectee answers unflinching. 「I love my nation-strat. Right now Tai-kun is the only thing keeping the other Hives from gutting the Mitsubishi, and on the inside no one would be surprised if the Chinese, Koreans, and ex-Greenpeace move to expel Japan from the Hive and let us take all the heat. I respect what O.S. was, but anyone who takes a shot at Tai-kun right now, whether it's you or Sniper, is my enemy.⌟

Warm wind at ground level announces that the predator has landed. ⌜You passed that test fast.⌟

The chief bodyguard looms bravely between the hunter and her ward. ⌜Who are you really?⌟

The monster has a second bone, and sinks its teeth into the rose wet flesh still clinging to it. What was this bone, they wonder. A goat? A stag? A dog? The thought of eating any once-living mammal turns most stomachs in our vat-meat age, but for these cornered six, with the adrenaline of the hunted surging through them, the monster's supper invokes a more terrifying taboo, conjured inexorably by fear, imagination, and the one name which is our era's synonym for cannibal. ⌜I'm Mycroft Canner.⌟

I smell urine on the wind.

It is no lie, not as they understand the name: a title of honor, Most Wanted, Archfiend, Devil. Those of the underground who are willing to believe that "Ghost" exists have long suspected their monster was *this* monster. He was too otherworldly, a trackless killer who cared nothing for rank or power, or even sides. He dealt only in barter, accepting food or arms or tradable treasures, and delivering in return, not only death, but terror's torture, and, if the client requested, bodily tortures too. One who would show his victim Hell hired that Hell here. Only one name in our century has created Hell on Earth, and since Saladin and I shared those deeds, so he deserves to share my name.

⌜You don't look like the Mycroft Canner we saw on the news.⌟

⌜Don't I? Here.⌟ The visible sliver of opening in the front of Apollo's captured coat wriggles like a snake as Saladin gropes beneath the folds of Griffincloth and loosens the straps of the piggyback harness. He spins as I step down, so the coat lifts from me all at once, revealing my dappled Servicer beige and gray, while Saladin settles in beside me, my wonderful, beautiful monster, his back against my back, invisible except for a slice of grinning face. ⌜Better?⌟

I pick up the light and aim it at them now. The six are clustered tight, their faces, some Japanese, some not, all ashen. The archkiller Mycroft Canner might loom dark enough in the media's memory to be the stuff even of mobsters' nightmares, but the Mycroft Canner who stood upon the Rostra sixteen days ago is worse, the tool of MASON and of MASON's Son, and of His other fathers, Andō, Spain, whose resources are matchless, untouchable, and angry. If my Saladin is childhood's fear, the unknowable evil in the closet's depths, I have become adulthood's fear, fear of power, law, illustrious contacts, police resources, covert agencies, and sweet judicial murder. Not only the wounded guards whimper. I know I should not enjoy this task so much, reader. It is sinful of me. April the twelfth is a High Holiday, the highest, Yuri's Night, the day mankind first broke Earth's eggshell and touched our rightful Space—a day for hope, for thanks, for recommitment to the Great Project. But I am weak, and it has been so long, reader, so very, very long since last my Saladin and I stood back-to-back and tasted fear-sweat.

「D-did Tai-kun send you themself?」 the protectee asks, almost bravely.

「Others too, but yes. You see why you can't pay me more than I'm already getting.」 It is Saladin who speaks, more fluent than I in the ways of the mobs, whose need for subtle killings have fattened him these thirteen years with hunts to ease the boredom.

「What do you want?」

I answer this time. 「To discuss the black market.」 I take off my hat. 「There's going to be a war.」

「So I've heard.」

「War profiteers will get very rich, very fast.」

「It had crossed my mind.」

I like this young one, not afraid to seem afraid—Saladin chose well, approaching the heir to the group rather than its inflexible patriarchs. 「In wartime,」 I continue, 「a lot of small crimes earn large punishments. The Hives are all preparing to wield lethal force again, not just Blacklaws and MASON. Death will soon be a lawful penalty.」

「That had also crossed my mind.」

「Groups like yours can waste a lot of lives and time working against us, or you can work with us, and get rich safely while we vent our . . . energy . . . on bigger enemies.」

Pressed hot against my back, Saladin punctuates 'energy' with a zealous slurp of flesh. It drips, meat on the bone, in a way no meatmaker steak does, the living juices of the animal still quick inside the tissues, as if seeking a heart to give them life again. One thug retches audibly.

「Tai-kun wants us as allies?」

「Tai-kun」—our Master's Mitsubishi nickname drips like syrup from Saladin's tongue—「has never heard of you, but They trust me to scent the powers of the underground.」 He cannot smile without baring fangs. 「I like you.」

「What do they want us to do? Hunt down Sniper?」

⌜Take a potshot if you have a chance, sure, but hunting's more my strong suit. Yours is business. The powers that be want your black-market channels flowing, to lubricate distribution of goods to civilians when normal channels inevitably fail.⌟ I catch the scent of marrow as the bone cracks. ⌜Accept our terms, and we'll see to it that your problems with the authorities are minimized.⌟

The protectee nudges the largest guard aside, striving to make eye contact against the dark and glare. ⌜What are your terms?⌟

⌜So long as what you leech from official stockpiles doesn't exceed two percent of our stores of food and materials, or one percent of medical supplies, then you may find that the efforts to stop your operations fall slack, while those of your people who do get caught may find evidence lost and prosecutions bungled. Take more than that, and repercussions will be in deadly earnest, and will start with your bash'.⌟

⌜What about weapons?⌟ the young boss asked. ⌜Two percent of goods, one of medical supplies . . .⌟

⌜Your current avenues for arming yourselves will stay open, but if you touch war weapons you risk death; no leeway there. Also, you'll minimize use of deadly force against our people, obviously. And no selling the lion's share of the supplies to our enemies rather than to civilians. Once things break down every bash' on Earth will be desperate to stockpile everything it can; get rich off them and leave the war to soldiers.⌟

The protectee pauses. ⌜You think the Transit System will go down?⌟

Saladin beams pride at his chosen contact's quickness, or seems to through the digital translation of Apollo's stolen vizor. ⌜Or at least flow much less freely, yes. Sabotage is easy. But you're used to working around the traceable. You have your own transport, slow, clumsy, filthy, but you have it. We want that flowing, moving goods where we can't, and more.⌟

⌜More?⌟

⌜When the need arises, we'll pay you to move food and supplies into a specific place or, more important, to move people out.⌟

⌜You want to use us as a rescue service?⌟

Saladin cocks his head. ⌜Why not? You're equipped for human trafficking. In six months we may have land vehicles enough to do it ourselves, but you could do it tomorrow.⌟

⌜Our touch isn't exactly gentle.⌟

⌜Needs must. You can rob them some, extort them some, recruit them if you can, but hand them over to us safe and uninjured and we'll pay you well for every head. Plus, do this well, and we'll also help take out any black-market rivals that crop up to interfere with your profits. We'll even give you a list of other groups in other territories that have made the same deal with us, so you can keep out of one another's way.」

The scent of power and profit cuts through fear. 「A global underground?」

Saladin nods. 「For a global war.」

I stiffen; something was off about that nod. I know my Saladin so well by sound. This is a new sound, not fabric, not skin, but the creaking friction of Griffincloth rubbing against the tooled leather collar that now rounds his neck. I hate that collar. It is a lovely object—I'll admit that—gilded scrollwork tooled into Madame's favorite shade of burgundy, an object much too lovely for the wild thing he is, but that isn't why I hate it. I can't hate it for being wrong either, since it is in all ways right, the culmination of my Saladin's renunciation of all things human. Madame brought my feral cynic off the streets and into the salon which is the center of truth and power, and where, after thirteen years, we can at last lie safe in one another's arms. But I still hate it. I hate the new callus its rubbing has traced across his neck, and how its leather odor mixes with the sweat upon his skin. It's changed him. And it isn't mine.

「What assurance can you give that we'll really be protected?」

Saladin smiles. 「The assurance the gardener gives the insect; we will try not to step on you so long as you destroy more weeds than crops.」

「Not very comforting.」

I take over. 「I can offer the assurance that Jehovah Mason believes it is important to protect human life, as do the King of Spain and . . . others.」 It was not the time to try to force the unready into believing in Achilles. It may never be. 「If you do what we ask, you will win the gratitude of princes. That is worth a lot, especially now.」

A pause—a wise, long, thinking pause. 「I'll need more details, if I'm to persuade my bash', and more proof that this deal is real than just your word.」

Look at my Saladin's beautiful victory grin. 「Whose word do you want? MASON's? Spain's? Madame's? Name your prince.」

All stiffen. 「Is Madame part of this too?」

「Everything and always. I thought the underbelly knew about Madame long before the public.」

「We did, but not as much as we know now. After recent events, you must understand we're reluctant to get closer to such an unpredictable force.」

I answer this one. 「Madame doesn't care about this, or about you. This is about saving lives and preserving some semblance of an economy. That's not Madame's concern, only her Son's.」

Again the young boss pauses for thought. 「I'll talk to my people and see what else we need from you to move on this. How can we find you?」

「I'll find you.」 A shimmer betrays the vizor's edge across Saladin's cheeks. 「Oh, there is one more thing I'm supposed to ask you for.」

「What?」

「Whichever of your people sold the real Canner Device to Merion Kraye.」

「What for?」

「Fun.」

「No, not fun,」 I correct quickly. 「Information. Perry-Kraye may be gone, but their network of allies likely isn't, and we don't know that the extermination of Europe's leadership is the end of their plan. We need to know all we can about their contacts, for the near future as well as for history.」

Frowns pass among the guards.

「You must understand, Ghost, Canner, whatever, why I'm skeptical that even I could convince one of our people to hand themself over to you.」

Saladin purred at the compliment. 「Fair enough. Have the guilty party call Romanova's police, ask for Detective Desi O'Callaghan, ask them for Deputy Commissioner Bo Chowdhury, ask them for Papadelias. Be helpful and I doubt the law will want to waste its time prosecuting the peon of a middleman. Might even help exonerate Japan a bit if they can focus blame on Perry-Kraye. Good for you.」

「I can't promise anything at present.」

「Fine, but I know who it was, and I know their bash'mates, and I can start mailing them finger bones if it would help.」 He smiles. 「Would it?」

「Not necessary, thank you.」 Dignity is strong in this one. 「One more question, Ghost.」

Saladin enjoys that title. 「Yes?」

「Who gets all this when the war's over? You're laying the foundations for a unified global underground. Who controls it in the end?」

The beast's eyes narrow. 「You lead a luxurious life, getting to think so far ahead. Right now the powers that be are working on surviving next week. If you want to try to make yourselves kings of the underground, go for it. No one has time to stop you, but you know what?」

「What?」

「If I had extra resources right now, I'd use them making sure the human race survives.」

Chapter the FIFTH

Strangest Senator

Written July 16–19, 2454
Events of April 13
Romanova

MOST EVENTS ARE CLOSE FOR ME, READER, AND FAR FOR YOU, but some, like this, we watch from equal distance, as Jehovah's twin enemies, distance and time, render us both impotent. I lived through the Senate Meeting of April the thirteenth, 2454, but I could no more touch those marble benches than you could stop the arrow that deprived Achilles of his first Patroclus back in Troy, or he, wading knee-deep through the mud-blood of the Scamander plane, could reach forward to save your life, or Bridger's. Before the crisis, I often walked the streets of Romanova, but now the mob knew me. Would look for me. The police had closed off the Forum to anyone not on critical business, but among the billions of the Earth there were enough who could concoct critical business to form a mob. They packed the streets and ringed the Rostra, pilgrims pressing close to where one could still see Jehovah's blood upon the stones. I don't think the stain was kept in place for science or police tests anymore. I think no one dared touch it.

Records of the Senate meeting must survive to your day, reader, if anything does, but I ask you to watch it again with me, through me, and see as I did the subtext, the strings of power which tugged the Senate from the depths. The benches were full again, all two hundred Senators present, but I could swear more of them wore temporary sashes than had their senatorial stripes dyed into the cloth. Of the twenty-seven Mitsubishi Senators more than half were new appointees attending for the first time, and fifteen of the twenty-two Humanist Senators were doe-eyed proxies. The block of Masons stood intact, and I saw no unfamiliar nowheres among the Utopian contingent, but I spotted a replacement or three among the Cousins. On the front benches, where Europe's chosen habitually gathered, I did not see one familiar face.

Jin Im-Jin, Speaker of the Senate, took the dais now, her thin Korean eyes almost vanishing as she massaged her temples, overburdened by more than a full century's wrinkles. The Speaker's sash sat comfortably across her chest, gold-trimmed ocean blue fabric pledging that, despite the coded Brillist sweater underneath, today she served not Gordian but Earth. No, the feminine feels wrong here. Speaker Jin's demeanor was unmistakably paternal, not a stern Father like the Emperor, but Grandpa, too friendly to be quite imperious as he presides over a gaggle of squabbling grandkids who each think the other's slice of pudding is unjustly large. It took Jin Im-Jin seven cries of "Order" to achieve even a tolerable approximation of silence.

"I hereby call this, the Second Special Emergency Session of the Three-Hundred-and-Tenth Universal Free Senate to ord—"

Before the final syllable took wing, no fewer than five Senators leapt to their feet with the selfish urgency of game show contestants. "Motion to Bring to the Table a matter of . . ." The rest was muddle, one Senator shouting "Universal Emergency," another "Imminent Global Disaster," another the ever-primary "Urgent Defense of the First Law," all those stock phrases which have the power to trump and hijack Senate procedure.

Speaker Jin Im-Jin took a deep breath as the ranks of Senators burst into hubbub. "Order! Order! This emergency session was convened to . . . Order! Order!" Grandpa's face made plain the true complaint: Is anyone in this room *not* having a temper tantrum?

Seeing Grandpa's exasperation, Grandma rose to her feet, Charlemagne Guildbreaker Sr., ever-smiling champion of order and courtesy, whose wooly beard, white against the dark warmth of Persian skin, has for decades been Romanova's symbol for calm. Charlemagne was no longer Minister of Labor, nor even technically the leading Mason in the Senate, but had passed those honors on in order to graduate to the more essential office of assisting the Speaker as the Unofficial Nonpartisan Resolver of Unnecessary Bickering. When the children dropped the ball, Grandma passed it back to Grandpa to serve again. "Incidental Motion, Member Speaker."

"The Chair recognizes Mason Guildbreaker Senior."

In pictures which predate her beard, Charlemagne is the image of her grandchild Martin in poise as well as face, but a decade in her office as keeper of the Senate's much-tried civility has so softened Charlemagne that today they hardly seem the same stock. (I know it is strange for me to call any Mason "she," reader, but see Charlemagne with Jin Im-Jin and you will agree with me.) This is not to suggest that Charlemagne no longer serves the Emperor—the imperial gray band of a *Familiaris* on her arm proves she is a Guildbreaker still—but while Martin's ba'pa Senator Charlemagne Guildbreaker Junior now serves MASON on the Senate floor, Senator Guildbreaker Senior's role in the Empire's agenda lies in accelerating all agendas, trusting that most changes moving in the world are shaped by MASON's will.

"Thank you, Member Speaker." Guildbreaker's cottony beard puffed as she nodded. "Motion to Suspend the Rules. Given the impossibility of establishing straightforward priority among all the urgent motions, I move that the Chair review all the new motions and improvise an equitable emergency agenda."

A junior Mason "Seconded!" at once.

"All in favor?"

The Ayes had it.

You must not think, reader, that MASON's dictates mold the Senate like wax. Sixty-one Masons among two hundred votes is not near a majority, merely enough to steady or to tip a rocking boat.

"Motion to Suspend the Rules passes," Jin Im-Jin confirmed. "And before we move on, I want to point something out. After we're done today it will be easy for one or another of you to raise objections alleging that today's decisions are invalid because we failed to follow one or another procedure. To those already planning such objections I say this: right now this Senate is the only body on Earth with any hope of stabilizing things. People are dying every day in riots which are getting worse, the economy is groaning"—a pointed glance at the still-not-admitting-they-were-striking Mitsubishi— "and we have a better shot than anyone of fixing things. If our authority is undermined, if the public sees us as weak, or squabbling, or impotent, or, worst of all, illegitimate, there will be nothing left but seven very angry Hives and a lot of very vulnerable Hiveless. Yes, we're on rocky ground as far as procedure. Yes, half the Senators in this room are sudden replacements chosen in questionable circumstances. Now is the time to demonstrate that, in spite of everything, we remain a competent and fair governing body, and that we will solve this. If anyone tries to undermine what we do here today by raising objections to procedure after the fact, you won't just have blood on your conscience, you'll have destroyed the best and freest government the world has ever known. So speak now or forever hold your peace."

These flushed and scheming Senators could not muster any unified voice, but they did at least manage unified silence.

"Good," Grandpa Jin continued. "Now, everyone who's introducing an urgent motion, pass your drafts to the clerks. Meanwhile, you each get twenty seconds to describe your business and why it matters. Everyone else, sit down!" His glare added: and shut up! "Are there motions both for both Senatorial Orders and Senatorial Consults?" he asked.

Diverse 'Yes'es confirmed.

"We'll hear Orders first, then Consults."

Did you spot it, reader? Another old Imperial victory immortal in these neutral-seeming words? The Universal Senate may issue Orders to its many arms: to its court, the Sensayers' Conclave, the Censor's Office, Papadelias and his police, the Housing Board, the Archive, but the Hives are their own free beings, like children at a school, free at any time to ignore the teacher's advice if they are prepared to accept the consequences. Since ancient days there has been a name for Senatorial recommendations that carry the force, not of law, but of the Will of the Leviathan, but the name is Latin, and we cannot say *Senatus Consultum* without implying that the Latin-speaking Masons somehow own this, much as we half believe they own all Romanova, built for us by MASONS past. So we instead say 'Senatorial Consult,' which translates to 'Let's pretend we aren't thinking about Masons right now.' Of course we are.

"First, the Chair recognizes Hiveless Fracciterne."

"Thank you, Member Speaker." The implausibly tall old Haitian bassoonist was accustomed to being recognized first, and accustomed too to serving as a neutral mouthpiece when multi-Hive coalitions cannot compromise on which should lead debate. "On behalf of thirty-two of my peers, and for the sake of ensuring the stability of global discourse, and to mitigate the current trend of innocently intended but nonetheless dangerous violations of the antiproselytory aspects of the First Law, I call for the urgent passage of a Senatorial Order to the Sensayers Conclave, commanding that they present, within forty-eight hours, a plan to facilitate safe global dialogue about the unavoidable theological questions involved in the supposed resurrection of J—" She caught herself. "Tribune Mason, focusing on—"

Jin Im-Jin's mace slammed. "Twenty seconds up. Next, Mitsubishi Zhao."

The young but dominant Senator from Wenshou was famous for modeling her vocateur tailor bash'mate Xiaodan Zhao's lavish fabrics, and for the day's gravity she had selected from her closet, not the traditional bright spring buds of March, but a nightscape with hints of blade-slim grass and fireflies that actually pulsed. "I call for the urgent passage of a Senatorial

Order that Commissioner General Papadelias assemble a Special Task Force to investigate the so-called O.S. conspiracy, and report to the Senate before any trial is considered."

"Thank you. Are there any more motions from Senators for Senatorial Orders? No? Motions for Senatorial Consults, then. Mitsubishi Mudali."

Former Minister of Wildlife Madhur Mudali straightened the antiquated Greenpeace coat which today conspicuously replaced her customary Mitsubishi jacket, and sat much better over the folds of her dhoti. "I call for the urgent passage of a Senatorial Consult recommending that the Seven-Hive Council demand that the Hives known as the Humanist Union, the European Union, the Mitsubishi Group, and the Cousins' Society draft proposals for the reform and correction of their governments, and that those Hives which fail to present satisfactory proposals to the Senate-within-one-month-be-considered-for-expulsion-from-the-Alliance." Her voice turned to a high-pitched race as she saw Jin Im-Jin raise the mace, but she finished just in time.

"Thank you. Gordian Petőfi? Gordian Petőfi?"

"What, me?" Gordian's celebrated psycholinguist Tisza Petőfi, her European pallor failing to hide delight's flush in her cheeks, was almost too absorbed in the rich array of specimens before her to recognize her own name. "Oh, I withdraw my motion. Mitsubishi Mudali's covered it."

"Any other nonredundant motions? Cousin Podrova?"

Volga Podrova's Russian paleness showed, not flush, but fear-blanch. "On behalf of twenty-two colleagues, I call for the urgent passage of a Senatorial Consult recommending that the Seven-Hive Council examine, expel, and dissolve the Hive known as the Humanists."

Grandpa glared. "I thank you for your brevity. Are there any more motions from Senators before I turn to motions from others?"

This silence was, I think, the first thing to truly please Jin Im-Jin all day.

"Good. Have the Minor Senators any motions or recommendations?"

The ten Minor Senators were all in attendance, youthful voices without the culpability of votes, who sit in the front row and speak for the millions who are old enough to realize that they live under a law, but have not yet passed the Adulthood Competency Exam and earned the right and burden of making said law.

"No new motions, Member Speaker," Xinxin Hopper spoke for the group, sixteen years old and the pride of the great Beijing Campus, "but my peers and I wish to claim Minors' Priority to speak first when the

Senate considers Hiveless Fracciterne's call for a Senatorial Order to the Sensayers Conclave, since we feel Minors are at special risk of being hurt by the current lack of guidance for structuring dialogue about the alleged resurrection of Tribune J.E.D.D. Mason."

Here was something sensible enough for Grandpa to smile at. "Your request for Minors' Priority is recognized. Now." Jin Im-Jin turned to the Officials' seats that flanked his dais. "Acting Censor Jung Ancelet Kosala, I believe you have a motion?"

"Yes. Yes, I do," the wishing-he-were-still-just-Deputy Censor answered with all the force of desperation. Ten days without the boss—and worse, without myself and Toshi too—had not been kind to Su-Hyeon, and his purple uniform had served as pajamas for so many nights under his desk that even his tiny breasts showed through the wear-sculpted fabric. "Getting through all these urgent motions is obviously going to be slow and complicated, but I'm actually the one who convened the Senate today, because it's been ten working days since this crisis began, and Censor— former Censor—Ancelet's order that the market be frozen, and some other stuff they did before resigning, is going to expire at noon today, but since the powers of an Acting Censor are different from those of a Censor I can't renew most of it unless you formally make me Censor, and if I don't renew it by noon the economy is going to—"

"Five seconds," Speaker Jin warned.

Su-Hyeon turned purple. ". . . do a bunch of stuff that's bad!"

Grandpa smiled. "Thank you, aptly put. Before we deal with any other action, since this one is mercifully uncomplicated, we have a motion on the floor to confirm Jung Su-Hyeon Ancelet Kosala as Romanovan Censor. Is there a second?"

Several rose to second.

"Does anyone want any further discussion of the Acting Censor's motion?"

"Point of Order, Member Speaker."

Had anyone else dared interrupt, I fear Grandpa would have thrown something.

"The Chair recognizes Mason Guildbreaker Senior."

Grandma's gesture was more bow than nod. "Thank you, Member Speaker. Given the current crisis, everyone in this room must realize that we may need to enable the emergency executive powers of the Censor, as set out in the Alliance Charter. No one in this room will doubt that Acting Censor Jung Ancelet Kosala can fulfill the standard duties of Censor

masterfully, but I think many of us would be more confident in this decision if we had a chance to hear the Acting Censor briefly answer whether
they feel prepared to accept these emergency powers, and serve as the temporary Executive Officer of the whole Alliance should the need arise."

"An apt point, thank you, Mason Guildbreaker Senior. Acting Censor,
what have you to say?"

Here it came, young Su-Hyeon's moment. Not so long ago, barely a
heartbeat by the Earth's long reckoning, a young Julius Caesar stood like
this, a young Mark Antony, a young Octavian not-yet-Augustus, receiving
the Senate's ear as crisis looms. "Take me," Power whispers. "The Senate is
a flock of sheep, that may bleat and graze at leisure in summer's peace, but
in winter's extremes it needs a shepherd. It could be you. In this self-
hobbled government that has no real executive, no head, no swift hand to
catch it as it falls, there is a shepherd's crook, a scepter waiting with the
name of Dictator upon it, which this Senate will hand to he who can best
charm the terrified. Speak your piece, young statesman. The temporary
kingly crown they are about to lend you could be yours to keep, if you
seem leaderly enough in this audition. Make them love you. Make them
yours."

Young Su-Hyeon frowned. "Former Censor Ancelet would not have left
such a critical position in unready hands. I have no more to say."

I have never felt prouder to call anyone colleague; Fortune had offered
Su-Hyeon her finest bribe, and the youth declined.

Jin Im-Jin's smile approved as much as mine, and he said something
warm in Korean to young Su-Hyeon, the old Brillist and young Graylaw
sharing an honest moment in their native tongue before protocol made them
revert to stock phrases and common English: "Thank you, Acting Censor.
I hereby call the confirmation vote. All in favor?"

None opposed. The secretary entered the confirmation as Senatorial
Order 2454–173, and Censor Su-Hyeon bolted for the exit like a man on
fire.

Back on the Speaker's dais, Grandpa's smile was all condescension as he
watched the others watch the departing Censor: See, kids? Accomplishing
things! It's what we're here for! He turned to the next impatient face. "Deputy Commissioner Chowdhury, you also have a motion?"

"Yes, Member Speaker." The trusty deputy whom Papadelias made his
primary ambassador to the Zoo (as Papa calls the Senate) was born to a
Graylaw bash' in Bangladesh, proud runner-up in the 2411 Youth World
English Spelling Bee, and had been first a Humanist, then, leaning Green-

peace, tried the Mitsubishi, and was now a Whitelaw Hiveless. "This is already on the agenda for today," Chowdhury began, "but should be decided before some of the honorable Senators' urgent motions: I have here from the Universal Free Court an urgent request for a Senatorial Order telling the Court whether to accept or reject Ockham Saneer's petition for a solo trial with the plea of *terra ignota*."

"*Terra ignota?* For O.S.?"

"That's insane!"

"You can't argue for one minute that O.S. was legal!"

"*Thank you, Deputy Commissioner!*" Speaker Jin screeched, "For this timely reminder. Is there any oth—" He trailed off into silent, mouthed Korean, likely profanity. Who could blame him? The ceremonial paper draft held aloft by the figure who rose before him now was not the pale blue pages of a proposed Senatorial Consult to the Hives and Hiveless, nor the sunny yellow of a Senatorial Order to Romanova's administrative organs, nor even the white or gray of common draft bills, but a coal-black page inscribed with pale ink, shimmering like steel. One hundred and thirteen years serving in Romanova and even Jin Im-Jin had never seen one.

"Order!" the Speaker had to scream. "Order! Order! Minister Cook, you are proposing a new Black Law?"

"Yes, Member Speaker."

"Today? You're proposing a new Black Law *today?*"

"Yes, Member Speaker. As an urgent motion to address this current crisis, I propose that the following be added to the list of Universal Laws, quote: It is an Intolerable Crime to take action which will cripple a child's ability to participate in and interface naturally and productively with human society and the world at large."

Chaos erupted as only volcanoes have the right to do. "The old Eighth Law." The dire misnomer cut swathes through the crowd like the curse it was.

The midwife of this chaos smiled calmly. You know this name well, reader, though this is the first time you have seen her: Minister of Education Lorelei "Cookie" Cook: educational theorist, teacher, boxer, poet, Cousin-born with one stray Brillist among her ba'pas. Judging by the bags around her eyes, Cookie had hardly slept the fifteen nights since her name had appeared on Tsuneo Sugiyama's ill-fated *Black Sakura* Seven-Ten list, and the depravation leant a predatory energy to her carriage, which I have rarely seen a Cousin muster. Cookie is of that free and easy human type that is too mixed to have bonds to any nation-strat, or even to any continent, her face neither dark nor pale, her hair wavy and dark, her round face ever cheerful in her wrap of many colors, with orange shoes, Nurturist mismatched socks, and bulging pockets promising fun and tissues. When she was twelve years old, Cookie's essay "The Adulthood Competency Exam: Why I Will Wait" secured her election as a Minor Senator. She retired from that post at twenty-one, completed law school, managed the Senate snack supply, then took the exam and joined the Cousins at the tardy age of thirty-six, clerking for Minister of Education Carlyle Kovacs Warsawski until, at forty-one, Cookie herself became a Senator and Minister of Education on the same day. So far so cheerful, but many a creature's cuddle-soft underbelly belies its ready claws. If there can be a Prince of Thieves, reader, a Pirate King, a Bandit Chief, then there can be a Queen of Nurturists. Of the bills Cookie has personally introduced into the Senate, a quarter have touched on set-sets, and her bash' has personally raised thirty-seven children 'adopted' from set-set training bash'es that have broken up. 'Broken up.' The savvy public knows the difference between when ice 'breaks up' from the sun, and when it is shattered by some conniving submarine. It is always strange for me, seeing the Nurturist leader's face clean and whole. When service used to take me to Tōgenkyō, I often saw the set of darts Danaë's broodlings kept on hand to help them fidget as they brainstormed, and I saw too the photograph, hanging ever on their dartboard's cork surface and replaced with a new copy whenever one dart too many made the old one fall to shreds: the image of Lorelei Cook. After seeing it so full of holes, my mind insists that the Cousin's cheeks should be pockmarked, or at least heavily freckled, but Cookie's is a smooth face, clean-shaven, and expressive as an actor's.

Grandpa was not pleased. "And what, Minister Cook, is urgent about reintroducing a two-hundred-year-old defeated Black Law?"

Cookie did not flinch. "Set-sets created, enabled, and maintained O.S., and did so without a hint of conscience, because the brainwashing which passes for a set-set's childhood keeps them from even understanding what a human being is. And the children publicly identified as set-sets are not the only ones involved in this crisis whose development was crippled by parental manipulation which intentionally destroyed their ability to think rationally about their crimes. We have proof, developmental records, testing, neural maps. What was done to young Eureka Weeksbooth and Sidney Koons should not be legal. What was done to Director Andō Mitsubishi's adopted children, Masami, Toshi, and the others, should not be legal. What was done to young Cato Weeksbooth, Ojiro Sniper, Ockham and Thisbe Saneer, and Kat and Robin Typer should not be legal. What was done to young Dominic Seneschal, and Ganymede and Danaë de La Trémoïlle by Joyce Faust D'Arouet in Paris should not be legal. What was done to Tully Mardi, crippled on the Moon, and to young Mycroft Canner and the other Mardi children by the think-tank experiments at Alba Longa should not be legal. I think multiple cases of mass murder are proof enough that this should have become law when it was first proposed two hundred years ago. This is not just urgent, Member Speaker, it is two thousand murders overdue."

It is not Speaker Jin's place to rebut, merely to enforce order, but in his impartial silence he has a certain slouching confidence which projects the fact that he could easily expose the stupidity of your claims, small child, if that duty were not better left to your fellow children. That confidence faded before Cookie's rhetoric. Invocation, I should say, for Cookie's words summoned all our terrors—the assassinations, *Black Sakura*, the grotesque charms of Ganymede and Dominic, Mercer Mardi's heart's blood dribbling down my chin—all conjured by one word of power: set-set. Cookie's good at this, reader. She's very good. Even when Laurel Mardi and I were Minor Senators, long after Cookie's tenure, things she had done and said in that little-great office were with us, inspiring, guiding, like an allegorical statue. Now that same skill made Jin Im-Jin pale. "I trust there is not any further urgent business to be added to the mountain," Grandpa half asked, half growled, "before I adjourn for ten minutes to draft a new agenda, my draft to be approved by simple majority when we reconvene?"

A new voice: "I have business." Quick gasps ricocheted across the Senate as the wolf among the sheep flocks rose from her Tribunary throne. Like old vines strangling a garden statue, so black coils draped her fit and fertile frame: her diagonal Tribunary sash of blue-and-gold-edged black, the Hiveless sash black around her waist, her own black hair, and the coiled leather belts which held the empty scabbard where her dueling rapier would nest again as soon as she left Romanova's strict security. Only three of the nine Hiveless Tribunes were in attendance that day, the others absenting, perhaps for fear of a repeat of the Brussels attack. Present representing Whitelaws was Dr. Chambeshi Rhymer, an emigrant to our Alliance born in the Great African Reservation, now a stained-glass collector, psychopathologist, and former president of the World Institute for Suicide Prevention

Research; representing Graylaws came Jay Sparhawk, master gambler, sailor, marine ecologist, and longtime first mate of the flagship *Ahab's Folly*, around whose salt-white sails the flotilla city Neverland assembles whenever the Seaborn nation-strat requires a capital; finally, attending for the Black-laws came India's brave daughter Castel Natekari, baking hobbyist, retired leader-by-conquest of the Algheni Group, and long-unchallenged Rumor-monger of Hobbestown. At age twenty-two Natekari had been kidnapped by a brutish fellow Blacklaw and endured three months' captivity before planning, luck, and guile conjoined to grant both her escape and her re-venge, as sweet and cold as ice cream. Three months by choice. Her late captor was as upright a Blacklaw as herself, and had obeyed the Fourth Law's stricture that he leave his captive's tracker intact, and with it her ability to call for aid to Romanova, whose agents would have saved her in an instant if only she would submit herself to its Gray Laws, and the po-lice which guard them. Castel Natekari, who rose now to face the Speaker's bench, would not renounce her Blacklaw pride to save such little things as liberty, or life.

Grandpa frowned. "Tribune Natekari, you can't veto Minister Cook's Black Law draft until we actually call a vote."

"My business is not about the Black Law." The Tribune held up her own blue paper. "I call for the urgent passage of a Senatorial Consult an-nouncing that Ojiro Cardigan Sniper, having committed the highest act of treason known to the law by attacking the secularsanct and inviolable per-son of a Romanovan Tribune, is declared a traitor and enemy of the Alli-ance, no longer guarded by any law, and that all those who possess the legal liberty to take a human life may, with the Senate's endorsement, kill Sniper on sight."

The Humanists flew fastest to their feet.

"That's outrageous!"

"Kill on sight?"

"Blacklaw savagery!"

"You can't condemn someone in absentia!"

"Without a trial!"

"Sniper shot a Romanovan Tribune." Natekari did not have to shout for her voice to cut through like a siren. "On the Rostra. Any law or body which would protect them so defies reason and justice as to be unworthy of human allegiance."

Now half the Senate rose.

"Sniper is a monster!"

"Sniper had good cause!"

"I see no reason for us to listen to protests from the representatives of a Hive of sociopaths."

"That's right! The Wish List proves all Humanists are guilty of murder a hundred thousand times!"

"Well, I see no reason to recognize as Senators any of the cronies in Spain's coup!"

"Shouldn't you be on strike, Mitsubishi?"

"Order!"

"Spain's kid's coup, you mean."

"Better to have Spain's people here than Senators appointed by a Parliament that supported O.S.!"

"I see no reason to listen to Cousin Senators who are all pawns picked by the Anonymous!"

"I see no reason to listen to a pervert who's married to a product of the same brothel where all this started!"

"How dare you!"

"Order!"

"Everyone knows Sniper and J.E.D.D. Mason planned all this together!"

"Order!"

"Arrest J.E.D.D. Mason!"

"Arrest Joyce Faust D'Arouet!"

"Order!"

Grandpa could not curb the hubbub, nor could his gavel, but the swish of cloth did, soft but omnipresent like the unfurling of a great tent as sixty-one Masons rose to their feet in unison. The object of their strict respect strode in, almost out of breath, through the Senate entrance, his suit of imperial gray cold against the warmth of marble. "*Me creato Senatorem.* (I create myself Senator)," Caesar decreed.

The youngest Masonic Senator had already rushed to meet his Emperor, and instantly handed off his Senate sash, whose band of gold and blue settled comfortably across the broad gray shoulder of Cornel MASON's suit. By Romanova's Law the Hives may choose their Senators as they see fit: by election, examination, lottery, or, in this case, *Dictum Absolutum*, changed whenever MASON wills. On calmer days, if Caesar thinks a motion merits his presence rather than his proxy's, he sits quietly among his fellow Senators, doing his honest best not to abuse the weight which his great office should not carry here. Today Caesar was not subtle. He did not glance at his seat, nor at the Speaker, but marched straight across the Senate floor to Tribune Natekari. To her alone he said something, soft but strong enough to bring a smile to her eyes. She took and shook his right hand, and set in his left the slim blue paper, so it was with his black-sleeved arm that MASON held aloft the call for Sniper's death.

"Mason MASON, will you take your seat?" Jin Im-Jin ordered.

Caesar turned slowly to the Speaker, passing the draft pages back to the Tribune, who beamed through the coils of her black hair, like a predator thinking already of the feast it will make once the prey is caught. "Will you recognize me, Member Speaker?" MASON asked.

Grandpa frowned at Father, but her Brillist eye could read him well enough to know he was a better choice than chaos. "The Chair recognizes Mason MASON."

"Thank you, Member Speaker." Caesar took two paces toward the Speaker's bench, clean strides, untainted by that psychosomatic limp which sometimes betrays his will's distrust of his synthetic left foot. "Though it is not yet officially on the table, I would like to say something in response to the renewed introduction of the Set-Set Law, and I believe my comments will prove relevant and productive for all the motions introduced so far, and for the drafting of an emergency agenda. May I speak?"

Grandpa smiled at the courtesy of MASON's pause. "Carry on."

"Thank you." MASON cleared his throat, and took from the closest desk one of the antiquated paper volumes with the Alliance crest round on their covers, which nest one on each desk, so like a hymnal. "'Collected Laws of the Universal Free Alliance,'" he read aloud. "'Section One: the Universal Human Law Code. No Law or Right may be justly called Universal which is in any way relative, debatable, dispensable, or based on any belief or custom whose universality is not proved by those guides of Reason and Necessity which are truly unchanging in all generations of the human race.

"'Authorities, which have many names, among them Government, State, and Hive, are created by a compact of members desiring to be governed by common law and defended by common force. Each such Authority has just scope to restrict, define, and defend those who have voluntarily submitted themselves to its governance, yet it does not lie within the scope of such an Authority to create Universal Laws, nor to force its governance upon any unwilling person, nor to prevent any person from voluntarily dissolving ties with it, unless the motives for that dissolution be criminal and unjust.

MASON's fellow Senators sat stunned at first, as in a dream when danger takes a strange shape: a pillar, or a color, or a sea of crawling balls, yet the dreamer somehow knows that they will Get You! This was not happening. This happened in histories, in legends, not the mundane Now. The Minor Senators on the front benches squealed and clapped. Then the grown-ups erupted.

"The Set-Set Filibuster?"

"Member Speaker, Motion for Cloture!"

"Seconded!"

Speaker Jin Im-Jin looked . . . I cannot say. So many decades give his face a subtler repertoire than my young eye dares read.

"Seconded! Member Speaker, did you not hear me?"

"Motion for Cloture is made and seconded!"

Discovery's joy, was that what touched Jin Im-Jin? The delight of finding that there is still courage in the younger generations? I think I saw encouragement, too, a kind MASONS rarely receive: Go for it, kid!

"'Likewise it lies not within the just scope of such an Authority to use its force against any person who is not its subject, unless that person has violated one of its subjects. Further, when the subject of one Authority violates the subject of another, the Necessity of Peace demands that the Authority governing the victim not use its force against the violator without first laboring in good faith to reach a compromise of punishment and action acceptable to both Authorities.

"'It is therefore concluded that no such Authority may justly be the source of any Universal Law.

"'And yet, because it lies within the power of a human being to inflict such damage upon the human race as to compromise its future, and to inflict such damage upon Nature as to endanger all present and future life and to inflict such damage upon the Produce of Civilization as to undo the life's labors of past and present generations, and to commit intolerable crimes which so outrage the common conscience of humankind that they cannot be suffered—'"

"Call the Cloture vote, Member Speaker!" Charlemagne Guildbreaker Senior broke in. "We have enough to vote it down!"

Grandpa sighed relief. "Pause a moment, will you, Mason MASON? All in favor of the Motion for Cloture?"

"Aye!"

"All opposed?"

A fierce "Nay!" rose as in chorus from the Masons, Humanists, Utopians, Hiveless, and not a few others.

The general babble did not approve.

"Member Speaker!"

"Member Speaker, in the name of reasonableness!"

"These things are genuinely urgent!"

"*Ordeeeeer!*" Who knew the tiny centesexagenarian had such a scream in him? "Senators, you brought this on yourselves. I have not seen the spirit of this House so abused in a century. Mason MASON has the floor, and if they choose to use their time to make you cool your heels and think again on the foundation of our law, that is a wiser use, both of minutes and of oxygen, than any of you is making. Some of you might think about using this time to excuse yourselves and talk to one another about how to settle some of your proposals, rather than all attempting to hijack this floor which should not be used for private bickering. Anyone who wants to leave and come back with saner proposals, go! For the rest, you will listen to Mason MASON politely and quietly, or you will be removed." Earth's Grandfather waited to see if any would dare meet his eyes. "Carry on, Mason MASON."

"Thank you, Member Speaker." Caesar cleared his throat again. "'Paragraph five: And yet, because it lies within the power of a human being to inflict such damage upon the human race as to compromise its future, and to inflict such damage upon Nature as to endanger all present and future life, and to inflict such damage upon the Produce of Civilization as to undo the life's labors of past and present generations, and to commit intolerable crimes which so outrage the common conscience of humankind that they cannot be suffered, it is therefore necessary that certain Universal Laws bind all human beings to that necessary minimum of restrictions upon their general license without which civilization and the species itself cannot endure. These Universal Laws being necessary, it is also necessary that there exist an Authority capable of expressing and enforcing them . . .'"

Many Senators did leave as MASON continued, a disorganized exodus as the hubbub of negotiation started even before they reached the door. With Caesar's nodded permission, several Masons followed. Grandma stayed, and Grandpa, and many of the oldest Senators, the youngest too, and the Hiveless Tribunes, who rose to their feet to hear the letter of their beloved law pour over them. More than half of those who stayed, like me, shed tears, less at what Caesar was doing than at where he stood to do it, for, as he spoke, his false foot and his true rested with equal firmness on the round brass plaque which broke the Senate's marble pavement like a moon against the night's black: "Here, on the Twentieth day of January, 2239, Senator Mycroft MASON filibustered six hours and sixteen minutes against the passage of a new Black Law and was assassinated."

A long, unsteady whistle wafted from Achilles's lips. "He really means it, your Cornel MASON. He really thinks he's ready to kill and die for this."

I handed Achilles a bowl of fresh-picked wild figs, gathered by we Servicers in whose low company the hero chose to watch this great tumult of state. There were sixteen of us, picnicking on a hillside close enough to Romanova for us to see the Roman roofs in the mid-distance, and for city scents to drown out the salt winds from the coast.

"Of course MASON's ready," a brave Servicer voiced. "If anybody in the world is ready to kill or die for something it's the Masonic Emperor."

Achilles's filth-matted curls still had gloss enough to shimmer in the mix of sun and campfire where we roasted hard-earned sausages and yams to supplement our little feast of baker's discards and found fruit. "Perhaps, but no one knows for certain if you're ready to kill, not until you have your hand at an enemy's throat, or an enemy's hand at yours. Still, for this era, it's impressive to see how completely he believes he's ready."

"Do you not think we're ready, sir?" asked another Servicer, who sat behind us as we watched the Senate broadcast together, some on our lenses, some on the screen which tech-shy Achilles preferred to forcing man-forged devices into his god-given eyes.

Achilles smiled. You would not expect Achilles to have so many smiles in him, but the old hero loves life, for all his wrath and violence, and with the warmth of friends and loyalty around him he does not conceal it. "I think you're as ready as people of this era can be, but when you have a blade in one hand and a soft throat in the other, that's when you discover not everyone's mettle is battle-strong. We'll find out whose is and isn't soon enough. Now"—he reached out his hand—"show me."

The young Servicer recoiled. "What?"

"What that is inside your jacket that you've wanted to show me since we got here."

The others laughed healthy, patronizing laughs at this, our youngest, thwarted in imagined subtlety. I told you, reader, I would show the backyard whispers as well as the great deeds.

More obedient than shy, the young Servicer pulled out a wad of long-suffering papers, crumpled and flattened, drenched and dried, torn and taped, used and erased and used again, scraps only a prisoner or exile would cling to. But as we waited for our shy companion to sort the papers, I heard Hobbes's specter calling, and his Great Teacher Nature, and godlike Achilles heard their calls too, lifting his eyes back to the time-cracked screen where the Emperor read aloud the blood-soaked foundation of our liberty.

"Are they my laws?" Hobbes asks. "Your Black Laws, are they the fourteen Laws of Nature I wrote up, teased out by craft and Reason from the character of Man and his primordial War of all against all?"

A few of these laws Thomas Hobbes would find familiar, that specter whose shadow still darkens our philosophy. Yet, just as the first man to mint a coin could not imagine stocks and banks and usury, so the Beast of Malmesbury could not see far enough past sword and field and banditry to imagine a world where equality and equal rights were no longer in debate, or where a man might push a button and exterminate a city.

"'. . . it is therefore necessary that certain Universal Laws bind all human beings to that necessary minimum of restrictions upon their general license without which civilization and the species itself cannot endure. These Universal Laws being necessary it is also necessary that there exist an Authority capable of enforcing them.'"

Let us review again, reader, with our Achilles and with Hobbes, what must seem antiquated as you gaze back at our savage present. Yet to Hobbes, who draws close now to read beside you, these laws are an undreamt-of future, real application of what was for him a thought experiment. And for Achilles they are even stranger, this mad claim that laws are not handed down by kings, fathers, or even Father Zeus, but excavated from Nature herself by the philosopher's spade. Reread with them.

"'Therefore the Human Assembly, embodied in the Senate of the Universal Free Alliance, assembled in accordance with the Carlyle Compromise, proclaims this LIST OF UNIVERSAL LAWS, which represents the extreme minimum of restrictions which Reason and Experience prove necessary for the continued welfare of the human race. [Amendment of 11/12/2239: Except for the Eighth Law] all human beings are equally subject to these Universal Laws, and all Authorities established by the human species for its governance and protection are equally empowered to enforce them upon those who have chosen to subject themselves to said Authorities. This same Human Assembly hereby institutes the UNIVERSAL FREE COURT to be a final court of appeal to protect and enforce these Universal Laws when all other civil authorities fail, and grants to the Court those powers necessary to carry out this mandate.

"'Whosoever, being of sound and mature mind, should, with full understanding or through gross negligence, violate or attempt to violate one of these Universal Laws, if that person is not appropriately punished by some other Authority, may be detained, tried, and, in the absence of mitigating circumstances, appropriately punished by the Universal Free Court.'"

"Such power!" Achilles must marvel inside. "A universal court that anyone can turn to! In my day, if the wronged had no ally or king to muster force, there was no hope of justice. Even Trojan Paris's great crime saw no trial but war."

"'Whosoever should plan to violate one of these Universal Laws but does not attempt to carry out the act may not be prosecuted or punished in any way by the Universal Free Court, but the Court may take appropriate measures to prevent the execution of such a plan.'"

"Such mercy!" Hobbes too marvels, "to say that thought without deed is not a crime! In my day almost as many were executed for opinion as for deed, and even to imagine the king's death constituted treason."

"'Whosoever, not being of sound and mature mind, should violate or attempt to violate one of these Universal Laws may not be punished in any way by the Universal Free Court, yet if said person is expected to commit more such actions, and if no other Authority takes action to prevent the commitment thereof, the Universal Free Court may take the minimum action necessary to prevent said actions, for the sake of all humanity.

"'As the Object of these Universal Laws is the continuance of human civilization, not any judicial agenda of correction, retribution, or moral enforcement, so the Spirit of these Universal Laws demands that they be enforced minimally and generously, and with Humanity, not abstract Justice, as their final arbiter.'"

Do images of our statue survive to your day, reader? Justice, Temperance, and Reason, sketched by Thomas Carlyle and translated into stone outside his courthouse here in Romanova? In darker ages Justice stood alone before courthouses, but in Carlyle's vision her sister Temperance stands to one side holding back her sword, while from the other side Reason lifts away her blindfold, so Justice can finally see the contents of her scales. The Minor Senators dress up as these figures for festivals. Perhaps it was hubris for Carlyle to change Justice's image after so many centuries, but such enlightened hubris even gods might forgive.

"'The Code of Universal Laws, commonly known as Black Laws:

"'First Law: It is an intolerable crime to take an action likely to cause extensive or uncontrolled loss of human life or suffering of human beings. [Clarification by Senatorial Consult 2144–3: proselytizing outside Reservations violates this law.]

"'Second Law: It is an intolerable crime to do significant and measurable damage to Nature or the Produce of Civilization, or to take an action likely to result in extensive or uncontrolled destruction of the same.

"'Third Law: It is an intolerable crime to kill or seriously harm a Minor. [For the definition of a Minor see Senatorial Order 2144–8 'Minors' Law' and Senatorial Order 2144–33 'Rights of High-Functioning Non-Human Animals and Artificial Intelligences.']

"'Fourth Law: It is an intolerable crime to deprive a human being [or nonhuman Minor] of the ability to call for help or otherwise successfully contact fellow human beings. [Clarification by Senatorial Consult 2191-21: destroying or removing a tracker or the means to access and use a tracker violates this law.]

"'Fifth Law: It is an intolerable crime to inflict torturous and unnecessary suffering upon a living animal which is not a human being and thus incapable of fully informed consent.

"'Sixth Law: It is an intolerable crime to interfere with or disregard reasonable directives issued by a police officer, firefighter, doctor, or other agent of an Authority carrying out a mandate to enforce these Universal Laws or to protect the human race, intelligent life, Nature, or the Produce of Civilization.

"'Seventh Law: It is an intolerable crime to break a legal contract which one has made voluntarily without duress or pressure, and with full understanding of its terms, conditions, and consequences, unless an unforeseen change in circumstances renders the contract's terms destructive, absurd, or cruel, in which case a settlement must be found which is as fair as possible to all parties who have acted in good faith throughout.

"'Eighth Law [passed by an amendment of 11/12/2239, known as Senatorial Act 2239-19 or the True Eighth Law Act]: We do not anger the Leviathans. This Eighth Law applies exclusively to those, known commonly as Blacklaw Hiveless, who bind themselves to no laws but these Universal Laws, and it may be applied and enforced only by the same.'"

"What's this?" Our Hobbes cannot restrain himself. "What's this? I see relics of my handiwork in these other laws, the Sixth and Seventh especially, and this Eighth Law seems to echo my own Fifth Law of Nature—that for the sake of peace every man must strive to accommodate himself to the rest so as not to stir things up—but why does my own word, 'Leviathan,' appear in this law and not elsewhere? And what use has a government for a law so vague, and which cannot be enforced by the law's own officers, but only by certain excepted people?"

Well observed, Master Hobbes; this law is not for the government, it is for those with none. In the centuries that you have slept, there came into existence beings who choose not to join one of those mortal gods, as you called them, that have gone by the names of tribe, and Hive, and state, and kingdom. Instead, these people choose to fend for themselves, motes as they are among Leviathans. The Blacklaws are bound by the Eight Universal Laws alone, an option which the great Carlyle insisted must remain open, or else our liberty-to-choose would be tainted with hypocrisy. Blacklaws are, naturally, much mistrusted by the vast and well-resourced majority, so, like ambassadors from some isolated tribe only provisionally recognized as civilized, they have learned to live always on their best behavior. The fish that rides the great whale's belly must not bite the giant whose least effort can crush him and his thousand kin. For the ninety-five years that the original Seven Black Laws stood alone, this Eighth, unwritten, was etched into the heart of every Blacklaw: We do not anger the Leviathans. Blacklaws themselves punished infractions of their private Eighth Law with anarchy's gruesome severity. When 2339's frenzied Set-Set Riots led to the first ever motion to pass a new Black Law, which might have given the noble title of Eighth Law to the Set-Set Law, the Blacklaw Tribunes were swift to move that their unwritten law be set in ink, securing its eternal place of honor as the true Eighth Law of our Universal Free Alliance.

"This is a strange new world you bring me to, Mycroft," Hobbes answers. "But why do they invoke my word, 'Leviathan'? Why do they not say Hives, since Hives they mean?"

Ah, modest Master Hobbes, you—

No need, Mycroft—this one even I can answer. Have you forgotten, Friend Thomas, that the ancient Blacklaw Capital, of which Blacklaw Tribune Natekari held the post of Rumormonger, bore your name? Hobbestown was no anomaly. This little race of Blacklaws considered themselves your children, these strange courageous minds who read about the war of all on all that you so feared, chose to live in it.

Straight to the mark, good reader, you are right. These are Hobbes's children. But you say 'were'; have they not lasted to your era, then? Our rare, brave Blacklaws? I would ask you of their path, their fate, but I know you cannot answer, noble reader; yours is a better world than I may know.

"'Supplements to the Universal Laws.'" Caesar's eye gleamed almost smugly as he paused. "By the way, if when I finish the three supplements, one of my fellow Senators were to appear with a draft agenda which puts the day's urgent motions in some reasonable order, and includes provisions for postponing some of the more problematic ones for a few days so all sides can prepare for the debate, I might be inclined to stop rather than reading out the entire lists of Gray and White Laws."

Across the capital, agents of every power worked faster.

"'First Supplement: the Consensus Laws, commonly known as Gray Laws. In compliance with Senatorial Order 2144–3, the Universal Free Court has assembled a list of balanced and reasonable laws intended to reflect those laws most commonly recommended by all human beings for the preservation of the common peace. Prohibitions apply primarily to violence against persons or property, theft, deception, exploitation, and other destructive behaviors. All Minors and persons not of sound and mature mind, as well as all adult persons who have not registered to be governed by a different Authority or by the Universal Laws alone, and who are not residents of Reservations, are automatically protected by these Consensus Laws, may demand the enforcement of these laws from the Universal Free Court, and may, in appropriate circumstances, be detained, tried, and punished by the Universal Free Court for violating them. A person who is not a Minor may choose to adopt the Consensus Laws at any time, or to renounce them and be governed by the laws of some other Authority or by the Universal Laws alone, unless the motive for said change is criminal and unjust. [Clarification SC 2144–14: the Universal Free Court will make public a list, known as the Blacklaw Registry, of all persons who have renounced these Consensus Laws and elected to be governed by the Universal Laws alone.]

"'Second Supplement: Minor's Law. In compliance with Senatorial Order 2144–5 no Minor, unless born in a Reservation, may renounce the protection of the Consensus Laws and be governed by the laws of another Authority or the Universal Laws alone. A Minor is defined as a sentient being, regardless of age [or species], who has not passed an examination demonstrating sufficient mental competency to make moral, legal, and life-or-death decisions, or who has passed such an examination but can be demonstrated to have lost said competency and can no longer pass a comparable examination. No person shall be prevented from taking such an examination for any reason including age [species, or synthetic origin]. No limit shall be placed on the number of times a person may take such an examination. The Office of Minors of the Universal Free Alliance must make the opportunity to take such an examination available to any Minor within 24 hours of request. Such examinations may be offered by the Universal Free Alliance Adulthood Competency Exam Office, or by any other Authority whose examination process is approved by said office.

"'Third Supplement: the Character Laws, commonly known as White Laws. In compliance with Senatorial Order 2144–104, the Universal Free Court has assembled a code of behaviorally restrictive laws intended to reflect those laws most commonly agreed upon by those human beings who believe that the prohibition of certain activities and the requirement of certain others is conducive to the formation of good moral character and health, and thus beneficial to the human race and the fulfillment of human potential. Prohibitions apply primarily to such arenas as recreational violence, mind-altering chemicals, harmful cultural artifacts, and potentially exploitative sexual activities, while requirements apply mainly to arenas such as health, education, working conditions, and happiness. Any person, including a Minor, who has not registered to be governed by the laws of a different Authority may register to be governed and protected by these Character Laws in addition to the Consensus Laws and Universal Laws, may thereafter demand protection and enforcement of these laws from the Universal Free Court, and may be detained, tried, and punished by the Universal Free Court for violating them. A person may choose to adopt or renounce the Character Laws at any time, unless the motive for said change is criminal and unjust.'"

Perhaps never in history had so many eyes stared prayerfully at the Senate door as when MASON began the final supplement. Hiveless Fracciterne answered their prayers, the proud old Graylaw entering with a stack of papers held aloft, like the last tuft of leaves as autumn claims a lanky poplar. Other key Senators trailed behind their spokesperson like a V of geese: the many motions' movers, Mitsubishi Zhao and Mudali walking together, European Higginbotham, Cousin Podrova trading glares with sitting Humanists, the redundant but supportive Gordian Petőfi, Blacklaw Tribune Natekari with her cat-soft steps, Deputy Commissioner Chowdhury looking substantially calmer than when he left, even Cookie, whose Black Law draft sat at the back of Fracciterne's stack like one diseased leaf. Many other key Senators walked with them: Senator Charlemagne Guildbreaker Junior and other lead Masons, four of the sharpest Brillists, six European nation-strat representatives, and, accompanying Minister of Education Cook, nine more of our Alliance Ministers, including the Ministers of Culture, Communications, Health, Strat-Relations, Reservations, even the Minister for Extraplanetary Affairs, irrelevant but beautiful in a coat which gave the other Senators space suits. Grandpa Jin Im-Jin beamed as he accepted Fracciterne's papers.

"Are you finished, Mason MASON?" Speaker Jin asked as soon as Caesar paused. "If so, Hiveless Fracciterne seems to have a new motion."

The Emperor gazed on his little blue book long enough to put the fear
of MASON into the crowd once more, then smiled. "Yes, that's enough
review, I think. Thank you, Member Speaker, colleagues, for your kind attention."

"Thank you, Mason MASON. The Chair recognizes Hiveless Fracciterne."

"Thank you, Member Speaker. I have here a draft for an emergency
agenda, which covers all the urgent motions, plus some elements of today's
original agenda, and has the consent of all the movers of all motions. We
propose that the Senate take an expedited emergency vote on each motion
in turn. Each motion will be presented by its mover for three minutes, then
a single opposition spokesperson will have three minutes to speak against,
and then we will take an electronic vote. Any motion passed by a two-thirds
majority and not vetoed by a Tribune will be carried, any voted down by a
two-thirds majority will be dismissed, and those where no two-thirds majority is achieved will be put on the formal agenda for the next session,
which we recommend commence two days from now. The only exception
is Minister Cook's proposed new Black Law, which all agree is too grave a
question for an emergency vote, so it will be deferred until the next session, without a vote today."

As Jin Im-Jin skimmed the ceremonial papers, the network shared the
pure text with the lenses of the millions watching. Grandpa frowned. "You
included Cousin Podrova's motion for the dissolution of the Humanist Hive
among the questions to be voted on today. Do you not think that one, like the
proposed new Black Law, is too grave for such a hasty hearing?" The Speaker
looked less at Fracciterne's gaggle than at the twenty-two Humanist Senators
still on the benches.

"No, Member Speaker. We believe that can be resolved today."

It was the Humanists' nods, not Fracciterne's words, that calmed the
Speaker, their silence promising that, at some point in the basement negotiations, enough votes had been pledged to keep the Hive secure.

"Any objections to this proposal?" the Speaker invited.

The new agenda passed unopposed, one last gasp of unanimity.

"First on the new agenda, we have a modified version of Hiveless Fracciterne's motion for a Senatorial Order to the Sensayer's Conclave, commanding that they present, within forty-eight hours, a plan to facilitate
safe global dialogue about the supposed resurrection of Tribune Mason.

The modification calls for the Senate's order to give no specifics as to what the Conclave's plan should entail, just that they develop one, and that the Minor Senators be invited to the Conclave to participate in its development. Do the Minor Senators wish to exercise their reserved Minors' Priority and speak to the matter?"

Young Xinxin Hopper rose again. "Member Speaker, so long as we are invited to the Conclave to participate in the plan's development, we are content."

Grandpa smiled. "Hiveless Fracciterne, you have three minutes."

"I don't need three minutes," Fracciterne replied serenely. "At this point every human being on Earth has watched the video of Tribune Mason's apparent resurrection an average of eleven times. The number of Alliance Members requesting visits to religious Reservations has increased by a factor of sixty-three, and only capped out at that level because most Reservations have a daily max on Alliance visitors. I suspect most of you would love a chance to sit on a couch for an hour and talk to your bash'mates about what happened on the Rostra without having to go to Tibet to make it legal. Conclave Head Julia Doria-Pamphili is in jail, and we haven't heard a single coherent announcement from the Conclave since their arrest. The Conclave needs to do something, immediately, and we need to order them to. That's all."

"Fracciterne's draft nominates European Vega to speak against. Any objections?" Grandpa's scowl promised that any who spoke up would go to bed without dessert. "Vega, three minutes."

I did not know this tall, athletic Spaniard, but had seen her from time to time in the king's halls. "I shall match concision with concision. Cumulatively, religious wars have killed more human beings than there are alive today. There is no more dangerous fire we could be playing with. The Sensayer's Conclave is our fire crew. We do not order them to go in unprepared. If we rush this, we risk wasting our best and only resource. That is all."

"I call the vote on this motion."

The electronic vote, like the captive lightning which carried it, was swift.

"One hundred ninety-two in favor, eight opposed. The motion passes. Is there a veto?"

As the world waited for the Tribunes' silence to affirm the vote, fear quickened Achilles's breath, the Servicers' too, for those who sat with me had heard the alarm beep of that crass and alien pacemaker which, at Papa's order, thumps on within me, replacing the homemade creation Saladin and I implanted in our lusty youth. "Mycroft? What's wrong?"

Reason calmed me swiftly. "It's alright. I'm fine. It's not *the* eight. Vega must have been one of the nay votes."

"What?"

"One-ninety-two to eight can mean all Hives and Hiveless united against the eight Utopians, but that wasn't the case here."

Such a mix of frowns. Many of my fellow Servicers had Hives once, or at least birth-bash' Hives, so the remnants of allegiance cling like cobwebs to their thinking engines, and the remnants of majority as well: they were not Utopians.

"Let the Senatorial Order be sent."

The printer in the Speaker's desk produced the artifact at once, and a Senatorial courier placed the rich gold sheet in its deep blue folder and bore it down the center aisle with all the careful pomp the cradle of a newborn prince deserves. Across the Forum in the flowered courtyard of the Sensayers' Conclave, a hundred rushing feet rushed faster.

"Next, Mitsubishi Zhao's motion for a Senatorial Order for the Commissioner General to assemble a Special Task Force to investigate the so-called O.S. conspiracy and report to the Senate before any trial is considered."

The face to watch during these minutes was Deputy Commissioner Bo Chowdhury's, scowling as Zhao presented what we all knew was really a delaying tactic, Papadelias and this Commission set up as time-wasters to slow the gears of Law. Report everything to the Senate for interminable discussion? All before even beginning to prepare for the first of what must be many long trials? What blessed breathing space such a move would offer to the guilty, especially to the Mitsubishi Directors, and the fox-crafty lawyers their great fortunes could buy. If this passed, months would drag on before brave Ockham Prospero Saneer could stand before a bench and say *terra ignota*. Judging by Chowdhury's knit brow, had this been a bar he would have started the discussion by punching Zhao in the face.

"Thirty-one for, one hundred and sixty-nine against. The motion fails."

The Senate could see through this transparent ploy. Well done.

"Next, Tribune Natekari's motion for a Senatorial Consult declaring Ojiro Cardigan Sniper a traitor and enemy of the Alliance, no longer protected by any law, and granting license that those with the legal liberty to take a human life may kill Sniper on sight. Tribune Natekari?"

Natekari does not usually let herself finger her empty scabbard while she speaks, but did today. "By attacking the secularsanct person of a Romanovan Tribune on the Rostra, Sniper made a direct assault on the sovereignty and authority of the Universal Free Alliance, and on human liberty itself. Extending legal protection to such a traitor would amount to a declaration that Romanova will not guarantee the safety and liberty of a Tribune to speak, or to use our veto as we are charged to, to protect the universal liberty of the Hiveless and all humankind. Either Sniper is an enemy of the Alliance and has no protection under it, in which case those who have the right to kill must have the right to kill Sniper, or this Alliance must admit that it cares more about the conscience of the majority and the partisan desires of the Hives than it does about fulfilling the mandate of its charter."

"Thank you, Tribune Natekari. Minister Luo has volunteered to speak in opposition."

I wondered briefly which quick-thinking genius had nominated the Minister of Public Safety to oppose the motion, with her spotless Whitelaw sash, her maternal, Venus-round build, and her voice of universal trusted calm. This tamer of floods and earthquakes tames crowds as easily.

"Romanova does not kill. This Universal Free Alliance has never executed a human being, and should not begin now, and that is what this would mean if it passes, even if an independent Blacklaw carried out the deed. We did not execute the war criminals of the Church War, we did not execute the assassin of Mycroft MASON, we did not execute Mycroft Canner, and we should not execute Ojiro Cardigan Sniper. We are different from past governments, and our lack of capital punishment is a part of that difference, symbolic perhaps but still important. Every life on Earth will be fundamentally changed if this Alliance kills. I know many of you will object that this is Whitelaw thinking projecting itself into areas of Universal Law, and that I am thinking of the moral effect this will have on the character of our government and its people. If you think that, you're right, I personally am thinking like a Whitelaw, but to you I propose three other important reasons to oppose this motion, that have nothing to do with the principles of Character Laws. First, we need Sniper alive. We need information only Sniper can give us about O.S. and this conspiracy, and the reasons for the attack on Tribune Mason. Without information to calm things, the present crisis could grow even more heated, endangering the security of this Alliance and the entire world. It would be irresponsible for this body to permit the destruction of such a vital tool for peace. Second, assassination is assassination, and it would be the deepest hypocrisy for us to authorize an assassination even as we put on trial those incriminated in the O.S. assassination system. We cannot justly and rationally examine the moral and legal questions raised by those who have claimed that Hives have the right to kill if we muddle that process by radically changing the Alliance's own policies on killing at the same time. Last, and this may seem similar to my first but it is fundamentally different: there is a lot of talk these days of war. Some think we're on the brink. I think we're not, but I do think violence breeds violence. If Sniper is killed there will be violent repercussions, globally, which might claim many lives. Voting to kill Sniper would kill hundreds, probably thousands of others, and possibly start a war. We don't need to do that. Justice will be done—no one doubts we'll punish Sniper appropriately once they're captured—but those other deaths won't be justice, they'll just be deaths."

"Thank you, Minister Luo. I call the vote."

Can you believe, reader, that I felt no envy? I had expected to, watching someone else attain the bloody prize my youthful planning had so hungered for: to make the Romanovan Senate—the greatest body of our united Earth—debate whether or not to kill a human being. But after I had shared so many meals and afternoons with Sniper, envy was not in my mind; friends' deaths I fear.

"Ninety-nine in favor, ninety-three against, with eight abstentions. The motion will go on the next session's agenda."

Eight abstentions. This time my pacemaker's alarm did not fade so soon. Murmur's speculation filled the Senate seats as the Utopian island sat in conspicuous silence. I shuddered, and through the cameras I saw fresh strain in MASON's brow as he tried to read the faces beneath those vizors. Clean hands, Utopia? The Europeans, Cousins, even Gordian's Brillists glared as the eight of you sat there with your clean hands, reminding all with this haughty abstention—or so the others felt—that you and you alone are neither tainted nor injured by O.S. This wounded majority will not forgive that.

"Next, the request from the Universal Free Court for a Senatorial Order instructing the Court whether to accept or reject Human Ockham Prospero Saneer's petition for a trial with the plea of *terra ignota*. Human Carpenter has volunteered to speak in favor."

"Thank you Mem—"

"Murderer!" Shouts rose at once.

"You expect us to sit here listening to you defend your crimes!"

"How many names did you put on the Wish List, Carpenter?"

"Order!"

"You shouldn't even be here! You should all be on trial with Saneer!"

"I don't think we should admit into this chamber any Senators elected by a Hive which has picked nothing but mass murderers for two hundred years!"

"Order!"

"Everyone elected by the Humanists should be arrested!"

"Drag them out!"

"The Europeans, too!"

"I wasn't elected."

Wonder washed the hate and fear from all eyes as the Strangest Senator rose to her feet. Aesop Quarriman wears her Senatorial stripe dyed into an athletic jacket, where Romanova's gold and blues thread carefully between the bright Olympic rings. If the Mitsubishi can assign their Senate seats by service exam, the Empire by Imperial fiat, Utopia by multiplex occlusion, then the Humanists are free to fill their twenty-two seats as they like: twenty-one by popular election, with the last reserved for a heroes' hero, the Olympic Champion, chosen anew at every Summer Games. The achievements of a heroes' hero cannot be briefly listed. One could count Quarriman's personal golds and silvers, her world records, or the stunning total of five hundred and eight medals which the Humanist Gray Team claimed over the three Olympics for which she served as Team Training Leader. For those who value heroes more for heart than brawn, one could add that, at the Panama City Games of 2450, Quarriman—though she was front-runner and less than a mile from the finish line with its promise of another Olympic gold—was first to abandon the marathon when a sudden sinkhole swallowed up a group of spectators, and Quarriman's too-good example would not let any of her fellow runners leave the site for the four hours it took to dig every last person free. But none of these is her true pride. That lies in Antarctica, her birthplace and her team's birthplace, the Humanist Gray Team, created when the Esperanza City Winter Games of 2280 made Antarctica the sixth continent to host the Olympics, adding a sixth ring to the Olympic flag and a sixth team to the competition-hungry Humanists. The addition was much needed. While some Humanists compete for nation-strat teams, so many prefer the Hive to any strat that, even when the Humanists divided into five separate colored teams—Black, Red, Gold, Green, Blue—each of the five still outnumbered every other Hive or strat team two to one. The addition of the Gray Team made the balance saner. But Quarriman is no complacent Antarctican. In ages past merely surviving on the frozen wastes was achievement enough to mark a hero, but nowadays electric heat and flying cars make mere survival easy. But Quarriman wants to see her icy homeland truly inhabited, loved, played in, not just cowered from as children cower from Nature in a pillow fort. This coming August, peace and Providence permitting, the Olympic bid which Quarriman herself spearheaded will see its culmination as Esperanza City becomes the first Antarctic city to host the Summer Games. When she runs her next marathon across the ice of Earth's harshest wild, Aesop Quarriman will at last merit her Champion's title in her own eyes.

"Can I say something?" Quarriman asked, raising her hand as if in school.

"Please do," Jin Im-Jin invited warmly, his face aglow with delight as the Strangest Senator broke her accustomed silence. "Human Quarriman has the floor."

"Thanks."

The athlete stretched as she rose, bouncing in her light, pliable Humanist boots, science's finest polymers folded in elastic layers as natural as muscles around bone, protecting and padding while leaving the foot as mobile as if it were still bare. It was no easy task fitting the metallic bands of so many Olympic medals among her boots' folds, while the short stripes of her shared team medals sparkled in a dense line from her heel well up the calf.

"When I first heard about O.S.," she began, "I was really upset. Like a lot of you are. Then, when I heard more, I started feeling worse. Because, even though I didn't know about it, it was done partly for me, for my Hive, by my Hive. Now they're saying it wasn't even for the Hive but for world peace, which means not just we Humanists, but everybody has to feel dirty. And it's horrible to accept that this wonderful world we've made is made from killing people. But then I started thinking about what the geographic nations used to do. I'm no expert, but I read a bit about it this morning, and from what I can tell, even to the end, the geographic nations never had any consistent policy on what secret nasty things they were and weren't allowed to do to each other, and each other's people. Even when they made rules, they let each other get away with breaking them all the time, because they all wanted to be able to use those extreme means to protect their own. Now it turns out that the Hives have been doing the same sorts of things, with O.S., and the Canner Device the Mitsubishi made, and I wouldn't frankly be surprised if we discover more things like that. It's not exactly the same as the geographic nations, but it's legally and morally confusing in the same way. The pretend-we-aren't-doing-this strategy has failed. And frankly, this new blame-everything-on-the-Humanists strategy isn't going to work either. Romanova needs to make an official policy about covert actions, one that admits that, if O.S. really did facilitate world peace, then Romanova needs to come up with a substitute for that, another way to make peace, before O.S.'s good effects wear off. Minister Luo was brave enough to use the word 'war' here where everyone else has been avoiding it. O.S. was a terrible means, no one will deny that, but when you pull the keystone out of the arch the rest falls down unless you do something. We need a real legal answer to what means Hives and Romanova itself can and can't use in future to fill the gap left by O.S. Otherwise we don't know what will happen except that it'll probably be really bad. Now"—her face stayed frank—"maybe some of you are thinking I should shut up and keep out of this because I don't have much experience in law and politics, but in this situation none of you do either. We're in unknown lands. We should all admit it. A witch-hunt-type trial isn't going to solve the real problems, but a real *terra ignota*, where experts give us advice, just might. That's what I think."

The Speaker waited. "Thank you, Human Quarriman. So you are speaking in favor of the Senate accepting the *terra ignota*?"

"Oh, uh, yes."

"And is that all you have to say?"

Quarriman scratched at the red-brown cloud of hair around her ears, not organized enough to be called curls. "Is that enough?"

"Yes, thank you." Speaker Jin smiled. "Minister Cook has volunteered to speak in opposition, if there are no objections. Minister Cook."

Achilles fingered the invisible hem of his Utopian coat and whistled, low under his breath, asking in silence what we all did: What favors did you trade, Queen of Nurturists, to get the others to agree to let you be the opposition voice?

Lorelei Cook rose, and I must admit that the cheery colors of her bright wrap in my lenses made my back relax a little after so much black and gray. "Thank you, Member Speaker, honored colleagues. While I appreciate Human Quarriman's honest comments"—she smiled warmly—"by asking us to grant Ockham Saneer a *terra ignota*, the Humanists are asking the Senate to publicly declare that we believe the systematic murder of more than two thousand people might have been legal. The *terra ignota* plea is primarily intended to settle property disputes and social policy conflicts. Using it for a case of repeated and willful homicide is absolutely absurd. There is no doubt or blurriness about the law here. Gray Law and all Seven Hives' law-codes, including Humanist law, clearly forbid homicide, except in a few cases like self-defense, and even that is recognized only by some Hives. Whatever the supposed social benefits of O.S. may be, calling it self-defense is like saying it's self-defense for one job candidate to poison a rival to get the position. This motion is tantamount to a request that we let the guilty Hive governments keep on murdering people, since, if the trial found it legal, it would give them carte blanche to murder whoever they like in future in the name of a supposed greater good. Anyone who defends O.S. is asking the rest of us to walk around with bull's-eyes on our chests while they strut around safe because they've cut a deal to be put on the do-not-target list. This is hypocrisy of the worst kind and . . . what . . . what?"

Murmur, rising like locust song, made Cookie trail off. A change had come over all the faces in the Senate House, and it took the cameras some moments to track the Senators' stares to their object: Olympic Champion Aesop Quarriman, who had ripped a paper form in half, drawn a bull's-eye on its blank back, and pinned it to her jacket just over her heart. She said nothing, but smiled proudly as she dared Minister Cook to meet her eyes.

Cook fortified her composure with a long breath. "Human Quarriman, this disruption is—"

"If Ockham Saneer told me that my death would save ten thousand lives," Quarriman interrupted flatly, "I'd let them kill me. Would you?"

"There it is," Achilles whispered.

"What?"

"A side."

No words now, not from Cookie, the Speaker, or the crowd as the rising clamor churned too much for ears to sort. As the cameras kept their lock on Quarriman, a Humanist colleague beside her took the other half of the torn paper and made himself a matching bull's-eye. Others followed rapidly, Humanists, then one brave Mitsubishi, five, some Europeans, the Blacklaw Senators, and Tribune Natekari, who beamed as if she had just crossed the border back into her own wild country.

As when a good dog, endearing and obsequious, when playing tug with bash'kids plays too rough, and the ancestral predator shows through for a moment in the good dog's unintended snarl, just so the schoolteacher softness fell from Minister of Education Lorelei Cook as she fixed on Aesop Quarriman a glare of open war.

"For and against O.S.?" I asked. "We had those sides before."

"Not recognizably," Achilles answered as the cameras zoomed in on the spreading bull's-eye. "Now there's a symbol, and not an ignoble one: kill me if it will serve the human race. Many have worn lesser sigils proudly. Many will wear this one. When you can tell friend from foe, you can make battle lines." Flush rose in the great commander's cheeks, flush of anticipation, anger, readiness. "With this you can make war."

Hush fell on all we Servicers, memory's hush, but not our own—inherited memories of shields and crests and bright, fluttering standards, passed down to us through history and fiction.

"Shouldn't we have a symbol too then, sir?" asked the young Servicer who sat behind us. "A clear way to tell friend from foe."

Godlike Achilles frowned, the blood-rush still bright in his face. "I haven't forgotten." He took the stack of battered papers and leafed through them, while I leaned close enough to peer over his shoulder. They were sketches, childlike figures fit for a world of boxy houses and lollipop trees, but the clothing, not the figures, was the artist's focus, flat torsos and stiff arms sporting a variety of colored stripes and insignia, while the main part of the figures' costumes, rendered in tea stains and thumb-smeared graphite, were recognizably the tan and gray mottling of a Servicer's uniform.

"These designs are terrible," the great commander pronounced.

The young Servicer gave a little whimper. "Sound in concept, I hope?"

"No, not even sound in concept," the veteran snapped, hotly. "Color-coded rank hats? Those are worse than wearing a bull's-eye on your chest! If you want your commanders to survive a week, you want no difference in uniform visible from more than a few meters away. Marking them out like this is madness! Think, child, the enemy's *name* is Archer! . . . I mean, Sniper." The others peered, concerned, while Achilles shook his head, trying to shake off the heat rising within him as he scented war.

Speaking of names, Mycroft, should we not have names for thy convict brethren? They were omitted in thy first book at Kosala's insistence, to protect the Servicers, but this new chronicle is uncensored, made, not for thy contemporaries, but for me alone. I am not about to track down thy coconspirators by name and rat them out to Papadelias. Why not use names?

"Well said, friend Reader!" Hobbes seconds heartily. "There is no harm in telling us, rather great good. Achilles's former captains, Menestius, Eudorus, Pisandrus, Phoenix, Alcimedon, they will never leave men's memory since Homer graced them with eternal fame. Do these brave Servicers deserve less?"

Deserve less? If anything, those sitting with us here, who follow battle-hard Achilles not by birth but by choice, deserve fame's elegy even more than the ancient Myrmidon captains. Yet still I hesitate to use real names. It is not you, my distant masters, whom I fear. It is hope. What if one of my friends survives to the war's last day? And what if, in the war's wake, the thrill-puffed victors think to beat the beaten further with purges and show-trials? Should our side be the losers in this war, and should this chronicle surface as the victors gloat, then I might have the survivors' executions on my much-wounded conscience if I include their names. Better to guard them safe with anonymity, and let them write their own accounts at the war's end, if they survive.

Such caution is not unreasonable. But if thou wilt not use true names, Mycroft, at least use false ones, some contrivance to end this intolerable vagueness: "young one," "another," I shall never keep it straight.

As you command, reader.

"Sir, if the sides are taking shape now," Eudorus braved, the most athletic of our little company, "and if you're sure that Sniper is our enemy, does that mean we finally have a goal? A side of our own?"

Achilles's brows narrowed, like a javelin thrower's fixing on his target. "Why do you want to die for me?"

Eudorus grinned. "I'm hoping for at least fifty-fifty odds of survival, but—"

"No." The Great Soldier had no time for flippancy. "If you fight for me you'll die. Why do you want that?"

Eudorus paused as gravity set in. "Mycroft expl—"

"Mycroft could talk a fox into skinning itself." The famous runner spared me a fast glance. "Ignoring Mycroft, why do you want to fight, and kill, and die for me?"

"I . . ." If Eudorus had had an answer, the words died unwinged in his throat as he endured great Achilles's glare.

"You Servicers are protected," Achilles reminded us, rising to his feet. "You're neutral, more Hive-less even than the Hiveless. You know how to forage and feed yourselves, and no side expects you to participate in this at all. Keep your heads down and you'll survive if anyone does. Why choose death?" The hero fixed his glare on face after face, the question keen in his eyes as he tested all: Why die for this? For me?

A few of the Servicers managed to meet his eyes at least, but even the oldest of them, wise Phoenix, struggled to voice an answer.

In the hush, those of us with half an ear still on the broadcast heard as Speaker Jin and her weary allies in the Senate marshaled calm enough to call the vote. Ockham Prospero Saneer would have his *terra ignota*, one-thirty-eight to sixty-two, no veto. The hate-hot eyes of Cookie and her opposition scanned the ranks, jumping from bull's-eye to bull's-eye, counting enemies.

Menestius: "I'm willing . . . to risk my life . . . in this . . ." one Servicer ventured, screwing up her courage, "because I'm not so coward as to hide when the world needs saving."

Achilles: "You should be. Hades is no perfumed paradise, if it exists for you at all."

Menestius: "Some causes are worth it."

Achilles: "You think mine is?"

Menestius: "Yes. You want to end the war."

Achilles: "Everyone wants to end the war."

Outis: "But you don't want anything else."

Achilles: "I want many things. Believe me, I want many, many things."

Outis: "But, unlike everyone else in our era, given a choice between two plans in which Plan A has an eighty percent chance of preserving the Hive system and a one percent chance of exterminating the human race, and Plan B would almost certainly destroy the Hives but would definitely save the human race, you wouldn't pause to think about plan A, would you? You'd put humanity's safety first, whatever it meant for any side or faction."

Achilles: ". . . True . . ."

Menestius: "Exactly! You aren't biased by our times. You aren't feeling violated by O.S. You don't have a Hive to protect. You weren't raised to hero-worship Thomas Carlyle and Romanova. This might end in anarchy, or dictatorship, or the return of geographic nations, but however it ends it needs to end with humanity surviving. None of us can face that choice without being distracted by the temptation to preserve the world order we've grown up in. You can."

Achilles: A long pause. "True. But what about all of you? I won't trust anyone with mixed loyalty to guard my back. Think carefully, each of you: will you genuinely follow me, obey me absolutely, even against the world order you've grown up in? Will you generally serve whatever side I take? Wholeheartedly? I could decide to join the Masons and make them masters of this world, or I could decide to wipe their Empire off the face of the Earth. Following me means accepting either path, any path, and dying for whatever side I take. Will you do this?"

Menestius: "Yes."

Achilles: "Why trust me that much? What if I exploit that trust? What if I use you to make myself Emperor of half the world, and then throw you away?"

Phoenix: "You would never do that."

Achilles: "You've only known me ten days."

Phoenix: "We've known Homer a lot longer, and from Homer we know how much you hate war." Old Phoenix choked up saying it. "You don't want to rule, you want to live. You wouldn't fight for selfish reasons, only when there's no other choice. Most of us believe you are what Mycroft claims, Achilles. You may be the greatest soldier who ever lived, or didn't live, but even you need an army at your back to win a war. You need us. Why are you trying to convince us not to fight for you?"

The hero paused, and I wondered briefly whether he was listening once more to the Senate. Now our law's great scales were weighing two fates for the Humanists: give them a second chance to defend their actions and revise their ways? Or issue an immediate demand that the Humanists dissolve and become Graylaws, or else be expelled en masse from the Alliance, and made in one stroke all Earth's enemies. The problem and its banter were enough to distract me—child of this era as I am—but I doubt the son of sea-nymph Thetis heard a word of it; when Achilles's mind strays, it strays far.

"How many of you are there?" he asked at last.

The assembled captains reviewed each other. "You mean Servicers total, or just those that want to follow you?"

"Both."

Old Phoenix answered. "There are just under two million Servicers in the world right now. Last tally about a hundred thousand are ready to take up arms for you. Another five hundred thousand definitely don't want to. The rest are undecided, but I suspect a lot will join up once there's something more formal to join."

"A hundred thousand already." Achilles's hands shook. That frightened me. His shock was natural enough—the fifty ships Achilles brought to Troy from Phthia, with fifty men in each, had been a mighty force in the days when all Greek states together could not boast a million souls. The thousand ships that Helen launched brought fifty thousand men to Agamemnon's call, and now I handed Achilles twice that force, all scavenged from the criminal caste our law had thrown away. The King of the Myrmidons, Homer's Achilles, should indeed have trembled at a number with six digits, but not my Major. He should have memories of the World Wars, of fleets of iron massing vast as cities, of soldiers in their millions bloodying Europe's shores. He should have memories of space ships, and of billions. Had those versions of the Major faded so much already? Was the script which Bridger's dying fantasy set for this world so fixed on Troy?

"This world's too big," Achilles said at last, looking to me as if it were my fault. Perhaps it was. "A hundred . . . five hundred . . . divided by . . ." He counted on his fingers. "A hundred a day will take about a month."

I smiled. "To meet them all?"

He did not return my smile. "To have their oaths. I won't have a soldier at my back who isn't mine by oath. Would you?"

He did not press me to answer.

"They could take it in batches, I suppose," he half mumbled, his mind still slowed by math.

"Do you have a specific oath in mind?" Outis asked first. "I've been drafting—"

"Nothing complex," Achilles answered. "Just 'I swear by all I hold inviolable that I renounce all other ties, and from this day shall live, and fight, and kill, and die only for Achilles.' Will you swear that?"

They would and did, our convict captains, each hesitating just long enough to prove that they thought hard about the words before they spoke them. They had expected him to make some such demand. I had told them how, in ancient days, a soldier's loyalty was sworn, not to his state or homeland, but to his general. The great conquests—and tyrannies—of early history were enabled by that personal bond of command, which made armies flexible, able to switch sides, even switch wars, when their commanders willed. With this war's chasm opening before us, many-sided, we needed that again. The fourteen Servicers I brought today were not mere friends or chance companions, but the leaders of we who are allowed no leaders, elected by charisma and notoriety to represent the others in this first meeting with our chosen commander.

"Not you, Mycroft."

He would not let me take the oath. Nor could I have, reader. Too many ties.

In lulls between the oaths we learned that Fate had spared the Humanists, that day at least. Fifty-one Senators voted to dissolve the Hive then and there, but one hundred and forty-nine voted to give the Humanists a second chance. Only fools were shocked. Cornel MASON commands sixty-one votes and, despite paternal rage, Cornel MASON still dreamed of peace. "The motion fails."

Menestius: "What's next, sir?"
Achilles: "Next we build a training camp. You're not an army yet."
Eudorus: "We've been training."
Achilles: "I'm about to punch you in the face."
Eudorus: "What?"

Achilles: "You say you've been training. I'm about to punch you in the face. Block."

Eudorus: "Okay. Readyyykkhgghhhh!"

Even my eyes did not see the blow, just blood's brightness as the proud young Servicer crumpled from fighting posture to a fetal curl.

Achilles flexed his fist. "We build a training camp, deep in the woods, somewhere untraceable. Mycroft, find a place."

"Already found."

I got a fast, questioning glare, but Achilles did not ask whether I had anticipated his need, or whether I kept a ready inventory of abandoned places for my own purposes. "Assemble your best hundred there, then. Three weeks with them, then they split into groups and each group trains another hundred. If the world survives that long."

The others mustered brave smiles. "We look forward to working with you, sir."

"It won't be me who trains you. I'll come by when I can, but I have Hive leaders to deal with, and battle plans to make."

"Then who . . ."

Child-bright wonder lit the Servicers' faces as Prince Patroclus clambered from Achilles's pocket.

So, as my companions asked eager questions of Earth's second-greatest soldier, I settled back to watch the last emergency vote of the now-calming Senate. Greenpeace Mitsubishi Madhur Mudali's motion passed, again one-forty-nine to fifty-one, and proud Jin Im-Jin handed down the Senatorial Consult to the Seven Hive Council, giving the Humanists, the European Union, the Mitsubishi, and the teetering Cousins one month to prepare proposals for reforming their governments, or else face the Senate's wrath. A firm date. What would our makeshift army not have given for a firm date for the war? To know how fast to train, when to move our goods and weapons, how much quality to sacrifice for speed? One certain prophecy in wartime is worth a thousand times the treasures haughty Agamemnon laid so long ago at great Achilles' feet.

And now we have that prophecy. My chronicle will reach it soon, the day of resolution when my first, best Master, in His Inhuman Wisdom, ended, in one blow, the storm of doubt and hope that had assailed us, planting in their place the certainty of war. As I write these words we have forty-four days until the Will to Battle turns to Battle. No doubt, no constant watch for smoke on the horizon. Forty-four days.

Chapter the SIXTH

Lex Prohibit—The Law Forbids

Written July 22–23, 2454
Events of April 14
Romanova

"I saw what I saw. J.E.D.D. Mason—Jehovah Mason—came back from the dead. It's fact. The public can't avoid discussing it, whatever the law may say. Here, play the tape again."

"Yes, play it again."

"We've played it twenty times."

"Is it true that not even the Censor's database can identify the child who flies in out of nowhere, with the flying sandals?"

"*Hermes's* sandals."

"Careful."

"Yes, it's true, no success identifying the child so far."

"There! There's a flicker on the tape for a couple seconds, surrounding J.E.D.D. Mason. You see it?"

"Yes, I've seen the glow."

"It's residue from whatever visual distortion they used to fake the injury. It has to be. The whole thing is an elaborate fake!"

"That's one theory."

"What do you think it is, then?"

"Do you want an honest answer?"

"Of course."

"I think it's God. Don't all of you?"

The faces of the sensayers who crowded the benches turned as pale as the statues of past Heads of the Conclave, whose portraits lined the courtyard around them, just as long ago in true Rome monuments to past Head Vestal Virgins had stood eternal vigil around their sanctum. It was too beautiful a day for even secret councils to resist the call of April kissed by sun. The Conclave members, and the Minor Senators who had joined them for the day's debate, had chosen the courtyard for this meeting, where spring's first waterlilies graced the pond with crowns of color, while high above the winds chased skeins of cloud along the Tibernovus toward the sea.

"Starting without me?"

"J-Julia!"

It was she, Julia Doria-Pamphili, not yet a statue but the living imperatrix, who strode into the citadel whence her pseudopriestly legions govern the omnipresent, silent kingdom of theology. Today she wore not only her slim black-and-purple sensayer's scarf of velvet and satin, which twined about her shoulders like a serpent, but her full robes, the puffed and rustling archaism of academia, which strikes our eye as mad, but made sense in the arcane days when universities were born, and the surest proof of membership in Earth's elite was still that one could afford to waste two yards of cloth on sleeves. Julia did not close the robe, of course, but let it flutter open, baring at the front her suit of sheer black silk, its custom tailoring proclaiming her membership in Earth's elite today.

"Julia, but . . . you were arrested!"

"You've never heard of bail?"

Julia's dark eyes smiled, but she ran her fingers along the coil of her black hair too. I knew that gesture from times she has lost games, or learned of plans falling through. A bitter sign. He is neither fool nor green, our Papadelias, the unwilling but devoted Commissioner General of Romanova's law. Papa knew Julia's resources: her family fortune, her ties with Madame and Dominic, the web of craven parishioners Dominic taught her to snare. With zealots ready to throw their fortunes at her feet, her resources were infinitely grander than her wealth on paper, so any bail amount a judge would consider reasonable, Julia could raise and discard without a second thought: a million, ten. No financial tether, then, could keep deadly Julia from slipping away and making her next appearance in a broadcast at her beloved Sniper's side. But Papa is Greek, and Greece knows Rome, and the Doria-Pamphili line could not be more Roman had they laid Julius Caesar on the pyre themselves. Papa had asked Sciarra Colonna, Duke-Prince of Paliano and Prince Assistant to the Papal Throne, to post Julia's bail, a mere twenty grand—pocket change to a Colonna prince, but as iron a leash for Julia as one could wish for. They do not die easily, these ancient families. With centuries of intermarriages, rival cardinals, old feuds, and coats of arms with papal keys above them hanging side by side in palaces older than bail itself, Julia would not dishonor the Colonna bash' for all the gold in Troy.

"Julia," one of the braver Conclave members ventured, "with all that's happened we haven't started the process to remove you from office, but given the charges aga—"

"I took the liberty of inviting some guests," she interrupted. "Jehovah, please, come in—no need to linger in the doorway."

All froze upon seeing the Addressee. His head was bandaged, not from Sniper's bullet but from Science, whose tests had cut His flesh deep, seeking the miracle's residue. His suit of antique black had always been a mourning suit, His protest against His Peer's creation Death, but it felt different now that concrete tragedies made so many wear black with Him. He Who Visits from Another Universe can never be said to change expression, nor is there much alteration to the bearing of the flesh that He inhabits so distantly, as a puppeteer inhabits his marionette. Yet somehow the flush of spring and sun awakened an energy in the limbs of His youthful earthly body—Jehovah's Peer, Who governs Nature, bade her grant His Guest the full flower of the human form, however little He might use it.

"I hesitate to enter Another's sanctum," He said as He crossed the Conclave's threshold, "but I am relevant."

For three breaths, no one could do more than stare.

"Yes," one sensayer found strength to answer. "Yes, you are relevant. Thank you for making the time to come."

"What is more important?" No one could face His pure black stare and think the question was rhetorical.

"Nothing," they agreed.

Julia smiled. "I asked Jehovah to come, in case some of you had questions. It should make certain decisions easier."

The others nodded stunned thanks, and raised no protest as Julia took her seat as Conclave Head. Her smile was all victory as she fingered the new pin she wore upon her breast, Quarriman's bull's-eye O.S. sigil. Only a day had passed since Quarriman created it, but the sign was already common on the streets, and even two here in the Conclave wore it. But it felt different on Julia, pinned beside the temporary clip-on chest monitor which oversaw her new heart. Had you forgotten Sniper's second shot? After it fled the Forum, with Dominic still clinging rabid to the car, the living doll stopped at the jail in Antwerp and fired a second bullet through the window and clear through Julia's heart. She had a new heart now, fully artificial, thumping coldly on within her cold chest. I have seen many strange species of courage in my years, but one of the strangest was this, to pin above her still-raw wound the bull's-eye invitation: shoot me again, my love, if your cause demands it.

"I will answer anything you ask," Jehovah offered, "excepting matters on which one of My Earthly offices requires silence."

Several of the sensayers blinked as they reviewed the imperial gray armband which held the insignia of His many offices. The crisis and its power vacuums had promoted Him: no longer merely a European Parliamentary Counsel but a European Council Counsel; no longer a Humanist Bailiff but Deputy to the Humanist Attorney General; no longer a Clerk of the Cousins' Chief Counsel's Office but an Advising Member of the Board. It takes a rare mind in such days to forget Jehovah's part in earthly politics; here sat many who can.

"Come on, then," Julia prompted. "Ask away." She waited, smiling, to see who would dare speak first among her many . . . what would you say they are to her now, reader? Her peers? Enemies? Vassals? Rivals? Pawns? Rebels, perhaps, eager to expel and depose her, but willing still to let her buy her way back in, in return for bringing the priceless Answer to their questions?

"What really happened on the Rostra with Sniper?" The chief rival to the Chief Sensayer was Jess Tilden-Crowner, Austrian and Brillist-raised but now Mitsubishi in a mixed Brillist-Mitsubishi bash' composed entirely of sensayers, except for one vocateur mechanic.

He Who Visits does not believe there is such a thing as too much truth at once. "Sniper's bullet pierced this skull, destroyed this brain, and killed this body, whereupon I reverted to existing only in My universe, *post quem* this body was resurrected by a miracle worked by This Universe's Maker through His agent, a child narratively resembling Asclepius here known as Bridger, whereupon My consciousness returned, both to this flesh and to this universe."

The heartiest of the sensayers still took some seconds to process and recover. "Your universe?"

"The one I generate, sustain, and Am. It differs greatly from this one. I agree with your Maimonides that divine things are often more easily defined by what they are not than by what they are. My universe does not have time, space, limit, ignorance, discovery, exploration, hope, solitude, or death."

Fear dashed among their glances, and a few hands wriggled as scholarly instinct drove them to bring Maimonides's works up on their lenses. In saner days they might have slipped into debating Crescas and the old scholastics: Anselm, Abelard, Duns Scotus, medieval questions alive and evergreen. No time now. "You have a private universe?"

"Not private. There are many beings there. But I am its sole Author, so it is Mine. I am a God, and, there, I am the only God, omnipotent and all-creating. Your own Creator, the Maker of this universe, is My Peer. He made this flesh so that I might visit His universe and here perceive His works. It is a dialogue between Us. During My visit I have experienced some forms of human suffering, so I sympathize with what you endure for Our dialectic, but I know no other way for Us to communicate."

In my wayward childhood I read as many forbidden things as I could lay my growing hands on, including Geneva Mardi's sensayer training books. There are several formulae for handling a parishioner who says he is *God*, or who says he is *a god*, but none for one who claims to be *another God*. I wish there were more people in this world whose answers I could trust when I ask if they believe Him.

"Why are you having this dialogue with our Creator?" one sensayer asked, definitely not any formula's next question.

"For the same reason you open your eyes," He answered, "and engage in dialectic. I and My work are better because I respond to My Peer's. I *deich* . . . I *mostr* . . . I show . . . *oui*, 'show' is English . . . I show also, or rather I will and do and have show showed Him works of Mine, equally alien to Him as His to Me. He made makes and will make you and all His creatures be what you are because He is, always has been, and always will be responding to what He knows of Me. If the human is by nature a social creature, then We Two—My Peer and I—though We Are Creators not creatures, Are social with Each Other." He paused. "Apologies. My own sensayer Dominic Seneschal excels Me at expressing this in English, but he is occupied at present as proxy custodian of the Mitsubishi Hive."

They could not fault the excuse.

"And your assassination and resurrection, what was the purpose of that?"

"*Nescio.* I don't know." He caught His own Latin slip. "My Peer your Maker Wills that I meet Him incrementally, as you do. I did not choose My death, but I am glad I died. It freed Me from several painful doubts, and greatly clarified the nature of Our dialogue. I am also glad He brought Me back to learn more of Him, and of His." Jehovah rarely meets others' eyes. "*Ainiku* I regret to inform you that I still do not know whether or *non* your Maker provides you an afterlife. I long to free you from that question, since I know its pain, but I experienced only My universe, not death in His."

The thought of the Great Answer swept across them like winter's frosty breeze.

The Great Answer? Surely, Mycroft, that title must be reserved for proof of Divinty's existence, not merely of the afterlife.

Must it, reader? It has been so long now, I forget what life was like before He placed His Signature before my eyes. His Existence, for me, is an answered question, while the other still burns late at night when Pascal's truths break through. Still, what portion of mankind, I wonder, truly worries more about whether this cosmos has a Mind and Maker than whether the fragile, priceless ego must someday fade?

Hobbes: "The lesser portion."

Reader: *"You think so, Thomas? Even when the scholastic ancestors of these sensayers, their Aquinas and Maimonides, strove page on hand-scribed page to prove their God's existence and nature?"*

Hobbes: "I know the depths of Man. The endless war to guard his life reminds him at each skirmish that someday he must make the great leap in the dark. Deep down, all fear is fear of that. Besides, there are many like Aquinas who find the old proofs of God convincing, and plenty like Mycroft who have seen the Pattern enough to believe they recognize the Author's Hand, but far fewer to whom ghosts, angels, or logic have proved the afterlife with equal certainty. Don't you agree?"

"The child who resurrected you, you called them Bridger?" The brave sensayer who pressed on fastest was Andalusia Whitewing, a pale and towering redhead, and the only Cousin in a primarily Humanist bash' which boasted sensayers, an architect, a journalist, a seamstress-nanny, and a wall of awards and honors to rival any in Buenos Aires.

Jehovah turned. "My Mycroft knows more of Bridger than I."

So fixed were their souls' eyes on answers, reader, that, with the Addressee before them, they had not noticed the cannibal-parricide who lingered by the door.

"Mycroft Canner!"

"My Mycroft translates for Me when My English fails."

I stayed on the threshold, pinned by my twin duties obey His summons and to guard this sanctum from any profane presence, including my own. This is the most sacrosanct of houses, reader, and I the most unclean of men.

"*Gib Laut,* Mycroft," He commanded, "Bridger *ni.*" (Speak, Mycroft, of Bridger.)

"B-B-Bridger"—my own voice echoing off the hallowed marbles scared me—"was . . . a child of Providence, created without parents and, as proof of that, without a belly button. Bridger could bring toys and dolls to life by touch. A miracle. Inexorable Providence made me Bridger's guardian. I was chosen to raise and protect them for thirteen years. Te-te-ten days ago Providence snatched Bridger back, now that their work was done. I... I have some proof, and can send for more. But, if I may dare advise you, h-honored Parents of the Conclave, I don't think you have time for these questions now. Ἄναξ Jehovah will answer any question you pose Him instantly, honestly, and completely, since to Him ignorance and pain are indistinguishable, so refusing to answer a question is a form of torture, and He will never inflict torture upon a feeling thing. But that means He's too kind to remind you that the purpose of this meeting was not to discuss the implications of His and Bridger's existences, but to address the current Senatorial Order, and figure out a way to help the public cope with talking about the resurrection, to guard the First Law, and the peace."

"Quite right," Julia confirmed at once. "The question of Jehovah's resurrection is an empirical one as well as a theological one, and I suggest we stress that dichotomy in our public strategy. We may be able to get people to calm down and reserve judgment if we say that science should get to answer first. We should have several independent, official scientific teams launch investigations, and we should post continual updates of their findings in a coordinated forum which we administer, so we can certify the phrasing and presentation as neutral and nonproselytory. People will wait for those answers, at least some people. We should also discuss the possibility of temporarily suspending the normal group approval process and letting all sensayers make their own decisions about permitting bash' group sessions and other small group sessions. Practically every human being on the face of the Earth requested a sensayer session this week, and group sessions will ease that backlog fivefold if not more. Would you all support that?"

They were too saturated with questions to keep up with hers.

"Also," she pressed, "there are some elements of public curiosity we can settle quickly. Jehovah, dear, would you support the release of a public statement saying that your experience—I think 'experience' is a safe label—has left you with no new information about the nature of death or the afterlife?"

"*Ja ... sí ... oui ... yoroshii ...* yes."

She laughed again—Julia rarely laughs except at those she has good cause to fear. "Do the rest of you support that?" She waited, looked around, then sighed. "All still in the awe stage, are we? Jehovah, are you okay with letting scientists look at you?"

That delay, always that delay as His thoughts condense themselves from universe-broad currents into words. "Many already have, but more may, yes."

"I-is there a scar?" It was our Minor Senator Xinxin Hopper who dared ask, sitting on a side bench with her fellow Minors.

The Addressee turned toward Hopper, clean motion without excess, as shadows turn away from sun. "There is a circle where the bullet entered, where the skin is white and no hair grows. You wish to see and touch it-*ne*?"

All eyes widened at the invitation.

"Yes, please!" Hopper answered with childhood's eager ease.

"May I touch it too?" I did not know this sensayer, and I hesitate to reveal which of the Conclave was the bravest by so much, but Posterity will wonder. It was Gilliard Gerber, the tireless Swiss Graylaw and essayist, who has several volumes in every good sensayer's library. Gerber is bash'mate of a former Graylaw Tribune, and personal sensayer to, among other notables, the new Censor Su-Hyeon, and most of the renowned Kosala bash', to which the Ancelet bash' was recently grafted.

"Then come."

Jehovah reached, quickly but carefully, to pull back the opaque over-layers and reveal the transparent under-bandage. Gerber, drawing close, reached, just as quickly and carefully, for a gun.

The snap was not a gunshot, rather a mass of action everywhere, as when the force of a downpour is thunderous by itself without the help of bolts from Hephaestus's forge. I had no chance to act. I was blinded by the Sun, not the star that warms us but a sigil which appeared before me, crisp and dazzling with arrow-sharp rays. This strange sun slammed me back against the wall beside the doorway, pressed me hard, and only as it pressed me did I recognize the strength of human flesh beneath the light. "Stand down, Mycroft. All's clear."

The sun released me slowly, still looming between me and the action like a bodyguard, backing away enough for me to see its full form. A stylized sun sigil blazed on the back of a long coat, the rest of which only now flickered into visibility, its hood and sleeves the angry black of shadow-clouds. I could just glimpse a vizor's edge through the hood's mouth. The sight of Utopia calmed me like clean wind as I peeked out around the looming Griffincloth. Gerber was on the ground, pinned by two dragons and a crystal cheetah in whose transparent jaws the gun sat stark. I could not see Jehovah, but near where He had stood a wall of clustered nowhere coats surrounded a column of golden-orange light, higher and broader than a man. The column sizzled as it repelled a trespassing leaf, much as magnets repel their kin. The other sensayers and Minor Senators were on their backs on the grass, fumbling as if winded, while a brace of Asian dragons snaked their ribbony patrol above them, rage-flared nostrils dusting the sensayers with jets of air. Robots patrolled above that, round like children's tops, smaller than those that guarded MASON and Spain, but the same ingenious genus, peppering the courtyard with the dots of their laser sights. Amidst these wonders a car descended through the open courtyard, black but dazzling with lights. Well before the car touched down, Masons in the black-piped gray uniform of the Imperial Guard leapt from its open doors to ring the scene. It all felt like a dream.

"Let no man lay hand on My attacker." Jehovah's order rose clearly from within the protective circle of Utopians. "This Conclave and its members are sacrosanct." I could see Him now, dark within the column of golden light. I could see too the darkly hovering U-beast—something between a turtle, a stingray, and a saucer—which floated above him and projected the protective field.

The lead Masonic guard approached. "*Porphyrogene, te occidere conavit. (Porphyrogene,* they tried to kill you.)"

"Let no man lay hand on My attacker," He repeated. "*Vestalis contingenda non est.*" (A Vestal must not be [contaminated/touched]—NOTE: these are my rough translations since Mycroft, as usual, refused.—9A) He continued in English: "All here are sacrosanct, save yourselves and My Mycroft."

A rainbow archaeopteryx scanned the winded sensayers with a buzzing light, omnichrome and piercing, then settled on one Utopian's shoulder. "No other weapons found."

The guard stood firm. "*Me paenitet, Porphyrogene, sed auctoritas tua IMPERIUM MASONICUM non rescindit.* (Apologies, Highness, but your orders don't override MASON's AUTHORITY.)"

Static flashed just then, the wall of coats around Jehovah turning to harsh white blankness as, across the rolling surface of the Earth, all the worlds Utopia dreamed of turned to emptiness. Four seconds, five, six Utopia mourned someone, and we all froze, and breathed, and thought of our mortality.

"You've ruined this, Gilliard." Julia brushed grass from her crumpled robe. "Working with Jehovah, we could have calmed things down."

"You mean we could have handed the Conclave over to them." Gilliard Gerber wriggled in the dragons' grip. "TM's already 'helped' the Hives enough to plant themself and their lunatics deep in all seven, and now you want to give them Romanova!"

Julia spun, catching every eye in turn. "We need to keep this incident from getting out. The public needs stable sensayers right now. A disaster like this could be the last straw."

The lead guard frowned. "If MASON consents."

Julia had no time for fools. "This isn't MASON's jurisdiction."

"I don't care. Jehovah is my son."

The voice came from above. None of us had noticed a second car's arrival, but none could fail to spot the swarm of glittering defensive robots which schooled out around the Emperor as he descended from it. His personal guards followed, one with a freshly bloodied nose, and, if I know Cornel MASON at all, I know which fist it was which struck the guard who had dared tell Caesar it was too dangerous for him to come in person to retrieve his Son. MASON's guards are all *Familiares*, and their lives are in his hands as much as his in theirs.

"MASON . . ." Even Julia took some seconds to blink away the shock. "If I call Papadelias—"

"Then it will be Papadelias I bully over this, instead of you." Caesar had no more time for Julia. "*Vulneratus esne, fili?* (Are you injured, son?)" He waited. "*Fili?*"

Silence always lingers over Jehovah when He sees Utopia mourn, deep silence, as when, in childhood, He would demand a father who could not come just then, or grope for a book beyond His arm's reach, or ask to meet an author long dead: our mortality stings humans hard, but impotence stings Gods hard too. "*Incolumis, pater,*" he answered at last. "*De mortalité Mea Par Meus εὖ admonuit.* (Unharmed, father. My Peer reminded Me of My mortality skillfully.)"

"*Bonum. Fortasse Eo curabis.* (Good. Maybe you'll listen to Them.)" Robots and monsters traded electric hisses as Caesar advanced. "*Egomet iam te admonui. Omnes te admonuerunt. Dimidium gentis humanis mortem tuam petit. In Sancto mane!* (I already warned you myself. Everyone warned you. Half the human race wants you dead. Stay in the Sanctum!)"

"*In sancto sum.* (I am in a sanctum.)" Jehovah gestured at the marble walls, guarded by inviolable, iron-girded tradition, and nothing else.

I could not see Caesar's face, but could imagine exasperation's red flush deepening its bronze. "Take the *Porphyrogene* to the car."

The English command obviously aimed to part the Utopian wall so the Masonic guards could reach their stubborn Quarry, but the battlements of seas and stars stood firm.

"*In volantem, fili. Nunc.* (In the car, son. Now.)"

The Visitor lingered. "Mother Gerber." He knew well the names of all His Peer's high priests. "Were you actively aware of Your Creator asking or commanding you to kill Me? Or did it seem to be your own initiative?" His voice is ever soft. "Please answer."

We all needed to know.

"It was my initiative," Gerber replied, clean words, clear. "The world can't stabilize with you in it. You must see that. Now get out of here. MASON can carry me off and destroy me if they must, but leave the Conclave alone."

"Thank you. I go."

Now with the Alien's consent, Utopia parted.

"*Nobiscum si libet, Porphyrogene.* (With us, please, *Porphyrogene.*)" Caesar chose his guards carefully, smaller than himself but larger than his Son, large enough to sweep Him with them as a flood sweeps timber toward the whirlpool's mouth, or, here, the car's. As MASON saw his Son settled into the waiting seats, with guards on either side to keep Him there, the human pillar that is Caesar eased at last from quaking fury to his customary stone.

"Wait, Cornel!" Julia's rich alto called out as the Emperor turned to climb in beside his Son. "Are we all agreed that this incident should be hidden from the public?" She said 'all,' but it was MASON's nod she waited for.

He gave it.

"Good. Valor, pull the fire alarm to give us a cover story. Andalusia, go outside to make sure no one's out there spreading rumors. Utopians, am I right in guessing you've been blocking satellites and cameras and whatever else might record us since this started?"

Vizors exchanged quick glances. "Yes."

"Good, then keep it up, and see if you can doctor some images to make things plausible, then you and your beasts vanish to wherever you came from, quickly as you can. As for you, MASON, it's obvious you're going to carry off Gilliard and whomever else you like, so just carry them off and go. The longer you stay, the more people will notice. Go! Get! Shoo!"

Only mildly fazed by the Chief Sensayer's condescension toward their Imperial Master, the guards approached the would-be assassin, but had to stand back like any mortals while the dragons kept their prey. The Utopians who had ringed Jehovah had now fanned out around the courtyard, their long coats transforming the Masons' uniforms, one making them into living calligraphy, another into trees shading a sun-swept lake whose lily pads supported toy-sized tenements and halls and clock towers, where prompt frog denizens hopped about in coats and hats. The Masons frowned as they waited for the dragons to withdraw. There was no obvious cause for the delay, but the twitch of silent Utopian lips and fingers showed they were consulting some broader constellation. At last the glassy cheetah dropped the confiscated gun into a Mason's waiting bag. Then all at once there were no dragons, no cheetah, no archaeopteryx, no thrum of robots with their lazer lights, and no Utopians. The world felt dim.

"Wait! MASON!" It was the ex-Brillist Mitsubishi, Jess Tilden-Crowner, who was brave enough to call to the departing Emperor.

Caesar does not rise from his seat lightly. "What?"

"Tell us J.E.D.D. Mason isn't your successor."

His eyes grew dark. *"Lex prohibit conloquium de Imperatore Destinato."* He translated himself: "The law forbids discussion of the *Imperator Destinatus.*"

Tilden-Crowner pressed on. "Sniper's whole cause is fired by everyone thinking J.E.D.D. Mason's going to take power in every Hive. Just announce they aren't your successor and it'll all die down."

MASON's words were stony as the obelisk in Alexandria, where the grim law stands inscribed in all the great languages of the ancient age when it was supposedly carved. *"Lex prohibit* discussion of the *Imperator Destinatus.* This is your second warning. There will not be a third."

Tilden-Crowner has deep reserves of courage. "I know you want us to know it isn't them. That's why you adopted them in the first place, since it's common knowledge that a *porphyrogene* never becomes Emperor. But people are paranoid. Just say it publicly, that they aren't your successor. That's all we need to end this!"

MASON nodded to the one among his guards who wore the gold and blue cording of a Romanovan deputy over his Masonic gray. The guard at once placed a heavy hand on the offender's shoulder. "Jess Tilden-Crowner, I place you under arrest for public and repeated violation of the First Black Law, action likely to result in extensive or uncontrolled loss of human life, which, as clarified by Senatorial Consult 2147–129, covers public discussion of the *Imperator Destinatus.* You will come with me."

I saw little more, nor did I have time then to wonder whether Julia had somehow planned this, too, the elegant removal of her most ambitious potential replacement.

Those who took Tilden-Crowner came for me, too. I do not resist MASON's agents unless the need is dire, but I did cling to a railing long enough to grope and find by touch the now-invisible Utopian who had shielded and pinned me in the moments of crisis. I shouted my test. "Delian!"

They spun. They all spun, a heavy whish filling the courtyard as all the invisible Utopians turned as one. I was right. Someone else might have mistaken it for a trick of the coat's stormy lightning, that sun sigil that had blinded me when the Utopian first appeared—but I knew that shape well, from the flyleaf of Apollo's *Iliad,* and from a grimmer source. When Saladin patrols an alley in Apollo's captured coat, its Griffincloth turns Hive Members' customary dress to how Apollo imagined their wartime uniforms: Europeans to updated historic uniforms, Cousins' wraps to nurses' scrubs in azure and warm cream, Mason's suits to gray-piped black and purple. From time to time Saladin passes a Utopian, nowhere overlaying nowhere. When he does, Apollo's program does not replace his comrades' coats, but instead stamps that blazing sun sigil onto each Utopian's back. Delos is the sacred birthplace of Ἄναξ Apollo and his sister, deadly Artemis. Apollo's Delians; Apollo's army. I released the unseen figure, and said nothing more, not as MASON's guards sat me beside my Master in the car, not as their medic checked us, not as we flew across the noon-bright sea toward Alexandria's fortressed *Sanctum.* What could I have said? It was no accident if Utopia had flashed the Delian sigil before the eyes of the one person on Earth most likely to recognize it. They had their army. While Achilles struggled to turn servicers into soldiers, and Saladin to turn thugs into a commissariat, Utopia wanted me to know that they, at least, stood ready.

"I should not have come to the Conclave."

Jehovah's face and voice were still expressionless as He sat beside me, but I could feel His pain, as if my soul were its own sense, able to perceive anguish in another, or in Him at least. Which ancient was it who called the soul a sense? Aristotle?

"It wasn't your fault, Ἄναξ," I consoled. "You couldn't have known what would happen." I forced myself to use English with Him, playing my part in regenerating His ability to sort languages. "The Chief Sensayer summoned You to help Your Peer's priests, You couldn't refuse that. You shouldn't refuse that."

"Yet I did harm."

"It had to happen." I forced a smile. "You know that, Ἄναξ. There is Providence. All that happens serves the Plan, and Your ongoing Conversation. Or are You afraid that, because His Providence does not dictate Your actions, You might act against the Plan and thereby change or harm it?"

"That is not My fear. My Peer wants Me to change His Plan or else He would not invite Me."

"What, then?"

"Thinkest thou that My Peer knows how terrible harm feels to His creations? Or is His experience too removed from theirs for empathy? And if the latter, is it so for Me? If I make My creatures suffer, as He makes His suffer, would I realize it?"

Never again, reader, let me call myself anxious when the great Anxieties of This Infinite Being so dwarf such petty spheres as Earth, and Time. A whole universe could be in torment and He might not know. "I'm sure that isn't true, Ἄναξ, You care so much. I'm sure You'd know."

"Yet how could I? If the mote cannot perceive the workings of the Whole, how can the Whole comprehend the anguish of the mote?"

He does not know how to weep, this kindly Visitor so unfluent in the subtleties of body. So I wept for Him. "I'm sure You can perceive suffering, Ἄναξ. You're learning. You're learning even now."

SOURCE: *Rosetta Forum*, 4/14/2454, 5:30 PM UT
ARTICLE HEADLINE: **CONCLAVE PROGRESS**

TEXT: Spokesperson Andalusia Whitewing describes the Sensayers' Conclave as "optimistic" about the plan they will present to the Senate tomorrow in response to the Senatorial Order that the Conclave address the theological questions raised by the attack on J.E.D.D. Mason sixteen days ago. The plan will address both private and public discourse, and proposes action to be taken both by the College of Sensayers and external bodies. An account of J.E.D.D. Mason's own experience of the attack is also expected. Scientific investigation of the incident is under way, and Whitewing urges everyone to be patient and await the results. Despite reports of their arrest earlier this week, Conclave Head Julia Doria-Pamphili led the deliberations, which, according to Whitewing, focused on seeking a way to satisfy the safety requirements of the First Black Law without interfering with the course of science, or stifling individual dialogue. Deliberations took a turn for the dramatic when the fire alarm system was triggered by two type Yulóng-AI766 dragons, which strayed onto the Conclave roof in the course of removing the equipment Sniper used to escape the Forum after the attack. The dragons' operator apologized for the error.

CHAPTER THE SEVENTH

Grace

Written July 24–26, 2454
Events of April 14
Zürich, Palma de Mallorca, & transit

"YOU CAN'T GET THEM OUT OF HERE SOON ENOUGH. WE'VE handled politically sensitive prisoners before, and our share of whackos, but this has shut us down, completely shut us down. We figured we'd have to keep them away from other prisoners, but it's just as bad with the guards. I know that look a prisoner gets when they see a—if you'll excuse the expression—a piece of ass they can't resist. Half my staff has that look now, more than half. And who can blame them? The nutcase won't wear clothes. Ripped the uniform to shreds whenever we dressed them by force, just stood there totally stark naked and . . . distracting. Do you have any idea how distracting—"

"Yes, I know."

"They won't eat," the warden ranted on, "won't drink, won't sit down or even lean on anything."

"I see."

"They just stood there naked in the center of their cell until they passed out from exhaustion. Got a concussion on the way down, then flipped out when they woke up in the infirmary, attacked the sheets."

"Of course they did." These gentle interruptions came from the companion who followed behind me and the warden, his soft steps precise, not like a guard's stiff march, but like a dancer's.

"Why? Why attack the sheets?"

"They weren't silk."

"So?" I smiled at the warden's obliviousness as he rambled on. "I wasn't told about the ex-president being allergic to cotton or anything."

The view through the infirmary door before us cut short any answer. Milo's Venus shattered at my feet could not have raised worse sobs in me.

The prisoner's sun-gold mane was sweat-tarnished, his alabaster skin faded from moon-pale delicacy to death's-door sickness. His fingertips, once so delicate it seemed they could have plucked one flake from a snowbank, were all bandages and scab, his perfect nails cracked from the clawing struggle of the arrest. The injuries of his fall were still with him, bandages on his cheek, around his ribs, his ankle, while newer gauze across his forearms failed to conceal more recent injuries, where he had attacked his own arm after the medics dared mix liquid nutrients with his royal blood. Soft fetters prevented him from increasing the self-damage, but his frame was so weak that he did not as much struggle as quiver in his bonds, like a dragonfly whose death throes are indistinguishable from the breeze that continues to stir the carcass hours after life has left. Zeus himself would not have recognized his Ganymede.

« Be easy, Your Grace, » I called as I broke through the clinging prison wraiths to reach the duke's bedside. « We're here to move you to more proper quarters. »

French stirred him. The duke's eyes slit weakly open, still as bright as the Hope Diamond with its trail of murder. He knew me, and I saw his starved cheeks flush with healthy scorn. Scorn too can be a form of relief, reader. In a world of scum unworthy to raise our eyes to his, I at least was scum who knew it.

« His Majesty has made arrangements, Your Grace. You will be moved to La Almudaina. »

My companion drew close behind me. « We are sorry it took us so long to arrange matters, La Trémoïlle. »

Ganymede's throat released a gasp of voiceless breath, but it took his cracked lips three tries to shape that breath into a whisper. « . . . Ss . . . Sfu-uu . . . Sp-ain . . . »

« Spain ? » Folly's blindness left the warden's eyes at last as he gaped at my companion. « You! You're—Your Maj— »

The King of Spain held a fast finger to his lips. « Today I am simply an agent dispatched by Romanova to facilitate the humane treatment of this prisoner. »

« Nothing inhumane's been done! » the warden almost screamed. « I've seen to it! I've worn myself ragged seeing to it! »

The king did not raise his voice. « I know. Your efforts have been a credit to your office, but you are not equipped to handle this prisoner's special needs. In the duke's world a nobleman hangs with a rope of silk, not hemp. »

« What? We don't hang— »

« It was just a simile. You haven't done anything wrong, it's just how the duke was raised. You must think of Their Grace as a time traveler. To them this place, which would send a son of royal blood to prison without his silks and servants, is insane. Imagine yourself in a prison from a thousand years ago, or a thousand years from now, where your treatment was incomprehensible, and violated a thousand unspoken social rules that your captors did not share. Even if your captors tried their best, if you couldn't communicate the problems you would not fare much better than the duke has here. »

The king's own hands helped me free Ganymede's wrists from the padded fetters. His Grace was too weak to raise his head, but not so weak that I could not feel him trying as I lifted him straight enough to sit. It had to be me they sent. The duke would not have tolerated a stranger, and, besides myself, the only servants trained to know his needs were his own, not trusted by the powers, or Madame's, not trusted at all.

« Drink, Your Grace. »

I saw the warden's eyes widen as Ganymede's lips, which had spat back like poison every drink the prison had offered, accepted my silver flask of alpine spring water.

"It is not your fault, warden. You did all anyone could have." I could not see the king's face as I nursed the duke, but his tone had the edge of tears. "It was their upbringing."

The jailer frowned down. "Raised so they can't live normally. Like a set-set."

Isabel Carlos II did not answer.

The duke sputtered. « Da . . . naa . . . »

« Your noble sister is safe, » the king replied at once, « I spoke with them today. » Here strictness replaced softness. « We require Your Grace's parole that you will not attempt to flee, or cause disruption, while in our custody. »

« . . . ha . . . y . . . wuu . . . » I could not make out a syllable, but between gentlemen it was enough. Sniper itself could have burst through the brickwork now with an army at its back, and the duke's word would have remained his bond.

I held the silver flask again to Ganymede's lips. I choked up seeing him like this, reader, his white cheek, which had once put lilies to shame, pale like a grub that should not yet have been uprooted from its tomb-home within the black decay of earth. Not that I have any great love for the duke—rather it felt as if Nature herself were lessened, wounded, by having her master-work so despoiled.

« Is it true, Your Majesty, » the warden interrupted, joining us in French, which made the question feel more private, « what they say about your . . . I mean your relationship to the *Porphyrogene*? » I suppose he should be commended for managing to wait so long with answers dangling close.

« People say many different things about Epicuro Mason, » Spain answered mildly.

« Is it true you're their real father, like Sniper said? »

The king paused only a moment. « Yes. »

The warden gasped, though I think it was less the truth that stunned him than the ease with which His Majesty admitted it; never forget how many of history's kings have waged wars to avoid acknowledging a bastard.

I brushed off the tendrils of prison wraiths which stuck like cobwebs to my arms and fingers, lest my unclean hands further distress the duke. « Are you ready to be moved, Your Grace? »

Ganymede tugged at the collar of his hospital smock, his bandaged fingers too weak to rip the cloth.

« We have proper attire waiting, Your Grace, but they wouldn't let us bring it in. »

Even before prison's starvation, Ganymede had been delicate enough to carry easily in my arms. Feeling his warmth against me, reader, I could well understand how hopeless had been the warden's efforts to inoculate his staff against desire's epidemic; Saladin's dear heart, ever master of my own, could not keep my hands from trembling with the thrill of touch.

The waiting car had a satin dressing gown, soft slippers, an inlaid comb, and a meal of broth, champagne grapes, fresh-squeezed mandarin juice, young cheese, wine from Ganymede's own vineyard, and a fresh baguette, still warm. Broth and fruit's sweetness breathed quick life into the duke's lips, but he did not speak; parched membranes or politic caution kept him silent. The king spoke instead, a gentle summary of the events the prisoner had missed. He spoke of the proud-hearted Humanists, how they had united behind Ancelet, who snatched from the dust Ganymede's lost presidential crown and bore it in conscientious stewardship. He spoke of the angered hordes at Odessa, and the more calculating horde which had exploited the riots there to strike at those who use Brill's arts to rear unearthly set-sets. He spoke of the Mitsubishi general strike which still stretched on, of Sniper's spreading bull's-eye sigil, of the Senate's triumph over chaos, and of the second Senate battle coming on the morrow, when the Conclave would present its new prescription for salvation. He spoke of the *terra ignota*. I, who weep too easily, strove at least to weep in silence. His majesty was too kind. Every actor he mentioned he made seem full of dignity and purpose. Even Tully. I would have called them poison incantations, the videos which leaked from my coward enemy, fertilizing the thorny weeds of war. The king called them instead « the prayers of one who, despairing of peace, hopes at least to warm the war with meaning. » As my tracker continued to scroll through hate-filled newsfeeds, the kind king felt as miraculous as lost Mommadoll.

« Majesty! Dear Majesty, they've tried to kill our darling Son! »

The car had not even landed before Madame's voice burst in, making Ganymede shudder beside me like a rain-soaked nightingale.

« What? » Spain tried to block the doorway as he stepped out, but I caught a glimpse of fluttering frills. « Is Epicuro hurt? » he asked.

« Not hurt, Cornel's guards took care of it. He's with Cornel now, but they tried to kill Him! Right in the Sensayers' Conclave! It's too much! Too much! »

I leaned and peered past Spain to see Madame, dark in a hooded traveling cloak which would have completely shrouded her skirts if not for a sea breeze which exposed the amethyst-trimmed black of her gown beneath. She was pale, her painted cheeks a waifish purple rather than her usual sensual pink, and so artful is her mask of makeup that, even though I know its falseness, the change felt real enough to awaken empathy.

« The attack was inside the Conclave? » The king gasped.

I was glad His Majesty could not see my face and the guilt upon it. I had witnessed the attack on his Son myself, of course, but Caesar, Conclave, Jehovah, and Utopia had all commanded that I hide the truth; a king, however kind, did not trump that.

« Yes! Inside the very Conclave! It's unthinkable! Cornel and Julia are hiding it from the public, but if it can happen there it can happen anywhere! He's in such danger! Anywhere He goes they want to kill Him! Our dear, darling Child! I can't stand it! Majesty, I think I shall collapse from fear! »

Madame made good on her threat, collapsing in the king's arms, which knew from practice just where at the bodice's edge to grab and catch her as she fell.

« Madame, you should not be here. » He rotated her body so she faced toward him, and away from us. « How did you get here? »

It was a fair question. Over His Majesty's shoulder I spotted servants, some in the king's livery, some in suits, all sheepish at their failure. She should not have been here, and, as the duke shuddered beside me, I knew how completely her presence spoiled his promised sanctuary. La Almudaina would have been perfect for Ganymede, an ancient fortress-palace on the island of Majorca off the Eastern coast of Spain, long in Spain's family, with sandy stone, arched walks, and battlemented towers overlooking palm trees and calm waves, all warmed by a vigilant but temperate sun. Here on Majorca's shores, watched by Spain's private guard, the fallen duke president would enjoy the same sort of dignified exile as Napoleon and the many fallen kin of ancient Caesars. Now, instead of the Mediterranean's healing kiss, there was only the floral syrup of Madame's perfume.

« Oh! » she screamed, flinging herself past Spain, toward us. « My Ganymede! My poor! » English fails here to capture her wailing French. « What have those barbarians done to you! »

The duke lacked speech still, but I saw the healthy flash of murder refresh itself in his eyes. I don't believe this hate was for his own downfall. Madame had knowingly let Danaë's destroyer, Merion Kraye, parade through Parliament, through Paris, even enter Ganymede's own palace, shielded by a new face and the pseudonym Casimir Perry. Would Hector have forgiven Helen had he learned about the time the wily destroyer Odysseus—vulnerable and alone—crept into Troy to spy, and Helen recognized him but let him sneak back out again, and told no one? Odysseus's death might have saved Troy, and Perry's might have . . . no, I dare not speculate. Even with the war less than six weeks away, I dare not guess which side is Troy.

His Majesty Isabel Carlos II caught Madame by her corseted waist before she could assail invalid Ganymede with kisses. « I told you to stay at Las Huelgas. » His stern eyes turned on his guards, who bowed apologies from the periphery.

Madame's smile was frantic and warm at once. « My love, how could I stay away? With our Son threatened? And my dear Ganymede barely alive thanks to this unforgivable treatment? How could I not come at once? »

The king made her face him. « You can't be here. The others were reluctant enough to let me take Their Grace into my care, but they were adamant I permit them no contact with others involved in the conspiracy. That includes you. »

« Me? » Painted lashes fluttered over eyes sparkling with innocence. « Oh, that's absurd. This is all a conspiracy against me, not one of mine, remember? I'm no more involved with O.S. than is Felix! Or Cornel! Ganymede is my ward. I raised him since infancy. I know what he needs, his favorite foods, how sensitive he is. Let me nurse him. If anyone can coax him back to health, I can. »

Ganymede, still in my lap, breathed hard. 'Ward'—here was a cold term. Was he an orphan, then? She merely a 'guardian,' this woman who had crafted him and his sister gene by gene from the ducal genome she had purchased? Who had rented the womb that carried him? Who oversaw his birth, his education, and held him a thousand times against her breast in childhood, but never once to nurse? Madame has many 'wards,' bred and polished in her boudoir. They have no other parent, but she has only one Son.

The king still held her fast. « I'm sorry, Madame. If anyone found out you two even came in contact, they'd ship Ganymede straight back to the public jail again. Let me take care of things. You can send the twins' old nurse over if you want, but you yourself can't be here. »

She gave a pouting frown. « Erlea says you're talking about abdication. »

Spain choked. « What?! »

Hobbes: "What?!"

Reader (laughingly): "Oh, poor dear Thomas."

Hobbes: "The Leviathan cut its own head off in the middle of a war! He'll have more deaths on his conscience than any man living or dead!"

Reader: "Yes, well, you for one are dead for the moment, friend Thomas, so the king can't hear you, and I already agree with you, so there's no point reiterating here."

Hobbes: "Without the sovereign, society turns back into a nest of beasts! All Europe will tumble into chaos! All the world!"

Reader: "Calm, Thomas, calm. It's not as dire as that. Leave this to Mycroft. You know he has your volume in his pocket even now, filling out the empty bulge where Apollo's Iliad *lay so long hidden. Intervening centuries may keep you and me from interfering, but Mycroft is contemporary with these events, and has the king's ear. Our little Greek is not about to let Spain doom Europe."*

How saintly your forgiveness, master reader, to forget my many failures and still rank my powers so high. I will try my best to dissuade the king— or rather I already did my best, since I am writing now of events three months in my past—though I do not believe I deserve any real credit for steering His Majesty off this upright but disastrous course. Madame was not about to miss her chance to be a queen.

* * *

The king's hands twitched around hers. « Why have you been talking to my Prime Minister? I told you to stay at Las Huelgas. »

« Erlea came to me. Besides, »—she planted a quick kiss upon the royal cheek—« you know I already love and honor Your Majesty, but until the wedding I've no obligation to obey you. Now, see sense. You can't abdicate. »

« We are not going to talk about this now. »

She hung on his shoulder. « I know it's improper for the king to take a spouse of ill repute, but the Spanish nation-strat needs your stabilizing hand right now as much as Europe does, and they don't mind. They know you're marrying me because you're a responsible father who wants to do right by his Child, whatever the mother's circumstances. They'll understand, and love you the more for it if you stay king. »

« We are not talking about this now. You need to go back. »

« But— »

« Joyce, you're still a Blacklaw! Far more people hate you right now than hate Epicuro, and some of them could kill you without any repercussions. I can't protect you if you won't stay in my protection. Please go back! »

He wrestled her, grappling her lace-trimmed elbows while her taut bust strained against him. In her excess of energy she seemed almost like a little dog, heedless of the dangers of the crowded street, which cannot understand that its master's restraining discipline is for its own safety; I say almost, for such a dog's eyes sparkle with confusion, not with teasing cunning.

« Madame, if you want to remain your own free, independent person then you can run around and scheme and stage melodrama to your heart's content, but if you intend to marry me you must act as my family, bash', and state require us to act. You can't do this. »

She wiped lint from his collar. « Your Majesty likes it when I do this. »

He steeled himself. « You still can't. Mycroft, help Their Grace out of the car, and then escort Madame back to Las Huelgas and make sure they stay there. »

« Yes, Your Majesty. »

« Mycroft! » Madame turned her eye on me, and then her fan, blue lace over oiled ebony and heavy enough to split the skin of my eyebrow as she struck me. « Some watchdog thou art! » A second blow, a third. « Thou'rt supposed to keep Jehovah away from danger, not escort Him to where there are assassins! »

I squinted against the blood which trickled into my left eye, but had no right to defend myself with word or hand.

The king restrained her. « Dignity, Madame. Please step aside, and let my nurses see to the duke. »

Three nurses had arrived, and a litter draped with silk to bear the invalid to his museum-worthy cell. Protect the duke, that was my only thought as I made myself a living wall between His Grace and faux-frantic Madame. I laid him on the silks, and helped the nurses wrap him gently, like a statuette of gold and ivory packed for transport. Madame tried to reach past me, to tuck in her darling duke with her own hands, but I blocked her. « Into the car please, Madame. » I grasped her arm and steered her toward the car, hard.

« It's not right! » Her eyes and lips shot hot protest at His unwavering Majesty.

« I'll come to Las Huelgas myself as soon as I can, » the king promised as I corralled her into the car's black cradle, « and I'll check on Epicuro, too. »

« My Ganymede . . . »

Isabel Carlos II nodded his royal gratitude to me as I climbed in beside his stubborn future queen. I saw Ganymede too give me a last glance, cold and dismissive, and so infinitely less disdainful than my station deserved that I could not mistake it for anything but heartfelt thanks. With my left eye still squinting against the blood, and my right distracted managing the unhappy conjunction of skirts and closing car door, I did not spot Madame's mancatcher until its blades closed around my throat.

« Thou'rt so hard to get a hold of these days, Mycroft. It's unfair of Cornel so monopolizing thee. »

As she twisted the inlaid handle, the stiff pole toppled me forward onto my knees on the car floor and pressed my face against the opposing seat. I jerked against it, but the fine blades which ring the inside of the collar are every bit as ruthless as their mistress. Practiced hands—not hers—bound my wrists behind me, and I could hear but not see the car's far door close. Madame had an accomplice, then, someone who had approached the car from the far side, unseen while the lady's fuss over 'her' Ganymede had drawn all eyes. I clenched my jaw as I felt someone try to force something between my teeth.

Madame clucked. « Don't be stubborn, Mycroft. We don't want thee biting thy tongue when I short-circuit thy pacemaker. »

That we did not, and, as I felt the car speed skyward, leaving escape behind, I parted my jaws obediently. I was glad to have a prop between my teeth as electric thunder made my frame convulse. My pulse skipped, and the remnants of the flesh part of my heart staggered like a cripple unused to tottering alone. The tracker at my ear went silent, and my lenses flashed one last white burst, then went blank.

« Disgusting! Dog, thou'rt positively infested with Utopian vermin! »

Hands brushed my shoulders, and a shower of ants and a slim snake fell on the floor around me, sparkling with luminous static as their short-circuited Griffincloth skins searched for instruction. « Do they make flea collars that work against U-beasts? If not yet, I must demand that they design one. »

A sob rocked me, not fear but gratitude learning that such magnanimous spirits as Voltaire Seldon and Mushi Mojave, who had ten times Madame's right to heap tortures upon me, had instead planted these precious sentinels to guard my life. The strangest surprise in all this was that Madame's accomplice, with the bit already between my teeth, did not gag me, but pulled it out and let me speak.

« Madame, » I choked, my words half muffled by the cushions that pressed against my face, « if you wanted me, you only had to— »

« Hello, stray, » her accomplice growled, low.

All at once it made sense: the deception, the restraints, the scene Madame had staged to make me so fearful for the duke that I had dropped my own defenses; the hands which now bound my ankles lest I kick for freedom were more practiced even than her own. « Brother Dominic, » I sputtered, « please— »

« Thou'rt going to help me kill the blasphemer. »

As a ribbon dancer uses the subtlest play of fingers to make her silks weave cyclones through the air, so, with a tiny twist of her mancatcher, Madame turned me to kneel at Dominic's feet. I had not seen him since just after the assassination, when I flew off on my last doomed effort to save Bridger, leaving in the hospital the bandaged wreck of Dominic Seneschal, and the body bag which contained the once-living Sniper doll whose synthetic fingers had pulled the fatal trigger. I gasped as I looked up. Medicine does wonders, but Dominic's recovery was still a wonder half worked. His hands and face were masked in a wetly wrinkled gossamer membrane, meat-scented like an amniotic sack, which fed and monitored the new muscles and skin which the doctors had grafted on to replace what had been flayed off by the friction of Dominic's impossible ride on the outside of Sniper's getaway car. In another week the skin and lips would set again into that cruel, conniving beauty which commands all Madame's creations, but for now the canvas was too wet to look like anyone. Dominic still wore black like his *Maître*, but the elegant French tailoring was half covered by a Japanese haori jacket, an embroidered geometric pattern, black on black, with the gold-trimmed red trefoil of the Mitsubishi Executive Directorate glaring on either breast like blood.

« Do you mean Sniper or today's blasphemer ? » I asked.

« The Chief Blasphemer, » Dominic wheezed, as if even repeating the epithet fouled his tongue. « Today's can pollute this Earth a few days longer; I hear she never pulled the trigger. »

I gulped, wincing as the mancatcher's steel prongs scraped my throat. « Sniper is our Master's enemy, and ally to my personal enemy Tully Mardi; I'll willingly— »

« I did not say *thou* wouldst do it, » Dominic growled back. « Thou wouldst offer her a fast, dignified death. » His facial membrane stretched and crinkled as he leaned close. « The blasphemer loves thee like a bash'mate, does she not, Mycroft? »

I hate hearing Dominic discuss Sniper in French, which lacks the 'it' pronoun the living doll so loves. "You know it wasn't really Sniper who pulled the trigger. It was the doll."

« The doll died at my hands first, but the blasphemer was the mind and will and architect. Is Kraye guiltless of the thousand murders perpetrated by his pawns? » The harsh German of Perry's true name rolled like a curse off Dominic's tongue.

I frowned. "Right now I think much of the world would say Madame is guilty of them, since Kraye was originally her pawn."

Madame twisted the mancatcher just enough to let me catch her smile. She was enjoying this, the world as it should be, the pedigree bloodhound she had purchased for her Son exerting fresh dominance over the stray He had led home. I will never call myself a mutt. My blood remains as Greek as Patroclus's, but in my childhood path, which should have led me straight to service at Censor's or Caesar's side, I did stray.

"But it shouldn't be you that does this," I pleaded, "not now, not either of you. Think of your fellow Blacklaws. With Natekari's motion to kill Sniper under debate, if Sniper dies now everyone will accuse the Blacklaws, and it'll be ten times worse if Blacklaws really did it. Use someone else. Use pawns. Use thugs. Brother Dominic, use your new Mitsubishi resources. Use me. Use anyone but a Blacklaw!"

Madame straightened my hat. « Mycroft, though knowest this is too personal to leave to others. »

« Then use me! » I begged, switching to desperate French to please them.

« Thou canst not do it; thou art too close to the blasphemer. »

I bristled as the old beast in my depths bristled as well. « You doubt my ability to kill someone I'm close to? »

Madame's musical chuckle ricocheted across the upholstery. « Never, dear stray; we doubt thy ability to kill someone who's been studying thy methods for thirteen years. Landing a wary fish requires novelty. »

The old beast calmed. « Then why involve me at all? »

« Thou art bait. »

I half liked this plan. « You've told Sniper where I'll be? »

« I shall drop notes at the homes of some fans, coaches, teammates. Word will reach our target. »

« But Sniper won't come in person, » I warned. « Sniper wouldn't risk it. »

Dominic snorted. « Of course not. Any idiot could smell a trap, but when the blasphemer's pawns find thee half dead, she won't be able to resist carrying a loved one home to heal, will she? »

« Half dead? What . . . ? »

« When they find thee, thou shalt be slowly bleeding to death from a rapier wound. In the thigh perhaps . . . just back here. » Dominic's touch on my inner thigh was keen as flame. « Or perhaps in the back, a more commonplace target. »

« Ἄναξ Jehovah will never forgive you if you kill me, » I warned.

« Thou shalt not dare tell Him it was me. But thou'rt right, it must be carefully done, or else thou might indeed bleed out too fast, and die, and that would make our *Maître* very sad—perhaps even sad enough to come to me in tears. » With one membranous claw still on my thigh, Dominic grasped my chin with the other, tilting my head back against the blades. « Thou shalt be good and hold very still while I stab thee, yes? Or wouldst thou rather help me make *notre Maître* very sad? »

Fear tinged my eyes with salt. Fear. It was strange. For all the wait and war and worry as humanity churned toward its likely end, I had not had this fear, personal, fanged with loved ones' pain, not since [Bridger died.] (Mycroft's draft left this sentence incomplete, but the intended end was obvious.—9A.)

« You won't be able to track me once I'm in Sniper's hands. » It was my last defense. « They're a professional, Lesley and Tully too. Whatever device you plant to trace me with, they'll find it. »

« There shan't be a device on thee, Mycroft, we're leaving thee alone. And I shan't track thee. Doubtless thy beloved aliens are already conjuring their hordes to hunt for thee. » Dominic lifted Voltaire's now-lifeless swiss-snake from the seat. « I'll follow them. Ah. » He smiled, and from the flicker on his lenses I guessed the car had flashed its landing notice. A few minutes' flight, then. Our destination was close to Majorca; Europe or

North Africa, not farther. « Now, Mycroft, » Dominic pressed, « thou hast play-sparred with the blasphemer—tell me all thou canst about her weaknesses. »

« No, bad Dominic! » Madame gave the too-keen bloodhound a chiding fan-strike. « Now's the time to be gracious, not cruel. We're about to send dear Mycroft to potential death. It's time for last requests, not interrogation. » Her vise of blades tipped me back enough to see her kindly smile. « Come, Mycroft, what wouldst thou? Last messages to send? »

I had plenty, but none that I would speak to her; however harsh my trials, I trust even Providence over Madame.

Dominic bore me blindfolded from the car to somewhere. Then he bound me to a chair, removed my blindfold so I could learn as much as possible from seeing Sniper's people, and delivered one swift stab to the side of my back as promised, during which I held obediently still. Then he left me. It was a bare room, with no hint of light and no clock save the dripping and increasing scent of blood. Dark held no fear for me, nor death when I had been closer so often, but the consequences of this plan, success or failure (Sniper's victory, Sniper's death), those I feared. I fought the fear awhile by reviewing the chapters of my history which must come next. By humorous chance I was then writing the chapter where you, reader, first met Dominic—*Canis Domini,* as I had not yet titled it—and next, what should I write next? Carlyle day? Yes, that would show you the Censor's office, and the Pantheon. Anemia's haze was just starting to weigh upon me when dim light and footsteps entered from a door behind me. I tried to speak thanks, but managed only a groan. It was a single person, caution-silent, neither fast nor slow. They bent low over the ropes that bound me to the chair, then plunged a blade into the wound already in my back and stabbed deeper, hard, twice. The scents of guts and urine joined the blood drip metronome, which sped now to a stream. I whimpered. My attacker withdrew quickly and closed the door behind them, leaving the dark complete. Now fear reared dragon-fierce inside me, pain, cold, numbness as my blood's departure reduced muscle to meat. Consciousness fled too fast for me to complete a prayer.

Enemy Sanctum

Written July 27–29, 2454
Events of April 15
Somewhere east of Europe

MYCROFT? MYCROFT! THOU CANST NOT DIE NOW WITH THY work unfinished. *Who will tell me what this Dominic creature found in the Saneer-Weeksbooth bash'house? And how the O.S. melodrama cascaded disaster by disaster toward the world's upheaval? I forbid thee to quit my service with thy history barely begun.*

See, reader, it was you who saved me back then, you who called in duty's name and forbade my staggering soul from taking the soft hands offered by the twin horsemen Sleep and Death. I had finished only seven chapters of my history, and, as the crimson dripping starved my brain toward rest, yours was the first voice which called to me of duties yet undone.

Hobbes: "Well done, friend Reader. Our stubborn guide is not easy to keep alive."
Reader: "True, Thomas, true. Mycroft has many well-honed instincts, but not self-preservation."

I know, reader. Undeserving as I am of rest, it is so tempting. And it would have been so painless this way—that is what the part of me that could still think thought in that dim hour. In the pitch black I would not even have to know at what moment darkness gave way to eternal darkness. But you would not let me quit, nor would my other masters, whose voices joined in chorus now to nag me back to life.

MASON: "Live, murderer. Live and serve and suffer."
Papa: "Your sentence isn't up."
Reader: "Nor is thy task."
Sniper: "¡Hang in there, Mycroft! I'm with you. ¿Can you hear me?"
Saladin: «Don't waste the death of Mycroft Canner on something like this.»

Spain: « Our son needs you. »

Anonymous: "¡You're my successor! ¡You may not die without passing the office on to safer hands!"

Faust: "You're stronger than this, I'm afraid."

Mercer Mardi: "Remember what you hear here, Mycroft. It's important."

Bridger: "You can't run away, Mycroft, not you. I know it's hard what's coming—so hard I ran away—but you can't. I'm sorry. I love you."

Achilles: "He's right. The gods will ask much more of you before they let you rest, old friend. They always do."

Apollo: "You still have ships to board."

He: ⌈"«Bleib . . . quedate . . . reste . . . μείνε . . . mane . . . mate . . . stay.»"⌋

Smell pierced the veil first after the voices: laundry starch and hygiene. Touch followed: cotton softness, mild wound pain, straps around my wrists and ankles (comforting proof that whoever had found me knew me well), and a warm hand holding mine, child-thin and clinging. Soft light showed me a plain ceiling, a small white room fastidiously bare, and Sniper sleeping, slumped against my bedside, diffuse white sunlight making its soft skin glow. Serene closed eyes and a hint of smile on its sleeping face gave it a doll's perfection, while its black hair, just long enough to fall untidily, tempted one to brush the black locks back in place and pose the head straight. Someone had draped a towel in lieu of a blanket over Sniper's sleeping shoulders, and its hand nestled in mine. To this day I don't know whether, before its operation, the now-hermaphrodite was male or an Amazon, but if I had known, seeing Sniper beside me now I think my mind would have rebelled at assigning it a sex, as if I were asked to sex the sky, or fleeting clouds.

"Try anything and I will kill you, Mycroft, whatever Sniper says."

It took some seconds for my eyes to find the speaker, but only a moment for the sight to redden my eyes with rage, renew the wound's sting, and make my hands twitch hard enough to squeeze Sniper's fingers hard. The Enemy, Tully Mardi, alive and well and watching us from a stool in a shadowed far corner. Tully Mardi. He must have had an expression, a pose, complexion, some blank, generic clothes to reinforce his claim of distanced objectivity, but I could not see them. I saw Hell, Hell vapors cancerous in the air about him, black claws of cremation ash, and gunpowder, and burning homes, and blood vaporized by technology's inhuman thunder. I saw the war. Had the Enemy's throat been within my reach, reader, even with the brace that defended his Moon-weakened spine against Earth's gravity, I would have snapped his neck.

My squeeze stirred Sniper. "Mycroft! You're awake!" Such healing warmth was in its voice! Not like fire but like a nice day after drizzle's doldrums. "How do you feel?"

"Alright," I smiled. Usually I think harder about that question, but this was the time for reassurance, not for truth.

Keen, dark eyes searched my face for signs of pain. "What happened?"

"Dominic Seneschal stabbed me and left me as bait to lure you into rescuing me, so they could follow our movements, track you down, catch you, and torture you to death, likely over many days, so Natekari's bill to make it legal to kill you would have a chance of passing before they finish you off."

Really, Mycroft? Truth is a weapon, and thou givest so much to thine enemy?

And why not? Sniper's love, concern, and questions were a friend's, reader. Let us be honest friends for a few minutes, before we must be adversaries again.

"Dominic left you to die?"

I smiled. "They knew you'd save me."

"We very nearly didn't. That knife to the back went deep. Our doc's astounded you pulled through."

The second stab; I did not think it wise to talk about that now.

"I told you it was a trap." Tully's voice is always urgent, calling through the war vapors around him as if every word were some last message screamed over a dying radio as the invaders' tanks close in. I know I should not heap such scorn on Tully. He's my fault. Still, this is the child of Luther Mardigras and Mercer Mardi, ransomed from my rampage by Apollo's blood, and reared in Luna City by the vanguard of Utopia. Not since the days of Brill himself has one researcher's work expanded the charted regions of psychology as much as what Mercer Mardi dictated to the recording while the pain and shock of vivisection opened each new petal of uncharted madness to her, one by one, while Luther Mardigras was the indefatigable, fun-armored heart that first drew together the Mardi bash' which loved this world so much they dared scheme to destroy it to save a better one. The child of such a pair should have ridden on sphinx-back across an Earth that did not deserve to touch his feet, while on his coat the avatars of human intellect should war like angels through the cityscape of man's cyclopean unconscious. Instead he whined.

"You shouldn't have brought Mycroft here. [Mycroft flayed my father alive then burned him in a wicker man.] You're risking everything for mere nostalgia." The middle phrase was not spoken, reader, but I could feel it leak through Tully's words, whispered by the smoky tongues of hate that wafted from him.

Sniper smiled. "Don't worry. Our precautions are enough."

Tully leaned forward, war's claws expanding from his motion like infernal smoke rings. "We can't know that. [You've seen the photos of Mycroft bathing in my mother's bloody bile.]"

Sniper's smile faded. "If you don't trust my precautions, go take better ones."

Hate answered fast. "I'm not leaving you alone with Mycroft Canner. [They made my big ba'sis watch them eat her own roasted fingers.]" Tully brushed neglect-frayed hair out of his eyes, whose lenses glittered bright with data. "Mycroft is not your friend, Sniper. If they pretended to be your friend once—even if they really *were* your friend once in their own mad way—that's over. [We played together, Mycroft, Ken, and me. The police had me identify Ken's frozen dismembered trunk when they finally found it. I was eight.]"

"Stop being such a grown-up, Tully," Sniper snapped back. "Mycroft and I can be enemies in five minutes or tomorrow. Now is pretend time. We all need that sometimes."

"We can't all have it! [We treated Mycroft like family, and they ripped out seven of our bash'members' hearts and ate them. Ripped them out and ate them!]" Tully's fierceness stirred the Pillarcat, Halley, which coiled about his ankles like a great, furred muff. The U-beast yawned, green cheeks stretching cutely too far around its feline fangs, while the yawn's ripple bristled down and down and down and down the fur of its snakelike length, each pair of legs stretching in turn in a slow, drowsy spiral. Even Tully's obscene vapors dared not touch Apollo's dear Halley. I hungered to stroke its velvet length, to coax it to wind about my shoulders, as it had so often before they widened to a man's. Tully did not give the dear beast a glance. "This is war."

Sniper frowned. "It's not war yet."

"Yes it is." It was I who answered, or rather Hobbes through me. "War is not just battle, but that tract of time wherein the Will to Battle is so manifest that humankind can no longer trust itself to keep the peace. We are at war."

Sniper gazed down, not frowning, a clean face, like those contemplative angels that Botticelli or Raphael achieve, where the seraphs and cherubs are not mere rows of hosanna-singing ornament but intellectual beings, gazing with a complex, inhuman awe on Christ or Mary, whose coming sufferings their eternal vision makes so clear. "The only one that has to die is J.E.D.D. Mason."

"That isn't true." I nearly threw up hearing myself and Tully speak the words in synch.

Sniper shook its head. "If J.E.D.D. Mason dies then the plot to merge the Hives ends, instantly and forever."

"They aren't the one plotting," I corrected. "Ἄναξ Jehovah has no interest in ruling anything. It's others plotting, using Them."

"That doesn't matter. J.E.D.D. Mason could be an evil mastermind or completely innocent, the plan still ends when they die."

"But that won't stop the war," I countered. "There's still O.S., the Mitsubishi landgrab, the Nurturist anti-set-set violence, the CFB. Why make things worse? In the Senate yesterday it was the Masonic bloc that voted down the motion to disband the Humanists. Do you think the Emperor will continue to protect your Hive if you kill their Son again?"

Sniper's frown was slight, as when one tries to draw a neutral face but some unintended curve conjures melancholy. "I never said I thought J.E.D.D. Mason's death would end all the crises, just that it will save the Hive system. I know more than you think, Mycroft. Joyce Faust D'Arouet designed their child to be a Hive-eating monster. Take over or destroy, that's what they're for, they can't stop themself any more than Eureka can switch off the computer and walk away. No Hive is safe while J.E.D.D. Mason lives. Wars over land or set-sets are their own catastrophe, but J.E.D.D. Mason has to die for the healing to begin. Just like I have to die, right?" It smiled now, its eyes bright with a razor rim of tears.

The violence of the sob which wracked my shoulders startled even me. "Sniper . . . No, Ojiro now," I corrected myself.

"Sniper feels more right, from an old friend." It smiled gently. "I saw the look on the Emperor's face when they shook Natekari's hand. Dominic Seneschal's not the only one on my tail who has no intention of handing me over to the authorities alive. Am I wrong?"

My throat refused to answer for a moment. "I don't know Caesar's plans, but I know Caesar. They'll kill you with their own hands if they can."

Sniper winked. "Reckless. I'd shoot me from a hundred yards away, if I had to kill me."

I realized now that Sniper had not reacted when I said it wanted to kill MASON's Son *again*. Few are so ready to believe what really happened. "The doll . . ." I braved, "the one that fired on the Rostra—"

"How's it doing? Well, I hope?"

"It's dead. Dominic killed it. Or it ran out of life, hard to say which."
The living living doll turned away. "Pity."

"Did you plan the assassination together?" I asked. "Did you meet?"

Sniper mussed its own hair, hiding its expression with a forearm striped
with the residue of Lesley's fading doodles. "Never face-to-face. We spoke
over trackers. It was easy enough for it to prove to me what it was. It already
knew my . . . our . . . plan, it just had to get me to let it do the main deed
while I went after Bridger." Sniper caught my eyes now, grave. "Where is
Bridger?"

I broke here, reader. Rather, I was already broken, but now the glue failed.
I screamed as sorrow's whirlpool ripped through the fragile surface of pretending. It was not the first time. I'm told I was hardly verbal the first three
days after I lost him. I barely remember the series of pale faces, Martin,
Papa, Voltaire, Apollo, Outis, Heloïse, that kept the suicide watch in turn.
Even now as I write, it is Martin's turn to sit with me, doing his own work
over his tracker while keeping sharp watch for a smuggled blade, or the jaw
clench if I try to bite my tongue. I lost him, reader. Bridger, everything. I
had him and I lost him.

"What method will you use, Mycroft," Tully cut in, "when you kill
Sniper?" Phantom faces in the Enemy's shadow laughed. "Which of the two
of us would you kill first, if you weren't tied down right now?"

Tully's words were petty, bitter, childish, sickening, effective. Hate
stopped my tears faster than reason could have. "I wouldn't, not here, not
now."

"No appetite?" he taunted.

I snorted. "If you fear for your life, Tully, turn yourself in. Right now
you're only guilty of sedition and inciting to riot. In jail you'd be safe, safer
than free."

He laughed, and the phantom faces laughed with him. "If Mycroft Canner's become a bad liar, the world has lost something."

I closed my eyes. "Tully, while it's true I'll never rest in peace until I've
killed you, you're low on the list of reasons I will never rest in peace."

Sniper squeezed my hand.

The Enemy's voice hardened. No, 'the Enemy' is too vague, now that
we have so many. I should use Tully's true title: *my* Enemy. Greek differen-
tiates the political enemy, πολέμιος, whom one might face across the battlefield with honor and respect, from the personal enemy, ἐχθρός, who may
be a fellow-countryman or even a grudging ally, but who seeks your ruin
and you his in a lifelong, irredeemable vendetta. Ἄναξ Jehovah understands

this difference, Caesar too in Latin's *hostis* and *inimicus*. Tully understands as well, in feeling if not word, as the hunger gnaws at his scarred heart, as it does mine. Sniper may have become a πολέμιος, my faction's foe, but Tully is the only creature on this planet I will call ἐχθρός. My Enemy. "I won't let you get this close to me again," he taunted. "[Come on, monster! Try it! I'm right here, your last, elusive prey. Try it, come at me, rip those bonds and help me force Sniper to kill you!]"

I could not resist staring at his fragile neck. "Tully, I know you two aren't alone here. Even if I were confident that I could kill you both in my condition, your allies outside would kill me. I'm not an acceptable loss. I'm needed."

"What for?" Tully did not lean forward but his ghosts did, claws light as perfume drifting closer.

"As a translator."

"And?"

"And to help Ancelet with duties they don't have time for anymore."

"And?"

"And—" Well played, my Enemy. Only then did it occur to me that I was a prisoner, and this an interrogation.

"You must have more on your agenda," my Enemy prompted, Halley's green coils mixing with the smoky claws around his ankles.

"I have no agenda," I answered. "I'm the prisoner here. I have the right to silence." I am the world's slave and any free man may by rights command my obedience, but never Tully!

"All prisoners have agendas, particularly you."

I turned to Sniper. "I saw Ockham a few days ago. Prospero, I mean."

"How are they?" Sniper asked with a ba'sib's eagerness.

"Strong," I answered. "Bearing up as a hero should, and being treated like one. President Ancelet let me sit in when the two of them met. I wish you could've seen it. They were perfect. President Ancelet is perfect, you couldn't ask for a better emergency leader, whatever happens."

Sniper's smile glowed. "And the others? How are the others? Thisbe? Cato? Typer?"

My smile died. "I haven't seen them. Any of them." Guilt, reader, rarely do I encounter a new kind to add to my long list. It had not occurred to me to ask to see them, even to ask after them. In fact, I could not remember the name Thisbe rising in my mind since her arrest, except in a list of suspects or witnesses. She would be mourning too for the child we reared together, we strange godparents, the Major, Mommadoll, myself, and she.

Duke Ganymede had nearly died in the jail where Earth's forgetfulness had left him; what of Thisbe?

Mycroft, Thisbe fancied herself a witch, ready like Lady Macbeth to rip the child from her teat and smash its head. You think she too loved Bridger?

Yes, reader, I do. Love and murder are not so antithetical. Remember, I too willed Bridger's death once. I asked Saladin to kill him, to save him from Dominic, and Saladin failed because even my dear predator had not Cynic armor enough to stave off love. We all loved Bridger, reader. Even you.

Shame urged me to change the subject. "Sniper, President Ancelet asked . . . well, not overtly . . . implied heavily, let's say, that they wanted me to find you and deliver a message."

"We don't want it," my Enemy answered cold.

Sniper spun. "Tully!"

"We don't want it, not from Mycroft."

"It's from my president, Tully. I'm O.S., not your private fantasy army. I have an oath of office to fulfill."

The ghost mist churned around Tully's Moon-weakened shoulders. "Mycroft's a skillful liar, knows us both too well, and is our enemy. If your president wanted to reach you, they could find a better messenger."

Sniper's frown should have been grave, but on that face even the blackest rage retains a sweet, doll-like edge. "Tell me the message, Mycroft."

"President Ancelet is open to using O.S. and other violence if necessary to protect the Humanists, but wants to try peaceful solutions first. They want you to wait, not stir up the public, and not attack Ἄναξ Jehovah again until peaceful remedies have had a chance to try and fail."

The allies traded glances. I would not have called them allies before that moment, but that wordless deliberation which passed from eye to eye occurs only between allies, friends, or lovers; they were not friends.

"How long does the president want me to wait?" Sniper asked.

"They didn't specify at that meeting, but I know they helped engineer the order that passed the Senate, which gave the Humanists and other troubled Hives a month to draft reforms. A month from the Senate meeting, that's, what, May thirteenth?"

Tully half laughed, half coughed. "In a month, will the rest of the world be any less convinced that every single Humanist is a murderer? I doubt it."

Sniper pursed its lips. "Mycroft, Dominic Seneschal is trying to kill me. Lots of people are trying to kill me. Every day I wait, I increase the risk that I'll fall before I get J.E.D.D. Mason. Trying peaceful solutions first means gambling with losing the one permanent solution we do have. Does the president understand that?"

"I'm sure they do. But there may be a way to get your enemies to wait too."

"How."

I frowned. "Sniper, did your bash' actually consult the Wish List when you planned hits and crashes? I know Eureka read it, but did you ever act on it?"

It frowned back. "Does it matter? Our Hive had a system for voting for people you'd like to see bumped off, and we also actually did bump people off. There's no alibi for that."

"Yes, it matters."

"Why? Nine hundred and eighty-nine million humanists, almost nine-tenths of the Hive, added votes to a list of people they wanted dead. Even if there were no such thing as O.S., if I were in a different Hive I'd be freaked as all get-out. They say the Humanists are all murders. Morally, they're right."

"But did you consult the Wish List?"

"Why does it matter?"

"Because I'm writing a history of the last two weeks: the assassination, the investigation, O.S., Bridger, everything."

Good, Mycroft. I had wondered when thou wouldst remember thy true task.

Tully bristled, enough to make Halley bristle. "Propaganda."

"No," I corrected, "it will tell the truth, as much as it can. I'm writing it since I knew more of those involved than anyone, and because I'm certified insane, so my testimony can't be used in court. I can tell the truth without compromising the trials at all."

Tully's gaze was blacker than his phantoms. "The truth? Unusable in court? Who does that help?"

"It helps Truth."

Tully and Sniper both gaped, not expecting this particular vein of madness from this madman.

I sighed. "What Ἄναξ Jehovah finds most callous about Providence is not when millions die, but when a child lies dying in a gutter, and the child's death does serve some higher Purpose, but the child can't understand, and dies thinking the suffering is meaningless. Ἄναξ Jehovah can't stop death from happening, but He can at least give we who are about to die as much truth as He can. That is His consolation."

"That's insane," Tully spat. "This is war. Information is a weapon."

I took a long breath. "Either Ἄναξ Jehovah is insane or Ἄναξ Jehovah is the only sane being on Earth. But even if you don't think truth helps in wartime, tell me, Tully, what would the rest of the Mardi bash' have answered to this: Which will matter more to the human race in two thousand years, an old war starting one month earlier or later, or a record of the mistakes we made that started it, so posterity can study them, and avoid making the same mistakes again?"

Young Reader: "I want the record, of course."

Hobbes: "Really? A month more or less of war can change the outcome also, change your world."

Young Reader: "And what would you know of my world, interloper? It has already changed. Mycroft is here to show me why, and I shan't let him rest until he finishes."

Hobbes: "Apologies, Master Reader, I meant no offense."

Reader: "Oh, pay that other voice no mind, friend Thomas. That is my younger self complaining, the one still waiting for the eighth chapter of Mycroft's first history."

Hobbes: "Your younger self?"

Reader: "The one still reading about the seven days of transformation. I did not know you then."

Young Reader: "Know who? Who is that?"

Hobbes: "Ah, I see! The earlier reader, who chided Mycroft back from bleeding out. Apologies, my friend. You sounded so like yourself."

Reader: "Forgiven, Thomas. A most understandable mistake. And you, young reader, if you would take some good advice, acquaint yourself soon with Thomas Hobbes. He is a relevant companion, quick to slice away distraction's weeds, and afflicted neither by rose-tinted optimism nor by Mycroft's puppetlike surrender. A good companion for our journey, and a useful midpoint as we grope toward stranger minds."

Hobbes: "Thank you, Master Reader, too kind."

Young Reader: "Hobbes? Why Hobbes? I thought Voltaire was Patriarch of that strange age which Mycroft claims has so infected his."

I: "In peacetime you do want Voltaire, reader, in days of growth, reform, and progress when we may cultivate our gardens; not when the light grows weak."

Young Reader: "No time, Mycroft, for these, thy interruptions, thy speculations, thy Patriarch, thy Hobbes. You think I would stop to bone up on archaic statecraft when I have yet even to meet Madame D'Arouet?"

Hobbes: "I can hear your elder self laughing. Can you, young Reader? Well, in time it will be you."

"But why bring this up now?" Sniper asked. "This history?"

"Because Ἄναξ Jehovah wants permission from every single living person in the book before we publish it, including both of you. That means we promise to show you the finished manuscript before it's released, so you can verify that the parts with you in them are accurate, and that you're comfortable with how you're portrayed. It also means Ἄναξ Jehovah will insist that all parties refrain from attacking you two until the history is complete. Whatever Caesar's rage, when their Son and Truth unite in one request, Caesar will listen. That buys you time." I smiled. "We have grounds for a truce. It's fragile, self-interested, and secret, since the police can't legally stop hunting you just to let me write a book, and it will probably only last a month, but even a month will give Kosala time to—"

Never again do I want to hear a set-set scream. It was broken, breathless, not the strong, clear screams we hear in media but a neglected voice, discovering in its pain the untried limits of its own power. Have you ever watched a creature struggle against an injury it cannot understand: a fish too sick to swim that gasps and thrashes; a twitching, broken bird; a half-crushed ant; a rat I once saw that fell and broke its spine, and crawled on gamely with its forepaws, dragging the rear legs behind like limp, furred tassels, heedless of the death by hemorrhage that must follow, so inevitable and so near. Such victims are too uncomprehending to know their sufferings, let alone to raise angry eyes to Heaven and ask, "Why?" Neither could Eureka Weeksbooth.

Sniper sprang like lightning to the door. From my angle I could not see much beyond the doorway besides a patch of wall, but hearing painted a clear enough image of the writhing set-set.

"¿What's happened?" Sniper asked, leaping through to (crouch? sit?) at its ba'sib's side.

Without my tracker, my lenses could not pick up the set-set's text reply.

"¿What news? ¿What's happened?" Sniper pressed again.

This was April the fifteenth, reader, a day the world will wear black if we live to see another April. It was Tully who found the news first. "They just indicted all of you."

"My whole bash'?" Sniper asked.

"No, your whole Hive." Tully's war-wraiths twitched like the tails of self-satisfied cats. "They just indicted every living Humanist as accessories to the last sixteen hits O.S. made, plus two hundred and fifty thousand counts of conspiracy to commit murder."

"Two hundred and fifty thousand?"

"That's how many names are on the Wish List."

So it began. Across Earth's star-crossed circumference, angry billions find their hate vindicated: "See, they are all murderers! A thousand times! To law! To arms! To prison with them! Every bloodstained Humanist!" While this brave Hive which had, until now, comingled with the others as comfortably as clover among the grass now stands betrayed: "¡False friends! ¿You dare brand me a murderer? Not content to openly destroy us, you resort to judicial disenfranchisement. ¡One short step from judicial murder! ¡Damn you! ¡Damn you and your lies and your Alliance! ¡Damn you all to War's Hell!"

But it means nothing, good sense tells us. This charge is mere chaff, vacuous, absurd, as sure to be dismissed as if some merchant losing ship and fortune to the Moon-caused tides sued the Utopians. So Reason thinks, but evil was in the details, evil enough to make Thomas Carlyle roll over in his Pantheonic tomb. Codefendants. A codefendant may not fill any office in a trial. Now no Humanist could get near Prospero's trial, or Ganymede's, not as investigator, polylaw, expert witness, nor as judge. Nor as judge, reader. If you asked a Member of our great Alliance which is more precious, all one's worldly goods, or one's right to have one of one's Hivefellows—or for the Hiveless Lawfellows—among one's judges, even the most gilded miser would hesitate. By Thomas Carlyle's inviolable decree, a Polylegal Tribunal requires three judges from three different Hives—or Laws for Hiveless—one chosen by the prosecution and two by the defendant, and we always choose one from a sympathetic allied law, one from our own. Whatever diabolical prosecutor schemed this backstab, whatever hate-puffed judge accepted the indictment, they will now have O.S. tried by outraged Cousins, vengeful Masons, clinical Brillists, terrified Europeans, suspect Mitsubishi, distant Hiveless, more distant Utopians, and not a single Human. Will the Mitsubishi face the same when Andō goes on trial? Would Europe, had Perry left anyone alive to prosecute? News flies. Mobs form. Fools rush in. The wise, who know the full stakes, rush in faster. Somewhere in the stratosphere, some light-souled schoolchildren returning in a Moon Bus gape down as they see the constellations of city lights flicker like candles, and their young hearts wish to run, to turn back, to pull the shelter of the Moon's cold rocks like blankets over them, and shiver until Earth's wrath is done. Gravity does not grant wishes.

The set-set's sounds continued, not articulate enough for me to call them screams or moans, just the weak sounds of a throat so rarely used. The Pillarcat cried too, that part of it which was still Nature marking Nature's pain with yowls.

"It's started," Tully announced, the bile-black leakage of the war ghosts burbling in their triumph: how dare your generation hold us back so long! "The streets are filling: Romanova, Brussels, Tōgenkyō, Tokyo, Paris, Buenos Aires." Data gleamed in Tully's lenses, sharp enough to make him shake. "World War."

"World Riot," Sniper corrected, still invisible beyond the door.

Fists and fire were the easy choices. In a park in Augsburg, a mob fell fast on a Humanist in a Black Team Olympic jacket. In a pub in Singapore the bull's-eye sigil parted the crowd into two lines, and one side remembered faster than the other how flame and alcohol combine. Chance and photos made a few martyrdoms famous over the next days, but there were no *causes célèbres* that night, just whatever shards of the eruption one caught by chance. If four people on Earth truly saw the impact unfold on April fifteenth, one was Tully, another the new Censor Su-Hyeon, a prisoner in his office as the Forum turned into a sea of fists, and the other two were Sidney and Eureka, one in Romanovan custody still running the cars, the other with us.

"¿Eureka?" Sniper managed to make its tone soothing. "Eureka, breathe with me. I'm here. ¿Feel my hands? You're in a room. I'm with you. You're not in any danger. Breathe."

A pause to read the set-set's text response.

"¿What are you watching? ¿The movements? ¿Cars? ¿Casualties? Show me. Use the projector."

Even eclipsed by door, the light's burst blinded me.

"Tully!" Sniper burst back into sight now. "Talk to me, Tully. What are your projections? What are we looking at?"

We have so many oracles: Sidney, Eureka, Ancelet, Su-Hyeon—I should have known Tully would be one too. In thirteen years, he had not lived up to a twentieth part of his parents' legacy, but neither had he ignored the training notes left by his ba'pa, the late Deputy Censor Kohaku Mardi. I itched for my tracker, but itched more to see the data which sparkled across Tully's lenses showing him—what? What was he watching? Heartbeats? Euros? Weapons? Those garage-built missiles, which had reduced Brussels's Parliament to ash, doubtless had brothers waiting. Billions of lidless, electronic eyes watch Earth, and Tully's software digested that data, painting on his lenses the near future of our bloodshed. He'd had a decade to personalize his system, but I knew what heart beat within its prosthetic shell: Apollo's program, the same that ran his coat and filled his nowhere with troops and ruins, and predicted for some passers uniforms, for others death.

"It's a dark start." It was not Earth's gravity that made Tully's words slow, but it did exaggerate them. "It won't wipe out the species, at least not soon."

"How is it for the Humanists?" Sniper asked at once.

Don't think the question heartless, masters. Sniper's eyes too grew wet at the thought that the race which conquered Everest might fall back into the dark, but O.S. has sworn to protect the flame that led us to that victory, and the Games which celebrate it.

"Hard, but you're hardy," Tully answered. "You'll endure. Six months into this war the Humanists will still be a central, fighting power." He frowned as Sniper's stare asked for more. "Anyone who thinks they can see reliably more than six months into this war is as mad as Mycroft."

"Overall casualties?" Sniper pressed.

Tully breathed deep. "It isn't the worst scenario I've seen, but on a casualty scale of one to five it's four or five." There should be a name for that kind of soft, pursed frown that tries to comfort. "The realistic options may all be four or five."

"Stop it!" I didn't try to keep myself from screaming. "Sniper! Tully! Call them! Calm them! You're the figureheads! Every power on Earth will be on the air crying for calm now—Ἄναξ Jehovah, Kosala, Ancelet. Join them! Talk the Humanists down!"

Ares glared smugly through his avatar Tully Mardi. "You know we need this war, Mycroft, or the Mars War in 2650 will end the human race, forever. Apollo showed you that."

He did, and did again now, Apollo, always with me in the alley where we fight the war's first battle still: Apollo, I, Seine Mardi, and my Saladin. Apollo has more than beams and darts in his Utopian arsenal. He has prophecies which he projects at us during the battle, unthinkable visions of a lifeless Earth, just rocks, and shapes which hoped once to be more than rock, frozen but for the slosh of mud-tides and a dwindling rain of shooting stars, the debris of our fledgling satellites with no one left to wish upon them as they fall. Through that illusory future Hell we charge, my Saladin and I, charge the corner that shields the deadly archer who would destroy our present world to prevent that future. Do you remember who wins the battle, reader? Apollo or us? Sometimes I remember, but sometimes what I remember makes no sense.

"You don't need *this* war," I screamed back at all of them, Sniper, Apollo, Tully. "I know we can't avoid war, but it doesn't have to start like this. No one's ready. Put it off! Put it off until Kosala has time to stock the hospitals. Put it off until someone has a plan!"

My Enemy's eyes grew colder than his ghosts'. "You think we don't have a plan?"

How cold were mine, I wonder? "One you're prepared to implement? Tell me, Tully, look me in the eye and tell me you don't want three more weeks to move your pieces into place. Tell me you don't want three more days to teach a few more kids how to survive for five minutes out there! This isn't an opening volley, it's a world brawl. Stop it."

"The next start might be worse."

"How could it be? There will be more food! More medicine! Stop! Stop it! Please!"

I am lying to you, reader. I just realized. Reading back these last few paragraphs I recognize my fantasy, not memory, taking control. It should have been me who served my masters well and talked these rebel leaders into prolonging peace. I failed. I lay there sobbing, useless. It was my Enemy who made these arguments. It was Tully Mardi who saved the world.

"Stop blubbering, Mycroft!" He backhanded me, a strange blow, ill-aimed but strong, the semipracticed strike of one who has trained long on punching bags but never flesh. "Get me a direct line to Papadelias! Now! Mycroft, can you hear me?"

I didn't recognize the lump between my fingers as a tracker microphone until that moment. "Pa-papa?" I stammered.

"Yes, Commissioner General Papadelias. Call them. Now. They'll answer you. We can still stop this!"

I made the call, uncomprehending, and Tully snatched back the microphone the instant "Mycroft?" sounded urgent through its drum.

"Commissioner, this is Tully Mardi Mojave. Sniper and I want to help calm the chaos. We think we can talk our supporters down if you can get Ancelet and the other Hive leaders to calm theirs down. We'll piggyback a video on this signal, but we need your pledge, with witnesses, that we get temporary immunity, that you won't trace this call to track us down, and that you won't send anyone after us for, say, forty-eight hours after we get things calm. We want to save lives as much as you do, but we won't sacrifice our cause or our freedom to achieve it. Do we have a deal?"

Silence. "This plan will subtract evil. I can secure cooperation's pledge from every force on Earth whose pledge means anything. Amnesty is yours forty-eight hours beyond those hours we spend together on this good. Will you reciprocate?"

"I . . . who is this?"

"I Am Jehovah Mason."

I blushed at my mistake, but panic and autopilot had overridden Tully's instruction of which Master I should call.

Now the silence was Tully's, panic, not a rabbit's frozen panic but Reason itself in crisis, as when tedious arithmetic reveals slowly to Galileo a different Plan and Maker than the ancients knew, or when fragile Carlyle Foster sees a dying soldier turn to plastic. Tully Mardi was with us on the Rostra, remember? Jehovah's bloody brains spattered his clothes too. The public, with their static-blurred video, could doubt the miracle—not he. Coward. Coward you are, my Enemy, and always will be. Coward who had over the phone the undivided attention of a God, and knew he did, and stood there, dumb.

"Yes!" Sniper snatched the microphone. "We'll reciprocate: no attempts on your life by me or any of my agents for forty-eight hours after things calm down. You have my word, and if it was true what Mycroft says that you're offering a truce for a month while they finish writing their history, I'm open to that too once we get this calmed down."

Again the silence before He Who Visits speaks. "Dominic's pledge does not mean anything."

O.S.: "What?"

The Addressee: "Other powers' pledges I can secure, but Dominic's pledge does not mean anything. You harmed Me. Whether measured in hours, weeks, or seconds, My Dominic will not pause his hunt."

I: "Where is Dominic?" I shrieked it loudly enough for the microphone to hear me.

The Addressee: "*Yahari Mecum. Pericul'est. Continuitas tua Me solatur, Mycroft.* (With Me, of course. There is danger. I'm glad you're alive, Mycroft.)"

I: "*Tecum* . . . (With You.)" The tongue of white-hot panic in me faded. Dominic was not coming. Dominic would happily watch the world burn if he could defile the blasphemer's corpse amid the coals, but he would not leave our Master's side in time of danger. No one may harm his God; no one but him.

The Addressee: "Will you return My Mycroft?"

O.S.: "Possi—"

My Enemy: "Never!" Tully tried to snatch the microphone, but Sniper danced back.

O.S.: "We'll discuss it later."

My Enemy: "Are you insane? We're talking about Mycroft Canner!"

O.S.: "We have worse enemies."

My Enemy: "*You* have worse enemies."

O.S.: "Other issues later, crowd-control first."

My Enemy: "Do you like dental torture? Mycroft does."

O.S.: "Later! The world's on fire. We can spat after we've put it out. Well, J.E.D.D. Mason, do we have a deal?"

The Addressee: "Why do you not call Me Jehovah?"

O.S.: "What?"

The Addressee: "You exposed that name to all your species. You have the strength to use it; others may learn that strength of you, if you show it."

A new light kindled in Sniper's eyes, comingled curiosity, intrigue, aggression, pain, as when a child, used to crossing wooden swords with a younger ba'sib, suffers his first seriously bruising blow, and awakens to the fact that he faces no toddler now, but an opponent. "Jehovah. Do we have a deal?"

"We have."

Their efforts took many hours, and equipment which apparently the next room had, leaving me alone with my wounds. Sleep, with less death in it than before, visited me in spurts, but it is no use to you hearing how the mobswell looked to me in fever's dreams. You want reality. Their efforts worked; this possible version of war died unborn, but not quickly. Censor Jung Su-Hyeon dispatched predictions to Romanova's forces with electric speed. Papadelias made hard, brave choices of where to send his few, brave men. Two thousand, three hundred and thirteen people, by our last count, died that night. Hundreds of buildings burned. Millions of tons of food and kitchen fertilizer disappeared from shops and warehouses. All capitals became police states. The transit network closed all flights, except those away from danger areas and toward hospitals, shelters, or home. Authorities dismissed rumors that organized packs of servicers had separated crowds in Athens, defended set-set bash'houses in Los Angeles and Mexico City, and put out a flaming barge that threatened Chongqing harbor. Utopia hid. Kosala pleaded for calm, Spain for dignity, Ancelet for patience, Jehovah for humanity. MASON told the world to go to its room. Sniper pleaded for, of all things, strategy: "This situation needs a single bullet to the head, not a flamethrower into the crowd. These riots are unworthy of Humanists." Tully made public his predictions of the real consequences of what the mobs were doing, and once he made his numbers public, Censor Su-Hyeon released his own, not quite identical. The world went to its room.

It was Martin Guildbreaker who came for me in the end: Martin, the world's most trusted man. He is trusted of Caesar, of Papadelias, of our dear Master, of the Senate, of the Senate's grandmother his own grandparent Charlemagne Guildbreaker Senior, trusted of Ancelet and Faust who read men well, and of Andō and Spain who watched this young Mason grow up at their Son's side. In my delirium, Martin later told me, I started listing aloud his many trusts and merits, as if drafting in my head some brief biography which might have made it into my first history had sleep not claimed the memory. Caesar had sent Martin for me, with Cannergel cuffs and the order that he manacle my wrist to his to prevent escape as he escorted me back to Imperial custody in Alexandria. Seeing me bandaged and barely able to stand, Martin cuffed me all the same. Only as he helped me to my feet did I realize a goodbye kiss from Sniper had likely not been a dream.

"Tell me as much of what happened to you as you're willing to," Martin ordered, "but don't fill in the gaps with lies, not tonight."

I slumped against his shoulder, comfortable like sun-warmed stone. "Someone tried to kill me. Stabbed me. Someone who had the means to spy on Sniper's followers, who must have heard them talking about my capture and got to me faster than Sniper could. And whoever it was wanted to make it look like my original kidnapper was responsible for my death, so stabbed me again in the same spot."

"Your original kidnapper?"

I would not answer. Do you find my silence strange, reader? Dominic does not have to remind me aloud of the power he has to harm many I care about. Think of Voltaire and noble Aldrin ever in his power, reader. Think of Saladin. "How did you get Sniper to give me back?" I asked.

Martin told me what he believed was my true ransom: the three terms confirmed between Sniper and our Master. Term one: my history would be completed as planned, but each fresh chapter would be sent to Sniper's faction as soon as I completed it, so Sniper, Lesley, and Enemy Tully could veto or edit my words. Term two: Sniper would write a chapter of its own, to explain its disappearance on March twenty-seventh, and was free in that chapter to exhort my readers to join its deadly cause. Term three: Dominic and I would be watched carefully over the next weeks, and the Enemy notified if either of us made a move against him before the truce was done. I rejoiced at heart: these were fair terms, reader, happy terms that would make my history better in the end. But Martin was deceived: these were not the true price exacted by Providence for my release. The price was that they spoke.

The Addressee: "I will help you speak with your captured bash'mates without revealing your location. Live transmissions are easily traced, but Papadelias will facilitate exchange of text or recorded messages. They will be monitored, but neither censored nor admissible as evidence."

O.S.: "Tempting."

The Addressee: "I will also aid you in communicating with your supporters. Back channels breed doppelgangers."

O.S.: "What?"

The Addressee: "There are now as many lies circulating under the names of Ojiro Sniper and Tully Mardi as there were under the name Voltaire when all Paris knew there was no greater draw for readers than the title of their banished Patriarch. Fugitives cannot control which words carry your names."

Hobbes: "I had that problem too from time to time! Upstart nobodies circulating underground pamphlets with my name on them when I was forbidden to publish. Infuriating!"

Reader: "Yes, I have seen the phenomenon from the other end. It is maddening slogging through tome after tome of false Seneca or Canner to find the real works."

The Addressee: "One supposed Ojiro Sniper wrote today *que* My Emperor father must join Me in death to end this, and another that it was not Perry but young Censor Jung Ancelet Kosala who masterminded all. I want to help you help the public weed out such doppelgangers. I will let you share the system the Anonymous uses to let the public sort author from impostor. That web of checks and riddles has stood two centuries impregnable."

O.S.: "Clearer channels would be very useful. And in return I release Mycroft?"

The Addressee: "I would be happy if you released Mycroft."

O.S.: "I thought that's what you were bidding for."

The Addressee: "Bidding?"

O.S.: "Why else would you offer me so much?"

The Addressee: "To decrease evil."

O.S.: "What?"

The Addressee: "Separation and confusion cause pain, a form of evil, and prevent the joy and creativity which are the fruits of human contact. I do not wish you pain, nor to decrease the sum of human happiness and achievement."

O.S.: "Wait, you . . ." Now it was Sniper who needed silence to collect thoughts. "You're offering me all this just to keep us from being lonely?"

The Addressee: "It is My small apology for My Peer's cruelty in creating separation. Political and filial obligations prevent Me from releasing your bash'mates, but I will allow as much contact as possible."

O.S.: "And communications with my followers? Why give me that?"

The Addressee: "Lies too are evil."

O.S.: "Are they?"

The Addressee: "Ὃντος . . . pardon . . . existence is truth; lies unmake truth and so unmake existence; that is evil."

O.S.: "That's really why you're doing this?"

The Addressee: "Of course."

O.S.: "Philosophy aside, you realize this strengthens my side, right? If I'm struggling against impostors, it slows my plans. Give me a clear line to the people and you make it easier for me to get what I want—and what I want is to kill you."

The Addressee: "You are principled, self-examined, *recta, destacada,* driven by worthy causes, and loved by one I Love. I can respect a universe where it is you who kills Me, but not one where I am murdered by a lie."

O.S.: A pause. A sigh. "You're one of these impossibly good people, aren't you? So the longer I talk to you the more I'm going to regret having to kill you?"

The Addressee: "I am thus far omnibenevolent."

O.S.: Again a pause. "You understand it's hard to believe anyone really thinks like that, not just in this day and age, but any day and age."

The Addressee: Again that deeper pause, as thoughts unfathomably vast, beyond both space and time, contort themselves into mere syllables. "I wish to restore to you that familiar company which understands your thoughts and language as no other can, and so reaches through the darkness of miscommunication which isolates every human soul; your shortest name for this concept is bash'. I wish too to give you Truth, and the means to share what Truth you have with Earth now and Posterity beyond. These things I freely give. It proves again your Author's love of symmetry that you have the means to give the same to Me."

O.S.: "You mean . . . Mycroft?"

The Addressee: "My translator and historian. I do not need Mycroft to kill you and Tully Mardi Mojave; many could do that. I need Mycroft for Myself."

O.S.: "Bad luck it's you that has to die."

The Addressee: "Luck?"

O.S.: "Bad luck it's you they picked to make tyrant of the world. It should've been a selfish dick like Andō or Perry, or someone horrible like Dominic, so no one would regret seeing their head blown off. Even President

Ganymede chose to play the game, so it's fair they've gone down in flames. You didn't choose this. You should be in the Sensayers' Conclave writing weird philosophy, not in the Senate, and not in my gun sights. It's stupid luck it's you that has to die."

The Addressee: "There is no luck, nor Fortune, only Providence."

O.S.: "You think you were chosen for the greater good?"

The Addressee: "There is a Purpose; that is not the same as Good."

O.S.: "What purpose?"

The Addressee: "It seems I have not given enough attention to that question. I thank you, My adversary, for reminding Me. You are wise. I grieve that you too will so likely die in this."

Thus, while had I slept and the world cooled, these two had met mind to mind, and poisoned the clean title of adversary with the taint of affection. I got the transcript later from Martin, who watches our Master more closely than ever now, not spying secretly, but watching with the full consent of He Who is watched. But for that night, as Martin helped me from the recovery bed, I still believed my ransom had been painless.

"Shall we walk a bit, Mycroft?" Martin invited gently.

"Thank you, *Nepos.*"

A little exercise was welcome at this stage in the science-hastened re-knitting of my tissues. While the Imperial guards carried a stretcher ready, Martin let me lean on him and walk up from the now-abandoned basement to face the smoky sky. We were somewhere in India, a festive downtown: clubs, galleries, spice bars, and walkways lined with windows packed with desire. The sun had not quite set, but smoke's interference gave an early wake-up call to what few evening lights survived. The musk of snuffed fires wafted from all sides, and to our left a sea of shattered glass sparkled like faerie fire around a freshly gutted improv club. My tears began when I saw the composition kiosk of the club's Amadeus set-set gutted in the street, its strings and cables draped across the ruins in triumphant garlands, like the intestines of a defeated giant. Graffiti covered the walls with slogans, opposing slogans, sloppy Hive sigils, and bull's-eyes. One bull's-eye had a crosshairs, and letters scrawled at its center to be the target: JEDDM. The silent shops had a sense of violated shock to them, as if affronted that we should catch them empty, like a theater set glimpsed in its naked frailty after the show. Looting had been everywhere. I can hear our Master Hobbes whispering over your shoulder, reader, saying this proves again that we are selfish, wicked beasts, but I think goods left unguarded breed forethought, not greed, a hunter-gatherer's rational defensive fear of future chaos: If law and trade break down, will my fight for survival need this loaf? This coat? This spoon? We walked three slow blocks, passing an ironwork sculpture ripped into makeshift weapons, and a brawl preserved in spilled paint, footprints bright as wildflower chaos. The arched gate of a Utopian district loomed on our left, with four sentinels beneath, luminous in coats of tide marshes, 1450, 1950, and space-view sunset, watched in turn by three stern unicorns, a giant spider, and a whirlwind of silver-sleek winged snakes that thrashed like flying mercury. Apollo's sun sigil did not show upon these coats, but I knew the Delians for what they were. In the square outside the gate someone had been burnt in effigy; it almost didn't matter who.

Martin paused our walk now, judging my tears enough. "Tully Mardi wants more of this, Mycroft." His voice was soft. "And Sniper wants to kill *Dominum nostrum*, kill them again so they stay dead. Both threats would've been eliminated today if you'd called Caesar, or Dominic, or me, or anyone who would've followed through and killed our enemies. I know today's secret truce may prove a good thing in terms of raw casualties, but it puts *Dominum* in greater danger, and that endangers the new age they will bring to the Empire and the world. You know that's not an acceptable price, not just to postpone a thousand deaths. Promise me, Mycroft, once this truce is over, that you'll never again give up a chance to destroy our enemies. Promise me."

Sobs wracked me, too fierce to let me even nod, but Martin understood. I think he understood things I didn't. I asked him, once my sobs subsided, if he knew what it was going to be like, Jehovah's new world, which Martin has spent all his life protecting since that childhood day Caesar made him *Vicar, Nepos, Familiaris,* and *Minister Porphyrogenito,* all at once. Martin smiled. I have rarely seen a man so comfortable saying, "No."

CHAPTER THE NINTH

❧❧❧❧❧❧❧❧❧❧❧❧

Repercussions

Written July 30–August 1, 2454
Events of April 15
Burgos

"MADAME"—MARTIN GAVE A STRICT BOW—"YOUR IRRESPONSIBLE abuse of Mycroft Canner is completely unacceptable."

I did not tattletale, reader, but Martin Guildbreaker is no fool. With a scrap of paper and an offhand remark by Cato Weeksbooth it had taken him and Papa four days to expose O.S. Do you think he could not unmask my kidnappers within an hour? Martin stopped off to confront Madame before even returning to Alexandria, bringing me—the living, limping proof of her transgression—still handcuffed to his arm.

"I can guess your goal," Martin continued, the slow, forced patience in his voice an imitation of his Emperor's tone but softer, as a blade of bronze is softer than a blade of steel, "but Mycroft is a fragile and unique resource, and it was sheer luck that they survived this. The consequences for others aside, you must realize how Mycroft's loss would have crippled our ability to communicate with the *Porphyrogene*."

"Not nearly so much as death would." Madame gazed up at Martin, her face uncommonly candid, as when the curtain falls and actors become people once again. "I will not see my Jehovah die, Martin, no matter what I must destroy, or whom."

On the last word her gaze shifted, not to me, but to the Emperor who stood beside us, summoned by Martin's call and radiating cold rage like the marble of a hillside monument which marks some unforgiven massacre. I doubt I would have had the strength to stand in the presence of Caesar's anger, even if I had had the strength to stand at all. Instead I slumped on the ground beside Martin. The rustic mosaic floor was not perhaps the best bed for a wounded man, but Saladin was, wrapped around me, his warmth coaxing my thinned blood to move again as he explored with touch and tongue the parts of me our enemies had marred. Sun warmed me too. Martin and I had reversed the sunset on our flight from parts east back to Europe, and late afternoon blazed down between the columns that ringed this ancient courtyard, Spring and Sun working their annual conspiracy to nurture weed flowers in every crack. The warmth was welcome, but even more welcome was the glare, which hid with silhouette the face of the other figure who sat on a stone rail to our right, chaperoning us: His exhausted Majesty Isabel Carlos II. No, reader, we are not in Paris anymore. Madame's estate was riot's first victim. The sparkling halls, whores' dorms, flesh pit, and silk-walled salons, even the nursery where a young God learned to speak, are now burnt waste. We are in the ancient Abbey of Santa María la Real de las Huelgas, just outside Burgos. Here the Middle Ages put forth their best stone face, fort-thick walls and slit-thin windows, somehow still managing a feminine delicacy in the ruffling of terra-cotta shingles and the curve of the rounded apse. The abbey is one of the oldest pieces of the Spanish royal estates, host to kings' treasures, reliquaries, retired dowagers, and, frequently, royal weddings. Here king and queen become one flesh, and one dust too in the royal tombs whose intricate sarcophagi were tended once by nuns, now by nation-strat-appointed custodians. Before war drove God out of politics, the ruling abbess here was one of the most powerful women in all Europe; now Isabel Carlos II prayed that these cloister walls might be enough to hide Madame.

"There are arenas in which I have never trusted you, Joyce"—MASON stepped forward—"and others in which I have."

"As it should be, yes." Madame was exquisite as she sat on a bench of sun-washed stone, her oceanic gown of mourning black sparkling with constellations of gemlike somethings stitched into the fabric. "You know I feel the same."

"Do you realize how thoroughly this has destroyed what little remained of the latter?"

"Yes, I believe I do, but I had the chance, Cornel. I had to take it, and I had every right to take it."

"You had no right—"

"I had every right!" Her words ricocheted around the cloister's square. "Nature makes rights, Cornel, not Romanova, or Thomas Carlyle, or you, or any man. It's a mother's natural duty to protect her child, at any cost. I'd rip a man's throat out with my teeth if I had to to protect our Son, even your throat, Cornel, and I'd rip out Mycroft's in a second!" Her chest heaved within her bodice like a chick struggling in its shell. "Someone had to do something."

Already MASON's voice was weaker, steel dulled to iron. "I am doing all that can be done."

"No, you're doing all you're willing to do—no, not even that much. You're doing all you think you ought to do, without even considering any action that's unbefitting of your office. And that's what you should be doing. You're the Emperor. I'm not. So while you sit in your tower governing billions as you're supposed to, I'm doing what I'm supposed to be doing: anything I can to save our Son!"

Anger's storm surged in Caesar, but broke as he met Spain's eyes. The king's presence urged decorum, as a library's solemn walls force tirades to couch themselves in whispers. MASON breathed deep. "You're right. I am limited by my office, and that also means there are limits to what I can let you do."

"To Masons, yes, but I haven't harmed a Mason, have I?" She faced him straight. "The only limits on what can be done to Mycroft Canner are the ones you personally set. I trusted that, as Jehovah's father, you would be willing to risk one little *Familiaris*."

MASON frowned. "I do not have sole claim on Mycroft's life."

"Legally you do."

"There's more to it than law."

"What matters more to you, Cornel? The wishes of a dead Utopian who never shared your feelings, or our living, breathing Son?"

Fierce as a bear, Caesar charged and seized Madame by her porcelain-white shoulders—or he tried to, but the last step failed him, his ankle twisting at the scarless seam of his transplanted left foot. He toppled forward, cracking his forehead against the wall, and would have fallen bodily on Madame if Saladin had not caught him. My own Saladin. He had sprung up to defend his mistress, as a guard dog should, and when MASON stumbled he was too close to fight off the human instinct to help a falling man. He caught the Emperor under the shoulders and steadied him, at least until MASON's eyes caught sight of his savior. The Emperor jumped as if the fingers on his back were scorpions, and struck with his elbow, bloodying Saladin's nose as he knocked the monster away.

"Oh! Cornel! Are you alright?" Madame's touch was all nursing, pawing at the Emperor's forehead where it had struck the stone. "Your poor head! Let me see. You're bleeding!"

"I'm fine!" MASON stormed back, batting at the security robots which swarmed in from the corners, bleeping. His guards burst in at once, Spain's too, followed by both their on-duty physicians and a flock of Madame's maids. An absurd pause held us as the doctors scanned and bandaged Caesar's forehead. I did not watch. I had a wounded Saladin to soothe and taste, and blood salt dissolved the present as sun dissolves sleep. My name awoke us.

"You're right, I misused Mycroft," Madame was saying as the door thumped shut behind the last departing guard. "I presumed you'd permit it to save dear Jehovah, but it was still presumption on my part. Either bring me to court for abusing a Servicer, or decide you're not going to prosecute and move on, but don't expect me to feign contrition, and don't pretend you too don't want to ignore the law and kill our Son's enemies."

"An Emperor does not ignore the law; I make it."

She brightened. "You mean Natekari's motion to declare Sniper an enemy of the Alliance? Oh, pass it, Cornel. Pass it, please! It would make things so easy!"

"I may pass it, but there are other ways, within my laws. The Empire faced assassins long before we built Romanova. We are not unprepared. That's why I don't want you interfering." He peered at her portrait face. "I want you to promise me you won't try anything like this again, and I will hold you to it."

She blinked. "To keep away from Mycroft? If you insist."

"Mycroft is not the issue. After this I'm not lending Mycroft to anyone again, no matter the errand."

"But Caesar!" I dared cry.

"Silence, Mycroft."

"The others need me! Ancelet! Achilles!"

MASON's kick flew with the full violence of hate, not at me but at Saladin who held me, slamming him square in that jaw which had ripped Apollo's flesh. Saladin yelped, and Madame clicked soft disapproval through her frown, as one should at misbehaving pups whom a guest has justly disciplined. I gave Caesar his required silence.

"Madame," the Emperor demanded anew, "promise me you won't try to use your own means against O.S. This isn't just bribery and nepotism anymore, it's war. Leave it to government."

Madame crossed her arms in a sparkling, lacy huff. "You want me to keep my hands out? Cornel, I don't play at that era when the lady was shut up in a dollhouse fussing over the silver; I play at the era when she had a secret hand in every plot. Whatever you may say, I shall pursue Jehovah's enemies to the world's end, with my full resources and liberty."

"Now's not the time. The world knows you're at the heart of this. They're

hungry for an excuse to prosecute you, or lynch you. Think of the consequences for your fellow Blacklaws. It's hard enough fighting Cook's Eighth
Law motion with set-sets involved in O.S. If you draw any more attention
the Nurturists will turn on Blacklaws in a heartbeat, and many will turn
with them."

The surprise in Madame's voice might have been genuine. "You think
they'll use our Jehovah as an excuse to take away Blacklaws' children?"

"They won't have to, they'll use Dominic, and Ganymede and Danaë,
and Heloïse, don't forget Heloïse ran into the Senate in a nun's habit, and
that's not the worst of it. When people put it together that a Blacklaw started
all this—"

"Merion Kraye started all this."

"You started Merion Kraye," he answered flatly. "What about the real
Eighth Law? You haven't just angered the Leviathans, you've set us all on
fire! Don't pour salt on the burns. It's a wonder the other Blacklaws haven't
already called a lynch mob down on you."

"I'm not a Blacklaw anymore."

"What?"

Madame blinked, as if surprised at his surprise. "I registered a few hours
ago. I'm a European now. And a Spaniard."

The Emperor turned on the king, slightly too quickly. "You're going
through with it?"

Fatigue made His Majesty's soft voice softer. "We are."

"You're actually getting married." Caesar had to hear it out loud, even
if in his own voice.

"It is the honorable thing."

"Honorable? Honorable is doing your duty by your Hive and nation.
Do you honestly think your people believe that taking responsibility for a
bastard is worth abdicating at a time like this?"

"No, I don't." Isabel Carlos did not meet Caesar's eyes.

"But you're going to abandon them anyway?"

"No, I won't."

"Then you don't intend to abdicate?" MASON's tone grew night dark,
almost urgent. "You told me a King of Spain can't marry a prostitute. You
promised me!"

Madame smiled. "We took a poll. Seventy-something percent of Europe wants His Majesty to keep the crown after the wedding, including
ninety-something percent of the Spanish nation-strat. It's heartening having such a warm welcome from my new people."

Caesar does not curse, not even under his breath. "Spain, you know Madame only wants this so they can visit the graves of Madame de Pompadour and whatever other famous royal mistresses, and gloat about becoming a real queen."

Spain's gentle eyes met MASON's as he corrected, "Empress."

"What?"

What should we call the emotion that made His Majesty's lips tremble so? Apology? "You know the Senate has ordered Europe, as well as the Humanists and Mitsubishi, to present a draft for the correction of our government after O.S." A weary breath. "Popular support is for an imperial system, based on yours. They will, I expect, choose me."

"An Emperor? A European Emperor?" So many monarchs would fix the piercing gaze of rivalry on a new peer—instead MASON . . . relaxed, until he too showed that fatigue I saw on Spain's face, like charioteers' fatigue, their arms exhausted from wrestling too-powerful beasts through Ares's frenzy. Wise men do not envy Emperors.

"It doesn't matter why Madame wants to marry me," Spain said at last. "Honor demands it, and the people, my people, approve it."

"So whatever the public wants is suddenly permissible?" The Emperor crossed his arms. "Isn't that the logic behind the Wish List?"

The king shook his head. "The will of the public does not make the marriage permissible, merely acceptable. I don't yet know if we will have permission."

"Permission?" Caesar repeated. "From what, if you already polled your Spaniards?"

Madame cocked her head. "We're going to Rome next week. Didn't Jehovah tell you?"

Martin's fist, cuffed to mine, clenched, the motion barely palpable through the Cannergel which lined my special cuffs. Something was about to transpire, something Martin had anticipated, planned. Arranged. The middle voice, that is how I often think of Martin. There was a third option in Homer's Greek between active and passive verbs, the middle voice, a subtle space between the doer who creates or kills and the recipient who is created or is killed. Between these opposites lies he who causes but does not do the deed himself. The patron touches no stone, yet builds the cathedral; the judge wields no sword, yet strikes off the traitor's head. Martin says nothing, yet this conversation is his creation, born from the conjunction he has carefully assembled: MASON, Spain, Madame. Even when Odysseus planned the horse, he did not saw the boards himself. Martin expected something, something worth making his Emperor come here.

"I trust you mean you're going to Romanova," MASON pronounced.

"No, real Rome. The Vatican Reservation." Sunlight on Madame's painted face made her smile too bright. "His Catholic Majesty and I have much to arrange."

Law's sting made Isabel Carlos II rise at once. "I will not have this conversation without a sensayer present."

« Majesté . . . » Madame purred.

"No. Playing around in Paris as we have was crime enough, but I will not break the First Law while standing in my family's ancestral nunnery."

"Are you going to have Jehovah legitimated?" The question broke from Caesar like storm over a mountain peak.

The king marched with perfect posture toward the door.

MASON blocked the exit. "Are you going to Rome to get papal dispensation to marry a prostitute? Or are you going to legitimate your bastard?"

I could not see the king's face, but I could see the tremor in his jaw. "I'm sorry. I know it's against our arrangement."

"I will not let you make Jehovah your heir."

"Prince Leonor is dead."

"There are others in line for your throne."

"It has to be my child."

"You have cousins."

"I had cousins; death by Merion Kraye."

A different, blacker anger joined the rage already rumbling through MASON. "Kraye killed your entire family?"

"I have a great-great-aunt who is one hundred and sixty-six years old and succumbing fast." Isabel Carlos II turned back toward us, composed again and perfect as a marble bust. "You have your continuity in law, MASON." He held his hand out. "Ours is this blood. It flowed through queens, saints, emperors, and it flows through my one surviving child. I cannot change this fact, not even if it means breaking my word to you."

Even optimism sounded rough in Caesar's throat. "You're not too old to have another child."

"True"—Spain nodded toward the Lady—"and we will try to have another child, Joyce has promised that, and if we succeed that could solve everything. But I could also be assassinated tomorrow. I'm holding the European Hive together with nothing but residual family trust. Neither Spain nor Europe can feel safe unless I have a successor."

MASON's stance solidified, his left foot's imagined weakness eclipsed as danger eclipses pain. Martin's grip solidified at the same time, his hand and arm supporting me as I slumped against him, bracing me—for what?

"I will not let you make Jehovah your heir," MASON pronounced.

"They are my heir."

"I will not let you make Jehovah take the Crown Prince's oath of loyalty to you and the Spanish people."

My stomach heaved, but Martin's support kept me from writhing hard enough to strain my wound. An oath? Jehovah take an oath? The manacle that bound my arm to Martin's could be broken or, in desperate times, the hand gnawed off, but to the Great Scroll's Addressee words are more real and more unalterable than breathing, fact, or matter. The stuff that His Peer's world is made of. Prison wraiths surged around me, dense as Tully's war-cancer, weaving their spiral bonds of smoke-ribbon like maypole dancers in my mind. A God sworn vassal to the King of Spain? Divine Infinity and all His Goodness yoked to the self-interest of one arbitrary nation-strat? You did not see Him, reader, in the weeks before He was sworn in as Romanovan Tribune, how He pored over its oath of office with linguists, lawyers, sensayers, family, strangers, performing desperate and stubborn exegesis on every word until he satisfied himself that He could understand and execute the pledge to "exercise My judgment to identify and oppose laws which strip too much of human liberty." So much thought He gave to an oath He could shed with resignation any second, as crabs shed their cramped shells. That was nothing to this—a lifelong oath of loyalty to the Spanish people? I retched again, and lost myself in a maze of insane solutions. Have Spain annex the whole Earth? Replace Jehovah's bone marrow to purge him of the blood of kings? Travel back in time and murder Charlemagne before he could bear children? Surely, reader, you have wandered in the mire of half-sleep, and forged from dream logic plans that waking must call mad.

Martin spoke up at last, for my sake. "*Caesar, Mycroft domum ferendus est.* (Mycroft must be taken home.)"

Black-fisted MASON glanced at me with rage's crimson still darkening his cheeks. Then he turned to Spain. "We will discuss this more another time."

"Why?" The quick, light question would have sounded natural on other lips, but coming from the king, who fashions his words so gingerly, it sounded like a curse. "In this matter we are not people but peoples. Neither Europe nor your Empire can compromise on this. Discussion will not resolve it."

MASON's brows furrowed. "What will?"

Gentle, still so gentle, the king, as if he sees with every breath the millions that a king's too-hasty word can ruin and so, Leviathan among the Lilliputians, steps on tiptoe. "Hopefully not violence." His eyes beamed empathy. "I owe you an apology, Caesar. I let harm come to your *Familiaris* when you kindly lent them to me. I gave you my word of honor that I would return Mycroft Canner safely as soon as we completed the transport of the duke, and I failed."

"The fault was not yours." MASON would not look at Madame.

"The promise was mine," the king answered quickly. "The stain is on my honor."

Caesar frowned long at the king. "You can't maintain this, Isabel. You can't be an honorable gentleman and be with Joyce. They're a whore. I don't mean prostitute—you and I both know prostitution can be an honorable profession in its way—but Joyce actively wants to live up to the old archetype and be a filthy, treacherous, honor-destroying whore. Right now you're the only evidence the world has that there can be a morally pure leader anymore. Joyce will tear that all down. For fun. To prove they can."

The king smiled, soft. "Joyce has the right to tear it down; they built it up."

"What do you mean?"

"When Madame and I convene for our . . . trysts . . . Madame plays Vice and has me play Virtue, and we've been doing it for twenty years; after enough play a part becomes habit."

The Emperor shook his head. "I don't believe you're a good man just because of that. I think you always had this in you, Madame just brought it out more." He limped a step toward the door. "Same as with me."

Martin did not yet help me to my feet. "Caesar, may I address Madame a moment, before we go?" he asked.

MASON had a smile for a Guildbreaker scion, even here. "Of course."

Madame herself perked, adjusting her skirts as if to get the rustling over with before the next scene of an opera. "What is it, Martin?"

"It would benefit you at some point to recognize that, like the *Porphyrogene*, I too have grown up. My Emperor has given me literally unlimited resources, public and clandestine, and the trust of Romanova gives me even more, all dedicated to the service and safety of *Domini* Jehovah. I could likely have captured Sniper today if you had made me your accomplice instead of, or in addition to, Dominic. I caught you, after all."

Madame's smile had a lively, rolling glow, as Hera or Demeter wear in frescoes. "My dear Martin, Dominic I can predict."

Martin frowned. "I do not exaggerate, Madame, when I say I believe myself to be possibly the most predictable person on Earth."

"Of course you are, dear Martin," she answered, "but you can't keep a secret from Jehovah for five minutes, and only Earth's greatest fool would dare try to predict what He will do when you tell Him something."

Martin considered that a moment. "It is certainly true, Madame, that I keep secrets from *Domine* only in the most extreme situations, but that is because, if *Dominus* orders or advises something, it is the right thing."

She shook her head. "What He wants is not always what's best."

"False, Madame. *Dominus* always wants what is best. You raised them thus."

Spain and Caesar watched in quiet fascination as ever-calculating Martin judged it worthwhile to raise his voice in argument against immovable Madame.

"You flatter me, Martin," she replied. "Every mother wants to think her child is perfect, but I know it's not quite true."

"Perhaps, but *Dominus* is morally perfect if not absolutely perfect. What they order does not always lead to success, but it is always the best of all possible human actions. If Dominus says we should kill Sniper, we should kill Sniper; if they say we should not, then there are reasons we should not."

She laughed. "Jehovah isn't actually infallible, Martin, appropriate as your devotion is."

"No, Madame, nor are they omniscient, but still I believe no one in the history of the human race has ever erred less. It is not hubris when I say that I am myself reasonably wise, yet observation has proved to me that I am wrong much more often than *Dominus*. I know therefore that I choose the right thing more often when guided by *Domine* than when I choose on my own. To ignore or avoid their council, as you have done, Madame, is both irrational and immoral."

"Dear Martin"—she reached toward him, as if to cup his cheek in her hand—"not even you can think it's that black and white."

"In fact, Madame, I do."

"Martin the Manichean!" I screamed. I screamed it, reader, full force despite the pain, anemia, fatigue, and the utter inappropriateness of a slave interrupting kings. I couldn't help it. If at an outdoor theatre, with brave Antigone monologuing her last hours, you spotted on the hill above the stage a unicorn, elusive, pure, and real, you too would forget decorum and shout and point to let actor and audience alike enjoy the long-sought vision. "Martin! That's why our Master calls you Martin!"

It was an odd moment for dawn to break at last upon the dusty mystery. Martin the Manichean. Mycroft 'Martin' Guildbreaker had borne the nickname, and its cultish stigma, patiently since he was sixteen and the Master Who renamed him six. Why He chose 'Martin' we never knew. The Child Jehovah was too tangled in Earth's many languages back then to answer complex questions, and by the time He semimastered speech, the secret behind the nickname had already become a puzzle-quest which Martin felt he had to solve himself. On the ride back to Alexandria I apologized for blurting the solution, but middle-voice Martin only smiled, content that he had arranged the conjunction which unlocked the mystery. We had been on the wrong track all these years, thinking it must be Saint Martin, or Martin Luther, or some other historic Martin, or perhaps the bird, when the answer was in our Eighteenth Century the whole time: Martin the Manichean, the character from Voltaire's *Candide*. I got to watch Martin over the next days, as I worked on my history while he, in the corner, read, reread, and memorized his namesake's scenes. The ancient Manichean cult believed the universe was a great war between a force of Good and one of Evil. In such a world there is true right, true wrong, and Evil was not mere imperfection necessitated by our Maker's Plan but a Maker in itself, which schemes and undoes while the other loves and gives. This Manichean sentiment leaked quickly into other cults, especially those veins of Christianity which imagined the universe as a struggle between God and Satan, instead of a play where God the Author scripts out rebel Lucifer and loyal Michael with equal absoluteness. The Manicheans had vocal enemies, the Platonists, Saint Augustine, many who argued that light is something, shadow its mere absence, so Good is Real but Evil merely a diluted good, like fabric with too many holes to hold. So fierce were the Christian counterarguments that later generations used the Manichean heresy for target practice, re-proving its folly in theology exams to demonstrate their syllogisms. Soon the Manichees became Europe's stock stupid heresy, something only an idiot would fall for. But then she breaks, the Dawn of Reason with her rosy fingers, and brings us Montaigne, Descartes, and Pierre Bayle. Bayle raised the problem first, the ambidextrous Bayle, as Voltaire called him, forever seeming to write one thing with his right hand and another in a footnote with his left, confounding censors by hiding his arguments in pieces, as prisoners hide their tools. In his dictionary entry on the Manicheans, Bayle wrote that, for all the centuries of attempted disproofs, no one had ever actually made Good versus Evil seem truly unconvincing as a model of the world. What good was Logic if it could not best this oldest folly? A generation later, Voltaire's long-suffering Candide pauses in his troubles to muse on old Manicheanism, so abused a dead horse that no one could possibly be a Manichean anymore. Sheepishly his fellow traveler Martin confesses, "I am one, and I don't know what to do about it, but I find myself unable to see the world in any other way." Soon, reader, I would have the privilege of watching our Martin Guildbreaker read that line, and understand at last the blessing our Master had given him sixteen years before: "Live on in your black-and-white world, Martin my Manichean; I will never tell you you are wrong." So Martin would understand, and smile, musing on how rare and useful his black-and-white mind is in this too-distracting world— but that will be tomorrow. Today, in Spain's cloister, a lifetime's curiosity could not make Martin interrupt his Emperor's business for his own.

"My point, Madame, is that the pledge Caesar demands of you—that you not go after O.S. on your own—is easily kept; have me hunt for you."

The lady frowned chidingly at Martin. "We'd dropped that, dear."

"Enough, Martin." MASON's words were half sigh. "A Blacklaw's promise would have meant something, but I put no value in the word of someone who's been a Spaniard for half a day and already stained their king's honor."

Spain frowned, as I imagine Cassandra frowns when she watches her doomed brothers march to war. "I know small betrayals are habit for you, Madame, but once you become my queen they will also be high treason against the Spanish Crown, which I will be obliged to prosecute."

« Majesté! » Madame offered a plaintive stare, but no argument: even she could not bring logic to her side.

"You are entering a law, Joyce." His Majesty spoke firmly. "Of your own free will. You are taking vows of your own free will. There will be consequences to your actions henceforth, and nothing you do will manipulate me into lightening those consequences by the weight of one hair if you violate the honor—national and personal—whose preservation is the very reason I shall marry you."

MASON gave a sour smile. "You can't have everything, Joyce. You can't become a European and keep acting like a Blacklaw. You can't marry a Hive leader and still demand we treat you as Hive-neutral. You can't promise to live as a strict Catholic and pretend you'll maintain our polyamory. And you can't use tricks and twists and seductions and technicalities of the law to snare us over and over and expect us not to snare you in return."

"But I can still love you both."

She got them. One could feel it in their strides, their breathing, as they hurried wordlessly away in opposite directions, Spain across the courtyard, Caesar out to the world. Love. If social mores have one purpose, it is to armor us against the instincts that Hobbes knows made wild life so brutish, and so short. Here are the two most civilized men in the world, who teach admiring billions the difference between savage and citizen, yet, as their eyes meet over Madame, her machinations regress them irresistibly: two rivals who can no longer share one mate. Their pulses race, their faces flush, and Caesar's black-sleeved hand thirsts for Spain's throat for a moment, as it does for mine. She did this to them, reader, planned it and *enjoyed* it. I dared pray in that moment that, if these two great men must fall, they will not fall for her.

※※※※※※※※※※※※※※※※※※※※

Our Secret Truce

Written August 2–3, 2454
Events of April 15–23
Observed from Alexandria

IT FAILED. IT WAS INEVITABLE. NO ONE KNEW. THE PACT BETWEEN
Sniper and my Master could restrain Caesar, Papadelias, Spain, even Tully
Mardi for a month, but a leader's urging has only so much power over a
frightened widow with a jagged stone. Not a day passed from the fifteenth
to the twenty-third that did not see riot, fire, and somewhere or another a
peppering of death. Still, the Will to Battle was not yet Battle. When
every guest at a dinner has a motive for wanting the host dead, in one sense
it doesn't really matter who strikes first, the oppressed stepdaughter or the
vengeful rival—either way, the victim dies. Yet, in another sense, it does
matter which heart heeds conscience, and which breaks civilization's most
ancient law and makes itself a true hospiticide. Peace was our murdered
host, the dwindling chance, nurtured by Senate, Kosala, and Ancelet, that
our recent wrongs might be righted by Law. In one sense it did not matter
which act snuffed that hope first, but those industrious guardians who
bought us precious days deserve due credit, especially the strange ones.

Kosala: "This offer came from Dominic?"
Greenpeace: "Partly, though I developed the details."
Kosala: "To give me one point one million properties?"
Greenpeace: "Distributed fairly evenly around the globe, well located, mostly
    urban. You're welcome to renovate the existing buildings as needed.
    We'll offer an indefinite lease, no payment asked, on condition they are
    returned to their current owners when the crisis, and the recovery from
    the crisis, are done. No time limit specified, but the situation should be
    reviewed annually starting in four years."
Kosala: "And I'm to use these properties for what, precisely?"

Fine print spread, hypnotic as zebra stripes, across Kosala's office wall as Mitsubishi Greenpeace Director Jyothi Bandyopadhyay summoned her draft. "The current language suggests hospitals, refugee housing, soup kitchens, storage of humanitarian supplies, fire stations, and quote 'other comparable use.' We didn't want to limit it since no one knows what might actually happen in this conflict. Will we need quarantine sites? Radiation scrubbers? POW camps? We want you to decide what to use them for, since you're the one who's pledged to build a new emergency center in every city in the world."

Dark times, reader, when a million free hospitals do not make a Cousin's face brighten. "That plan isn't public yet."

Greenpeace: "Then both can be announced together. We want to give you as much freedom as possible to use this land to help the human race."

Kosala: "And you hope that giving us rent-free land for hospitals will defuse the demands for the Mitsubishi to give up your land monopoly?"

Greenpeace: "Monopoly is a strong word."

Kosala: "Majority."

Greenpeace: "Majority is a strong word."

Kosala: "It's also true."

Greenpeace: "You've been listening to too many of Tully Mardi's broadcasts, Chair Kosala. But, so has the whole world, and that's the point. If this proves to the public that the Mitsubishi are willing to share land with other Hives, that could defuse the tension. We all want the Mitsubishi strike to end. We're giving you this land as long as you use it for the public good, and we trust you entirely to decide what that good is. We'll appoint a committee—mixed Greenpeace and others—to review the sites periodically and make sure they're being used well, but it'll be pure formality."

Kosala: "Greenpeace? Not Mitsubishi?"

Greenpeace: "Well, Greenpeace Mitsubishi. We said Greenpeace in the draft because ..."

Because recent scars reopen easily. All Hives are Frankenstein chimeras, stitched from mergered peoples: the Humanists were born from the Olympians and One Big Party, the Cousins absorbed Rainbow Bridge and Schools Without Borders, Europe swallowed Volemonde and IBN; so many names from the heady decades after the Great Renunciation, when dozens of newborn Hivelets vied for slices of mankind. The fittest survived, but with the conquered within them, as conquered bacteria became the mito-chondria which feed the cells that crawl through volvox, trilobite, and coe-lacanth toward Mars. One suture is still fresh. To me it is history, but to Papadelias, Jin Im-Jin, Joyce and Felix Faust, sixty-four years ago is very liv-ing memory. Greenpeace, lean of members but fat with forests, farms, and mountains. In Greenpeace had gathered those who loved the land, the farmers, shepherds, seaherds, naturalists, Earth Mother's self-appointed guards. Here too, as the geographic nations died, accumulated their parks, wilderness, sanctuaries, refuges, and reserves, adopted by guardians determined to ensure that the Church War's carnage left the untouched untouched. India quickly became the Hive's heart, that exquisite subcontinent whose many peoples have always been so prudently reluctant to subject the small-est parcel of their paradise to outsiders' exploitation. Soon, in addition to owning most of India, Greenpeace guarded a quarter of the Earth, pris-tine, primordial lands, in business terms untappable. Untappable but real. How the Mitsubishi hungered for it, the land-crazed Mitsubishi who lust after the sweet curves of hills or the dusky laps of mountains just as much they do after rent-rich high-rises and commodity-plump factories. Those Hives that think only manpower is real power laughed when the Mit-subishi bought out Greenpeace, as when Prometheus duped Father Zeus with his trickster's offering of rich fat hiding empty bones. Some gods want bones. While for a European or a Humanist one life is one vote, every unit of property a Mitsubishi Member owns is one extra share in the cor-poration, an extra vote. A more valuable property might be two votes, twenty, a thousand. Even if each wilderness acre was worth a hundredth of a house, there were millions of acres. I know the Directorate, and the courting dance they play with the voting blocs that feed their power. All Directors come from land-rich families, but family property is only the tiny axle which anchors the great wheel of a billion supporting votes, bound to their chosen Director by promotion ladders, nepotism, debt, trust, and tribe mentality. Greenpeace's property brought two billion new votes into the Mitsubishi Hive, one billion to raise a Greenpeace Director, the other bil-lion to be wooed by the dominant voting blocs which vie eternally for the other eight seats. If Shanghai now had two Directors, it wasn't just because of property in Shanghai. It is no coincidence that crowd-courting Andō has always made his love of nature sanctuaries so very public. For sixty-four years, then, there has been no Greenpeace, but in history's terms the sutures are still raw, and when ex-Greenpeace Members smell blood on Mitsubi-shi hands, their minds are quick to chop 'they' off of 'we.'

Kosala switched to speaking Hindi with Bandyopadhyay here, the intimacy of their shared strat-language demanding extra honesty with it. She has kindly translated for me.

Kosala: "Do you think the Mitsubishi Hive might split?"

Greenpeace: "No, but there's been discussion| People will be more comfortable if it's clear that, if things do turn sour, these properties will still be governed by Greenpeace members, the slice of the Hive that's likely to be less involved in violence| The landgrab isn't Greenpeace's policy, after all|"

Kosala: "Are the properties being offered all Greenpeace-owned?"

Greenpeace: "No| Actually hardly any of them are, but the owners who pledged the land have agreed to Greenpeace Members overseeing things|"

Kosala: "How much of this land comes from Mitsubishi ruling families?"

Greenpeace: "Some, I guess| I'd have to check how much|"

Kosala: "And how soon can I have it?"

Greenpeace: "Today, if you want it|"

Kosala: "I do, but I'm going to sleep on it, run it by some people| Is forty-eight hours alright?"

Greenpeace: "Sure| Oh, there is one other proposal|"

Kosala: "Proposal or condition?" The backroom-savvy Cousin Chair pricked her ears as deer do at the rifle's loading click.

Greenpeace: "Somewhere between| We want the Cousins to help us push a Senatorial Consult through Romanova| Well, a Blacklaw clarification, actually|"

Kosala: "The set-set law?"

Greenpeace: "No, no| A clarification of the Second Black Law|"

"Now?" I cried aloud as I read the transcript later in the safety of my cell. "You'd bring another assault on the Black Laws now?"

Kosala: "The Second Law?"

Greenpeace: "We want Romanova to officially declare that engaging in combat in designated nature reserves, or transporting or storing war materials there, legally constitutes 'action likely to result in extensive or uncontrolled destruction of Nature,' and is thus banned by the Second Black Law| We have a list of about two hundred and fifty thousand individual areas we think are justified in being declared off-limits to the war|"

Kosala: "Doesn't the Second Law already restrict what can be done in nature preserves?"

Greenpeace: "Yes, but its past interpretations have all related to restricting particular types of equipment or materials| We want to argue that any kind of military action, even just having food stores there, or moving troops through, will give the enemy an incentive to destroy the area, thus endangering Nature|"

Kosala: "You're asking me to create borders|" I imagine Kosala sighing like some great shaman whose apprentice pledged to join the master's desert journey of enlightenment, but arrives for embarkation still clinging to a teddy bear.

Greenpeace: "I'm asking you to create borders around rainforests, and orangutans, and baby elephants| We need these borders|"

Kosala: "Creating peace zones means creating war zones|"

Hobbes: "More than that: creating a peace zone is the announcement that you have given up on peace. This will feed fear, and the Will to Battle with it."

Greenpeace: "That's the whole point| Creating peace zones, and by extension war zones, will show people that not only the whackos and criminals like Tully Mardi are taking the danger seriously| If the Mitsubishi and Cousins together—whom everyone sees as enemies in this, on the O.S. front and the set-set front—if we're seen jointly preparing for the possibility of World War, people will wake up and realize that Word War might actually happen, and they just might get off their butts and do something to preserve World Peace| That's what we both want| This way if we succeed there will be peace, and if we fail there will be protections for orangutans and baby elephants|"

Kosala: "This," Kosala's Hindi sounded so intimate here, so cautious: "This idea came from Dominic Seneschal, didn't it?" It is such a good thing, reader, that Kosala has drunk of Madame's poison, such a good thing that there is someone at the Cousins' heart who can recognize its taste.

Greenpeace: "Y-yes| Seneschal's a weird, weird person, but I can't deny they're a great Acting Chief Director| This is a good plan, and, in the public eye, it will be you and Greenpeace at the center, not the Mitsubishi, or Seneschal| Don't forget, Greenpeace is clean of any involvement in O.S., and we're in complete agreement with you Cousins in thinking that the top priority is protecting everything we can in this mess| A public Cousin-Greenpeace alliance will combat the Cousin-Mitsubishi enmity| You want the strike and riots to end too, don't you?"

The Cousins' great poison taster did more than hesitate before agreeing. She consulted friends, board members, experts, even, with Caesar's permission, Martin and myself, who know Dominic better than anyone outside Madame's. It was in that visit that she gave permission for me to add this transcript to my chronicle, and brought some brightness to my cell with her stories of growing food stocks and nurses' training. You must not think my captivity in MASON's sanctum dank, reader, nor he a cruel protector. It is a cheery room where I sleep and work, cozy with cushions, alive with screens which show me anything I wish, from light-swift news to warming dawnscapes. I have visitors: constant Martin, Ἄναξ Jehovah, Xiaoliu Guildbreaker, my Saladin, Mercer, Kohaku, sometimes playful Faust, exhausted Ancelet, or calm Geneva. Kosala was the steadiest of all through this, the reed that bends and springs back when the oak falls. But I could not help her understand Dominic. Nor can I tell you much of his activities. The Mitsubishi are my blind spot. I want to show you how Dominic did it. I want to trace, threat by bargain, how the bloodhound played that vast harp, stringed with favors and blackmail, which he had so long watched Chief Director Andō play. But Andō has his victory, his cunning surrender, not to the Master, but to His hunter whose shadowed path no one can follow—no one but Andō who laid out the course and waits, in prison's peace, for its completion.

"What does Dominic want?" Kosala asked me when she visited, healthily unashamed to seek help wherever help is found. "This proposal is totally reasonable and beneficial, and really looks like it might help the peace. Why would Dominic do this?"

I answered the truth. "The only thing Dominic wants, or ever thinks about, is Ἄναξ Jehovah. I wouldn't be particularly surprised if someone told me Dominic had a scheme to wipe out the rest of the human race just to eliminate all distractions. I don't know why he'd try to stop the war, or protect Nature, but that does seem to be what he's doing."

The Greenpeace proposal was not the only evidence of Dominic's unlikely peacemaking. That same day, April fifteenth, the Sensayers' Conclave presented to the Senate their plan for stabilizing public discourse about the resurrection. The plan reeked of Julia, and gave unprecedented liberty for small-group in-bash' religious discourse, enough so that some wise and bitter critics warned it would turn the world from ten billion independent minds into a billion bash'-sized churches. But every single Mitsubishi voted for it, and enough others to let the motion pass.

The fifteenth also saw a sudden announcement from the Mitsubishi which promised a bewildered Papadelias complete and open access to all Directorate records, and the personal files of Directoral families, back to the foundation of O.S.

"Suspiciously candid," Papa called it when he too took a turn on the couch between Martin's desk and mine, seeking our advice on Dominic's psychology. Papa was calm by then, but had not been when he first arrived, and hurled a list of curses that only a centenarian could accumulate against Martin and everyone: How could they have let Mycroft—*the* Mycroft, Papa's Mycroft—slip, however briefly, into mortal danger? But so skeletal a chest can only rant so long. After securing Martin's promise that he and Papa would work together to discover who stabbed me the second time, Papa was again a smiling font of sport-swift speculation. His smile was false, though. There is a twitch one picks up from abusing anti-sleeping-meds too much. I have had it for years, but had not seen it in Papadelias since the rich days of my capture. Papa didn't—couldn't—mention details, but World Riot is someone's job. Local city governments relied on Romanova as a backup, but the not-quite-untiring Commissioner General couldn't back up every city on Earth at once.

"What I don't get," Papa continued, "is why the Mitsubishi don't just sell off some land? No one's saying they have to give up Asian land. They could sell in Detroit, Dubai, Manchester, Naples, Halifax, their half of Athens. They could sell farmland, marshland, or those hunks of rainforest that just sit there being ecologically important and full of frogs."

"They think all power comes from land." Martin aided our speculation game. "Location doesn't matter, they won't sell their patrimony."

Patrimony? I chuckled at Martin, such a Mason, still measuring value in man hours, and human lives. It isn't the work ancestors put in to accumulating the land that makes the Mitsubishi cling for dear life. Land is real. Immortal, as the fruits of lifetimes' labors cannot be on Time's grand scale. Just as the ancient bronzesmith leaves no fingerprint on our towers of steel, so today's great achievements will someday be invisible within the great machines that are to us the future, and to distant generations trash. Yet after a million sunsets there will still be acres, dirt, and dawn. The Earth is real, and one who owns a sliver of her owns something eternal. I know why Martin couldn't see it. He never sees his labors as his own, only as part of the Masonic Leviathan whose projects outlast ages. But one corner of me is still European, and had Providence blessed me as it has blessed Papa with twelve acres of olive groves and grazing land where young goats frisk after their dams, it would take a harsher threat than politics to pry that property from me. If it were Greek, that is. My Greece I know, and love, and understand. Twelve acres near Detroit or Halifax are to me as interchangeable as empty euros. But perhaps the Mitsubishi truly are wiser than Europe, and truly can love all Earth the same.

Danger, Mycroft. Thy tone reeks of territories, regions, borders, not thy elastic nation-strats but the geographic nations whose battles were so bloody, and so long. Art thou already so infected by thy embryonic war?

Perhaps I am. Perhaps I always was.

"I think Martin's right, Papa," I said. "I think the Mitsubishi see all their land as homeland, regardless of location. We have to imagine they're all going to be as stubborn as we'd be giving up Delphi or Mycenae. We'd do worse than go on strike. I think that's why Dominic understands the Mitsubishi well enough to work with them; he's slightly French."

I don't know whether Papa quite believed me. I don't know whether I quite believed myself.

Dawn's kindling on April sixteenth saw fresh crises in the Senate, with the Mitsubishi at the heart of both. Up for debate first came Minister Cook's hateful reintroduction of the Set-Set Law, which heightened the fervor around the Mitsubishi strike. While the Mitsubishi administration claimed that the Odessa land redistribution edict was their only provocation, the world remembers the Set-Set Riots, and knows that the entrepreneurial Mitsubishi train and employ the lion's share of set-sets. The same session saw the first discussion of Natekari's motion to declare Sniper an enemy of the Alliance to be killed on sight, a proposal which spread bloodlust farther than any but myself had done in living memory. I want to tell you, reader, that the world was noble in restraint, like Spain and MASON. I want to tell you there were no more skirmishes, no toddler set-sets delivered bewildered to orphanage doorsteps. I want to tell you that when Voltaire Seldon next visited my office-cell his coat did not keep flickering with mourning static, that the photographs Martin failed to hide from me were fake, that these eyes never saw the rainbow-leaking limbs of a lynched dragon, nor its master's scarlet blood commixed. May I, please, master? May I gently lie?

No, Mycroft. Never. Not and still call this a chronicle.

Then pray, master, let me at least be brief. These days were darker, I think, than Martin let me know, if not yet dark enough for Achilles to call them war, as Hobbes does. I cannot tell all that happened. What I can deliver is a patchwork, more holes than cloth, of Dominic's maneuvers as the Mitsubishi walked the tightrope between strike and war.

Martin received the call first, one of hundreds I half tried not to listen to as he carried on his duties as *Minister Porphyrogenito,* and bearer of the *Imperium Vicarii.* "Am I correct, Acting Director," I heard him ask, "that this proposal actually comes from Acting Chief Director Seneschal?" Pause. "Tell them to call in person. Caesar does not deal with intermediaries." Another, patient pause, then, "Caesar also does not deal with lies. Tell Dominic to call directly." There was no malice in Martin's face as he ended the call, just mild efficiency, as when rain moves in to work its life-giving duty, parade or no.

The consequent conversation I received in transcript later:

Dominic: "Thank you for taking my call, *Votre Majesté Impérial.*"

MASON: "Don't waste my time."

Dominic: "I need your help to end the Mitsubishi strike."

MASON: "Your hold is too weak?"

Dominic: "The stakes are too high for me to win them over."

MASON: "Tell them they're destroying themselves. The people who are out of work or losing money because of the strike are spending their lost hours watching Tully Mardi's videos. Every minute this drags on brings another hundred people to the edge of riot, not anti-set-set riot, anti-Mitsubishi riot."

Dominic: "I know, *Majesté,* but every man has his sticking point, these Mitsubishi no less than yourself. They will not cave, not so long as there's any bill in motion anywhere, whether in Romanova, Odessa, or Easter Island, to force the Hive to give up land. But if you were to speak out and publicly oppose forced land redistribution, your word, and the votes it commands, would be enough."

MASON: "I support land redistribution."

Dominic: "I don't care."

MASON: "The landgrab is an economic bottleneck, not to mention poison for the Mitsubishi themselves. Land monopoly turns tenants into lynch mobs."

Dominic: "I said I don't care. The strike won't end unless you condemn forced redistribution. I didn't say you have to actually prevent it, just imply that you will."

MASON: "MASONS do not lie lightly."

Dominic: "Do this for me, and in return I promise to fight tooth and nail to get every Mitsubishi Senator to vote for Natekari's motion to kill Sniper on sight."

MASON: "That's no offer. You'll do that anyway. You want Sniper dead. Are you planning to rip their throat out with your teeth, or burn them alive?"

Dominic: "My plans are my own, *Majesté*, as yours are, and we both know that the only real difference between *Votre Majesté* and myself here is that I don't care whether or not it's legal when I do it. You want the law to kill Sniper. If you want that, you need my votes."

MASON: "It is legal for me to kill Sniper by the only law that matters: *Lex Masonica*."

Dominic: "Are you really going to pretend your law trumps Romanova?"

MASON: "My law predates Rome, let alone Romanova."

Dominic: "Do you really expect Romanova to accept that?"

MASON: "Romanova is a mere alliance. Either it respects the laws of its members, or it means nothing. Alliances come and go."

Dominic: "Fine, then. Every man has his sticking point, *Majesté*, and we all know yours. Speak out against land redistribution, or my Mitsubishi bloc will vote for Cook's new Black Law."

MASON: "What? That's insane. Mitsubishi use more set-sets than anyone."

Dominic: "True, but the bill will be vetoed by the Blacklaw Tribunes anyway. It won't become law, but you swore to fight it with your dying breath, and I'm prepared to make that fight Hell for you to get what I need. Do this favor for me and you have my twenty-seven votes; add your sixty-one, the Utopian eight, say twenty of the Humanist twenty-two, likely at least two Hiveless on your side, that's a hundred and eighteen votes right there, the bill's dead. Refuse and your side has ninety-one, while on Cook's side would be my votes plus the Cousins, Gordian, dissenting Humanists, probably the Whitelaw Hiveless, that makes eighty-four, which leaves you begging favors from waffling Europeans, plus you still risk the bill passing, then the veto, then Cook's push to overturn the veto, and while that drags on you know there will be riots, and Utopia will strike, just like they did in the days of *Son Majesté Impérial* Mycroft MASON. That's when it turns nasty."

MASON: "Cook's law is targeting you personally, *canis*, you as a Blacklaw and as Madame's creation."

Dominic will not object to being called a cur in any language. "Were I a free man, *Majesté*, I'd be in Hobbestown right now burning Cook in effigy, but I have a Hive to save. From itself. I'm sure you know the feeling."

MASON: "I am willing to publicly announce that I oppose any attempt to legislate the land question until after the Mitsubishi Hive submits its proposal for self-reform to the Senate a month from now. Is that enough to end the strike?"

Dominic: "That . . . yes . . . yes, that should be enough. I'll need to check with the other Acting Directors, but I believe . . . yes. We have a deal."

MASON: "Would you really be in Hobbestown burning Cook in effigy if you weren't busy doing this?"

Dominic: "*Votre Majesté Impérial* knows me too well. But I'm not going to give you a recording of me saying what I really want to be doing to Cookie, or to Sniper. And I'll give you some advice to pass on to Mycroft and Martin too. This isn't a threat, just a suggestion to lubricate our future interactions: if any of you catches the blasphemer before I do, call me and let me do the final deed. *Mon Maître est mon Maître.* It's my right and duty to avenge the blasphemy against *mon Maître*—no one else's right or duty—mine. Take that from me and you'll birth an . . . inconvenient . . . grudge."

Since I try to render everything in English, I have often struggled with the titles we closer servants use for He Who has so many. We His intimates are, as you must have observed, possessive servants, each craving to be somehow uniquely His. While any Mitsubishi may call Him Tai-kun or Xiao Hei Wang, any Spaniard *Alteza*, and any servant at Madame's *Jeune Maître*, Dominic alone may use *mon Maître*, Heloïse *mon Seigneur*, Martin *Dominus*, and I would feel bitter jealousy if any (save my Saladin) shared my Ἄναξ. Even MASON respects this strict division, and not from an objective distance, either, for I think he too would quake if he heard one of Jehovah's other fathers call Him *Filius*, or Him call another *pater*.

MASON: "More inconvenient for you, I think, than for me, *canis*."

Dominic: "True. That's why I sincerely hope you will take this advice, for my sake, and for yours. This is not a threat, *Majesté*. I do not imagine that I could destroy you, even if I had two Hives united behind me. I merely say this: if you crush me I will bite back, and you can't afford to be wounded right now. All I want is to kill a worm we both want dead. It is a small petition."

MASON: "I will consider it."

I do not know what answer MASON gave in the end. The Emperor did publicly condemn hasty land laws like Odessa's, and the Mitsubishi

strike did end. The Mitsubishi voted as Dominic promised. A bash's right
to raise its children as it wished triumphed one hundred thirty-two against
a bitter sixty-eight, casting Cook's resurrected Set-Set Law back into the
dust of history. As for Sniper—patriot, assassin, blasphemer, πολέμιος, self-
styled tyrannicide—Natekari's motion to declare Sniper an Enemy of the
Alliance passed, barely, a technical majority, ninety-eight to ninety-four,
with eight Utopian abstentions. A Whitelaw Tribune vetoed at once, and
before anyone could move to overturn the veto, that strangest Senator,
Olympic Champion Aesop Quarriman, very sensibly demanded that the
Court examine the legality of a bill which stripped a Hive of the right to
protect one of its own members. Now Sniper's sideways death sentence
lingers toothless in the Courts. Meanwhile, Dominic's hastily appointed
Acting Mitsubishi Senators can say with honesty: "I don't support O.S.
Look, I even voted to kill Sniper." Nicely played, Dominic. You make
Madame proud.

Inviolable

Written August 4–5, 2454
Events of May 1
Hobbestown

TO THE OFFICE OF GRAYLAW HIVELESS TRIBUNE J.E.D.D.
MASON, FROM THE OFFICE OF BLACKLAW HIVELESS TRIBUNE
CASTEL NATEKARI 4/17/2454: A community of concerned
Hiveless requests Tribune Mason's attendance at a Town Hall
Meeting to be held in Hobbestown City Hall at 4 PM UT on Friday
May 1st, 2454, at which Tribune Mason will be asked to answer for
their continued fitness for the office of Tribune.

ALL STRANGERS FEEL THE CHILL OF EXODUS AS HOBBESTOWN'S
silhouette looms up from the horizon, as when one emerges from the warm
and comfort of a theatre to face real air. Civilization's end. Here there is
no zoo glass between us and the lions. Hive badges still armor visitors, as
Roman citizens once marched through sprawling colonies armored by the
threat of distant law, but he who would visit Blacklaw lands consents to
witness murder in the street and place no blame. Here all things are possible, and all natives as honest as Saladin.

Hobbes: "Already! Oh, Jubilation! I had not dared hope to see so soon my
   backwards capital!"
Reader: "Backwards, friend Thomas?"
Hobbes: "Yes, backwards, Master Reader. My *Leviathan* aimed to describe and
   strengthen government, to remind ungrateful citizens why we so need
   it. Hobbestown is furthest from what I recommend of any place in history, and yet these Blacklaws call it by my name? I feel like I've spent

my life training young architects, but been thanked only by the ones who gave it up to become tent-dwelling nomads."

Reader (laughingly): "Ha! Well put, dear Thomas. Yet thanks is still thanks, and you know it is never bad to be remembered."

True, masters, true, and this Blacklaw capital fixes Hobbes's name in our age's memory like a burn scar. A sentry nodded to us at the gate, rising from a comfortable stool and lifting an eight-foot *guandao* pole-arm, whose moon-bright blade glittered atop the shaft she could no doubt wield as organically as Sniper its epée or Ancelet his numbers. Hobbestown uses no uniform apart from a Blacklaw sash, nor could one quite call this sentry part of a militia, since when she rose to escort us she called her replacement, not from any guardhouse, but from the passersby, one of whom volunteered to take her stool and drew a brace of pistols. Perhaps 'sentry' is the wrong word—honor guard? There is a warning bell beside the guard's stool, but it has never yet been used as anything but a reminder that, while ordinary cities blur into the bash'house-peppered countryside, Hobbestown's gates and walls still mean what gates meant when the Mycenaeans raised lintels of cyclopean stone. That my Master did not tremble as we crossed the threshold proves anew He is not human.

"The Six-Hive Transit System welcomes you to Hobbestown. This area is governed by no law but the Eight Universal Laws, commonly known as Black Hiveless Law. Minors and visitors protected by a stricter legal code are advised to keep their Hive or Law insignia clearly visible at all times. To view the list of suggested customs posted on the Hobbestown gate, select 'Blacklaw Customs, also called Natural Laws.'"

Hobbes: "Natural Laws? Are these my Natural Laws? Those nineteen rules found out by Reason, by which a man is forbidden to do that which is destructive to his own life?"

I: "Almost, Master Hobbes, almost. They are modeled on your list, but times and peoples change, and so too do the laws that Reason leads such peoples to."

Hobbes: "Changed? Balderdash! Such Laws are immutable and eternal. To forget any of them leads inevitably to war. It can never change that peace is endangered if one man tries to reserve to himself some Right which he will not share with everyone else, or if, in cases of revenge, men dwell on the greatness of the evil past, instead of thinking of the greatness of the good to follow, and so let private vendetta grow into public ruin.

Whether in my era, thine, or any, Mycroft, Peace and War and what creates them cannot change."

That I dispute not, Master Hobbes, and rest assured, the alterations to your laws are not so great as you fear. The fundamentals are unchanged, but our age cares less about primogeniture or Right of First Possession than your contemporaries did, and since our mores are more ubiquitous, we can cover more types of transgression with fewer words. Hobbestown's rules are carved, not posted, on her gates, and their honest roughness corroborates the rumor that her founding Rumormonger etched them with a pocket knife, not any artist's chisel. Romanova's eight Black Laws stand on the left gatepost, while on the right post stand Hobbestown's Eight Customs, also Called Natural Laws, enforced by nothing more than mob retribution, and crowned here by the Blacklaws' brave commandment:

STRANGER, GO TELL YOUR LAWMAKERS THAT, WITH THESE CUSTOMS, WE LAWLESS FEW LIVE WELL.

1. Here we endeavor sincerely to keep the peace, but when that fails, we defend ourselves with all the means at our disposal.
2. Here we remember that what we do to others, others can and will do to us.
3. Here we put reasonable effort into accommodating others, no more nor less.
4. Here, when we harm others, we either volunteer fair recompense, or accept vendetta; when we are harmed, we accept fair recompense, and do not let vendetta go too far.
5. Here we endeavor not to harm or monopolize communal things.
6. Here we do not act on rash rumor, but do heed well-weighed opinion.
7. Here we do not harm or hinder peacemakers, arbiters, ambassadors, or those working for the public good, nor do we undo their work without good cause.
8. Here those chosen to be arbiters try to be fair, and those who consent to have a disagreement settled by an arbiter accept the judgment, and let matters end.

Hobbes: "Fascinating. And tell me, Mycroft, how do my backwards children separate rumor from opinion?"
Reader: "*No more for now, friend Thomas, you have interrupted long enough; indeed were*

you less a friend I would say 'too much.' I am the reader here, not you, and it is at my
pleasure our chronicler serves."
Hobbes: "Deepest apologies, Master Reader. Such excitement can make even
    me forget the deference due to sovereignty. Forgive me?"
Reader: "Forgiven, my friend, forgotten. Now let Mycroft press on, and show both of us the
    famous Blacklaw capital."

"Straight forward, TM." Chagatai glowed with pride as she stepped
down from the car after our Master. Chagatai was still wearing her neat
housekeeper's uniform, formal enough for the grandest occasion. Over its
crisp darkness she wore a coat, heavy, sweeping, the kind of cut that reminds us how coats evolved from cloaks and robes of office, with the blue-
edged gray armband of a Tribune's Escort pale on her sleeve in slightly silver
silk. Her tasseled Blacklaw Hiveless sash—with our Master's Tribunary
crest in gray upon it—frisked about her right thigh, while at her left her
cutlass bounced, plump in its scabbard, a heavy blade which rarely gets to
play. If under this regalia Chagatai's frame was a little over-heavy, her belly
rounded out by cheerful dinners, the extra girth just made her so many
pounds of force more fearsome. "Do keep up, Mycroft," she chided.

Wert thou there too, Mycroft? Did not thy Emperor keep thee cloistered still in Alexandria?
At all other hours, yes, and his Son with me, but for this one journey it
was easy to secure Caesar's blessing. Hobbestown is, after all, the safest place
in the world. Are you surprised? Two Blacklaws might duel to the death by
daylight in her streets, but one who would break a law in Hobbestown, or
harm a visitor guarded by some foreign law, reaps punishment unmatched
in any court. A Blacklaw who did so would face real and lethal tortures
from his fierce Lawfellows, vengeance for angering the Leviathans, while a
Hive Member who dared break the peace in Hobbestown would face, first
the repercussions of his native law, and then the eternal hatred of posterity,
who would never forget the criminal who turned all culture to hypocrisy by
proving civilized man more barbaric than barbarians. Not even Tully would
dare.

"I'm coming," I answered, forcing my unsteady foot across the threshold. It was not fear that slowed me, reader, it was the sight of marvels. At
Hobbestown's gate, for caution's sake, all things reveal themselves: the many
robot guardians which crawl and hover undetectably about the *Porphyrogene*
uncloak, the Masonic guards who flank their Charge pull back their jackets baring hidden weapons, and the Delians materialize. All around me they
appeared: coats of cold stone, of faeries dancing in the autumn, of the swirling

deep, all with Apollo's sigil on their backs, grim enough to remind us that the Sun is merely our nearest taste of violent starfire. I had known for weeks that they were with us, invisible, these alien angels, but to see them step into existence all at once, each trailing the dreamworld they seemed to have sprung from . . . it was the kind of magic one can never stop believing in. No matter how grim this war becomes, even if our sins drive all Utopians into hiding, if I go weeks without seeing them, years, yet to our dying day we who saw them even once will still believe they might appear again, like wishes out of nothing, at our time of need. You must believe in them too, reader—your ancestors walked this Earth when they did, saw them, touched them, passed down whispers. Perhaps a thousand years have passed since any glimpsed them, but a thousand years cannot erase the hope that faeries might return if our belief and need are great enough, or lost King Arthur, or Utopia.

"Thank you for coming, Jagmohan." Tribune Natekari offered her Colleague a warm hand.

I know we must have walked the road from gate to Town Hall through Hobbestown's streets, yet I remember nothing but the nowhere coats flanking the Most Precious Visitor.

"I come gladly, Tribune Natekari," He answered. "You ask important questions."

Blacklaw Tribune Natekari smiled her sharp smile, sharpened by the scar she will not let science remove from her left cheek. "You seem better today. Your English is better." It was the warm observation of a familiar colleague.

"True," He answered, "though I remain grateful that you allow Me My choice of inquisitor and translator."

On 'inquisitor' He looked to smiling Chagatai, who was distracted now, distributing flirtatious glances among passersby. On 'translator' He looked to me. I suspect my bow looked more like a flinch as the Blacklaw Tribune's eyes fell on me. Do you expect kinship in her glance? Do you associate, as many do, my savagery with her wild kind? No. Her eye holds the same horror any sane person feels toward Mycroft Canner. She does not know me, nor my Saladin, nor how we hold her kind almost divine, as wise Greeks held happy Diogenes, and all the Cynics strong enough to break free from the puppet strings and live. She only knows that I made the world more bitter, more afraid of killers, more afraid of her. I made her world worse. But Chagatai knows me, Chagatai behind whom I hide, her homecoming swagger shelter enough to make me brave as she and Natekari trade greeting kisses on both cheeks. The pair have crossed swords, I suspect, or had sex. Or both. It can be difficult to tell the difference.

Chagatai knew the Town Hall's steps as perfectly as she knew the chapel-house she had kept for Jehovah in Avignon. That house was gone now, not burnt down like Madame's, but too vulnerable to remain His home, so Ἄναξ Jehovah donated the property to a university, to safeguard its collections, moving Himself to Alexandria's *Sanctum Sanctorum*.

Chagatai shooed our Master and myself like children through the Great Hall door as shimmering Delians spread to cover the exits with their sprites, and will-o'-wisps, and training. It felt like Olympus inside, reader, a hall of gods arrayed on creaking theatre seats which seemed to me like thrones. I do not mean universal Gods like Jehovah and His Peer, nor immortal gods like Zeus. I mean what you, Master Hobbes, named with reverence a 'mortal god,' that earthly power, charged to keep peace and defend its own, which answers to nothing between itself and the Immortal God above. States. Sovereigns. It is not possible to call them all Leviathans, tiny as they are, but each Blacklaw is as much a Sovereign as MASON. Oh, there was a balcony in the back of the hall for Hive Members, and some Whitelaws and Graylaws mixed in the back, but they were people, while the front rows seemed to my eye a ring of Emperors.

Thou canst not see it, Mycroft, but our Thomas here is smiling.

"Thank you for coming, all." In lieu of a gavel, Castel Natekari thumped her podium with the heavy, enameled pen which has passed from Rumormonger to Rumormonger through Hobbestown's colorful decades. It was in her office as Tribune that she summoned her colleague here this day, but her seat as hostess derives from her older office as the living encyclopedia of this black city and its (I cannot say citizens) inhabitants. Custom requires asking the Rumormonger's opinion before a Hobbestonian embarks on any feud, and her advice keeps many a youth from acting rashly on a rival's poison lies. Custom requires updating the Rumormonger on all gossip, and her patient perspicacity has recognized many a hidden mastermind when one name was involved by 'chance' in too many 'accidents.' Temperance she is, Prudence, Justice, and Force as well, ready to call her people to arms when a rotten branch needs pruning. I have shown you lynch mobs, reader, or their bloody wakes at least. How many fewer—set-set and Servicer alike—might have died in Odessa if the Hives had shared the Blacklaw custom that one may not lynch anyone without first asking the best-informed person in town whether we're being idiots?

"At Tribune Mason's request, Blacklaw Euphrates Chagatai will conduct today's interview, since I understand the Tribune is still recovering their full faculties of speech, and Chagatai has experience handling that."

Chagatai shed her sweeping outer coat and took the podium with a swish of her nearly-as-sweeping inner one. "Thank you, Tribune Natekari. I have a list of submitted questions, but I'd like to ask my own first. Any objections?" She scratched her silvered stubble as she waited for consenting nods. "Good. First off, TM, do you believe you can still adequately fulfill your Tribunary duty to represent the needs of the Hiveless against the Hives when you're so caught up in upper-level Hive affairs?"

How like a trial it would have seemed, the spectators' eyes locked hungrily on the defendant, had He been one who trembled. "Is that the most important question?" He asked.

"No, but it's what brought us to this room." Nods supported Chagatai.

"Clarify 'represent,'" He requested.

"Clarify 'clarify,'" Chagatai reposted.

"Represent as agent or represent as symbol? *Vous* . . . you-*tachi* chose Me Tribune largely *ut* as symbol, to remind Earth that One Who enjoys such trust and honor from the Emperor, Chief Director, and other powers is nonetheless still a Graylaw. I have served as your Proof that Hiveless matter to the Hives. If it is as symbol that I represent the Hiveless, I am fit for office while I am still perceived thus, yet unfit should I come to be perceived otherwise. Since I do not know how I am perceived, I cannot answer more completely. Is that clear?"

"Yes, very." Chagatai's smile made the wrinkles at the corners of her Mongol eyes turn kind. "And if the question is whether you can represent us as our agent?"

"The age's volatility precludes an answer. Tomorrow I may be stripped of all My other offices and left at liberty, or I may be crowned the ad hoc King of Spain, or I may have ceased to live."

What can one call that muted murmur when hubbub flies soundless over trackers, or typed on pocket screens by those supreme Blacklaws who choose to face life trackless like our feral ancestors?

"Questions from the list now. Let's see. A lot of these are about how busy you are, or are about to be. Will you be attending the court sessions when they examine the legality of condemning Sniper in absentia?"

"Probably."

"Will you attend Ockham Prospero Saneer's *terra ignota*?"

"I do not yet know."

"How busy will those keep you if you are involved? Enough to inter-fere with your duties as Tribune?"

"I do not yet know."

"How about the Olympic Committee? Is it taking up your time as the Games get closer?"

I had forgotten that He held this office too, the Humanists' best at-tempt to make Him partly theirs. "Some time is taken by it."

"Out of curiosity, do you know what they're planning to do about Sniper in the upcoming Games? They were supposed to compete."

"I know not yet."

Chagatai frowned at her list. "Do you still consider yourself Hiveless?"

"Hiveless I am."

"But do you intend to remain Hiveless? Is it important to you?" Cha-gatai did not add, 'as it is to us,' but her sash did, rustling at her thigh.

"Hiveless I remain."

"Why?" The housekeeper did not hesitate to press her Master hard. "You are twenty-one already. A lot of people are wondering why you haven't chosen a Hive yet. If you're remaining Hiveless because it means something to you, then most of us would agree you can represent us and the Hiveless life, but it's very different if you've put it off because your mother is forcing you, or the Hive leaders are pressuring you, or you're just too busy to take your Adulthood Competency Exam. We need to know the reason."

I must confess, reader, that most of the preceding paragraph is my in-vention. I have a recording of this interview but cannot even read this section without slipping into memory's blind daze. You're nearly seventeen, Mycroft, and brilliant. You could've passed the Adulthood Competency Exam years ago. Which will it be? Friends ask . . . teachers ask . . . Will you become a Mason? A Brillist? Kids ask . . . foster-ba'pas ask . . . Our feelings won't be hurt if you don't pick Cousin. Sensayer asks . . . MASON asks . . . Hive-less? Utopian? The Mardis, even those who don't ask ask: patient Aeneas, Ibis with her saccharine love-gaze, deep-seeing Mercer . . . You killed me with that question. All of you, you did. Seventeen years old. I had to be a blank thing when I did it, my beautiful rampage, the act of evil of a human being, not a Hiveless, not a Hive. I had no answer, no good reason to postpone the exam we all knew I could have passed. I wanted to live longer, enjoy our era's opulence, go to a Campus, study broadly arts and sciences, touch the Moon again, continue to discover Saladin's body as we both ceased to be boys. But you, with your curiosity deepening to suspicion, you wouldn't let me wait. I was already seventeen. I had to act, before someone who asked why I was still waiting recognized my lie.

"I know you always have a reason for what you do, TM," Chagatai pressed, eyes gentle. "Why have you put the exam off so long?"

The Great Scroll's Addressee forms all His words with care, as if the rest of us think ourselves typists, armed with delete keys, while He alone remembers that we carve our speech in the unhealing stone called Time. "The Adulthood Competency Exam," He repeated.

"Yes." Chagatai glanced at the minor's sash still around our Master's waist. "A lot of people have suggested that, if you took the exam and then officially chose to remain Hiveless, it would be a powerful declaration that you don't favor any Hive. That would reassure the Hiveless, and show the world that you don't intend to take over all the Hives, as Sniper alleges. It could ease the crisis greatly. Are you willing?"

"Ich werde die Prüfung . . ."

Chagatai cleared her throat to warn Him that His language had lapsed.

"I will not complete the Adulthood Competency Exam," He finished.

A frown touched Chagatai's cheeks. "Alright. That's your choice. But, Sniper is wrong, right?"

"Οὖτις . . ."

"No one," I translated, seeing Chagatai flounder.

". . . has perfect knowledge," He finished.

Many nodded support; these Blacklaw madmen are philosophers enough to still care about grand questions in the midst of petty ones. I might have heard, "Hear, hear!"

"I mean about you and the Hives," Chagatai specified. "This is another question from the list: Do you intend to take over all the Hives and merge them like Sniper says, or don't you?"

How many interviewers, intimates, even His many parents had not dared ask?

"I neither desire nor plan it, but it may occur. I do not know the future."

"Then you think it's possible? It might happen?"

"I have never sought an office, but through Another's plans I have received more offices than some ambitious people secure with a lifetime's effort. More may follow."

Chagatai nodded. "So, to clarify, you don't want to rule or merge the Hives, but you believe you may wind up doing so anyway?"

Cameras buzzed as close about Him as their operators dared. "Yes."

"All the Hives?"

"I don't know."

"Are there any in particular—excluding the Masons, of course"—
Chagatai glanced at His guards—"since we can't talk about the *Imperator
Destinatus,* though I do think we're allowed to point out the precedent
that no *porphyrogene* has ever been named Emperor—but are there any other
Hives in particular that you think you might likely wind up leading?"

He froze, the long, slow grind of many factors invisible beneath His
surface, like the workings of a lifeless-seeming mine. "All are possible."

Again murmur.

Chagatai smiled gently at our Master's endearing if inhuman honesty.
"I received this question repeatedly in a lot of different forms," she pressed,
"so I want to be absolutely and distinctly clear. You understand, TM, that
a lot of people are upset at the prospect of one person becoming head of all
the Hives, yes? People think it would mean the effective end of the freedom to choose our law."

Chairs creaked as many leaned forward.

"This I understand," the Guest confirmed.

"If you can establish that there's even one, *even one,* Hive that you think
you're definitely not going to take power in, then all the furor would end."

"Untrue'*st. Mitsubishi no* land majority *inita-que populi majoritas Masonica*—"

"Slow down, TM," Chagatai interrupted gently. "Give Mycroft time to
translate."

Even I took a moment to parse the Japanese possessive nestled between
English and Latin. "The Mitsubishi land majority and the Masonic near-
majority population."

"*Ja,* these," the Guest confirmed. "These would still be, exist, as would
O.S's crimes, and human grief, and guilt."

Chagatai smiled. "I meant that the danger to you would be over. No
one would want to kill you over that."

"All material beings are in danger in a war."

Chagatai frowned. "I know you'd never intentionally evade a question,
TM. Help us understand why it's so hard for you to answer this one."

"I struggle to understand the reason for this question. All things are
possible. Why must I specify *que* a specific thing is possible when all things
are?"

"I see." She too paused, searching for the right words. "I think what
this question really wants you to do is to differentiate between remote possibility and a realistic probability. For example, at this moment there is a
remote possibility that a giraffe might suddenly wander into this room, but

there is not a realistic probability of such an occurrence. So similarly there is a remote possibility that you or anyone might suddenly end up in charge of the whole world, but what we want to know is: is there, in your opinion, a realistic probability of you taking power in—and we're still not talking about the Masons—any other Hives?"

Long, so long, His silence. "Yes, such a probability is real. Should I endeavor not to?"

"Should you endeavor not to take over all the Hives?" Chagatai released a long, low whistle. "Many people would say yes. Certainly it would be safer for you." A darker silence, now. "I have to ask, TM, do you think, as Sniper does, that your death would end this crisis?"

"It did not the first time."

Silence.

"As this is not a sensayer session," Chagatai began in that loud, forced tone one uses more for cameras than for friends, "but a very public gathering, we will not discuss that issue at present. Tribune Mason, you did not attend the Senate debate over Tribune Natekari's motion to declare Sniper an enemy of all civilization to be killed on sight. Some of those in this room may very well personally carry out said execution if it's approved. We'd all like to hear confirmation of your personal support for the execution of the enemy who, by attacking a Romanovan Tribune, violated the one thing which every human being in our civilization has agreed to hold inviolate."

Not only Chagatai but many in the room tapped eager hilts, or grips, or quivers.

"I expect," Jehovah began, "that this crisis will not end until either Sniper's death or Mine, and also that, if Sniper is victor, then Earth will continue to depend on that . . . cowardly and addictive evil named O.S. Therefore it seems I must seek Sniper's death. Yet I believe, in all deeds, knowledge should be as complete as possible, especially in homicide, for death is irreparable. The torture of regretting having killed is *atrocissima* . . . too cruel. Therefore I will not have any kill for Me who does not know as much Truth as it is in My power to share, nor will I have Sniper die, though Sniper is My enemy, without the dignity of understanding. I therefore command all whom I have the power to command, and request of those I do not, that no one slay Sniper until the history I am currently having prepared is done. It seeks to explain the events which led to O.S.'s exposure and Sniper's act. When you have read it, then, those who still wish to may, if My consent conjoins with that of Romanova's law, help Me remove O.S."

Chagatai smiled, a proud, parental smile, not out of place on she who, despite Jehovah's many fathers, is the one to welcome Him home after long, strange nights.

"Ask Me whether Sniper killed Me," the Visitor commanded.

A frown now. "No, TM, not if you're going to talk about resurrection."

"If you ask Me, I must answer *sic et non.*"

"What?"

"Yes and no. Here virtue ethics opposes deontology."

Chagatai sighed. "You're talking about deed versus intent?"

"The Sniper who now lives bears the skill that killed Me, and the intent to have killed Me, but not the finger that sped the bullet home. Bridger was real."

Not only Chagatai, but all within the room froze speechless.

Even Jehovah, though Jehovah is never truly *within* rooms.

It was not His words that stunned us. His black eyes, like everybody's, shifted their focus suddenly far from this room, far from this city, to the news which rose in His lenses. "*Sanctum . . . conrupt'est?*"

I saw it too, in my news feed. I saw a world away, far out of reach, the first too-tiny plumes of smoke against the spotless marble.

"*Ecce,* Mycroft," this foreign God called softly to me. "All material things are mortal after all."

I zoomed in on the feed. A dark wound, that's what others have said they saw, a tight incision sliced into the side of Alexandria's great lighthouse tower, which bled irregular bursts of black smoke, clumpy like bubbles leaking from a sinking ship. I did not see a dribble, but a deluge, filth-black blood pouring from the wounded lighthouse, an endless torrent of living— no—un-living, moving black, as if this injury at last revealed the great reservoir from which are born all the specter trails and war-cancers that Tully Mardi leaks.

"Stay still and calm, all." Rumormonger Natekari does not have to raise her voice. "Something is happening at the *Sanctum Sanctorum* in Alexandria."

Obedient in their wisdom, the Blacklaws kept their seats, and all tuned in to witness the abomination. The Masons did not. They rushed to Him. They had planned for this, studied every millimeter of the room, of every room the *Porphyrogene* enters. Half manned the exit, while the others plunged in a spearhead movement down the center aisle to retrieve Him from the podium to their safe custody. The Blacklaws rose to block them, not all in one force, just a few, a stand of wardens, individual but terrible, like breakers in a storm.

"You dishonor us, Masons," Natekari's tone was as black as her sash, "to think we cannot protect a guest in our own house."

"It is our task to move the *Porphyrogene* to safety during crisis."

Lightning her glare. "You have already failed to protect your own *Sanctum Sanctorum*. This sanctum"—she gestured to the hall's aged wood—"remains inviolate." The Blacklaw Tribune shot a glance of warning at Jehovah's Utopian escort too, but the Delians stayed well clear, hololemurs and floating faerie lights watching in silence as the Masons faced the noble savages.

The Masonic guards halted, though not, I think, for fear of Blacklaw weapons. These Guards of the *Porphyrogene* were all at least three generations in the Emperor's service. They had not paused nor shuddered when Perry-Kraye and Ganymede fell through the window at Madame's, nor even when Sniper's bullet spattered their Ward's brains across His iron father—guards know their duties to a ward dead as much as a ward living—but they had shuddered when duty's script broke down as Bridger's potion gave Jehovah life again, and so they shuddered now as a new transmission leaked from violated Alexandria. Two videos. Cameras from the shore still showed the lighthouse from the outside, where a second black wound had appeared, at the top, a fresh explosion cutting through the gold-leaf surface of the tower's crowning ziggurat. The second image came from inside the ziggurat. We saw smoky air first, the doll-like figures of unconscious guards, Martin's singed desk and mine beside it, lunch detritus smoldering, my mattress. A jiggle now as the camera is borne out of my cell and up the stairs, a guard's room, then our Good Guest's simple bedroom, deep in the tower, safer even than the Emperor's palace below. A pause, another jiggle, up again, guards' rooms, a spiral staircase, up, and up, and now we see the *Sanctum* vaults themselves in their grand circumference, sliced open by the violators like a marble honeycomb. Chips and cards and papers dribble from the damaged chambers: sensayers' secrets, Censors' secrets, Gag-genes' secrets, the identities of past Anonymouses, truths men have killed for tumbling to the floor like dirty hail. The intruders care not. Their target is already open when we see it, the central vault, a block formed of an impenetrable glassy-black substance dreamed up by who knows what genius to guard the Empire's archsecret. Hands, gloved and trembling, push aside the fragments of the shattered block and hold the tablet to the camera. I guessed even then the almost noble hope which drove these criminals. It might not have been Him. Imagine, reader, if it had named Martin, or better, someone further from Him, some young *Familiaris* from a distant trusted bash'. We could have had no war.

IMPERATOR DESTINATUS IEHOVAH EPICURUS DONATIANUS DE
AROUET MASON ESTO. SI RECUSEAT, DUM PERSUADEATUR,
MYCROFTI CONFRATRIDOMITORI AGNOMINATO MARTINO
VICARIO IMPERIUM MASONICUM COMMENDEM.
—CORNEL MASON.

NOTE: I can't blame Mycroft for refusing to translate this, since it's still technically against the First Law even to read it, but since the whole world knows by now I may as well: "Let the Destined Emperor be Jehovah Epicurus Donatien D'Arouet MASON. Should they refuse, while they are being persuaded, I leave the MASONIC IMPERIUM to Mycroft Guildbreaker, nicknamed Martin, as regent.—Cornel Mason."—9A

No one said anything. No one said anything for a long time.

"I was there." It had to be He Who Visits Who broke this silence—no child of Earth's civilization could have. "I have been in that place, many days. They waited for this time, when I was not."

"Ἄναξ?" I used the Greek in public now that there was no need to hide what we were to each other. "Where's Martin?"

"Elsewhere," He answered. "Safe." Here was a small mercy, a drop of rain to give our desert life.

Some moments more we watched, the outside view of the tower showing emergency forces swarming the soot-stained entrance. Now the inner view cut out altogether, and something bullet-slim and blue shot from the tower's larger wound and flight-fell to the water. Only as its splash-foam thinned did I realize that what had seemed tiny at this scale must have been nearly room-sized, large enough to bear the violators to their well-planned but ill-deserved escape. A submarine?

"TM." Chagatai still managed to sound warm. "Everyone who's anyone is calling me to ask why you aren't answering your tracker. Shall I tell them to shove off?"

"Say I am safe."

"Your mom wants you. Ancelet. Heloïse. Dominic. Every newspaper ever."

"Say I am safe."

"Righto."

"How about Cornel? Has Cornel called for Donatien yet?" The stray voice interrupting from the Members' balcony was Felix Faust's. Did you think the age's sage and grand voyeur would pass up such an exquisite feast as the gestures and twitches of this Blacklaw company as they asked 'important questions' of his Nephew? "If Cornel hasn't called, you should worry."

"Why?" In any other meeting it would have been someone in charge, Natekari perhaps, who answered Brill's Headmaster, but in this company of sovereigns it was instead someone I did not know, a grave face in the second row, wise, to-the-mark, and, save for her sash and backpack, naked (as is a Blacklaw's right).

Faust liked the interruption. "It is my not-inexpert opinion that my Nephew is the only living being capable of calming Cornel MASON down enough to stop them declaring war on the whole world instantly over this theft."

"Theft? You mean exposure."

"I mean theft."

A pause. "You think they also robbed the vaults?"

The Headmaster nodded. "I think few creatures on this Earth could crack the *Sanctum Sanctorum* and not succumb to curiosity."

I felt the blood drain from my face. "The Oath of Office. The MASONIC Oath of Office is in the same block in the vault! No one but an Emperor has seen the Oath since thousands of ages of however-long-you-think-the-Empire-is-old ago!"

Faust applauded the wounds my fear inflicted upon grammar.

"Caesar angry." I slumped onto the nearest something. I often feel in my mind the vice of Caesar's black-sleeved hand upon my throat, but now I seemed to see it on everyone else's.

Still soft, Jehovah's words. "This demonstrates that My many offices do indeed conflict with My Tribunary duty." I was not quite sure to whom He addressed this. Possibly Himself. "My apologies, colleague Natekari. I believe My uncle is correct. I should go *ad patrem*."

She nodded. "Okay, people, get Jagmohan to somewhere safe and private. Now."

The prospect of a task woke the attendant Masons from shock's stupor. "We wi—"

"No, let them act now." Jehovah's pointing finger chose a Delian, shrouded in a cityscape of brass and moths' wings. "Masons should follow us, and mourn." To His colleague. "Acceptable?"

Natekari smiled at His perfect courtesy. "Go, and good luck."

A flash sea of flare-bright floating spirits stunned the crowd as Utopia snatched the Visitor to the safety of away. They snatched me, too, hands which, even without Griffincloth, were invisible through the tear blur which

turned the newsfeed in my lenses to prismatic glitter. They slung me over
something dark and furred and warm that vibrated with life or electricity.
Griffincloth fell across me, a coat shared by a Delian, whose tender darkness me kept me still, like a horse's blinders, as we rushed down paths of
patchy brightness and loud footsteps.

They set me down in Camelot. Or something very like it, a semicircu-
lar courtyard of stone, ancient in style but new and clean, hung with pen-
nants of azure, gold, and scarlet. In the distance to one side I saw the
thatched-roof denseness of a city, rich in market stalls and horses. On the
other side, a road led out of the still-closing castle gates, lined with other
edifices. What did I glimpse along that street? First a waterfall of mirrored
mercury, then a palace of ancient Egypt, cliffs of amber, a misty graveyard,
Mars—a city block of worlds pressed side by side as books stand side by
side on shelves. But the gates sealed quickly, and once the cockatrice finished its scan, they let me climb down. My steed turned out to be a black
lion, which sat down behind me so I could slump against its soft side rather
than falling upon the stone. Or rather, upon the Griffincloth, for there was
no stone here, nor mercury, nor thatch, nor amber, not really. It felt like a
kind dream, and it was kindness, kind Delians and kind Fate, which let me
enter Hobbestown's Utopian district. It is one of the largest Utopian dis-
tricts on Earth, block on block of Griffincloth edifices crowding their oth-
erworlds tight side by side, for Utopia—the tiniest Leviathan, a dolphin
half forgotten by the great whales—is happy to show its trust by schooling with the even smaller race of Blacklaws.

I spotted my Master easily, a patch of black cloth starker than our medieval setting should have had. Chagatai too stood out, incongruous, but
the Delians around them were all knights in armor now, or rather some
were, while others became long-robed sorcerers, a Viking youth, an elf king,
a flame-bright autumnal dryad, whatever persona each had programmed
their coat to generate when they stepped into this genre.

"Shall I call Alexandria for you?" one offered.

The Visitor was not looking at anyone. "Do I make the human race
worse?" He asked. "I make you violate the inviolable, a Tribune's person,
the MASONS' *Sanctum*, Hobbestown; I even make mankind a Deicide."

"TM," Chagatai coaxed, "MASON's ready to take your call, if you're
ready."

One last pause. "Ready."

The Griffincloth castle became at once a different castle, MASON's,
Alexandria, the ceiling of lapis and gold and candle-stars, the floor of chan-

neled marble. The Emperor was on his throne this time, blood-purple porphyry framing his square-cut Mason's suit. A new suit, reader. It was black, all black, death black, save only for the right sleeve whose gray cloth promised some faint possibility of mercy. I curled against the lion's inky mane and wept.

"I want you tracking their escape," Caesar began. "Every sea monster, and dendan, and hippocampus, and seahound, and panoctopus, and plasma-ray, and kraken . . ."

"You have them," Utopia pledged.

"You should not declare war today, *pater.*" Jehovah managed English.

MASON shook his head. "*Fili,* these laws are older than the word 'law.' The wheels are moving. The Empire defends itself. My enemies, all my enemies, all who in their selfish, fleeting factions sharpened the blade which has wounded my IMPERIUM, all will be destroyed. If Romanova tries to stop me, Romanova is a young and toothless power, and will hardly be a bump in my path."

"Not today. The day after tomorrow."

MASON squinted at his Son. "Why wait two days?"

"Because war will disrupt travel and keep all Powers occupied, including *Su Majestad el Rey de España,* so, in a thousand years, it will still be said that Cornel MASON declared war the day before his lover would have gone to Rome to seek permission to marry another and exclude him. I would not have that personal side effect make posterity forever doubt the justness of your choice."

Long and black the Emperor's silence, marred only by my sobs.

"There is precedent," MASON pronounced at last, "for granting enemies the option of surrender. I give them three days. If those who breeched my *Sanctum* all surrender to me, and return unread the Oath they stole"— here the Delians winced at confirmation of the deeper blow which fired MASON's rage—"then their executions will be . . . unprotracted." He locked his gaze on Jehovah, doing the best a human can to hold His eyes. "This same mercy I offer to Sniper, Tully Mardi, and to those who shelter them. Three days."

"This is wise patience, *pater.*" Jehovah's voice felt like hope, not that His tone changed, but even His lifeless voice felt light beside the Emperor's. "Three days may buy many."

Three days may, in fact, buy one hundred and twenty-eight.

The Temple of Janus

Written August 8–9, 2454
Events of May 2
Hobbestown, Burgos, Rome, Romanova

"I AM GLAD WE GO TO THE VATICAN TODAY, MYCROFT. NEVER before have I desired so acutely to speak with My Peer, nor about so specific an aspect of His Plan."

These were the only Words spoken by He Who Visits in our flight the next morning from Hobbestown to the convent, where we were to join His mother, thence to fly together to the reservation. I had not slept that night, for, when my eyes closed, I could see nothing but black-clad MASON on his bloody throne, and when they opened, the cornucopia of Utopia's wonders proved irresistible. Braced by an anti-sleeping dose, I wandered that night through Eldorado, through asteroid mines, through a giant's house, through Thebes, through a dusky Venice whose seas were inky purple and whose sky was sliced by vast Saturn-like rings, and through strange trees whose hollows merged into a black hallway where only shadows stirred. I was not alone. All night the Delian's black lion padded, soft and solid, at my side. The great beast's somber gaze reassured all bystanders that the cannibal did not range their lands unchecked. The lion condescended too to catch me with its furred and muscled softness, whenever the beauties made me faint. Most beautiful were the superhuman denizens these halls made of their populace, the nymphs and ancients, wraiths and aliens, that watched me with inhuman vizored eyes. The nowheres changed unpredictably, a shopping district on a plum-red moon transforming into eighteenth-century Kyōto as the computer's timer switched the Griffincloth from following one Utopian's program to another. Blacklaws stirred here too, human monsters mixing comfortably with folklore monsters in a collegial, commercial chaos under the real night sky. A child gave me an orange in return for a recaptured ball, to the quiet approval of its accompanying ba'pas, one Blacklaw and one flame-clad Utopian. Fate even gifted me a glimpse of one of the great prides of our age: the Lóngsphinx, a body which fuses feline with undulating Asian dragon lined by luminous translucent wings, which holds within an A.I. so advanced that, like those chimps and dolphins that we rear among us, this U-beast wears a minor's sash as proof that Romanova recognizes in it a sentience as precious as a human child. We made life, reader; we made a thinking thing. All this Utopia let me enjoy, as if they sensed that I would need a special kind of strength to face tomorrow. For hours at a time, I did not think of Bridger.

"I must have My sensayer."

That was the first weight upon me as we flew toward Spain. Though younger, less church-scarred Hives are not so strict, a European Member who would visit a reservation to discuss theology must bring their sensayer as chaperone, and, though Ἄναξ Jehovah remains a Minor, when in Rome He does as His Spanish father does. When we reached Las Huelgas, the whole nunnery was aflutter with preparation for the expedition, for Madame must have her ladies, and her ladies must have their escorts, and all must have their sensayers, so the visit multiplied like ivy from what had seemed a single chute. The young Master required no such complex entourage, but He did require His sensayer, and thus sent me to fetch him.

Good reader, how much I would have given to not step into that room. How much I would give to not remember now. But when such a Lord hands down commands, a man submits, even if it costs him scars. I did step into that room in Las Huelgas, and I saw there Carlyle Foster-Kraye de La Trémoïlle.

When we were ready to go, Dominic followed me out into the hall and—

When thou wert ready? Thou canst not leave it there, Mycroft. What happened? What didst thou see? How fares our Carlyle?

Oh, reader, do not ask, I pray you. It has not been easy shielding you thus far from Carlyle's state. Better that you remember the first Carlyle you saw, arising daily full of strength, a welcome friend in Bridger's wild garden, smiling.

I do not like to repeat myself, Mycroft. At my command thou servest. What didst thou see?

As you command, reader. To your judgment, however little I may understand it, I subject my flawed and failing own.

It was Dominic's cell, his books and stark necessities transplanted from Madame's so faithfully that the order of the papers, the icon of Jehovah on

the wall, even the smell seemed just the same. The bed was his same stiff
wood-framed palette with the thumb-thin mattress still upon it, and upon
that mattress lay Carlyle Foster-Kraye, tied down with wrists and ankles
lashed fast to the bed frame. Carlyle's Cousin's wrap and long sensayer's scarf
were nowhere, but a habit lay discarded on the floor beside the bed, Dominican black and white. Sweat made Carlyle's bare chest sticky, while dried
spit crusted the gag that stifled what I doubt were even words. Tear-crusted
eyes twitched with the inhuman wildness of one transported beyond the
here and now, while Dominic, as fired with zeal as I had ever seen him, sat
on a stool at the far corner of the room, reading aloud from the *Pensées* of
Blaise Pascal:

"The greatness of a man is that he can know he is wretched. A tree does
not know it is wretched. True wretchedness is knowing that one is wretched,
but it is greatness too knowing that one is wretched. This wretchedness
itself proves human greatness, for it is the wretchedness of a great lord, or
a deposed king . . ."

I vomited, there on the threshold. Beautiful and terrible Pascal, the
darkest author I have ever read, darker than Calvin, Kafka, the black friar
Savonarola, darker even than you, Master Thomas, for all your warring brutes.
You never tried to intentionally make your reader wretched, nor pried his
eyelids back and forced him to gaze into the Great Dark. Some acts are
too cruel, reader, even for philosophers. If William of Ockham's art we dub
a razor, and if Nietzsche subtitled his *Twilight of the Idols* "How to Philosophize
with a Hammer," then Pascal's is surely a flaying knife, petal-thin and cruel,
that peels the victim's skin back inch by inch, leaving no shield between the
tender soul and the infinite dark mirror. And he does more, Pascal, he bares
our race's flaws as well, civilization's cowardly underbelly. Pascal's French
is unsurpassed in elegance, his logic flawless, his message likely true, and
his goal nothing less than the perfection and salvation of his reader, but—
remember who it is that says this, reader—he is too cruel. Yes, I have read
him. I learned from him that all the activities of my life, all my duty, my
penitence, my love, all these are mere diversions to distract me from thinking about the only certainty: someday I will die. We all will. All human
achievement, our empires, good deeds, art, the Great Project itself, all are
distractions, invented by a race so weak we cannot sit still in a chair for five
minutes and face our finitude. What is Caesar but a man so rich in power
that he can afford to be distracted every instant of every day? A king in
office is fortunate in his distraction, but a deposed king has nothing to
distract him from the lesson that even kingship is one more game invented

by a race that will never grow out of fearing the dark. Yes, when I read Pascal, I fled. I admit it. I am a coward, and I do indeed use duty to hide from my fear, my guilt, my wretched human state. And now, before my eyes, our fragile, straining Carlyle, a prisoner with no means of escape, endures the lashing of philosophy's cruelest words . . . surely, reader, no philosopher in history has ever had a truer apprentice than had the Marquis de Sade in Dominic Seneschal.

Dominic inhaled the salt perfume of sweat and acid, my vomit the first to christen his new cell.

"See, Sister Carlyle? Our Mycroft, like thee, has been blessed with plenty of that 'greatness' named wretchedness, offered to the human beast by its unkind Creator."

The title 'Sister' warmed me, made me think of the bright young Cousin when I first met her, lively in her trailing wrap. Madame keeps trying to force us to use male pronouns for Carlyle, to remind everyone that the Carlyle Foster-Kraye she has ensnared here is indeed the Prince-héréditaire de La Trémoïlle, a future duke. But this broken offspring of broken politics is also still the kind Carlyle I met and wished I could call friend. Even Dominic is not so heartless as to call this diamond a spade. Let some unfeeling censor change our words, if when this chronicle is finally released Madame still has power enough to censor. We who truly care about Carlyle—even if it is Dominic's dark caring—shall respect her choices and say 'she.'

Dominic placed his finger between the pages of Pascal to keep his place, a motion no more reassuring than if he had taken a red-hot poker off my flesh to reheat it in the fire. « Well? » he invited. « What news? »

I gazed down at my vomit on the floor. It was a small splash, just a trace of citrus and goo, which worked its viscous way toward the brushlike soles of my Ahimsa shoes. These shoes, with their many bristles, used to be soft enough to let me step on an insect without harming it, but they were so worn down now that I suspected the nubs would prove deadly to passing ants. I need new shoes. Just as well. In war I will need better traction, and it was hard to think of ants when even Utopians were casualties. Besides, we now know that, even if ants are Gods, then, like Jehovah, Their deaths would not destroy Their universes, merely their Earthly form. See, reader, how even now my mind dodges and ducks away from thinking of that cell? And dread Pascal?

« Spit it out, *errant,* » Dominic commanded, addressing me by my domestic title as 'stray dog.' « What news from *notre Maître?* »

I couldn't look at Carlyle. I feared a mirror, feared seeing in Carlyle those same tormented eyes that I had had when I first saw Madame's, and learned that it might have been for nothing that I slew Apollo. The sensayer's vocation had been Carlyle's Apollo, a thing so noble that its very presence on this Earth proves Earth worth saving. Carlyle had sacrificed it, prostituted it, for Julia first, luring in powerful parishioners, pretending she believed it was for their good. Carlyle prostituted it again for Thisbe, and for me, concealing Bridger while pretending to her other parishioners that she did not hold in her hands the Proof that all hearts crave. She lied to them, to her parishioners. And then, when Dominic had tortured from her her confession of Deist hypocrisy, no sooner had Carlyle purged her conscience through that contrition, but she had prostituted her priesthood once again to Papadelias, betraying Julia, betraying Thisbe, lashing out in the same rash spite which now leads Cousins everywhere to perpetrate, in pacifism's name, atrocities. These are not my accusations, reader, they are Carlyle's, the many spines of the iron maiden of self-hate that she erects about herself in her despair. Dominic does not ply his art here without consent. And this was not the worst. The worst, the evil that made Carlyle think even Pascal's tortures were too light for her, was the revelation that her very birth had turned Merion Kraye into Casimir Perry, Madame's homemade Horseman of Apocalypse. And now I came to announce more damage done:

"Have you heard about the *Sanctum Sanctorum*, Brother?"

"I heard something had happened." Dominic followed me into English. "An attack."

"Persons unknown have breached the inner vaults, and publicly exposed our Master as *Imperator Destinatus*. They also stole the MASONIC Oath of Office, and Caesar has sworn his inviolate oath that he will make war to get it back, and . . ." I bit my lip.

Dominic's brows narrowed, but his forehead could not wrinkle—his freshly regrown skin was too elastic, virgin, like a child's. "And what?"

Bending to swab up my vomit let me avoid seeing Carlyle's desperate eyes. "And some of the Gag-gene files were there too, and have fallen into public hands, including . . . well, actually, the only one they have made public is . . ." I did not have to finish.

"Here's a true boon, Sister Carlyle!" Dominic cried. "Now our whole race knows thy guilt from beginning to end. There'll be plenty of help to remind thee of it now. How generous He is, this Local God, to send thee such a scourge."

I realized now that Dominic must already have seen what happened through our Master's tracker, or the news, or been informed by Mitsubishi agents. His questions were a performance, for Carlyle, a stroke of the flail of which I was one more knotted cord.

"So, are we at war now?" Dominic asked, stroking his scalp, whose newly replanted hair was barely long enough to show his tonsure. "If so, thou must help me dress at once."

"We are not yet at war."

"Whyever not?"

"Because Caesar has agreed to wait until Ἄναξ ... until we ... finish at the Vatican."

For that Dominic set down Pascal. "Then I must dress the sooner. Fetch my clothes at once."

"Yes, Brother." I nodded my obedience. "Ἄναξ Jehovah asked for Carlyle, too."

Everything changed, Dominic's posture, breath, as if an adversary familiar from the circumscribed play-wars of backyard football had stepped suddenly into adulthood. "Did He say why?"

"No, Brother. Nothing."

"Better 'Father' now, I think," Dominic corrected, "since I seem to be an abbot suddenly."

I winced at that, had guessed it from the empty habit on the floor beside the bed. Dominic liked my wince, I think, and studied anew his prisoner. "Release her, *errant*," he ordered.

"Yes, Father."

I freed Carlyle's right hand first, and she herself assisted with the other bonds, though sluggishly. I handed her her Dominican habit, rude white cloth with the black overlayer. I caught a lightness on her cheeks, almost a smile, as I handed up her nun's headdress, welcome concealment for the partly golden hair which reminds every gazer of Carlyle's partly golden ancestry.

"No. Court-wear, fool!" Dominic snapped, too far away to kick me. "In the wardrobe. We can't wear our habits at the Vatican, it makes the King of Spain uncomfortable."

"Yes, Father. Apologies." I helped Dominic change, his reconstructed fingers not yet quite equal to waistcoat buttons, or to easing his taut stockings over the calf. He wore his Master's black still, trimmed with black lace which lapped at black gloves and black boots, so the scarlet Mitsubishi crests on his haori jacket stood out like gore.

A garment bag held Carlyle's costume, virgin from the tailors. Its blackness almost matched her abbot's. Not even the Chevalier, Dominic's second in Madame's halls, may wear so much pure black as this. The coal-black satin had no colored trim nor lining, just embroidery along its seams in royal blue, which woke the blue diamond sparkle in Carlyle's eyes, dimmer than her uncle Ganymede's, but still as deadly as the glittering bait of old Versailles. It was a gown. I saw relief in Carlyle's eyes when she saw that, and I thanked Dominic in my heart for this kindness, which cannot have been an easy one; even the bloodhound pays a price for so opposing dread Madame.

"Thou'dst best shower before dressing, Sister Carlyle, thou'rt filthy." Dominic made for the door, his stiff hands struggling with the iron latch. "You may both catch up with *notre Maître* and myself when you're presentable."

Getting Carlyle into the shower was easy, but getting her into the gown and corset, whose workings were as alien as Sanskrit to both of us (I am no maidservant) required asking help from the nearest ladies. They were eager, but twittered throughout, over the gown at first, then over the beauties of the Prince-héréditaire herself, when they found their subtler flirtations went unscolded. Carlyle had no spirit to chastise them, just a compliant limpness as her silent inner self remained in someone's thrall (Dominic's? Pascal's? Julia's? Thisbe's? Perry-Kraye's?). I tried to defend her when, the gown complete, the ladies lingered to keep flirting, but they called me 'bad' and shut me in the bathroom, chiding my 'barking,' and in my office as 'that weird stray dog the Young Master brought home,' I could only let their game play out. I thought of calling Sister Heloïse, but she was at Casablanca. The Cousins' election the previous Tuesday had granted Minister Cookie and several of her Nurturist followers seats on the Cousins' Transitional Congress, though, to their credit, the Cousins also elected Bryar Kosala and many of her allies, and, strangely, rashly, inevitably, Heloïse. Heloïse had been much in the public eye: her speech to the Senate, her blood-smeared ministration to the victims in Odessa, and her spitfire remonstrations of the guilty in the riots' wake. The public, and the Cousins in particular, demanded more from this font of goodness, more than a Minor and outsider could provide. Heloïse had chosen the European Union to administer her Adulthood Competency Exam (the best option available in French), and applied to the Cousins the next day. She was no sooner Cousined than elected, and sat with the Transitional Congress at that very moment, presenting her latest studies of the violence.

Dominic returned to find out what kept us, and the fussing ladies scattered like maple seeds in wind before his glare. Their work was worthy.

Carlyle was stunning, regal like an elm among willows, her height exaggerated by the curved black hat which mostly veiled her golden curls, while her blue eyes' lack of focus suddenly seemed more faerielike than dead. Dominic's smile approved the transformation, and he drew from another bag a new sensayer's scarf, double-sided, Dominican white and black, which he draped across Carlyle's shoulders. Last, Dominic produced a Blacklaw Hiveless sash and bound it around Carlyle's corseted waist. It is as easy to leave the Cousins, reader, as to join them. I did not have to look at the sash to know Dominic's crest would be embroidered there, a sleek little hunting hound with black and white patched fur, bared fangs, and the motto *Canis Domini*—Dominic's warning to any other Blacklaw who might dare touch what was his.

When we were ready, Dominic followed me out into the hall with Carlyle on his arm, a picturesque but also practical arrangement, since Carlyle's steps were so hobbled by stupor and strange shoes that she genuinely needed to be led. Sunlight awoke a midnight-blue tint in some petals of Carlyle's skirts, further accenting the eyes that marked her noble lineage. How the ladies cooed over her when we reached the central courtyard. How ladies and gentlemen alike hungered to flirt, but Dominic's warning glare kept all well back. Madame's gentlemen were superfluous today anyway, gathered merely to flatter the beauties who would form the matron's train. Sensayers, not they, would accompany these ladies today, some domestic sensayers reared by Madame, some outsiders, mainly Cousins and Blacklaws, who mingled over a buffet of fruit and breakfast pastries. Three Masonic sensayers and one Graylaw had appeared to accompany Jehovah's Masonic guards, and there were Utopian sensayers too to guide His Delians, their Griffincloth sensayer's scarves matching their coats: a draping vine, a band of cloud, a snake. Spain stood with Madame, his three sensayers around him, for, determined to keep mind and soul fit for his offices, the king follows Conclave founder Mertice McKay's prescription to the letter, and sees three sensayers of different secret faiths. The Sensayers' Faith Registry, that too was kept for safety in MASON's *Sanctum Sanctorum*, or used to be.

You have not seen Dominic in our Master's presence before now, have you, reader? See how he stumbles, tramples flowers, feet, forgets the path, the ledge, the spectators, the world, staggering through all as if it were vacuum until he reaches Him. I believe Dominic goes blind in those seconds, that the world does actually melt away from his fixed vision. He forgets to breathe too, or rather he takes one breath, one fast awe-startled gasp when his eyes first lock on the black Figure, but he does not afterwards release that breath, as if he fears with exhalation he might lose the vision, too. I, who woke gradually from boyhood to love, do not know, but if love can come at first sight, as romance claims, and if it can erase the world, leaving nothing but the vision of the beloved, and if love is, as poets claim, a kind of Death, and burns away the past self so the lover's soul arises like a new-born phoenix to Love's promise, then I believe that Eros's arrow slays Dominic anew every single time he lays eyes on the One Who is so absolute his Lord and Master.

Inertia kept Carlyle on Dominic's arm as the human seas between them and Jehovah parted. I pulled her off just in time, fearing stunned Carlyle would topple as a far-more-stunned Dominic fell to his knees before his God. He always kneels. When he has approached his *Maître* several times within as many minutes he sometimes gains steadiness enough to only drop to one knee, or to bob and catch himself as they remeet, as you may have seen Catholics do before the altar. But the first time he draws near Him— indeed, the first few times in every encounter—he falls to both knees, stunned to that abject and awestruck helplessness that kneeling was supposed to imitate when some honest sycophant invented it in the primordial court of Gilgamesh, or earlier.

If the hand Jehovah extended to Dominic had held a knife to slit his throat, the bloodhound never would have noticed. Instead He laid it gently on his head. « I need thee more than usual today, My Dominic. I am glad thou'rt Mine. »

Tears leaked from the monster trembling on his knees. Do you find it strange? Object that *this cannot be that same beast which plotted to spill its Master's tears with such frenzied malevolence.* I say it is. Could a less beloved Master inspire such frenzy? I wonder sometimes how I react when I enter Ἄναξ Jehovah's presence. No one has told me.

"Carlyle Foster." Jehovah turned to her slowly, His black eyes stirring a shudder in Carlyle's half-bare shoulders. "If it were true," the Addressee began, "that you were created only to catalyze this crisis, then, that work done, you would not continue to exist. Therefore either you continue to exist only to suffer, and we learn from this that My Peer equates justice with pain, or else Providence plans more for you."

"I don't want it!" Most of the company was polite enough pretend they did not watch as Carlyle sobbed. "I don't want to be part of the Plan any-more!"

"You intend to follow Dominic in serving Me?"

"Y-y-e-es." Carlyle sobbed again, tears blinding her to Dominic's embarrassed glare as his still-standing protégé twice failed to use any title when addressing our Lord God. "The Plan is too callous; I can't respect its Author anymore."

Jehovah labored to condense his answer into English. "I shall never recommend the path of absolute filial impiety which turns a human away from its Creator toward Me, but if you do choose Me, I shall not reject you. In this universe I cannot rescript Fate, nor hear unspoken prayers, nor grant prayers beyond what My human powers can work, nor can I guard nor reach you after death. All I can offer is My Empathy, and the knowledge that I, Who Am Eternal and Infinite, though distant and here impotent, Love you."

Carlyle shuddered; sometimes we humans struggle just as much as our Maker's Interlocutor to force thoughts into words.

"But before you make this irrevocable choice," the Stranger God continued, "I will have you try every means to reconcile with your Maker and Natural Lord. Therefore you will come to Rome today."

"Ready at last, then? Good!" Madame cut in, her voice too cheerful; she knew how easily her Son's Mind might be turned off of her business. She must be queen. "Come, ladies! Escorts! To your cars!"

Last croissants were snatched and flatteries traded as the party scattered. Dominic rode with our Master and His guards. I found shivering Carlyle a seat in another car, with the king's three sensayers and none of Madame's creatures; well, none excepting Carlyle herself. As I watched her alabaster hands smooth the skirts about her, it was hard to remember she was born outside. No, wait, Carlyle was born inside after all, and has come home. I myself rode with some of the ladies' Blacklaw sensayers. It is illegal for a Servicer to leave Alliance territory, and illegal for any but a Blacklaw to knowingly enable it.

"The Six-Hive Transit System welcomes you to the Vatican Reservation. This territory is not governed by the Universal Free Alliance, and here the Universal Laws are not interpreted or enforced by Alliance standards. If within this territory you witness intolerable crimes as outlined by the Universal Laws, you may not interfere with local practice, but may report your concerns to the Alliance Ambassador to this Reservation, or to the office of the Minister of Reservations. This is a Theological Reservation. It is strongly recommended that Alliance Members who intend to participate in theological discourse be accompanied by a licensed sensayer; your own law may require this. For a list of the Reservation's laws, select 'laws of the Vatican City State.' For a reminder of your own laws regarding Reservation visits, select 'list.'"

I will not transcribe the whole Great Debate, though I did serve as a translator throughout. A recording remains in the Vatican Secret Archive, and will be made available to researchers after the customary seventy-five years. For now, let the Powers have their privacy. I shall instead show the periphery, those strange encounters possible in lands where men speak freely of such deadly things as God.

Our car touched down on the edge of the grand square before New New St. Peter's. Here, a threshold of ash black stone warned all comers that these grand columns and fountains were never really touched by Bernini's hand, that Maderno never sighed at this façade, nor was this central obelisk, with its time-worn hieroglyphs, worn by real time, nor touched by any real blood of a man called Peter. All was Blackframe. Shards of the real obelisk are kept inside the reconstructed basilica, among whatever other relics were hardy enough to have survived the bomb. All else, from the carved saints boasting their arms of martyrdom upon the rooftop to the graceful paving stones, is replica. There was much indecision among the Blackframe Project leaders about how to mark the Vatican, and other places where the building itself was art. Most of the official Blackframe substitutes made after the Church War are literally framed in black, the sculptures set on black bases, to remind the viewer that the originals were consumed by mankind's collective sin. But even a mourning generation hesitated to stripe the new Sistine Chapel or the new St. Peters's nave in black. The fixed boundaries of the Vatican Reservation provided a solution: a black stripe around the border warning not only that a different Law reigns here, but that, across this threshold, all the art is new, replacements, computer-planned and painstakingly crafted, standing in for the charred and mangled wreckage of lost Rome. Rome's other palace-galleries use the black stripe too: the Capitoline, the Borghese, the Palazzo Doria-Pamphili where Julia's cousins still dwell in their replacement palace and lord over their replacement masterpieces. All false. Our race cannot afford such losses again. What will this next war claim: Athens? On the Acropolis at least the tears we shed are still tears of connection: where I stand Socrates stood. In the Blackframe Roman Forum, by the Blackframe Coliseum or the Blackframe Pantheon, they are regret tears. Replicas cannot touch. That is what we all want, to touch what *someone* touched, a special someone, different for each of us, whose story reached forward through history and touched us. We want to reciprocate that touch as friends do. Who touches you, reader? Whose touch do you want to reciprocate, thwarting the walls of time? Raphael? Socrates? Machiavelli? Caesar? Homer? Hobbes?

"Jehovah! Welcome!"

"Good to see you."

"Welcome!"

"Glad you've come!"

"I thank you for your welcome, Monsignor Colonna," the Visitor answered, "Father Kaluza, Father Moye, Father Pillion. I come gladly."

It was not yet seven by the local clock, and the dawn-touched square stood empty except for the clutch of priests and Swiss Guards gathered to receive us. Oh, there were a few odd pilgrims and trainee sensayers here for their exchange year, but the crowds that flock to art were at the second reconstruction twenty miles eastward, which now serves as the museum, leaving the site of old Rome for the surviving Romans, and the site of the old Vatican for its old Church. The car that carried the king and would-be queen had touched down in the inner gardens, but Jehovah always insists on using the main entrance, out of respect for the architect, and for the Architect.

"Good, good." Monsignor Aurelio Colonna serves the Papal See as dozens of Colonna princes and cardinals have before him. He is a healthy man, an athlete in no small way, with some squash trophies, but paranoia poisons my memory. In my mind he is too pale, a touch of blue about his cheeks, his hair too thin. However safe science may claim Rome is now, radiation is our boogeyman. Just as ships claimed by cruelly placed but senseless rocks led man to name Charybdis, so every time some Roman leaves this world, even for the most natural reason, we blame the bomb. Just as well. They may blame me on the bomb too if they want to, if it would stop us using it again. "Their Majesty the King and their party," Colonna continued, "are joining Their Holiness for morning mass in the Sistine, and any here who wish to are welcome to join them."

Some did so wish; I did not. It was hard enough seeing in my mind's eye Isabel Carlos kneeling before the pope, genuflection before the altar, the whole medieval ritual, and poisonous Madame beside the king. To see it face-to-face—too much.

As one of the priests led Madame's ladies and their companions off to chapel, Monsignor Colonna turned to Jehovah. *"Imperator Destinatus."* The deep sympathy in his tone and wrinkles proved he had thought much about our Guest's new plight. "Dark days. How are you holding up?"

Jehovah's gaze lingered on the great basilica, built of nostalgia for its predecessor built of hope. "I have many questions."

"So do we all."

"Have any of My guests arrived?"

"Almost all. I told them we probably wouldn't get started before nine, since Their Holiness will need that long with your parents, but everyone's so eager they arrived early."

"Guests, Ἄναξ?" I asked.

I should not have interrupted my betters' conference, but in His Kindness He forgave me. "I said before, Mycroft, I have never elsewhen had so specific a question for My Peer. I must consult His ministers. I think . . ." Another pause. "I think that I should act." How to communicate, reader, His tone, the way He voiced it, uncertainty mixed with gravity, as if this were some new discovery. As if He had never *acted* before.

"You've done well already." The Monsignor patted His shoulder. "You saved the Cousins, ended the assassinations."

Colonna's words turned slowly into meaning in Jehovah's Mind, and meaning to new words. "I have hitherto acknowledged the filial and legal obligations which accompany My human existence, and the filial include the offices given Me by parents, but to complete what parents ask of Me is not to act."

"Who else . . ." I began, but trailed off as a glimpse of color among the columns made me pause and peer. It was a figure robed in orange and red, walking with two men in black with beards and broad-brimmed hats that instinct said were rabbis. I swallowed. "That's the Dalai Lama, isn't it?"

"The Panchen Lama," the Monsignor corrected. "Last I checked, Their Holiness the Dalai Lama was inside with the Zoroastrian and Hindu delegations, discussing the moral implications of earthquakes." He had a wink for me. "Your master sent me quite the guest list. And here, if I'm not mistaken, is another." The Monsignor nodded to a fresh car, just opening. "Julia, *mia cara!* Welcome!"

The somehow-not-yet-stripped-of-office Head Sensayer Julia Doria-Pamphili made a light leap from the car into Monsignor Colonna's open arms, and kissed him like a ba'pa—which, it occurred to me, he probably was, given the frequent interweaving of their houses. Rome has not that many noble lines left. "Delighted to come," she answered. "Is the rest of my Conclave running late or early?"

"Half and half. How's the new heart?"

"Better than the old one." She thumped her chest, where Sniper's bull's-eye sigil still sat. "It really is—oof! Felix! Watch it!"

Brillist Headmaster Felix Faust did not apologize, or even notice that he nearly knocked the Head Sensayer and Monsignor flat in his leap from the car. Mania. I know I suffer from mania often, but it is still unsettling to see it in another, a face so transported, so savage in its focus, raw. "Donatien!"

Julia rolled her eyes. "Sorry. I know Felix wasn't invited, but they saw me walking to the car and guessed. I couldn't shut them up."

"Donatien!" Faust panted. "You have to let me attend."

"*Onkel* Felix, as a Hive Leader you are not impartial."

"No one's impartial." Faust grabbed his Nephew's arm.

"You do not speak for My Peer in any trained or official way."

"I don't have to speak, I just have to be there: see, hear, smell!" Faust begged.

"You know you always speak."

"I'll try not to interrupt. I'll honestly try! I have to see this. All the theological leaders in the whole world, all together, and with You! Nothing like it has happened in—ever!"

Through five of His frantic uncle's racing breaths, Jehovah thought. "Take notes that further human knowledge as you watch."

The old Headmaster collapsed onto the stones as mania released him. "Thank you."

Now the Addressee too spotted the little clutch of black and orange and theology that watched us from the gallery. He turned toward the lama and rabbis, waved to them, and raised His voice to shout. "Thank you for coming! *Je regrette* that humans must exist in only one location!"

Murmur or laughter made them pause. "It's fine, Jehovah!" they shouted back. "No one minds the trip!"

"It was difficult choosing which Aspect's Reservation should be host!"

"It's fine! Rome's convenient!"

"That was not My only reason!" You must not imagine Jehovah animated here. He does not smile, or flush with passion, or crane his neck as He shouts. He seems as ever lost in daydream, but uses shouting to conquer, for a few modest meters, His old enemy Distance.

"No?"

"Increasingly since My resurrection I think on the concept of My Peer's Incarnation experiment! If it is true *qu'*He tested Incarnation on Himself before He used it on Me, then perhaps when He scripts His Providence He understands, as His human creations do, pain, time, distance, limit, hope, failure, *et* being loved! I like this concept! Such a Peer I can respect! And I fear less what He does to His thinking creations!" All this Jehovah shouted, clear across the courtyard before all, a comfortable shout, as when one shepherd calls to another across the dawn slopes to share news of some wild apples he has stumbled on.

Hush held us, and, briefly, held the theologians, too. "Why don't you come with us inside?" they shouted back. "We can talk better there!"

"I'm waiting for the miracle!"

"What?"

"I had My Mycroft send a message! He should come soon!"

"I'm here," a gruff voice answered, close behind us on the Blackframe threshold strip.

The whole company caught its breath.

Including Jehovah.

Including Jehovah, reader, Who left us now, as a child abandons his make-believe fortress when the game ends. We could see the speaker, or a sliver of the speaker, a line of face and chest barely visible between wind-rippled folds Griffincloth. Jehovah has learned, through long study, to smile. "Absolute welcome." He spread His arms. "Our meeting heals what was unendurable in both Our universes."

The sliver of figure froze on the threshold. "None of that. I am myself, Achilles, my own person, not a shard of Something bigger. You address me as a man, or I leave right now, and You don't find me again."

The barely living shell which hosts Jehovah's Essence paused. "You are three-quarters god, nymph-nursed Peliades, not human."

I had never seen godlike Achilles shy, not on the battlefield, not in council, not when taking on a giant twenty times his height, not watching Bridger handle the No-No Box, but here he hesitated, like a wild colt at the gates of the corral, warned off by instinct. "I am a man. I live among men, I die among men, and I blame and thank the gods for the blessings and sufferings they hand out, as all men do. I am not a god, or part of one."

The whole company stared rapt at this antiquated stranger in his muck-blotched camouflage, which eased into visibility as he switched the Griffincloth out of stealth mode.

"Then you come only for the war?" Jehovah asked.

The famous runner Achilles took two cautious paces across the mourning threshold, still ready, like wild game, to spring away. "Making war is all Fate tends to let me do."

"Making war." He Who Visits paused to wrestle words. "A strange verb phrase. War consists in unmaking: lives, creations, peace."

"I suppose so, but that's not how it seems to humans, not in the middle of it." The hero flexed his shoulders, narrow like the boy's they once were. "War is a thing we make, a vast, momentous, horrible thing. Making destruction is still making something."

"How Manichean."

Achilles shook his head. "Human."

"Am I not human, then?" Jehovah asked.

"No." It healed me, reader, hearing Achilles say it outright, as if someone had finally bandaged a long-open wound. Jehovah isn't human. "I've seen gods many times before." The hero frowned. "I know the difference between a human being and something shaped like one. Are You glad to have me confirm that for You?"

Jehovah paused, black eyes seeming to strain vision's limits as He studied the living miracle before Him. "You prove to Me that I am not what humans are, thus that this is not a race of deluded Gods who think they are not Gods. It is some relief to know humans are not all mad. But if they are not Gods, then there truly exists such a thing as a finite—perhaps even mortal—thinking thing. That deepens My concerns about the character of their Creator. Your Creator. My Peer." He didn't muddle his languages in this exchange, not once. How hard He worked, how long He must have planned, to do this right.

"If You're looking for reassurance that whoever or whatever runs Fate in this universe is nice and good," Achilles growled back, "I'm not Your man."

"I know."

The breaker of armies breathed deep. "Then what do You want from me?"

"Show Me your Creator. This I want from all beings, but expect most from you."

"I meant why did You call me here today?"

"Minorly because the Council I have summoned contains many of those living who most need and deserve to know that you exist. Majorly because I may be about to act, and if I do, I want you at My side."

Matchless Achilles glanced at me, then back at my Master. "You want me, too? You have Mycroft already."

"I thought before today that My Peer brought Me here only to learn. I was wrong. No humanlike being in this world's history has been handed as much power as I have, and there is about to be the greatest war. Providence admits no coincidence. My Peer arms Me because He wishes Me to act. Now. He cannot lend Me omnipotence, but he can lend Me all the substitutes humanity has forged, and He must intend that I use them."

The mortal son of immortal Thetis sighed. "Then You think we're both here only for the war?"

"I am not certain of the 'only.' I believe My Peer could have incarnated Me anyone, anywhen, anywhere. He incarnated Me here, now, Jehovah Epicurus Donatien D'Arouet MASON, Hiveless Tribune, *Imperator Destinatus*, Heir to the Throne of Spain, Gordian's Brain-bash' Stem, the new Cousins' Architect, the Mitsubishi Tenth Director, intimate Ally of every Earthly Power. And He made you. Will you join Me? Stay? Help?"

"Help? I don't yet know what You're planning."

The God held out His hand. No, there was more in this gesture than flesh's finitude; the God held out His Hand. "Help make My Plan."

Achilles's eyes fixed on that Hand, as if he faced a cup and in it equal chances of cure or poison. No, that's not right. He wasn't looking at Jehovah's Hand. I was. Achilles, I realized as the silence swelled, was looking at me. This was my fault, his eyes accused. I brought him here, not just today but that day, long ago, when I first found his hiding place. I dragged him out from toys and safety, paved this path for him, this Fate, this moment, all my doing. He was right, but I was right too. We needed him. I'm sorry, Achilles, but I would do it again.

"Take me to your Council." Achilles did not have to take Jehovah's Hand yet, but he did. He could have waited, pointed, bade Jehovah lead the way and followed, wary, independent still. Instead, eyes still on mine, he took His Hand. Matchless Achilles—did I choose for him?

"How do You like to be addressed?" the lord of the Myrmidons asked the Lord of Stranger Things as they turned together toward the colonnade.

"Honestly."

Achilles laughed. "I meant by what title. Like most gods, You have too many names."

"Let each choose for himself."

"Jehovah!" Monsignor Colonna called after them, and so in my eyes proved himself one of the strongest people in this world. "Will you introduce your new friend to the rest of us?"

The Addressee turned, as if surprised there were still other people in this world. "We . . . are new-acquainted. Let Mycroft do it. Mycroft knows him well."

The daggers of all eyes fell on me, the priests', Julia's, deadly Dominic's. "Mo-onsignor, this . . . this is . . ." I froze. I could not have finished the words alone, but the hero's own smile told me it was time. "This is Achilles. The . . . the actual ancient Greek hero from the *Iliad*, Achilles. Brought to life.

Except they're dressed like they're from the age of World Wars because they were created out of an old plastic toy soldier, by a child named Bridger, who was miraculously conceived without parents, and had no belly button, and could make toy things real, and was the kid you saw in the video, with the flying winged sandals who came to the Rostra and resurrected Ἄναξ Jehovah, Who was killed, actually completely totally really dead killed, by Sniper, and was actually really genuinely resurrected and brought back from the dead by Bridger, who then unmade themself to keep their powers from being used for evil during the war, but left behind Achilles for us, because the world needs an experienced veteran to teach us how to be soldiers again."

It poured from me easily once I began, so much truth, a torrent, like when a welcome blade finally lets the tiresome lifeblood drain away.

"A pleasure to meet you, Achilles."

There is no treasure in any bank vault to match the presumption of honesty, the willingness to believe that what we said—even what I said—was what we truly believed. They all presumed our honesty, every priest and rabbi and shaman and sensayer, throughout the hours of those talks. Not everyone thought everyone else was right—this was a conference of doctrinal adversaries—but everyone believed that what each person said was what that person honestly believed. Whether a man claimed that there is an afterlife, or that there isn't, or that three equals one, or that infinity equals one, or that He is a God, or that he is Achilles, all claims were respected. I do not know how many of the assembled believed Achilles was Achilles—perhaps none, since we had not yet made public the medical reports—but all believed that he believed, and faced him with respect.

"Jehovah, before you gather your guests, you should join your parents and the Holy Father. The issue of your legitimation is being settled."

"I am indeed obligated," Jehovah acknowledged. "I shall attend. Achilles, do you want to meet My mother?"

"Frankly, no. In fact, definitely no. In fact, never if I can help it."

Jehovah gave another deliberate, studied smile. "I shall endeavor to protect that wish. And I shall return to you as quickly as duty permits." He turned to follow Colonna. « *Au pied*, Dominic, Mycroft. »

Reluctant to leave Achilles's side, I fell in beside Dominic, on whose face I found a fixed, demonic glare. Achilles glared back at him, and only then did I realize how close fire was to fuel. Dominic had tormented Bridger toward his suicide; Achilles was Master Jehovah's new favorite person in the world. The bloodlust between them made me nearly drunk.

We left. Achilles stayed. Questions followed. For me they were the Holy

Father's questions, as I translated Jehovah's many attempts to say that, since He preexisted His human birth, He did not understand how the issue of legitimacy applied to Him. For Achilles they were all kinds of questions. Where do you live? (Wherever I can hide.) How old are you? (Eleven or three thousand.) Do you speak Ancient Greek? (Yes.) Do you think your existence means the Greek gods are real? (I hope not.) Greek metaphysics? (I sure hope not; that afterlife was terrible, and I'm not looking forward to going back.) Monsignor Colonna transplanted the conversation to a frescoed meeting room, where Holinesses and High Priests in the robes of every faith and unfaith mingled with the common costumes of Hive and Hiveless, mostly sensayers, not all. New cars from distant Reservations raised the attendance to seventy-six, each adding to the onslaught of questions, but no interrogation could tire matchless Achilles.

The King of Spain did tire, but persisted. For an hour I watched His Holiness Pope Celestine IX voice open reluctance to allow his longtime friend and spiritual son to bind his kingdom and himself to such a woman, but in the name of public fear about the succession, the pope granted the king's petition. Joyce Faust D'Arouet would undergo confession and contrition, and several weeks of counseling on her conduct and her faith, but she and Isabel Carlos II would then be free to marry. Their Son, conceived *after* the late queen's death, would be legitimated, and could then be proclaimed Crown Prince, and take the Oath of Office.

His Holiness Pope Celestine IX next led Jehovah to the meeting room, where the Holy Father warmly greeted every theologian as a valued equal, from Her Holiness Chief Sensayer Julia Doria-Pamphili who oversees the billions of the Alliance, to Dominic who mentors only Heloïse and Carlyle. I heard some style Dominic 'Their Holiness' as well, a title which he, as High and Sole Priest of a Universal God, deserves, I suppose, much as anyone.

Jehovah used no titles here. "Thank you all for coming. There is Providence. I have been made almost-Master of the world. There will be war. Achilles and I must decide what We shall do. I wish your aid in guessing My Peer's Will."

They debated seven hours. The transcript, as I said, belongs to the Vatican, but what I can show you instead is the view inside the papal library not many doors away, where Raphael painted the sages of Athens and saints of Heaven eternally in this same dispute over the nature of Earth, God, soul, and Man. See there immortal Plato, Aristotle, Augustine, Jerome, alive in paint, in their fat volumes, and in dialectic. Since the museum crowds are at the second reconstructed Vatican outside the city, these famous rooms serve as the pope's personal library, packed with books on Great Questions, and here wait those who are not admitted to today's debate: the King of Spain, a cluster of aides (who carried on their own debate while the masters worked inside), and Carlyle. Madame is at confession.

"Five minutes!" Faust howled. The king described this to me, a true howl of anguish as, four hours in, when he failed for a fifth time to hold his tongue, the Brillist Headmaster was punished with a 'time out.' "I'll shut up! I promise!" He hammered on the inlaid door that slammed behind him. He had tried his best. I had watched him throughout the conference, fidgeting, mouthing attendees' sets under his breath, then mouthing comments, then voicing them. His first interruption had been received politely, but that only encouraged more. "Shit!" He slammed the door again. "Five minutes! They could write ten commandments in five minutes!"

His Majesty confesses that he laughed. "Smart money said you couldn't keep your mouth shut, Felix."

Faust cannot glare; he finds insult, like every human act, too charming. "Carlyle Foster-Kraye?" He sat down opposite the lank but lovely figure. "Whatever are you doing out here, hiding under all that black and scowl? You should be in there, they'd let you in." He cocked his head. "You know, you're the spitting image of your mother dressed like that. Think of a number for me. Any number."

Carlyle did not even raise her sparkling eyes.

"Now there's some top-quality despair. If you won't give me a number, look at these forty-eight pictures of things eating bananas." Faust held out a tablet, since the ancient room contained no screens.

Absurdity awoke what charm could not. "Why?"

Faust stiffened. "I am Headmaster of Brill's Institute and Steward of Gordian, the First Hive, which birthed the best age this planet has ever known. When I tell you to look at forty-eight pictures of things eating bananas, you do not ask why."

Carlyle swallowed. "Sorry."

Forty-eight pictures of things eating bananas later:

"Well?" Faust prompted. "What do you think?"

"I . . . I think sharks look really weird eating bananas."

"Fine observation. Anything else?"

"No."

"What types of creatures were there the most pictures of?"

"Let's see . . . sharks . . . um . . . rabbits, monkeys, parrots, people . . ."

"There were twice as many pictures of each of the others than there were of sharks."

"Really? I guess I just remember the sharks because they looked so out of place."

"Correct. Now, tell me, Carlyle, if you have your parents' brains: Why are there so many Cousins involved in these recent riots?"

"Are you saying . . ." Carlyle blinked. "Are you saying . . . there aren't actually very many Cousins rioting? It just seems like there are because everyone notices Cousins more because Cousins look so wrong rioting?"

Faust knows when there is no need for 'yes.'

"Then who is rioting?" Carlyle's voice gained momentum. "And who's destroying the set-set bash'es if . . . if not . . ."

The Headmaster's eyes twinkled like liquid chocolate. "Cousins' wraps are slow to change out of. Not like taking off a jacket."

"A jacket," Carlyle repeated. "The photos. Lots of Cousins. The Masons and Mitsubishi are taking their jackets off before the riots, aren't they? And Brillist sweaters . . . and feet are hard to see, so no one spots Humanist boots." Intensity flickered in Carlyle for a few seconds before she slumped back. "Hmm. Funny."

Faust waited. "That's all I get? I give you the key to exonerate your Hive and all I get is 'Hmm, funny'? You are far gone."

The king intruded. "Does Bryar know this? Does Romanova?"

"Don't spoil it!" The Headmaster spun on Isabel Carlos II, his face almost a snarl. "That was for Carlyle to ask! And as it happens, I don't think Bryar does know. Now, I'm sure the raw numbers are somewhere, the new Censor will have them, and Heloïse, but they'll all still be distracted by how desperately they wish Cousins weren't there. Oh, if only some enterprising young Cousin who knew Bryar Kosala and Heloïse personally might bring this to their attention!"

Softly, "I'm not a Cousin anymore."

"Codswallop!"

Silence.

"You really are the most far gone thing, aren't you?" The Headmaster peered hard at the face, which did not peer back. "Dominic is very talented." He sucked a deep breath through his teeth. "Tricky, tricky."

The door relented now, and a young aide peered around the corner. "Headmaster?"

"Time flies." Faust stretched. "Well, if Dominic's had you for several weeks, I don't suppose I should expect to fix you in five minutes." A frown.

"You didn't even ask to join us in there, did you? You know that's probably why Donatien brought you here, so you could see it too."

Still silence.

"Come in. If five minutes with me won't cut it, we'll see if the best sen-sayer session in the history of the world can't thaw you a touch, eh? No objections!" the Headmaster snapped, too fast for there to be any. "There are bodyguards enough to carry you in by force if I ask them, and don't imagine Donatien brought you here just so you could spend the rest of your life kicking yourself for not walking through that door. Come. Come!"

Faust had to grab Carlyle by the wrist and haul her from the seat, but when resistance was more effort than obedience, she obeyed. I, within, was glad when Carlyle entered. The sight of Caesar in his death-black suit had destroyed my last hope for peace, but hope, like mold, grows back in many miniatures once the parent's removal spreads the spores. If I could not hope for peace, I could hope for smaller things, for Carlyle, for some healing ef-fect from the shower of spoken treasures traded here by shamans and imams and Brahmins and bhaṭṭārakas and rabbis and lamas. Carlyle was silent in the council, uninterpretable like a sullen child, but from time to time I thought I caught a glimmer in her eye, something warmer than diamond.

The only other interruption worth mentioning was that Madame's con-fessor, two hours into her recital, attempted to bludgeon her to death with a censer. It was inevitable, in retrospect, particularly since he was a Span-iard. The lady escaped with minor burns, but the priest was not so fortu-nate, since Madame learned self-defense from prostitutes, and is no stranger to clawing eyes. I heard recently that all his physical injuries have been re-paired; his mortal sin may take longer.

There were many at the conference I should have liked to speak with afterward—Jehovah, Carlyle, perspicacious Julia, the Pythia, Noam Ben Aharon, Leigh Mardi, Bridger, Dastur Jobs—but as the pope was working around to thanks and farewells, Jehovah whispered some few things to Achilles, then ordered that I be seized. The guards were quick, and silent Achilles watched without surprise or sympathy.

"Why?" I cried. "Ἄναξ!"

My Ἄναξ answered: "Because you would rather die than let Me do what I do now."

With that, I was given to Utopia's custody, thence to Achilles's camp of Servicer recruits—Myrmidons, I should call them, for they were battle ready—who guarded me strictly as we waited for the coming act, of which they knew no more than I. My pleas for freedom fell on deaf ears, but the Myrmidons shared the newsfeed with me as soon as Earth's cameras spotted He Who Now Does More Than Merely Visit. "There! The Forum!"

"Visiting the ruins on the way out?"

"Not Rome's. Romanova's."

There He was, reader, breaking the police line as He stepped onto the Rostra where His Peer's message had been received. There was the stain upon the stone, the dark of spattered gore, the clean patches where MASON, Martin, and myself had stood beside Him as His brains burst forth. Humanist President Vivien Ancelet followed Jehovah up the steps this time, wearing, not a presidential suit, but a bright Olympic training jacket. Four more members of the Olympic Committee joined them, two with Sniper's bull's-eye stark upon their breasts. These six together stood upon the bloodstain, and faced the Forum, empty, all crowds banished by precaution's curfew. Only the stunned police remained, and here and there a clerk or secretary, frozen mid-errand by the Tribune's unthinkable return. But there are always cameras.

"Since this war is Willed and must now be," the Addressee began, "let the sides mean something. I would not have the longest age of peace in human history ended over land rights, or majority, or prejudice, or sex, or set-sets. Many of you are prepared to make war to destroy Me, because you fear what Sniper fears, that I will control all Hives, and merge them, and end this world and its version of Liberty. I did not intend to do these things, until today. No one should doubt what has been proved: that, for three hundred years, this civilization's unprecedented peace has been enabled by assassinations. The current system cannot function without O.S. I believe that I am intended to replace it with a system that can. I believe that is My purpose on this Earth, here, now, though I know it is criminal for Me to voice this belief so publicly. Therefore I have decided. I shall use the power I have been given to seize control of all the Hives, and Romanova, by force if need be, just as My enemies prophesied. I shall destroy and remake whatever I must to create a conscionable world. This is henceforth My foremost Earthly goal. I do not yet have details; such a complex thing as a New World Order cannot be designed in haste. I cannot tell you, if you ask Me now, which of the institutions, rights, and laws you cherish will survive, and which I shall destroy. There may be seven Hives when I finish, or six, three, twenty, none, but whatever world I remake this world into will not include O.S. or the kind of moral compromise that birthed it. Humanity must outgrow such compromise. If you desire this change, My unknown new order, support Me. If you prefer the current bloodstained partial-paradise, support Sniper." He paused. "There. Now both sides mean something."

As wine leaks from a wineskin, leaving the once-taut structure soft and empty, so the strength had drained from former Censor Vivien Ancelet's dark cheeks during Jehovah's speech. Now life surged in him again, as if he had come around the farther side of terror and achieved anger. He brushed past the other Committee members and charged toward the speaker's spot.

Jehovah's hand and black glance bade him pause.

"But war must wait," the Addressee continued, that phrase alone granting the Humanist President some calm. "In ancient times when the Olympics came, all wars would pause as enemies watched side by side the sacred proofs of human excellence. Upon their modern resurrection, the Games were four times canceled and once delayed for the World Wars. Not again. On behalf of President Ancelet, My colleagues on the Olympic Committee, and of Myself, I hereby invite Ojiro Cardigan Sniper to join us in Esperanza City on August the twenty-second to light the torch at the Opening Ceremony for the Games of the One Hundred and Fortieth Modern Olympiad. I ask that there be no violence or interference, from anyone or any side, during these Games, or during their preparation. I believe that, if the human race proves capable of honoring this ancient custom, that will prove you are also capable of peace without O.S. When the Closing Ceremony concludes, one hundred and twenty-eight days from now, I shall return here to the Forum to personally open the Gates of the Temple of Janus, and declare the world to be at war."

As tears, commixing pride, relief, and grief, streamed down my cheeks, I looked, as all the world did, at the little temple opposite the Rostra, with its double doors at each end, roofed in vine-patterned tile and framed with leaves of stone. The Temple of Janus stands barely forty meters from the Rostra, almost a toy temple, shed-sized, small enough to be shaded by the laurel trees beside the Senate House, happy to be ignored. I have never understood Janus. He is one of those few gods the Romans didn't borrow from us: their two-faced god of beginnings, changes, doorways, enterprise, and many other vague, liminal concepts that are difficult for my mind to pry off the domains of more familiar deities like Hermes. The Temple of Janus itself I understand better. It was the dark twin of the Altar of Peace, not a gathering place or haven like the larger temples, but a declaration. When its double gates stood open, exposing the sanctum of the god of enterprise and change, Rome was at war. Only when golden peace touched every corner of the Empire could proud Emperors close and seal those gates. Few enough to count on one hand were the happy Caesars who had the privilege of draping binding garlands across those doors, and many were the generations who never saw them shut. Our copy of the little temple, faithful to the images on ancient coins, was built closed, its bronze gates sealed by its builders with garlands of carved stone in hoped-for permanence. Hope no more, builders. Hope no more. No hope for peace, at least, but He Who Visits brings a new and different hope to give us structure. One hundred and twenty-eight days, His test to see if the human species, which would shoot a Tribune on the Rostra, could respect, if not its own laws, at least its own excellence. We will pass. Thirteen days left now before the ceremony, reader; we must pass.

"Also—" He pressed.

"Enough," Ancelet urged. "Haven't you made enough enemies in the last five minutes? Let me speak. Let me calm things down. This was supposed to be about the Olympics, not you conquering the world."

Jehovah stood firm. "One last thing. I must introduce our guide in this time of testing." He gestured behind Him, to a small, fit figure almost ready to step out into the light. "President Ancelet, honored Committee members, human race, this is Achilles."

ʚ✿ɞʚ✿ɞʚ✿ɞʚ✿ɞʚ✿ɞʚ✿ɞʚ✿ɞʚ✿ɞʚ✿ɞʚ✿ɞʚ✿ɞ

The Five Gates of Esperanza City

Written August 12–14, 2454
Events of May 3
Esperanza City

HEADLINES AND GRAFFITI STAND THE PUREST CHRONICLE OF THESE next hours. "JEDDM Declares Both Peace and War" was my favorite, proclaimed by *The Romanov*, the world capital's paper cutting a keen and honest mid-ground between *The Times of India*'s "Olympic Spirit Inspires Global Truce" and the *Buenos Aires Herald*'s "Sniper Proved Right: JEDDM Plans World Conquest." That first night, vandals multiplied Sniper's bull's-eye sigil tenfold on walls real and digital, often with the addition of a crosshairs and "JEDDM" at its center, but by dawn a new corps of scribblers had largely obscured these bellicose scrawls with bold Olympic rings. The proliferating slogans "Use Peace Well" and "Valuable Days" I attribute to Cousins, while their *Rosetta Forum* boasted, "Olympic Truce Opportunity to Negotiate Peace Before War Begins." The Cousins' Board and newly elected Transitional Congress pledged to fight for amnesty from the Masons if those who violated Alexandria would surrender voluntarily. MASON did not respond to the suggestion, but none could doubt at whose command *Audite Nova* published a new photograph of the ravaged *Sanctum Sanctorum*, promising it would be followed the next day by another image, and another, with a daily countdown toward the Closing Ceremony that would be War's birthday: 127, 126, 125, 124. . . . today 12, tomorrow 11 . . . The *Brillist Institute Newsletter* on that first morning reprinted unchanged, even in their quaint historic fonts, the original articles which had announced and mourned the cancellation of the stillborn Games of 1916, 1940, 1944 and 2136. Brillist graffiti generally takes the form of 1-5-☺-19-♥-2-∞-1, but Hive symbols appeared among the numerals more often now, along with Sniper's bull's-eye, and exposure has taught me to recognize sets close to Eureka's, Sniper's, and Danae's brood. *Le Monde* and *El País* praised Jehovah's

forethought, audacity, and respect for tradition, and focused their headlines, with well-feigned objectivity, on the progress of the motion in the
European Parliament that the EU should, as it purged the residue of Perry
and O.S., restructure its very heart and place, above its Councils and Ministers, an Emperor. "Europe Needs a Conscience," one bold vandal scrawled
across the temporary House of Parliament, "One Europe; One Leader,"
"Integrity, Stability, Monarchy," "Bourbon Forever," "Empire Endures."
Meanwhile, Mitsubishi papers praised "Tai-kun's Truce," and His respect
for honor and method, a virtue *Asahi Shimbun* and *Black Sakura* praised Andō
for instilling in his pseudo-Stepson, though *Shanghai Daily* focused instead
on the need to "rescue" Xiao Hei Wang from the control of Alexandria, and
for someone—anyone!—to find a way to quench the other Hives' continued appetite for Mitsubishi land. So the Great Hives played at normalcy
as kids play House. The graffiti knew it was a show. If Providence makes
Master Jehovah Master of the world, all this will be His to solve or smash,
the precious Mitsubishi acreage, the throne of Europe, the power of life and
death over Cousin and Mason, criminal and set-set, slave and king. The
graffiti knew, as I did, that the only real piece of news was what Sniper sent
to *The Olympian* six hours after Jehovah's declaration:

> It is with the greatest pride and gratitude that I hereby accept the
> Olympic Committee's invitation to light the torch at this year's Summer
> Games, and I commend Jehovah Mason's honesty and courage. I agree
> that clear sides are what we most need now, clear options: the Hives,
> with all their strengths and flaws, or an unknown new order. In fact, I
> agree with Jehovah Mason's speech on every point but two. First, they
> question whether or not the human race will succeed at keeping this
> truce through the Olympics; I have no doubt we will succeed. Second,
> they believe that, when we do succeed, it will prove that we do not need
> O.S.; someday, I'm sure, the human race won't need O.S. anymore, but
> I am not so sure that day will come this year, or even in our lifetimes.
> And if the order to discontinue O.S. does come, it must come from the
> legitimate leader of my Hive, my President, not any outsider.
>
> To Romanova I say: let people wear what insignia they like, and de-
> clare their sides in all this honestly, as they declare their Hives or Law;
> if you use the excuse of the First Law to ban the bull's-eye, claiming
> that it incites violence, all you will achieve is mass paranoia as everyone
> doubts their neighbors, and paranoia makes people rash.
>
> To my supporters, those who wear my bull's-eye or want to, I say:

wear the Olympic Colors too, and, using them as a badge of unofficial office, form yourselves into voluntary peacekeepers, to take shifts watching places where friction between the sides is likely, and talk people down. No one in their right mind will oppose this truce, but many things can jolt a person from their right mind.

To my enemy's supporters I say: wear the Olympic Colors also, if you are brave, and join my peacekeepers as we uphold the Olympic Spirit and the peace it brings.

To my fellow athletes I say: I look forward to seeing you on the field of contest; let these be the best Olympics yet.

And to Jehovah Mason I say: you are the best of enemies, but it is my duty to defend the Hives, freedom of choice, and liberty, so I will kill you.
    —Ojiro Cardigan Sniper, Thirteenth O.S., May 3rd, 2454

We set off for Antarctica at once. The edge of the world. Here chaos was sculptress, castles of nature-hewn ice, ice walls, ice towers, serving nothing except the infinite glare of sun and frozen surface. We forget, I think, how the countryside we think of as "wild" has been reshaped so many times by life, how the jungle's false chaos is really a scripted mesh of symmetry, leaf matching leaf, child parent, every life-form acting out its role as strictly as the dancer spinning on a music box. Life's symmetry has had no hand in this Antarctic, nor adaptation, cycle, food chain. All there is as random as the Moon, and when a . . . *shape* of ice which has no name, as big as . . . *itself,* for it was the biggest thing that I had ever tried to label with a size, loomed before me, I tasted the terror that stands twin to the romance of touching a new world. Death. It was Death, beautiful and certain. We are a coddled species, reared in soft soil where we have but to cast seed to the earth for food to grow. Outside that cradle waits only freezing and starvation. Yet, like the first green sprout that raises brave leaves against the bare volcanic rock of some new island, so, bright with hope, here rose the domes of Esperanza City. Their surfaces of ice, or glass, or ice-glass, had no color different from the snow around them, yet their confidence felt like color in a world of black and white. Esperanza City has no need for spires, but we gave her spires anyway, shimmering ice-stalagmite towers sprouting dense as spring growth between her igloo domes, with flags fluttering from every turret, with science's magic to keep them thawed. She is a hybrid city. One Hive dreamed her, planned her, invented the tools and domes and scrubbers, but it was another Hive whose hands wielded those tools, and carved her from the living, lifeless ice where only brave men step. Do you doubt which?

"The Six-Hive Transit System welcomes you to Esperanza City. Visitors are required to adhere to some requirements of both Humanist Law and Utopian Law while in this zone. Due to its unique climate, Esperanza City also has important safety regulations, including the mandatory use of thermal skin. Since our records indicate that local regulations differ considerably from your customary law code, it is recommended that you review a list of differences by selecting 'law.'"

"What! Who are you? How do . . . oh . . . talking computer . . ." Achilles's exclamations had started as soon as the cheery voice began its greeting, and his hand shot to his ear, already red from his fiddling with the unaccustomed tracker. "Will it say that every time I go anywhere?"

"Unless you customize the setting," I answered. "Sorry, I didn't think to warn you."

Since he could not scowl at the side of his own head, Achilles scowled instead at the Blacklaw sash which now hung around his hips, still smelling of the gyro shop beside the tailors' shop where we had bought it. In deference to the public eye, the hero had consented to new clothes, still army green but no longer patched from thirteen years of wear. It made him feel more real. He had the tools of existence now: Law insignia, modern clothing, the ubiquitous tracker. He could walk into a bar without seeming an alien. He was still out of scale, a man's frame compressed to a boy's height, yet that suited him somehow. In a museum, a pharaoh's tiny coffin is still magisterial, as is our lithe Achilles.

"You can hit skip once the recording starts," I answered, "but only when going to places you've already been in the past year. You can also set it to text mode."

The Great Soldier snorted, impatient as a bull. "Talking car. There's good reason horses don't talk."

Did you chuckle, reader? A guard beside us did, but I could not, for fear has long since made me memorize my Homer. One of Achilles's horses spoke once, granted speech by white-armed Hera, and prophesied the hero's coming doom, before the beast was struck mute by those same Furies who will claim me when my own turn comes to face the famous horseman Death. It was no joke to us.

Kosala: "Get Jed to talk to me, Mycroft. Now. They will if you ask them."

The Cousin Chair called over my tracker, her voice raw after many hours of conferencing; certain calls a Servicer does not have the legal right to decline.

I: "I don't think this is an appropriate use of your call override as head of the Servicer Program."

Kosala: "I know you're trying to turn my Servicers into your own private army."

I: "They . . . they need to be able to defend themselves. Uniformed scapegoats walking the str—"

Kosala: "That isn't why you did it, and you know it. I never should've left you free to mix with them. I should've locked you in a box to never see the sun again, and I still could."

I: "Servicers are supposed to be at the service of humanity. Right now humanity needs—"

Kosala: "Everything but soldiers."

I: "I'm sorry, Chair Kosala, but you're wrong. There will be war. Ἄναξ Jehovah won't retract their declaration."

Kosala: "I wouldn't ask them to. This is the chance we needed."

I: "When the Olympics end—"

Kosala: "I'm happy right now. I know I may sound as pissed as you've ever heard me—and you should be scared of me right now, Mycroft, you personally should, because you are not making soldiers of my Servicers, and there will be consequences for you, big ones—but under all that I'm happy. You know why? You know that fantasy, where you get to go back in time to the beginning of one of the World Wars and change things to stop it? Or make it a well-organized quick war without any atrocities? That's the chance Jed's given me right now, and I'm not throwing it away."

I: "Providence—"

Kosala: "Is your sensayer's business, Mycroft, not mine. I'm preparing for the war, don't doubt that. I'll build ten thousand hospitals before the Olympics start, but war ends when the sides agree on the terms of the peace, and now that Jed's made sides for me to work with, it's my turn to negotiate the terms. I don't know whether I'll succeed on the hundredth day of the war, the thousandth, or the negative-twentieth, but I will make peace. I'm already making it. Now get Jed to call me back. I don't care what else you're doing. They have to convince Cornel to offer amnesty if those who attacked Alexandria surrender. This can't wait."

I: "I'll try, as soon as we're done here, but—"

Kosala: "Succeed. Don't make me send Heloïse."

I: "Y-es, Chair Kosala."

Kosala: "And keep Achilles away from my Servicers. It's bad enough Achilles lied to me, but—"

I: "Lied to you? How?"

Kosala: "They said they'd help me work for peace, while all the time the two of you were training your private army."

I: "That was no lie, Chair Kosala. Achilles wants to help peace, more than anything."

Kosala: "You both believe the peace movement is doomed."

I: "All mortal things are doomed: you, me, this peace, the Empire, this planet. Achilles doesn't choose sides based on how likely things are to succeed, only whether they're worth dying for." I waited. "Chair Kosala?"

Kosala: "I heard you. If you mean it then tell Achilles too that, more than anything, I need Jed to talk to me."

I: "I will." I meant the pledge, but did not do it then, not yet, not with the gates before us.

Which would you choose, reader, of the five gates of Esperanza City? Which you, Master Hobbes? I have not had the liberty to choose my gate at Esperanza since the earliest bloom of childhood, when, like all kids, I chose the Sport Gate, with its perfected slope, half snow, half ice, whose custodians invite arrivals to complete the journey into the city by sled, skate, sleigh, ski, every apparatus our playful race has conceived to turn freeze into fun. But you, who have the maturation of philosophy, may choose otherwise. The Nature Gate, perhaps? Whose long, camouflaged tunnel lets all spy at leisure on the reserve where horde on horde of ambling, hardy penguins glut themselves on the bounty Oceanus brings even to the lifeless ice? Or the wonder-garden of the subsurface Water Gate? Where the generators trail and throb like giant jellyfish, turning the sea's vast motions into energy, while the plankton nurtured on their tendrils feed the fish shoals, meat vats, and glittering krill on which the native penguins, immigrant humans, and itinerant great whales feast as equals.

Reader: "*I do not need to choose only one, Mycroft; all thy world and gates stand equally open to me, who commands history's pages.*"

Hobbes: "As for myself, I know nothing of these gates. But since you do, friend Reader, please choose for me. You are sovereign here, and know what I would choose as well as I do."

Reader: "*True, Thomas, and it takes little deliberation to assign you the City Gate, built aloft for cars that docked high on the central spire, beneath whose transparent parapet the whole metropolis, with its streets and lives and treasures, stretched naked before the analyst's*

eye. As for this time-stranger Achilles Mojave, do I guess right, Mycroft, that thou brought-
est him by the History Gate?"

Of course I did, reader. Homer's hero has leapt across millennia, farther, returning from the shores of gloomy Acheron. It is little to him to
step down on something so domestic as the icy crusting of the far side of
the world, but at the History Gate, here we have a wonder to thrill the hero's breast if any can, carried here at the greatest expense humanity has
ever committed to a single object. The great red stone is smooth now, worn
to a mirror by the pilgrim multitudes who come to set foot on our collective triumph: a patch of Mars. And at this gate too I hoped that the familiar sight of a camp pitched stubbornly against the hostile elements might
make this living ancient smile. To the right of the great stone, in the shadow
of the slopes and city, stand the preserved (and restored) cramped huts of
the old Esperanza Base, where humankind first learned to huddle through
the dread Antarctic Summer. To the left, a wall of Griffincloth shows not-
quite-live (data, like light, lags on the orbit-to-orbit jog) the huts and hy-
droponics where our Martian terraformers huddle through a more alien
cold. Burnished letters frame the Mars rock with the ancient motto of the
Esperanza Base: *Permanencia, un acto de sacrificio* (Permanence, an act of sacrifice). Yes, even Achilles pauses.

"Thank you so much for making time to come in person. I know half
the Earth must want to talk to you right now." Strangest Senator, Olympic
Champion Aesop Quarriman, offered her strong handshake as we climbed
down from the car. "The committee's received thousands of letters. Every
athlete and every coach from every team is with us, all the way." Her stance
had an energy here that never showed in the Senate, as if Romanova's benches
were mere stables, and this the open track where racehorses are most themselves. Quarriman wore a different bull's-eye patch now, stitched over the
breast of her Gray Team track suit, and so new that the snipped threads of
its predecessor still showed around its edges. Her old one had been gray
and white, but the new one was formed of concentric circles in the colors
of the Olympic rings. Her companions, committee members and aides alike,
wore the bull's-eye in Olympic colors too, improvised in cloth and marker
within hours of Sniper's call-to-non-arms appearing in *The Olympian*.

That bull's-eye's Target took Quarriman's hand as He stepped down
onto the red Mars stone. "The athletes' approval gladdens Me."

Wait, Jehovah is with thee? Mycroft, thou shouldst tell me when Jehovah Mason is pres-
ent in a scene.

Oh. Apologies. He is so absent when silent that I forget others equate His presence with His flesh. We were His escort here, and this His plan, a trip south to the world's end to see where the world's stage was being built to host these brave Summer Olympics in Antarctica. It took almost two hours to reach it, while all the time a thousand voices begged us over text and tracker: "Bring Him back! The Senate needs to speak to Him! The Seven-Hive Council! The Mitsubishi Directorate! The Censor! Every newspaper! The Law!" He did not answer. So, the cries which could not make Him halt rebound on me through the tracker which I can no longer remove.

MASON: *"Cum praesentiam instantem fili heredisque posco, non spero vos abisse narrari in Antarcticam.* (When I demand the immediate presence of my son and heir, I do not expect to be told you have gone to Antarctica.)" Rarely is MASON so angered that he forgets I am not worthy of Latin.

I: *"Caesar, potestatem non hab*—(Caesar, I had no power—)"

MASON: *"Persuasio sola potestas necessaria; illa tibi semper.* (Persuasion was the only power needed; that you always have.)"

I: *"Prohibere Eius denuntiationem non possem. Me habuit captivum.* (I couldn't have stopped His announcement. He had me imprisoned.)"

MASON: *"Quod scio. Nisi verum, acriorem verbis accitum habuisses. Filium mi duc. Nunc.* (That I know. Were that not true, you would by now have had a harsher summons than my words. Bring my son to me. Now.)"

I: *"Moxmox. Tibi iuro, tu primus post hoc eris, sed populo videndus est hos Ludos ante omnia habens. Responsum Eius Sicario est.* (Soon. You'll be first after this, I swear, but the public must see Him putting these Games above all else. It is His answer to Sniper.)"

MASON: *"Non est bellum Sicari quod postposuit, sed meum. Numquam post homines torrere argillam in lateres didicerunt murosque Orchoes sustulerunt Imperator Destinatus cognoscens et cognitus terram perambulavit, ut nunc Jehovah. Periculum summum, ita vindicta.* (It is not Sniper's war that this postponed, it is mine. Never since humanity learned to bake clay into brick and raised the walls of Uruk has an *Imperator Destinatus* walked the Earth known and knowing, as Jehovah now does. The danger is absolute, and so will be my retaliation.)"

I: *"Sed nunc tutus est. Tutus usque ad Augustum. Nonne maxime interest? Iam tempus ad parandum habes.* (But He's safe now. Safe until August! Isn't that the important thing? Now you have time to prepare.)"

MASON: *"Etsi consultor militaris et imminitus filius heredisque mecum adessent, pararem. Nec Jehovah, nec Achillem, nec temet, Mycroftem, oportet has horas terere—horas meas—ante vulgus Humanistarum fanaticorum ostentare. Quattuor menses vestris Ludis comparavistis, sed quoad super Ritus Inceptionis aurora oritur, quos praesentia mea etiam honorabit, spero illos qui titulum Familiaris ferant, itaque meorum laborum confisos comites esse postulent, illam fidem observare. Illos memorato.* (And were my military advisor and my endangered son and heir here with me, I would be preparing. Neither Jehovah, nor Achilles, nor you, Mycroft, has any business wasting these hours—*my* hours—parading before a pack of sport-crazed Humanists. You have bought four months with your Games, but until dawn rises over the Opening Ceremony, which I too will honor by attending, I expect those who bear the title of *Familiaris*, and claim thereby to be the trusted partners of my labors, to honor that trust. Remind them.)"

"Here, Senator." Jehovah, still before me, lingered with His hand in Senator Quarriman's; He is always awkward ending handshakes, easily distracted by the question of how much souls touch when hands do. "I introduce to you Achilles Mojave," He recited stiffly. "Achilles, I introduce to you Senator and Chair of the Esperanza City Games Aesop Quarriman."

The strange Senator smiled, eyes bright with wonder's fire as they feasted on the time-perfected body of the hero. "Delighted to meet you, Achilles. Thanks so much for coming. Everyone here is in a tizzy over the evidence they just released about you, and, well"—a frank wince—"seeing is the next step in believing."

Quarriman waited for Achilles to accept her offered hand, but he had paused on the car's edge, wary, looking at the sky, the tufts of ice upon the wind. I understood his distrust. Was it real? Was it safe? Was the ice wind about to bite as ice wind should? He, like me, could feel the subtle cobweb cling of the thermal skins which we all wore, but that protection does not feel quite real. Our senses quarreled. Eyes told us of impossible cold, flesh of comfortable heat, and lips and fingertips of the gossamer brush of something dreamlike. Reason knew we were safe, but another part of reason did not trust invisible science, not when iceberg mountains still promised so many ways to die.

"Time continues," Jehovah prompted.

With that last spur, Achilles's wind-swift feet touched Mars rock, and his hand took Quarriman's. "Thank you for the welcome, Senator. I prefer when people are honest about their doubts."

Awe warmed her smile as she felt his tiny fingers, and his lightness as he alighted on the stone, two heads shorter than she. "Oh, I believe the genetics they published, and the bone development and diet tests, you're an ancient Greek, medically speaking, it's just the part about how you came into existence that makes no sense."

"In most senses I agree," Achilles granted. "Though my return here makes narrative sense, and narrative is a powerful force in the world, at least for me."

Now feet, and claws, and paws, and swirling nowheres touched down on Mars. The Visitor's Utopian guards uncloaked as they arrived, and paused as they stepped down to stare at their feet, or weep, or bend to touch the Mars rock, the end of stealth an act of piety, not Reason. Piety too moved them to let me ride the soft black lion's back until I reached safe ice. I will not defile that stone, reader, not with the footsteps of he who deprived Mars of ever feeling Apollo's.

Quarriman clapped her hands. "Now, I've got the Artistic Director and the Security Director waiting for us inside, and I thought we'd head straight to the Opening Ceremony site." Her sport-fast feet led almost at a jog between the tents and Mars-worthy domes. "There's still plenty of time to change the torch design. We were thinking . . ."

I beg forgiveness, reader, if I fail to report the planning details, but I myself missed many of them, as the calls kept coming through my tracker.

Kohaku Mardi: ⌈You should be in the Censor's office now.⌋

I: ⌈I'm sorry.⌋

Kohaku: ⌈You've never seen numbers like these. All the grand dance we were raised on were the ripples of a tame pond; this is ocean.⌋

I: ⌈I've seen it.⌋

Kohaku: ⌈Says the owl, mistaking Moon for Sun.⌋ Remarks like that are Kohaku's signature, his rare union of poetry and concision that won, in one three-hour seminar, the heart and hand of Faust's prized Mercer.

I: ⌈You left your numbers. I've run projections beyond them before.⌋

Kohaku: ⌈Silhouettes, devoid of texture and reality.⌋

I: ⌈I have other duties.⌋

Kohaku: ⌈Mere avocation, Mycroft, you know that, and impious betrayal. Vivien and I gave years of our lives to teaching you, and, just as we'd opened in you that new eye which peers through numbers to the prophecies they hide, you stole me away, and stole yourself away to selfish crimes and self-important secrets. Now you've helped them snatch Toshi away, and even our teacher Vivien themself.⌋

I: ⌈They made their own choices . . . ⌋

Kohaku: ⌈You could have reminded them their duty is to the many, not the few. Toshi tempted by bash' and Hive, Vivien to save the Humanists, each privileging one minority. Humanity in our age has consented to turn its essence into math and submit all to the razor of the Censor, but when that self-same Censor refuses to put the good of the many before that of the few, fear for the many.⌋

I: ⌈I'm sorry.⌋

Kohaku: ⌈Don't offer to the starving the empty word 'food.' Do something. Get to the Censor's office. Su-Hyeon's grown straight and strong, but they're far from ready to rule alone.⌋

I: ⌈I'm needed here.⌋

Kohaku: ⌈Has it occurred to you that one of the reasons Tai-kun is letting Themself slip back into the mongrel tongue of Their childhood is that They have the crutch of you there to facilitate it?⌋

I: ⌈Papadelias.⌋

Kohaku: ⌈What?⌋

Papadelias. There he was before me. We had reached a broad ice thoroughfare, lined with igloo shops which bloomed from the Earth like moons, some smooth, some faceted. Their domes in turn nestled in the crannies of a vast, twining ice folly, not so much a sculpture as a doodle in three dimensions, whimsy braiding pillars and curves into an ice jungle which lined both sides of the roadway and crossed in undulating arches above us. The folly shimmered with internal lights, which in daylight played through it like rainbows through prism, but at night, which already dominated day in the maturing summer darkness, the eerie rainbow makes it seem as if cunning has sown the ground with seeds of fire, and reared the Southern Lights. And there sat Papadelias. He was at a café, sipping a self-heating mug of something whose steamy head wafted in white waves through the pure Antarctic air. An empty plate testified to the length of his wait, and his position to its intentionality. Of the dozen cafés in sight, many commanded views of the bustling iceway, its outer lanes textured for walking while the inner strip was smooth for skaters, but from this seat alone Papa could also watch the History Gate. Of course he had guessed which gate we would use. On spotting us, Romanova's Commissioner General rose, unfolding from his ice table ponderously, like an old albatross, not quite too time-beaten to manage the complexities of its wingspan. "No video."

He mouthed it. The trustee of Earth's justice would not say it aloud, not in this ant farm of activity. I understood at once. Why had Sniper's reply to Jehovah's challenge not been a video? Sniper would not send bare text. Sniper would stand bold on every screen, those coal-bright eyes, those athlete's shoulders, sporting at last in public the assassin's costume the living doll must have tailored for itself by now. Bare text? It would be more like Sniper to parasail into Buenos Aires and proclaim its acceptance from atop the obelisk, with fans supplying fireworks and marching band. We must make sure no one realizes. With humanity's honor and survival hanging by this truce's thread, Papadelias had come here, just as we had, to try to make sure no one realizes something is wrong with Sniper.

Papadelias only mouthed it, but there were a thousand Humanists in line of sight who might have read it on his age-dry lips, and worse, passing Utopians, Utopians with their otherworldly hippogriffs, and lightengales, and iridescent lazards, and who knows what technology within. Jehovah's Delian guards scanned all faces within eyeshot, and dispatched swarms of eavesdragons and butterslies to seek suspicion in the whispers of the many who had paused to marvel at this great conjunction: the Olympic Champion, the Commissioner General, the *Imperator Destinatus*, the Criminal of the Century, and Achilles.

"Someone do something distracting," I hissed.

"Chair Quarriman?" Achilles interrupted in the expansive, thundering voice which had carried his orders across assembled squadrons in the age before the microphone. "I have a selfish but important request to make, and I want to get it in before we're interrupted further."

Curiosity eclipsed suspicion in all spectators' eyes.

"What?"

"I want to compete in the Games, for the Greek Team, in track and field, but I didn't qualify formally because I was five centimeters tall during the try-outs, and I don't have a birth certificate because they didn't use them yet in the millennium when I was born."

Traffic stopped. If you have seen starvation in the poise of a beast, the stare of a vagabond, the tension of a mantis as it fixes every fiber on vigilance, then you know the hunger of the athletes passing in their bright team jackets as they locked eyes on the most famous runner in all of human history. I too had wanted it. I too had imagined those godlike arms taking up the discus and the javelin in the open field, though I had not dared ask. Quarriman herself swelled bodily with the thought, as if she were imagining scoring a starting line into the bald ice here and now to take him on. She placed both strong hands on Achilles's shoulders. "No athlete in the history of these Games would forgive me if I said 'no.' We'll find a way. I don't know if you'll be able to complete formally on a team, but . . . we'll work it out somehow and . . . Yes. Yes. Yes."

Applause exploded from the crowd of passersby, spontaneous as rain, and echoed through the humming ice above.

Did they believe, then?

That he is Achilles? I think the answer is: sometimes. They know the world is better if he is. Surely you have discovered that emotions let you sometimes tell yourself the possible is real, even without proof. Perhaps on some historical tour you have been shown an artifact: this might be the sword of Charlemagne, this little face of gold might be the tomb-mask of Agamemnon, this grove is where Robin Hood camped if he was real; you let yourself believe a little bit, even if you disbelieve, too.

Papa's shoulder blades cracked brokenly as he stretched. "May I join your tour? I'm off duty."

The Delians and their attendant monsters flashed their willingness to remove the intruder, but Jehovah was Judge here. "Do," He invited.

"This way." Quarriman beckoned. "Have you talked to the Greek Strat President, Achilles?"

"We're breaking bread together tonight. I still can't understand how filling out a form determines your homeland, but . . ."

Papa fell in close beside me, muttering in quiet Greek. «I thought after the near-fatal Mycroft-napping two weeks ago, MASON very sensibly forbade anyone to take you outside unrestrained.» At this point smiling, cautious Papa cuffed my right wrist to his left with gentle Cannergel. «You arranged this little visit?» he asked.

«Yes.»

He raised a chiding finger. «You have no possible excuse for not having invited me along.»

«True, Papa, I have no excuse.»

«Epicurus's stunt on the Rostra has this whole apocalypse teetering on Sniper's cooperation, and you didn't even think to ask Sniper first if they'd play ball.»

«That wasn't my decision.»

«You have to keep Epicurus talking to me, Mycroft. I could've warned them not to gamble. Start keeping me in the loop or I'll arrest the lot of you for . . . for . . . »

I couldn't help myself. «Inciting to not riot?»

«You know what isn't funny, Mycroft? Declaring war on the whole world without warning anyone!»

«I know.»

«One call, that's all it would've taken. Half my own staff is threatening to quit if I don't arrest Epicurus right away, the other half if I do!»

We hushed as the Bulevar Aurora Australis reached its choke point at the entrance to the grand dome, not trusting even the barrier of Greek to ward off eavesdroppers here. I had not expected such a change in the first cavern, whose spell had always lain in its lofty emptiness, as when one steps from cramped city alleys into a cathedral, whose height and light air feel more like outside than outside. Now the dome was full, not just with people, but with exhibits which assaulted us on entry with their polychromatic helpfulness. "Learn How Your Thermal Film Works!" offered a sparkling banner and accompanying booth. "Why Don't My Lungs Freeze?" "What Is Ice Grass?" "What Will the Runners Run On?" "Extracting Energy From Ice!" "How the Domes Were Made!" "Weddell Suits Make Freezing Water Feel Warm: Try It Yourself!" and, best but almost shy among its peers, "Martian Technologies at Work in the 2454 Olympics." I tripped over the black lion in my perplexity. Surely that last banner should have been on every booth, for I had seen every one of these technologies mentioned in some bulletin from the brave young outpost which was preparing our brave young world.

Again my tracker.

Julia Doria-Pamphili: « If Jehovah is War, and you're Death, and dear Madame is Pestilence, who's Famine? Do you think it could be me? »

I: « I . . . geh . . . Julia . . . »

Julia: « Do you know where I am right now, Mycroft? I'm still at the Vatican. You forgot to make sure they made me leave. »

I: « What have you done? »

Julia: « Nothing. » Her sweetest purr. « Just chatted. So many new, unpublished weapons these fine holy leaders have, and better, they don't know to think of them as weapons. I'm stocking my arsenal. Can't wait to get back to my rebellious little Conclave and slit some spiritual throats. »

I: « I can't chat, Julia, I'm on duty, as Servicer and *Familiaris.* »

Julia: « You have to talk to me, Mycroft, I'm still your court-appointed sensayer, and that's not about to change. No one would dare break up a match so clearly made in Hell. »

I: « I know, I . . . I'll give you a session soon, just, please, call back another time. »

Julia: « Why not now? Because Papadelias is there with you? You can tell your Papa, next time they set their sights to bring me down, they should remember that, while I do have the means to lubricate juries and make sure evidence is lost, I don't actually need to flex those muscles anymore. Plastic has been made flesh, a messiah resurrected, and an ancient demigod walks the Earth; Church is currently more indispensable than Law, so I'm impregnable. »

I: « Do you really want me to pass that on? »

Julia: « You would, if I commanded, wouldn't you? You sweet, whipped thing. »

I: « You can't claim credit for breaking me, Julia. »

Julia: « I know. They taught me envy, your Madame and your Jehovah. »

I: « Madame perhaps. Ἄναξ Jehovah taught you nothing if you envy Him. »

Julia: « Forty-eight hours, Mycroft. If you haven't scheduled a session by then . . . »

I: « Tully Mardi. »

Julia: « What? »

I: « Famine. And you know I'm not Death. Goodbye, Julia. »

At last the privacy of an ice-glass elevator delivered us to the greater privacy of the athletes' wing. Along the main hall, posters of sport triumphs alternated with the doors of private training suites, bright with team colors. It was not hard to spot the door with eight guards flanking it, all in Humanist boots, with the bull's-eye's Olympic rainbow bright upon the inky jackets of the Humanist Black Team—Sniper's team. Through the frosted window in the door I could see the familiar blobs of Sniper's preferred exercise equipment, its favorite posters of role models and teammates, and I heard the rhythm of breath and force as someone practiced fencing lunges. Jehovah knocked.

"Who is it?"

"Those you expect, the Law, and Mycroft Canner. If some of these are unwelcome, they may be excluded."

A pause. "The Law . . . you mean Martin Guildbreaker?"

"Ektor Carlyle Papadelias, who will, for the peace's sake and Mine, keep secrets."

As we heard the door unbolt, the diagonal black sunburst rays of Sniper's team jacket rippled like snakes behind the textured glass. Once I was inside, even the uniform and fencing mask could not make me mistake our host for Sniper. It was a good impersonation, even down to Sniper's gait, sprightly but careful like a spider's, but those were not the curves of Snip-er's sport-perfected calves, and an eye who knew to look for it could spot the stiffness of the binding which concealed breasts.

"May I introd—" I began as I closed the door behind us, but interruption killed courtesy dead.

"Where's Sniper?" Papa pressed.

"Missing." Lesley Juniper Sniper Saneer removed her fencing helmet to reveal makeup and a short black wig which simulated her beloved bas'sib to the millimeter. Her body was tense within the form-fit fencing whites, but she still somehow seemed lifeless to me, Lesley's customary vibrancy muted by the straight black wig which stifled the curls which should have clouded around her, like the windswept surface of a tree. "We thought your side had captured them, until your announcement made it obvious you thought they were still with us." Lesley swept the detritus of cups and socks and citrus peels off the room's chairs, and the sofa on whose clean blueness her doodles already twined like weeds. "Sit?"

"Thanks. How long have they been missing?"

"Since April fifteenth. The day Ojiro and Tully rescued Mycroft, and we worked out the temporary truce to stop the riots after the mass indict-ment."

My stab wounds panged. *That* day? One answer loomed, grim but easy. Dominic's trap had worked after all, and these nineteen long days the mon-ster had had the heretic at his lack-of-mercy. When my mind fills with horrors, reader, they are specific. Nineteen days; if Dominic had Sniper that long, the pentathlete would be in no condition to run, or fence, or stand, or likely speak again. But, no. It did not fit. A Dominic who had Sniper in hand would not still brood, claw at his Blacklaw sash, or waste hours on Mitsubishi board meetings and shareholder hobnobbing. Dominic did not have Sniper. I knew it, and from Ἄναξ Jehovah's face I saw He knew it too.

"And Tully?" I asked at once. "Sniper and Tully were together when I saw them."

"Tully knows nothing. They parted as normal when they both left you."

Papa frowned. "Who wrote that letter from Sniper that *The Olympian* printed?"

"I did," Lesley answered, helping herself to sport tonic and offering the same. "On behalf of O.S., I heartily accept the offer of a truce until the Olympics, and, as next in line to head O.S. after Ojiro, I am fully empow-ered to accept—Tully is not, I am. Unfortunately, thanks to the Olympic fever you've stirred up, the public is going to flip if we don't have Ojiro Car-

digan Sniper here to light the torch. I can impersonate them at a reasonable distance, but I can't run a pentathlon at Olympic levels, and I can't
stand up to the quality of cameras you'll have at the Opening Ceremony."
Lesley took as deep a breath as her disguise permitted. "Either we have to
find Ojiro before the Olympics start, or we need a very different plan."

Many different plans brewed in us in the hush that followed, punctu-
ated only by the churn of exercise equipment from the suite next door. Bad
plans, all of them. Mine was the worst. The dolls, I couldn't think of anything but dolls. If Bridger were with us he could bring one to life, bring
ten to life, create a cooperative one by dressing it in a Mason's suit, or one
of Heloïse's habits, or my own, to make it loyal to Jehovah. It would urge its
half of the world to yield to His inexorable rule. No war, and then He would
have leisure to rewrite the constitutions of the Humanists, and Cousins, and
Europe, all the Hives, and make a world that lives on without murder. No,
there would still be the Mitsubishi land problem. New land, then? A new
world? A time-ray to make Mars's terraforming finish overnight? No, Mars
is for Utopia. A new Earth, then, create two new Earths in her Trojan points,
with prebuilt cities instantly upon them, an Earth for every Hive, a fleet of
ships to swarm among the worlds, among the stars, and the Kind, Wise,
Divine Mind of our Good Master—Kinder than His Peer—to guide humanity through her glorious transition. All we need is Bridger.

Again a call over my tracker.

Apollo Mojave: "You would turn us back so far?"

I: "Not back, Apollo. Forward! New worlds! Now! Enough for all, without
any necessity of war. And when Mars finished at last, Utopia could move,
safe and unenvied, to enjoy your red birthright."

Apollo: "But would Mars finish, Mycroft? If we, who work so hard to reach
fresh planets, find them instantly at hand? Who would break their backs
making red deserts green for their great-grandchildren when unclaimed
paradises teem with fruit? A new world that does not require us to be
brave—how kind a poison."

I: "No! That isn't—"

Apollo: "You're right, not poison. It's a sedative, to lure the dragon into sweetest dreams. How long would happiness like that lock humanity in
slumber, lulled by this one sun? Five hundred years? Forever?"

I: "Not forever. The dream would wake us, the dream of voyages, of distant stars!"

Apollo: "Society changes, Mycroft, faster, faster, always, always. How many eternal-seeming dreams did our ancestors have five hundred years ago that we now laugh at?"

I: "We won't lose this one. It's as ancient as maps, as ships, as the first hand that grasped a walking stick and crossed a mountain."

Apollo: "Mycroft, we both believe that humans can, with time and industry, do anything, but one thing humans can definitely do is throw old dreams away. You know how many people these days never even venture to the Moon: too dark, too frightening, too far. Today only our littlest Leviathan has wings. You can't promise it won't forget what they were for if it swims happy with the others for five hundred more years. Or if it is swallowed up, as seven become one."

I: "Jehovah will protect you. Jehovah loves you!"

Apollo: "Cornel would have protected me to the world's end, but I broke their heart, and spilled their blood, and made them go be Emperor alone. Complacency is the enemy, Mycroft, not xenophobia. An old phoenix needs burning."

I: "There are better spurs to change than war."

Apollo: "Name one."

I: "Any!"

Apollo: "Name one."

Reader: The Olympics.

I: "Yes, reader! The Olympics! See, Apollo? Earth's ambition gathers here to break records, and bear that torch which guided ships to brave the ocean back when Ocean was an infinite and changeable god. Can't you trust that ancient torch to light the star-sea, too?"

Apollo: "No. Not when the complacent crowds, including most Utopians, will choose to watch these Olympics from their safe couches. Antarctica is scary. Tell me these Olympics don't have the lowest ticket sales of our era, and I'll concede that safe and happy people would still leave this comfortable planet to brave the icy vacuum between Earth and our nearest starry stepping stone."

I: "They might."

Apollo: "They might, but they might not. We must think of worst potential outcomes, Mycroft, not just the wished-for best. If what I fear is true, and we have no war, then complacency may set in, and make us stagnate in our comfortable world. If that happens, the Great Project, and every hand that helped it from the first caves to the Moon, will end here, on this first and only human world. If I am wrong, the worst that will happen is that we endure a devastating war for nothing, and still some-

day touch the stars. I will not risk sacrificing the future for the present.
I will not give up a thousand future worlds to save this one."

I: "You lost faith."

Apollo: "So did you."

I: "Never, Apollo! Never! I know it burned, the day you heard Mushi was
going to go study the ants on Mars because Utopia's top entomologist
said Mars was too dangerous, but one Utopian is just that, one Utopian. Mushi still had the courage to go to Mars, and many others have."

Apollo: "Liar."

I: "Apollo . . ."

Apollo: "You lost faith too, Mycroft. You know it. You lost faith the day
you made me choose between dying in my Seine Mardi's arms, or flee-
ing to the lonely Moon, and I, who was the firebrand you hoped to follow to infinity, chose death. Why did I do that, Mycroft? How can you
trust a world where I did that?"

I: "I can't! You're right! You're always—"

"Shhhh." A calm hand shook me. "Do you need to step outside?"

It was Papa, worry swirling his wrinkles as a stationer swirls the stripes
of paint that will stain marbled endpapers. Worry for me. Who worries
for me? Who shows concern, not for the tool I am, the duties I might fail
in if illness binds me to a sickbed's uselessness, but for me? I buried my
face in the breakfast-scented darkness of Papa's uniform and sobbed.
"They'll go to Mars. Promise me they'll go to Mars? They'll go to Mars."

"Shhhh." He put his arms around me, warm, warm in my mind even if
they were too dry and skinny to be literally warming. He let me lie like
that, and sob against his breasts, whose soft sacks, once plumped by suck-
ling children, old age has not quite consumed. "They'll go to Mars."

Lesley's words leaked in between my sobs and Papa's breath. "I could've
killed you when you walked in here just now. And don't think I couldn't
have, no matter whatever zillion security gizmos you have going. But I didn't.
And, unlike with Ojiro, it's not awe of the Olympics that stopped me, it's
the certainty that most of my Hive would be massacred if I attacked you
now. I agree with the lot of you that this mess will be less bloody if it's
started in an organized way on a set date. The Olympics are a good choice.
But for this Olympic truce to work we need Ojiro, safe and sound, and free.
If you find them, you can't just keep them prisoner, you have to return them
to me, free to lead their side. If you don't, Tully and I will speak up and
tell everyone you've captured and coerced them."

"You have My word."

"... And mine," Achilles seconded, though not quickly. There was a long, black pause first, and the words that came were bitter. Sniper is Jehovah's enemy, our enemy, and, more than anybody, cost us Bridger. Achilles, breaker of men, does not forgive.

"And you, Commissioner General?" Lesley asked. "Will you release Ojiro to me if you find them?"

"What?" Papa twitched. "Me? No way. If my people find Sniper, I'm arresting them. They broke the law. They broke it a lot. I'm a cop. I answer to the law. And the Senate. Sniper's going on trial, unless the Senate orders otherwise, or the Court decides to uphold the Senate's order to kill them on sight. I'm also arresting Tully Mardi, and Eureka Weeksbooth, and ..."—a pause as pleading lightness joined his voice—"... in the name of sheer human courtesy, would you please, please, tell me which of the Typer twins I have in custody and which ran off with you? I don't even care anymore about the legal awkwardness of charging an unidentified person with a crime, we've worked around that, I just really want to know. Do I have Kat or Robin?"

No smug eight-year-old ever surpassed the scorn in Lesley's voice. "How in the world should I know?"

Papa's laughter rocked me like a ship. "Fair enough. Oh, and I'm also arresting you, of course. In fact, I'll get it over with now. Lesley Juniper Sniper Saneer, I arrest you for murder, and conspiracy to commit murder, and violations of the First Law, and I know you'll have the goons outside keep me from actually taking you anywhere, but now I've done my job, and I can put you down for resisting arrest, and I figure it's easier if none of us bothers to actually stand up for this. Do you agree?"

Lesley's voice turned cold. "You answer to the Senate, fine." Her jacket's slick sleeves whizzed as she turned. "You're a Senator."

"That I am," Aesop Quarriman confirmed. "And the Senate meets in a few hours."

"To confirm Jehovah's truce?" Achilles pressed.

"No," Lesley and Quarriman snapped as one.

The Senator finished the thought: "Not Epicuro's truce. If we call it Epicuro's truce on the Senate floor, we set precedent for them dictating to the Senate, and that reeks of dictatorship. I've had some calls, though, and some of the Senate's legalese-speakers are assembling something they think will ... condone the truce without recognizing ... something ... I don't know the details, some way of doing this that means that Epicuro isn't taking over the world. Yet."

Force sharpened Quarriman's final syllable, and I remembered suddenly that the bull's-eye sigil had started on her breast. They were multiplying, these symbols for our many sides and stances. It would be a strange Olympic summer that did not bloom with flags of Hives and nation-strats, but the bull's-eye bloomed with them, O.S.'s supporters printing bull's-eye circles in their Hive colors: European blue and gold, Humanists' Olympic polychrome, Mitsubishi red and white with a dash of green for Greenpeace, Hiveless gray or black with Romanova's gold and ocean blue, and, here and there, the Cousins' azure and white, or Gordian's gold, black, and red. I wish I could say the crosshairs was rare, that grim addition to the bull's-eye which declares support, not just for O.S.'s past work, but for its current choice of Target. I peeked from Papa's shelter, just enough to glance at Quarriman, and see. Was there (Murder! Murder in this very room!) a crosshairs on her bull's-eye? No, her rings were clean. The Olympic Champion supported Sniper's principle, but not Sniper's plan. Not yet.

Lesley's eyes caught Papa's. "Have you already play-arrested Jehovah Mason? Like you play-arrested me just now?"

I felt Papa's quick intake of breath. A laugh? Sigh? Curse? They merge sometimes, like rivers into sea.

"Knowledge would facilitate My search for Sniper."

All sense of playful sparring left the room when He spoke.

Lesley: "What kind of knowledge?"

Jehovah: "Secrets: allies, homes, resources, vehicles, loves, enemies beside Myself and Mine. A human's path follows these things."

Acting O.S.: "You must realize why I won't reveal things like that."

Target: "I abuse neither Knowledge, nor Trust, nor the fruits of human misfortune."

Assassin: "Well, I don't give knowledge or trust to enemies."

Prince: "Then My search is unlikely to outstrip the police's." A nod of praise for the Commissioner General.

Rebel: "Not if you sabotage their investigation. You're powerful enough."

Tyrant: "From your lips, this request surprises Me."

Human: "What else are you good for?"

God: "..."

Human: "Well?"

Her question silenced Him a very long time, all the way through the remaining planning and confused farewells—confusing for Lesley and Quarriman, who did not understand why He stayed silent, how vulnerable He is to words. Even as Quarriman led us up the central turret to exit by the City Gate, the wonders of Esperanza City spreading lively at our feet could not distract Him from the Realities of Idea. What good was He?

"This city seems lively to you?" Apollo asked, gazing out with me across the domes, where clouds of black birds schooled like flakes of ash.

"Of course!" I answered. "See the seats and tracks expanding, stadiums rising, the great Games sprouting up before our eyes. Look there"—I pointed—"around the training fields, how the team colors mix like crocuses on snow? And the ice sculptures on the street where we arrived, you can see the whole long tunnel glowing like a . . . like a . . ."

"Like the life-force ghost trail of a slain dragon," Apollo finished for me.

I leaned over the parapet, noticing anew the manacle that made my wrist tug at Papa's. "If Mushi ever needs an example of what their ants can't do, it's this. The people look like ants from here, but ants just make more ants, plus things for ants to live in, but here we make glory. Can ants do that?"

Apollo joined me, the heaviness of his Griffincloth making my thermal skin itch as it brushed my hand. "They look like ants to me, working away. Where are the loafers? Window-shoppers? Grouchy old people? Locals waffling between two restaurants, or waiting for a friend?" He pointed to three Utopians on a nearby landing, unpacking two gryphonloads of sound system. "Everybody here is here on business. It's all still an experiment. 'Permanencia, un acto de sacrificio.' With the rest of Earth so comfortable, no one really wants to make a home somewhere so harsh, so cold, so far. Even Antarctica is too far. Tell me, Mycroft, how many people today would sacrifice their hundred fifty years of life breaking this ice if they couldn't jaunt home in a heartbeat? How many in three centuries will sacrifice theirs breaking red rocks on our harsh new world?"

«Mycroft?» Papa called from behind me, soft syllables with a sob's edge hidden in them. «Go rest, alright? Please? For me? Tell MASON I said you need it.»

«Let it be.» Achilles laid his godlike hand gently on Papa's shoulder. «I know it's hard seeing him like this, but he can't stop working, not him, not until Fate decides it's done.»

CHAPTER THE FOURTEENTH

Filial Piety

Written August 15–16, 2454
Event of May 3
Burgos

NATURE IS STRANGE, READER, SO STRANGE THAT, WITHIN HER improbable vastness, snow can touch August, sharks intoxicated by fresh water can grow briefly tame, poisons can sometimes cure, mad bees can forget what bees are and betray their queens, frozen frogs can sleep a hundred years and wake again, and, once in the lifespan of our species, Madame can shed sincere tears. « You look so grown up. »

That He did. I had never questioned why He manifested in the body of a youth, since angels and gods are usually youths in art and icon, but now, as His mother's tailor tested the new seams across His shoulders, He seemed indeed a different kind of Youth, no longer childlike—like Artemis or playful Hermes—but a Youth of strength—like Mars. It was His new coat. I can't guess how many museums and histories Madame's tailors studied to devise this web of buttons and cording, not the uniform of any specific historic nation-state but somehow invoking all of them, that whole vague European flavor of the age when being an officer meant blood and breeding. It was not all black. He Who Visits had been so determined all the years I knew Him to wear only what He considers the opposite of His Peer's color that I had never imagined Him in anything but black. Even now cautious Madame had been prepared to change it all to black in case he balked. But when He saw her first offering, a black coat trimmed with triple-stranded military braid in royal gold, the porphyry purple of Censor and Emperor, and the pure gray of Romanova's Graylaws—my Master, like me, recognized the right thing. This coat was shorter in the back than his old one, a thumb above the knee. His coats, like all worn at Madame's, are short in the front, but long on the sides and behind, with those pleated panels at the back which give Enlightenment-era coats a gownlike breadth, to drape across a horse, or swirl as one spins to sting a foe with blade or tongue. This new jacket had the same voluminous pleating, but was more crisply stiffened than usual, which lent vigor to His motions, like the hiss of a bustle. It is good, I think, to lend some extra impact to the rare occasions when He moves.

« What I do now puts you in great danger, Mother. »

She tucked back a wave of His off-black Spanish hair. « I've been playing the most dangerous game in the world for decades, my little Prince. No need to fret if You spill a little water in the ocean. »

I could not read 'fretting' in His lifeless figure, which stands still as a dress-up doll even when not serving as one, but I have not the lady's sensitive imagination.

« I may cause your death without Willing your death, » He warned.

« Sweetness, no one's going to cause my death except me. You do what You must to make Your bright new world. »

« A new world is betrayal. Change. If people's works have value, then once the first progenitors set patterns for life, all efforts at change become filial betrayal. »

« Not when what the parent truly wants is to see her Child do great things. But come, » she coaxed, « what really has my little Sage in such a fuddle? »

« A question, posed to Me by a human: What Good Am I? »

Coral lace fluttered against black silk as Madame planted her hands on the exaggerated platforms of her hips. « Jehovah, Dear, how many times have I warned You not to take it seriously when people use words like 'good' and 'evil.' Most humans, even those who've studied, apply no consistency or rigor to their use of those terms, so unless it was a sensayer—was it a sensayer? »

« Human, athlete, leader, officer, foe who wills My death. »

« You see? I doubt such a person even has a clear notion of whether Good exists as a universal or only in the speaker's mind. It's just the hollow specter of the word, Dearest, a shadow, no reality behind it. If You waste Yourself getting distracted by shadows, You may as well crawl into Plato's cave. Stand tall, now. »

She lifted a new tricorne from a box, trimmed like the coat in gold and gray and purple. Her Son accepted it, explored it with His sight and touch, and tried it on, a complete gentleman for an instant. Then He removed and hung it on a waiting peg beside the black original. Oh, Ἄναξ Jehovah never wears His hats; they exist only so he may remove them out of courtesy, while He stands under the starry roof of Another's House.

« But now I ask Myself: Am I Good? » He continued. Careful Jehovah always makes it clear, though pause and rhythm, when He means time's finite 'am'—I am in Spain, I am twenty-one, I am breathing—and when He means it absolutely in His universe before and beyond time—I Am. « If, as Plato and Aquinas hold, Good Is One with My Peer, then, Being Not-My-Peer, I Am Evil. But if, as Ockham and Mycroft hold, there is no absolute Good, and good is instead a human construct, a kindly and anthropomorphic perfection which resembles, not My Peer, but what His creations think they wish He were, then in such a sense I may be good, for I am kind, and want all thinking beings to be happy. But can I be called good if I merely desire their happiness, but do not attempt to achieve it? Achieving it would require Me to endeavor to twist My Peer's Plan toward kind and human things, toward compromise, away from war, yet He has laid out war before Me, and such rich questions to be tested by it, meat for Our Conversation. I am invited here by Him, not them, and am a poor Guest if I shun My Host's table to aid the garden ants. »

Madame had flinched, and loosed a dainty yelp midway through this, when her fingers, tucking the minor's sash about His waist, encountered the sudden undulation of a swissnake, prowling through the coat to test the many security systems Utopia had worked into the weft. Such a mother does not let her Son march forth armored by common cloth. Madame clucked at Voltaire, who bowed silent apology, while the tailor and valet who dressed the Great Prince snickered at the Utopian barbarian.

« You're quite right, my Little One, » Madame answered as she recovered her smile. « You must think of Your Great Conversation, against whose infinity any finite thing weighs as nothing, right? Right? » she coaxed, taking His chin in her soft hand. « Think, as You say, only of the Host. Your logic is almost perfect; I would criticize only by reminding You that ants are far more like humans than humans are like the Author of Sun and snow and soul and cyanide. Or like Yourself. »

Cyanide seemed a strange choice for her, death too quick for thought; Madame I associate with slow contagions, the kind that drip invisibly from host to host, as the dark sensayer arts she bares now dripped from her through Dominic, through Julia, through Julia's pawns and Conclave to a vulnerable world.

« I hate suffering. » Even with His face inches from hers, the Child did not meet His mother's eyes. « I do not want to be an Author of it, even as co-Author of the Great Conversation. »

« It's not Your deeds which make the suffering exist, my Sweet, it is the capacity for suffering which He planted in His creations, against Your good advice. » She flicked the side of His nose with a playful finger. « Now, come, let's go show Your father and the others Your new clothes. »

He to Whom Distance is an enemy took some seconds to process and recover from the slight but unwilled motion of His head which her nose-flick had caused. « I have a father here? Which? »

« It's all Your stray's fault. » She smacked me gently with lotion-perfected fingers. « Cornel turned up because they tracked Mycroft and realized You must be coming here, and Your dear Aunt Bryar also tracked Mycroft, and each of them quite refuses to let the other see You first. But Bryar couldn't come in person, just on screen, and You know His Majesty my fiancé doesn't want me to see Cornel without someone else to chaperone, so I invited Your Dominic to chaperone us, thinking the poor pup could use some wholesome French between this tiresome Mitsubishi nonsense, and then Your Uncle Felix just turned up, the way he does. Now it's quite the crowd. »

Saladin, sprawled on his belly in a window-shaped patch of sun behind his mistress's chaise longue, laughed. Can you see him, reader? How his bronze skin glows with Phoebus's touch?

« They're waiting for You through here, Sweet. » Madame took her Son's elbow, and, as a speedy valet held the door, plunged out into the hallway with a cheery whistle. « Saladin! Mycroft! Heel! »

We frisked after.

The royal nunnery's hallways had never anticipated the architectural breadth of the hooped pannier which mounded Madame's skirts to three times human width. The hiss of silk against the stone passage as she passed was so organic that what little of the real creature 'snake' remains within Voltaire's swissnakes hissed in answer.

Madame flashed a sharp glance back. "Do hush thy infestation, Seldon"— she refuses to grant the Patriarch's name to Utopia's creature—"or must I have their numbers culled again?"

"Apologies, Madame." Voltaire gave a stiff, respectful, bow. Hostage is a hard state, reader, even in a seat of comfort. Madame's Utopian hostages may not, like my Saladin, have literal collars to tether them to Madame's side, but for the hostages to stray across the threshold without her permission or her Son's would be a rebellion Utopia dares not attempt, not now. Whatever Madame fancies Utopia still supplies: servants, agents, clothes, synthetic queenly jewels, walls of Griffincloth to simulate her lost salons. And so they must, for fear has nocked a billion arrows, some aimed by fearmongers—Cookie at the set-sets, Tully at the Mitsubishi, Sniper at

Ἄναξ Jehovah—but most aimless still. Only a fool forgets the virtuoso pup-petrix who sits by, ready for her encore. The billion arrows of complacent Earth against Utopia: don't doubt she could.

All were on their feet as we entered the square hall. Faust, comically modern in his Brillist sweater, was pouring a glass of brandy. Dominic, be-side him, seemed uncommonly himself, his suit of Enlightenment black freed here from the Mitsubishi jacket which his new office required. On the screen between them, Kosala had the overperfect hair and fresh-pressed wrap of someone trapped between Important Meetings, and the kitelike shifting colors behind her showed she was still at her capitol in Casablanca. MASON was not with them. Nothing beneath the inconstant Moon is perfect, reader, not the crumbling slopes of Olympus, nor the fractal structure of the water-flea, so even here, as Earth teeters between a New World Order and Apocalypse, this Emperor, who guards more lives than any sovereign in Earth's throne-rich history, still had to use the bathroom.

Faust's eyes nearly vanished into the smile-folds of his cheeks as he caught sight of his Nephew. "Dominic, brace yourself."

The warning came too late. As the bloodhound set eyes upon his *Maître*—color! color on his *Maître's* shoulders!—the blood vanished from his cheeks. His eyes rolled back. A staggered pace buckled under him, and Dominic collapsed to his knees, further as even knees gave out, and he toppled forward onto his forearms, groveling on the stone floor like a man too starved to crawl.

"Marvelous reaction." Faust stepped in at once, with a light, stimulat-ing slap to Dominic's ear, and a dark stimulating whiff of brandy. "Breathe, my boy. In-one-two, out-one-two. Don't raise your head too fast."

Dominic did not try to raise his head, but shivered on the stones, grop-ing toward Jehovah's soft steps like a blind man.

On the screen, a Cousin's nursing instincts made Kosala frown, but could not make her wait. "Jed, I need you here ASAP. Our new constitu-tion's due in Romanova in just over a week. You know the Transitional Con-gress had meetings scheduled this morning, and suddenly Cookie and their faction are openly calling themselves a Nurturist Party and have a rival draft. I've put them off as long as I can, but I need you here."

"You still want Me there?" He asked.

"Of course."

"Then you surrender?"

"What?"

"The Cousins surrender?"

"What are you talking about?"

"I declared war on you. Do you surrender?"

"No, Jed, we're not involved in the war, remember?" Kosala answered, with a strange mix of forced sweetness and impatience. "The Cousins are neutral in this: hospitals, aid, peacemakers."

Jehovah stopped before Dominic's prone figure. "In the Masons' war on those who pierced their sanctum, in the Mitsubishi war for land, in the Humanists' for Hive-survival, you may be neutral. Not in My war. I will reorder this world, including you."

Kosala took a bracing breath. "That's what I'm asking you to do, Jed. That's why you're on the draft committee. Heloïse is right that residual gendered concepts are still a big part of how the Cousins understand ourselves. To make a workable new constitution the committee needs people who understand that, and how it affects the way the other Hives perceive us. That's why we need you."

"No committee. I am sole Author of this intervention. I will have your unconditional surrender."

Kosala attempted a motherly smile. "Jed, everyone likes your ideas. You're a voice of sense against Cookie's fearmongering. I'm sure the committee will take most of your suggestions, and you'll like the compromises they suggest."

Jehovah bent and placed His—should I say gentle or lifeless?—hand on Dominic's head. « I am content with what I have become. »

His touch dispelled the paralysis, granting Dominic energy enough to throw his arms around his Master's knees, and sob. Dominic's are not grief tears like mine, reader, not mourning in advance the battle-deaths Jehovah's war clothes promise. Neither are they joy tears. I would call them tears of raw catharsis, as Dominic's mind reorders itself around the all-transforming fact that his God can change.

Jehovah's eyes turned to Kosala's screen again. "And if I order the Cousins dissolved?"

Now the hard Amazon appeared in Kosala's face, that had made Achilles think of queens and goddesses. "You want to dissolve the Hive?"

"I may," He answered. "I have not decided yet the shape of My new world. I may dissolve the Cousins; I may dissolve every Hive but the Cousins; I may dissolve no Hives, all Hives—I know not. Thus I must have unconditional surrender." His eyes strayed to his silent uncle Faust. "From all of you."

« You have mine! » Dominic gasped, his breath still ragged. « *Maître*, I have the Mitsubishi now. I lay them at Your feet. Tell me how to use them.

Tell me to destroy them! Tell me to make them masters of the world! Tell me to turn plowshares into swords and scar Your Name into the Earth! Tell me to have them raise an altar to You on every acre of their dominion, and stain the stones black with the hearts' blood of Your enemies, and then their own! »

Madame's smile proved she followed Dominic's panting French, but the Cousin and Headmaster could only frown.

Even Headmaster Faust is ignorant of French? Surely like thee, Mycroft, this Grand Voyeur and people-reader has, in secret, taught himself all the languages of eavesdropping.

Never, reader. Faust is a pure Brillist. He even authored a commentary supporting Brill's arguments about how each language acquired forever changes how a brain thinks. He would never clutter the Germanic precision of his thoughts with something Romance.

« Thou art a foreigner among the Mitsubishi, » Jehovah answered, His gentle hand still on Dominic's brow, « thy authority young and fragile. Thou must use it in the spirit in which it was entrusted to thee by Hotaka Andō Mitsubishi, who remains one of My fathers, and must be honored as such. Thou shalt either honor and further the needs and wishes of his Hive, or renounce the custodianship of it and return to Me, alone. » He tilted Dominic's head back to make the suppliant face Him. « And I warn thee, My Dominic: if this truce fails, and violence desecrates the sacred Olympics, and thou provest to be the agent of that failure, I will not judge that the human race has failed My Great Test. Thou art a traitor to thy Maker, one of My creatures, My agent, not My Peer's, so thy works are not works of humankind, nor thy sins sins of humankind, but Mine. My Peer's creatures will pass or fail this Test, and if thou interferest, thou wilt only make the Test into invalid nothing. Nothing comes from nothing, not wisdom and not grief. Failure may indeed loose from Me the tears thou longest to see, but will not if thou art that failure's architect. »

Witness this Goodness, reader, a kind and absolute Goodness so alien to our own Maker and His iron Providence. Did you think Jehovah did not know? That the bestial desire which rules Dominic's every thought and gesture remained secret from He before Whom this dark and craven angel cannot master his legs, let alone his lies? Dominic hungers to taste the tears of his God, broken, grieving, struck to His Heart by some unforgivable aspect revealed, in His Divine Peer, or in Himself. That is the consummation this bloodhound lusts after. Onions have proved on two occasions that Jehovah's tear ducts function, but never since His Will gained mastery enough over His flesh to still the screams of infancy has emotion stirred

His Mind enough to spill tears in our Universe. Yes, reader, He knows Dominic's grim desire to see Him wretched, and accepts it, and . . . I will not say that He forgives it, since forgiveness would require Him to consider this love-treason in his worshipper's heart a sin. He does not. He Knows Dominic's desire, accepts it, and still He places His kind hand on Dominic's brow, and Loves, and calls him His.

Kosala's patience for fawning and French is limited. "Jed, you can't have a war between yourself and every single other person in the world. I mean, I know you have some . . ."—she hesitated, as you might, surveying wretched Dominic and me—". . . friends . . . but if you reject us all, all seven Hives, and alienate the Hiveless, which your world empire plan has definitely done, then you're alone. Even Sniper has a following, but right now you don't. You can't change the world by yourself. Work with us. The Hive system is an incomparably flexible and effective tool. Use it for what it's best at, that's what I'm inviting you to do, what we're all inviting you to do."

"If humankind chooses the old world over My new one, that is its right, and will settle My question. But I do not believe that I am so alone." Here I rejoiced to hear Him use time's finite 'am,' confirming that the feeble company we mortals give Him on this Earth has made Him feel that He *is* not alone, not here, not now.

"You will be alone if you make us all your enemies."

Silence.

Silence from all of us as Death in the guise of Caesar stepped into the room. His war-black suit stood razor stark against the stone wall, like a crack in a cliff-face, where inky shadows are the only bandage across Earth's wound. Capital powers lived in that black uniform, axe and sword and firing squad, while only his right sleeve, still imperial gray, promised that the merciful peacetime Caesar might return once war's Justice was done. Seeing the black suit in person, touch-close, made the nightmare real, as when you face the coffin at a funeral, and denial's rosy membrane finally breaks. Guards flanked their Emperor, dour as caryatids, while Apollo striding in their midst seemed a mere wisp, barely present as his coat's program added nothing to the ancient nunnery save the dust of abandonment. Caesar marched straight to his Son, took one lion-deep breath, then seized Jehovah under both arms, ripped Him from Dominic's embrace, spun and hurled Him bodily across the room, so He landed staggering and gasping against a stone bench opposite.

"*IMPERIUM deponam teque Imperatorem hoc ipso momento creabo!* (I will abdicate right now and make you Emperor!)" MASON shouted in Latin stark as stone. *"Furtim aut palam, ut malis. Auctoritas, IMPERIUM pristinum, fides absoluta meorum omnium ingentium occultarumque copiarum, meimet ipsius, Imperi mei, duorum miliardorum civium ex decem quos regere in numine habes: omnia tua fieri nunc possunt.* (Secretly or publicly, as you prefer. It can all be yours: authority, primordial IMPERIUM, loyalty absolute from all my vast and secret forces, from myself, my Empire, two billion people of the ten you aim to rule, yours, right now. NOTE: Xiaoliu Guildbreaker offered to translate this scene, since I wasn't equal to it.—9A)"

We flew to Jehovah's side, I, His fluttering mother, Saladin, even Dominic who crawled forward, too weak to snarl threats. He Who Visits from a Better Universe lay frozen just as He had fallen, half standing, half propped against the stone bench, His legs tangled, His eyes unfocused, lifeless on the outside, while inside—we who know Him well all knew—His inside would be the nightmare agony of panic. Dominic helped me hold Him so He would not fall, while I hissed in His ear. ⌜"«¡Ἄναξ! ¡This is Your Mycroft Canner speaking to You!»"⌟ I present the words in English, reader, but I spoke the mongrel tongue that sets Him best at ease. ⌜"«You are perceiving Your Peer's universe, the one You know well, a section in the world called Earth, in the region called Spain, in the refuge of the mother of Your human form, Madame D'Arouet.»"⌟

He made no motion, not even, for the moment, breath. This Foreign God struggles at the best of times to understand distance, as we humans struggle to conceptualize the invisible structure of the electron, which is neither a ball orbiting another ball nor a cloud of electric mist, but how else can we, who have no senses fit for microcosm, understand it? Now distance had betrayed Him. Location had changed without His Will or understanding. Did Location still exist? Did Earth? Did Time? Had His Peer erased His former universe, to turn Their Conversation to some fresh question explored in a fresh Creation? The perceptions streaming into His Awareness now, what were they? After such disjunction, the old universe continuing as before was no more plausible to Him than an entirely new one, reconceived from the laws of physics up as His Peer changes the Topic of their Conversation.

« I am here with you, *Maître!* Your Dominic! I still exist. »

⌜"«You are in Time, Ἄναξ. It is a day called the third of May, in a year called twenty-four fifty-four. We are in the crisis following the exposure of O.S., and—»"⌟

"Bellum denuntiavisti, omnesque sphaeras humanas hostes fecisti, (You have declared war, and made all this world your enemy,)" MASON broke in, fully aware

that, in this state, all words were real and raw before Jehovah, His only true reality, while color and flesh were still in doubt. "*Tibi constantia victoriae praebeo, atque mundi novi tui faciendi facultatem, dum consentias ac MASON fias. Lege.* (I offer you the certainty of victory, and the chance to create your new world if you accept and become MASON. Choose.)"

I had never before dared to glare at Caesar, but did now. In such a state, when all senses are traitors, MASON's question was the only real thing in this universe to reeling, trapped Jehovah. In such a state, if MASON had said: "*Consensisti,* (You have already agreed,)" Jehovah would have believed him—and Cornel MASON knew it. Saladin growled at the death-black Emperor. Or was it Dominic who growled? Or me?

Jehovah took a breath at last, then a second, and His fingers explored the stone before Him, rediscovering the alien miracle of touch. In the background, Kosala voiced obligatory objections to MASON's rough treatment of everybody's Son, but hollowly, as if she recognized, in the Emperor's still-shaking hands, the hurt and passion she too longed to vent. I think that was her interpretation of the outburst, that MASON intended to reprimand this wayward Child for the declaration of war which could not avoid the label 'betrayal.' Remember, reader, in these barbaric days few speak Latin. Kosala does not understand what Caesar said, what crossroad looms here—nor does Apollo, nor Faust unless he reads it in our gestures, and if Madame and Dominic's reading knowledge of ancient Latin lets them catch some words, Madame's face—not exulting—tells me she did not catch enough.

"*Lege.* (Choose.)"

⌜"«Ἄναξ . . . ¿Do you have questions? ¿Needs? Ask and your Mycroft will answer.»"⌟

"*Lege,* (Choose,)" Death pressed, for Death it is that Caesar has become.

The God replied at last, "*Mihi monstra Iusurandum.* (Show Me the Oath of Office.)"

"*Nullo pacto.* (No.)" Death leaned close to his Son, as close as the wall of my body would let him. "*Tibi Ius iurandum est ut ducenti antea generationibus, consentiendum antequam legendum.* (You must take the Oath as two hundred generations have before you, accepting it before you read it.)"

"*Nullatenus faciam.* (This I will not do.)"

"*Scis quid sim, quid IMPERIUM sit. Iusiurandum Imperium tibi et te Imperio coniungit, nil amplius.* (You know what I am, what my IMPERIUM is. The Oath joins the Empire to you and you to the Empire, no more.)"

"*Flagitas Me ut caecus in tenebras procedam et religari patiar.* (You ask Me to go blind into the dark and let it bind Me.)"

"*Te obligat ad nihil nisi conservandum rem optimam, fortissimam, simillimam aeternae umquam humanifactam.* (It binds you to nothing but the preservation of the best thing, the strongest thing, the closest thing to an eternal thing humankind has ever made.)"

"*Necess'est Mihimet scire leges.* (I must know the terms.)"

"*Nescias. Scientia Imperi ipsius utere, ullum iusiurandum conscriptum ab antecessoribus prudens confide.* (You cannot know. You must use your knowledge of the Empire itself, and trust that any oath authored by your predecessors is a wise one.)"

"*Etsi non est?* (What if it is not?)"

"*Egomet ipse auctor recentissimus Iurisiurandi. Nonne mihi credis?* (I myself am most recent author of the Oath. Do you not trust me?)"

I sobbed, and saw Apollo sob too, pale over Death's shoulder. Apollo had been with young Cornel in those first weeks after this Mason became MASON, taking, blindly and without hesitation, the Most Ancient Oath. Cornel could not discuss the contents even with his Apollo, but he could discuss the idea, the great one-way conversation between MASONS past and MASONS future sealed in those eternal sentences. Each Emperor must be Emperor alone, with perhaps some few years of guidance if his predecessor has retired without dying and stayed on as *Familiaris* to his successor, but one peer is a poor slice of that vast college of Emperors which stretches back into the shadows before Athens received her name, and forward, perhaps, reader, even to you. But there is one conversation. The terms of office allow, in fact command, each Emperor to take the Oath, but then to add or change three words of the text he himself received, though without violating the spirit of what stood before. Thus each MASON refines and guides, in those three potent words, the reigns of all successors. Thus, slowly, three atoms per generation, the Oath evolves to suit the changing needs of humankind. Emperors spend most of their reigns choosing their three new words. Cornel MASON would never expose the Oath, but in those first months after his initiation into this most ancient rite, I know he talked in abstracts with his dear Apollo, and Apollo told me once that MASON said that, if Apollo heard the Oath, he would be happy.

"*Pater, Ego quidem vix intellego quid Sim et quid faciendum Sit Mihi. Tumet ignoras. Numquam bibam dum apothecarius num medicamentum sit venenum incertus sit.* (Father, even I barely understand what I Am and Must do. You do not. I shall not drink while even the apothecary does not know whether the draught is poison.)"

Death closed his eyes. If I saw an oak tremble as he trembled now, I would fear some wurm had pierced the taproot. "*Numquam?* (Never?)" he asked.

"*Fortasse aliquando. Tempore mutante, non possum iurare 'numquam.'* (Perhaps someday. Within changeable time I cannot pledge never.)"

"*Contemplaberisne?* (You will consider it?)"

"*Contemplabor.* (I will consider.)"

Something in MASON's shoulders eased. "*Dum Ius iuras, non licet mihi ut mutes Imperium pati. Licet mihi te protegere, copias praebere, per dominationem mutationemque adiuvare omnium aliorum quos domitare legas; at si tumet Imperium mutare conaris, me oportet te omnibus viribus meis oppugnare.* (Until you take the Oath, I cannot let you change the Empire. I may protect you, lend you my strength, support you through the subjugation and transformation of all others you may choose to conquer, but if you try to change my Empire, I must oppose you with all the force at my command.)"

"*Verum'st.* (True.)" Jehovah found the strength at last to trust both stone and legs enough to twist around until He sat. "*Et dominationem mutationemque aliorumne favebis? Mi valde placeat socii fieri, pater, et gratum faciat.* (And will you support the subjugation and transformation of the others? I would be very pleased by this alliance with you, father, and grateful.)"

No pause before Death's well-planned answer. "*Tantum contra illos qui etiam sunt hostes mei adiuvabo: inter quos ullos qui corruptione Sancti Sanctorum conscientes comperiantur, qui coniurationes ad vitam Imperatoris Destinati adiuvent, etsi condiciones emendationis septimana proxima in Senatu praesentandae vitia corrigere deficiant, Humanistas, Mitsubishos, Europam, Consobrinos.* (I will only support you against those who are also my enemies: I include in this any who prove complicit in the violation of my *Sanctum Sanctorum*, any who support attempts on the life of my *Imperator Destinatus*, and, if the proposals for self-reform they present to the Senate next week fail to remedy the malformations at their hearts, the Humanists, Mitsubishi, Europe, and Cousins.)"

"Humanists, Mitsubishi, and Europe!" Felix Faust piped up. "I caught three Hive names in that! And was the fourth one Cousins?" His smile was playful, daring us to wonder why the Grand Voyeur chose this moment to remind us of his presence. We had mostly forgotten him, how his greedy eyes read our every twitch, even if the Latin flowed past him. Worse, I had also forgotten his poison sister, drinking in the gestures of her Son and former lover from behind her feathered fan. Was Faust warning us? A timely reminder from the old Headmaster to "young" Cornel MASON that the virtuoso puppetrix still plans her encore?

"If you're done for the moment, Cornel," Kosala ventured in English in the hush, "I do believe my business with Jed is urgent."

Death turned to face the screen. "You are right, Cousin Chair Bryar Kosala. Your business is indeed urgent, if you are discussing the new constitution of your Hive. Your instability endangers my subjects, and you may tell Lorelei Cook, and their Nurturist faction, and Sniper's fans, and anyone else who is obstructing the progress of your revisions, that if you cannot or will not repair yourselves promptly and to my satisfaction, then, whatever Romanova's judgment, when the Olympics end I will indeed join my son in war against you, to ensure a world where power rests only with those equal to wielding it."

Kosala sighed. "I don't think threatening Lorelei Cook will help."

Death glared. "I was not threatening Lorelei Cook."

Faust smiled.

Kosala smiled too, though hers was forced. "Cornel, please, let's keep this friendly."

Apollo's hand, soft on deadly MASON's shoulder, tried to calm him, but he shrugged it off. "I do not have friends, Bryar. I am an Emperor."

The World's Mom did not flinch. "You have friends, and you know it. Save the bronze-age propaganda for the public. I'm a politician, you're a politician, and we can negotiate as friends and equals, or you can sulk behind your mythos and pretend you're not the one plunging us most directly toward war right now. If you'd just leave it to Papadelias to track down Sniper and the *Sanctum* violators instead of launching a personal crusade against—do you even know who?"

Static flashed, Voltaire's coat turning to harsh white blankness as, for three seconds, four, Utopia mourned someone.

MASON: "The Empire defends itself."

Bryar Kosala suppressed a full snarl, but its ghost still manifested cough-like in her throat. "If you let me mediate, if you agree to be lenient with those who attacked the *Sanctum* if they'll come forward voluntarily, then we have a chance."

"Absolute crime reaps absolute punishment."

"*Iusiurandumne eripuerunt?* (They stole the Oath?)" Jehovah interrupted.

Caesar stopped breathing for a long moment. "Yes," in English, "they stole the Oath."

"*Vulgare ullo momento possunt?* (Then they could make it public any instant?)"

Death faced his Son. "Nothing could do more damage to the Empire, nor to the world, to me, to you, than the exposure of the Oath."

Jehovah worked hard on this English. "I neither recommend nor discourage, but amnesty may buy it back, still secret."

Caesar's answer took so long to come that it seemed as if we were waiting for some part of him to thaw, as ice slowly condescends to turn clear at the edges. "To those who surrender willingly," he began, turning to Kosala, "I extend this boon: that for them I shall summon a skilled executioner, while to those who hide, or flee, I will deliver death with my own unpracticed hand. A second boon I offer to one alone among them, the one who returns my Oath of Office, still safe and secret. All the others' names, after their deaths, I shall expunge from every record, every document, every account and history, by force if other Hives resist. I shall un-write their every word, erase them forever from human memory as I ensure *Damnatio Memoriae*. But to the one who returns my Oath I offer this: their name may instead live on in infamy—a curse, with Clytemnestra and Ephialtes—throughout the rest of human history. This is the amnesty MASON extends to those who make themselves archcriminals and then seek mercy."

I passed out. *Damnatio Memoriae*—damnation of memory. Sense, thought, even the precious *I* fled before such terror, headlong and willing into the fearsome dark that always waits a noose away. But even there I had no respite. I have lived too long beside Achilles, reader. The hero has only spoken three times in my presence of those fields of drifting shadow where the fallen dwell, but the intensity of his few words made Hades's lost realm feel so real that now it rose before me. I saw the crowd—no, not a crowd—a pool of mixing shades, too weak and empty to remain distinct from one another, like the many shadows of a tree's leaves. So many. So many and so blank. Some I recognized: intractable and lordly Agamemnon, towering Ajax, Julius the first real Caesar, the ancient poets with their laurel crowns, there satyr-faced Socrates arguing with Cicero, Aquinas, and Voltaire the Patriarch, there terrible and brooding Nietzsche, dread Pascal, there Mycroft MASON, with the blood-badge of his assassination proud upon his brow, and Mercer and Kohaku Mardi tracing notes and numbers in the sands that settle again into forgetful blankness breeze by breeze. But these proud forms were rare as weed-flowers among the grass. So vague the others were, reader. Empty, as the ancients warned us, drained of self as the forgetfulness of history dooms them to forget. Only life gives life, so here the helpless dead retain only that portion of themselves which we living still breathe life into by remembering. If a smith's shade retains his apron and artisan's thick hands, some signature on one of his creations saves him: I, Hlewagastiz son of Holt, made this drinking horn. If a smiling matron cradles dear ones in her arms, there stands in some wet yard a tombstone: Eva Kimelman, beloved wife and mother. Not vain-seeming now, the strict and sacred honors Greeks and Romans paid their ancestors. See, here comes a shade almost shapeless, terrible, no longer slim nor mighty, stooped nor noble, just a shape, and on its fleshless lips one phrase repeated: I am Hildebrand . . . I am Hildebrand. Somewhere in a dusty archive a baptismal registry records some Hildebrand, and, when that dry page molders . . . when it molders . . . I can't look. I can't! Behind the shades, the broad gray plain, that sea of shapeless gloom extending on and on across the mockeries of trees, that vast borderless shadow, millions on millions. Souls, reader. That gray waste is all forgotten souls, minds empty of memory, smeared one into another, stripped of self but conscious and eternal still. And to this absolute dissolution Caesar damns his enemies. *Damnatio Memoriae.* Keep it away! Away! Back, sea of shadows! Not me! I will never let you take me! I will carve my memory into history, by work, by force, by guile, in swathes of blood and ashes if I must! I will! I part my lips to shout my name into the dark, but grope for it, slipping away: I am . . . I am . . .

Thou art Mycroft Canner.

I am Mycroft Canner! I weep for joy as it comes to my lips: my name, my past, my self. Draw off, vain shadow! I will never be yours! I am armored against you forever now, with this strong Master Reader at my side. Draw off, and hear me laugh, and know that you will never have me!

The dead look up hearing my laughter, great Agamemnon rising from his game of dice with Ajax. But . . . that is not Agamemnon's face. It is inhuman, art's primitive parody, as anonymous as the generic face that decorates some urn or shield boss, and as far from life-mask as a child's doodle. What is this face? Can I even call 'eyes' these scratched slits between shapeless metal cheeks? I recognize it now: this is no flesh face but the death mask in thin hammered gold, doubly lifeless, doubly frozen, which archaeologists extracted at Mycenae from the king's supposed tomb. The mask thousands have seen in its museum case, a face the living know, while all who knew his flesh face are themselves dust. Is even kingly Agamemnon so forgotten? I cannot say that such eyes stare, but I stare, trapped by the frozen horror of the gold's cold surface, polished like a mirror, and in that mirror the reflection of . . . whose face is that reflected, reader? Mine? I do not know it. Is that the face you imagine for me? Fancy and shadow assembled at your

whim? Your favorite nose, a haircut you associate with murderers and
Greeks and slaves and tricksters? Where is my own face? Lost with the last
of those who knew me, lost forever and forever. I scream. I scream and
scream and scream until I wake again to life, Earth, senses, and Saladin's
tear-drenched shirt.

"Merci-ful C-aesar too just." The syllables stumbled planless from my
lips. "Unjust Fate force you spa-are me, me, the killer that bereft you Apo-
po-pollo, should have condemned, infli-i-cted me *Damnatio Memor-or-i-ae*, I
deserve it, I deserve, shadow, forever, but you spare me, still, me, necessity
of office, necessity of Earth makes you, too cruel, deprives you of revenge,
good Caesar, too pure for this twisted world, thank you, thank you, I'm
sorry, I can't curse the Plan that forces you spare me, unhappy Caesar, Earth
does not deserve you, thank you, thank you, thank you."

Kisses hushed me, Saladin tasting of sweat and feta cheese. He helped
my breathing slow if not my pulse. Caesar slowed that, standing over us,
still death black. I can't know if he understood my babble. Even had he not
been backlit, I had not the strength yet to read a human face. But he has
long understood, I think, what I finally realized then, that the world which
forces such unconscionable twists of circumstance upon this perfect Emperor does not deserve him.

「"«¿Mycroft, art thou now well?»"」 I saw Him too now, the God too
Kind to Will a thing like Acheron, standing close behind Apollo, who
leaned over me to administer some soothing substance by painless snake-
bite. Voltaire—sorry, reader—not Apollo, this was Voltaire.

「"«Yes, Ἄναξ, I'm myself again.»"」 Speaking His title made me so.

"Then I go to Casablanca," He announced in English for us all.

"You and Kosala have reached a compromise?" I asked. She was no longer on the screen, and the level of brandy in Faust's decanter testified that
Sleep had held me for some time in Hades's fields.

"No compromise," He answered. "I will help rewrite the constitution,
save the Hive, and then make war on it until I have its unconditional surrender."

Death's eyes, still recognizable in Caesar's face, forbade me to rise and
follow as Jehovah left. The Imperial car and Alexandria's strong citadel
waited for me. With a fresh check of my pulse, Voltaire proclaimed me fit
enough to be moved, if not to move myself, and Apollo and my salt-sweet
Saladin helped me onto Aldrin's unicorn, which bore me to the abbey gates.

"I hear father and Son might become enemies." It was Achilles's voice,
light-feeling after so dark an hour.

Death turned. A slim side garden framed the nunnery wall, and here Achilles had consented to wait as Jehovah paid His filial visit to she whose threshold the lionhearted son of Peleus knows better than to cross. The Great Soldier sat on a tree stump, baring his arms to Phoebus's rays, and fingering in his small, thick hands an iron-gray *Familiaris* armband. Aldrin stood with him, a living slice of man's next kingdom as Griffincloth turned a waiting car into a space-scarred shuttle, and the stubbled abbey lawn to asteroid.

"I do not think we will be enemies," Caesar answered.

"I'm glad to hear it." The famous runner rose and took a light step closer. "I would be gladder to believe it."

In his hesitation, Caesar must have tried to guess, as I did, how much Aldrin had repeated to the veteran of what Voltaire's swissnakes reported of the—should I call it a fight?—inside. "You still want to side with me?" the Emperor asked.

"Fates willing," the hero answered.

Caesar smiled. "And call me friend, and lead my Empire in battle?"

Achilles rubbed the gray cloth with his thumbs. "I prefer to fight beside someone whose mind I understand enough to call 'friend.' In this strange age that means almost only you." The 'almost' brought Achilles's eye to me.

A smile again; look, reader, while in the guise of Caesar, Death can smile. "And you want to destroy Sniper?"

The crack of the Great Soldier's knuckles told me that Bridger's shade rose before him, vivid and unavenged. "Above all others living on the Earth, yes. But I know what plan is taking shape on your lips, MASON. You are about to say that we can all be allies temporarily, that so long as O.S. remains a threat, you, I, Jehovah, even Papadelias and the Censor, are friends joined by a common foe. But that's not enough. I cannot join a man for the first half of a war, trust him with my back, my honor, while knowing that a second war is coming in which every blade I lend him might fly back at me. Strength deserts a battle line when trust does."

Caesar nodded. "I agree. But I do not intend to fight my son."

"He intends to fight you," the soldier warned.

"Then we must make Jehovah change their mind. We still have time to make them change their mind. Will you help me?"

What thoughts, Achilles, in your silence? Thinking on the many prayers of the Trojans, ten years of prayer that could not make the thundering father on Olympus change his mind?

"What side would you take if my son did turn against me?" Caesar asked.

Silence again.

Caesar pressed on. "You've already said you prefer to fight beside someone you understand enough to call 'friend.' I don't think anyone on Earth can say that of Jehovah."

"That's true enough." The hero sighed. "I've said it before, Mycroft, your Jehovah often seems a lot less human, and a lot less comprehensible, than Father Zeus, or Hera, or Athena."

I shook my head. "Not often. Always."

He smiled at my honesty. "I understand creating sides. I understand wanting to purge O.S. and remake the order that depended on it, but if an enemy stings me I gather friends and allies and conquer that enemy. I don't declare war on my own father, or my own people."

I saw a stony satisfaction in the set of Caesar's jaw. "All I have asked of Jehovah is that they accept their patrimony, honor the customs and duties of their predecessors, and be a good leader to the many subjects who choose to trust themselves to the Empire's promise of strength, justice, stability, and honor. I fully expect Jehovah to accept, but if they don't, would you really be happy fighting for someone who so betrayed their father?"

"I would find it hard," Achilles answered, slowly. "Very hard. You are the only part of this future we ancients would recognize. The only part that's like what we imagined. But I would also find it very hard to take a different side from Mycroft Canner."

I met Achilles's eyes, my strong, staunch comrade, but what was this in them? Doubt? Quiet shadows veiling private thoughts? Doubting what? Doubting me? My lips trembled. "Achilles, you wouldn't consider . . ."

"You know I've always obeyed the gods," the son of Peleus answered. "The gods that rule the world, command the storms, gods that made me, gods that hear my prayers. The *impius* Alien you worship, though brilliant, and wise, and even kind, does none of this."

"But He isn't *impius*. You know Ἄναξ Jehovah values filial piety above . . . above . . ."

"Above what?" There was sharpness in the matchless runner's tone. "Above what? Above fleeting turns of politics, perhaps, but not above His own ambitions. Not above this Great Conversation you both value so much, which, however grand, is also entirely selfish. In His inhuman way He honors His parents, but not as humans do. He honors the past, but not as people do who know they will someday join the ranks of the dead. He thinks as an outsider." Achilles's fingers dug into the armband in his hand. "He will never honor the ancients as we wanted to be honored, the way MASON does."

My fast breaths made the unicorn beneath me shift its nervous hoofs. "You must fight on Jehovah's side!" I cried. "With me. You must!"

Achilles took a long breath. "I want to. I would not choose to call either of you enemies, but if He would betray such a father . . ." A grim smile for Cornel before his eyes caught mine again. "What would His world look like? Tell me that. You don't know, do you? Not even you?"

I found the strength at least to sit up as I faced Achilles. "He does not yet know, so how could I? All I know is that the Will of Providence is inexorable, and that same Providence gave me to Him."

"And brought me back," headstrong Achilles answered, hot words, quick, "and while I still draw breath and feel the touch of suns, I'll follow my own will, not yours, or what you guess of Fate's. I agree I'm here for a reason, as you are, but if you're too broken to raise your voice and try to turn things toward a future you desire, I'm not. I say the ancients who died to lay the first foundations of this world deserve some say in what their works become. The living of this age are too accustomed to forgetting the dead, but we won't sit silent anymore, not while I'm here to speak and act. And in the name of the dead, who spent our lives and labors to give humanity what it has now, I say we will not choose a future built by someone who would betray and destroy such a father, such an Emperor, and such an Empire." The words boomed as the hero spoke them, rumbling like battle's distant thunder, and startled a flock of birds whose sharp silhouettes rose in a cloud behind him, schooling in their panic like so many flying blades.

"Then we must make sure Jehovah does not betray me." MASON stepped between us. "We must make sure they change their mind."

"How?"

"By being perfect in this war," the Emperor announced. "By achieving every goal. By crushing our enemies, supporting our allies, protecting our people, enforcing our justice, guarding our patrimony, and achieving our will. Jehovah wants to be powerful, efficacious, just. We will prove we are precisely that."

Achilles breaker of battle lines frowned across at me. "War is not that easy, nor that kind."

"I am aware that many kings and many empires have made such boasts and failed, but I am not any empire. I am *the* Empire, the dream of empires, constant since the first time a heart wished to call the space between horizon and horizon 'mine.' And you, Achilles, are *the* Soldier. Fight with me. We are both human and imperfect, so we will not achieve everything, but together we will come much closer than anyone else ever has or ever could. We will prove to Jehovah that this Empire is something they want to preserve—not just to preserve, but to become. Then they will join us, and let themself be reshaped by the ideals you and I share, and together we will make a future you will be proud to live in."

"I won't live in it." The hero's words fell gently, but with force, as a boulder shifts just an inch, and all in earshot tremble at the whisper-creak that could so easily have been avalanche's thunder. "I am Achilles. I don't win the war, I die in it." He turned to me. "You're not asking me to live in a world shaped by someone who doesn't honor the ancients. You're asking me to be dead in it. You know why I care what shape it takes."

I did, and choked some moments as again the shades of Ajax and Agamemnon rose before my eyes. "The Masons aren't the future, Achilles. You know that."

No one said anything. No one would, but glances crisscrossed among us all, Achilles, Aldrin, pale Apollo, Death, cautious glances, edged with suspicion, and with something lighter.

"MASON, why do you oppose the Set-Set Law?" Achilles asked at last.

Death spoke warily now, "Why do you ask?"

"Because I don't think you care about set-sets. I think you care about the right of parents to rear strange children, and not just your own son." Achilles's gaze strayed to Aldrin's false digital eyes. "Am I right?"

MASON nodded. "I will die for it if I must, as Mycroft MASON did before me."

"Why?"

Caesar drew strength as Apollo, still beside him, squeezed his hand. "An Emperor may use their power how they will."

"Not you." Achilles shook his head. "Not you. You want me to think it's for the memory of your Apollo. I do believe, as Mycroft paints it, that Eros's arrow pierced you as absolutely as it may pierce any man, but I still think duty rules love in your heart."

The Emperor stood tall. "This is my duty. The Utopians are one of the wonders of the human race, and since that race is mine to guard and guide, I will protect its wonders. Utopia will strike out and found new colonies, new worlds, as many have before them, and MASONS will link those colonies into our Empire."

Achilles's glance, at once playful and accusing, passed across me to silent

Aldrin. "Have you had a secret alliance with each of us," he pointed to himself and Caesar, "all this time without telling the other?"

Aldrin's lips parted, but Caesar cut in too fast. "My arrangement with them is not an alliance."

"What, then?"

"My own policy, unilateral and unreciprocated."

Utopia's nod confirmed.

"Then what do you intend the Utopians to do in the war?" Achilles asked.

"Nothing," Caesar answered at once. "They're uninvolved, neither guilty nor victim in the O.S. scandal, the assassination plot, the land mess, the set-set mania, any of it. Let them stay uninvolved."

"Even though they'd make such valuable allies?" Achilles tested.

"I'd rather see them home safe than beside me on a battlefield," MASON replied.

"Do you really mean that? You'll really let them stay out of the war?" I knew why Achilles doubted. He himself had tried so hard to stay away from Troy, donning women's robes to hide among the maidens, but the Achaean chieftains would not let this best of fighters live in peace, and sent crafty Odysseus to expose him.

Death scowled. "If they ask for aid it will be theirs, but I think it will be enough if I make sure everyone in the war realizes, as I do, how much more terrible it would be if Utopia, and what Utopia can unleash, got involved. Let them help Kosala if they wish, with food and doctors, but no more."

Achilles nodded. "Like priests, then. In the wilds of war, a wise man will hurl even an infant from a parapet to keep it from growing up to seek revenge, but, if he hopes for any future worth living in, he still honors the gods and spares their priests."

Utopia stepped forward at last, taking a friendly equidistance between the two commanders. "This is a dangerous time for us to be thought of as priests."

Goddess-born Achilles drew a long breath. "True."

"It is a dangerous time for you to be thought of at all," Death added. "I saw pictures from Esperanza City, when Jehovah's Utopian guards uncloaked. I know Esperanza is half yours, but still, I'd rather no one saw you siding with Jehovah. Or with me. Or with anyone. I've seen both flags in most Hive's colors but not mine, and not yet yours. Make sure it stays that way."

I did not understand then what Caesar meant by "both flags," but I would soon: Sniper's bull's-eye had inspired an opposite. The first one I saw was ragged, in Alexandria, rendered in rough paint on a cut-up shirt, but within a few days shops would dye real ones. The flag of the Alliance, the one which flutters over Romanova's Senate and her offices, has on it a ring of eight abstracted, bird-like Vs which circle the Earth's blue orb (the number eight was fixed by Kovács and Thomas Carlyle back when dozens of fledgling Hives threatened to drown the flag in Vs if they made one V per Hive; our founders never dreamed someday the flock would dwindle to our meager seven). But now the Alliance flag had birthed a sequel, improvised in the heat of pre-war, with seven birdlike Vs flying, not in a ring, but in a flock, like geese, one great V formed of lesser Vs, united. A V of Vs. The first time I saw it I did not have to ask, only marvel at the clarity of the sigil which now flutters over many houses, and in many colors: gray Vs on purple over a Masonic theatre, azure Vs on white over a Cousins' library, red and green Vs on white (plus one Korean blue) over a Mitsubishi farm. Many lintels boast both the Olympic rings and this new V of Vs flag. Anyone can use it, and each who raises the banner can imagine that his own Hive is the leader of the flock, that J.E.D.D. Mason is truly a [insert Hive here] at heart. I weep so often that it must mean little to you by now, but perhaps this moment may move you. There are so many flags. Thousands upon thousands, brave, brave bash'es who have learned of O.S., of the corruption in the CFB, of the Mitsubishi's Canner Device, of Madame, of the Hives' shame, of Romanova's shame, and want change, and trust He who now proposes it, vague as His newborn plan still is. Unite the Hives, the flocking Vs urge. I want a better world badly enough to smash this one to make it, and to risk my life alongside yours, J.E.D.D. Mason, by raising your banner and letting the whole world know I side with you. When the Olympics end, and Sniper's brazen faction rises to strike down both you and the new world you stand for, you will not face them alone.

"Can you answer my question now, Achilles?" Caesar asked as we waited for our summoned cars. "Which side will you take if, after we crush O.S., we fail to make my son accept my terms?"

Achilles sighed, glancing again at silent Aldrin. "You have both the past and the future on your side, MASON."

The Emperor's smile did not feel like Death's now, but like a living man's. "I thought Utopia might be the last thing making you hesitate."

"Second-to-last. You still don't have Mycroft Canner."

Caesar frowned. "Is that really enough to make us enemies?"

Homer's Great Soldier took a long time to answer, "No."

"Achilles!" I cried.

He turned to me. "It's not enough. He's right. I never, ever want to be on the opposite side of a war from you, but I won't fight against everything in this world that makes sense to me. I'm with MASON, even if you aren't."

"But—"

Achilles cut me off. "You love the Masons. You can't pretend you don't. You owe MASON your life and your obedience, and you love Utopia, and owe Utopia the same. But I know you love and owe Jehovah, too. If you don't want this to rip them apart, and rip you and me apart, then you'll have to help us make Jehovah choose the Empire."

"It's not my place to—"

Achilles's glare struck me silent before his words did. "You could talk the riddle out of a sphinx, and you're the one person on this Earth who speaks the private, hybrid language of Jehovah's thoughts. If any creature can do this you can. If Jehovah joins MASON then every cause you serve remains united. If He won't, we shatter. Do it."

"Do it." MASON repeated the command.

"Do it," urged Apollo.

"Do it," Achilles ordered one more time. "The side that has the two of us on it will win, and you know it. Make it a side we can respect."

I could not answer them. I could not answer even myself as duty, hubris, awe, and terror wrestled to stalemate in my mind. In dumb stupor I watched Achilles don the gray *Familiaris* armband. In dumb stupor I watched brave Aldrin and my salt-sweet Saladin go back inside to the captivity of Madame's. In dumb stupor, as we rode toward Alexandria, I endured Caesar's and Achilles's stares.

"Build me jeeps," Achilles said at last, as the capital drew close beneath us.

"What?" Caesar answered.

"Build me jeeps. Build me twenty, no, fifty thousand jeeps."

"You mean the old land cars?"

"You can build jeeps faster than you can breed horses, though horses are good too. We'll also need some sort of fuel, and trucks, sturdy ones that can cope with the fact that you don't have roads anymore."

"The world has moved past land cars. We have better."

"Do you have better that will still work when the world breaks down?"

MASON's brows narrowed. "You think someone will destroy the transit system?"

"If our enemies get control of it, I will. If we do, they will."

A slow nod. "We can develop something autonomous that will still work much better than a land car."

"Good. Do. But it'll take you a month or two to design it, especially if you're not going to ask the Utopians to design it for you. Jeeps, you can get the plans from a museum and start building them tomorrow. Build me fifty thousand jeeps, and when you have something better build me fifty thousand of that, but we'll still use the jeeps, just like we'll use wagons, and horses, and wheelbarrows, and sticks and stones. This is war. Better a spear than a rock, but better a rock than nothing."

MASON took a long breath. "Very well. I'll build jeeps."

"Weapons are a more complicated question. We'll look together at what the history of warfare has to offer that still makes any kind of sense."

We had landed now, and guards and Martin waited with salutes and reports. MASON ignored them. "Anything else?"

Stag-light Achilles leapt down to the waiting stone. "I've found a bull."

"A bull?"

"A fine bull, yearling, fed right, reared close to Parnassus. I'm going to sacrifice it to father Zeus and the other deathless gods, to ask them for victory." The ancient King of the Myrmidons offered Caesar his hand to help him down. "Would you like to join me?"

Emperor he may be, reader, heir to Alexander and Augustus, but there is a modern person beneath the death-black uniform, and that person took some moments to wrap his mind around the notion of actually, in real life, not in metaphor, drawing a knife across a living creature's throat and watching the red blood flow. "Yes," he answered. "Yes, I'd be honored to join you."

It was done, and done well, a satisfying ceremony, as I understood from the new vigor which armored both of them against the next chaotic weeks. I was glad. They are both men who need friends. I did not attend. I could not. I am a parricide. My unclean presence would make the sacrifice unfit, the prayers unheeded. Nothing in any universe can wash the blood of my adopted parents from my hands. These days that fact grows harder to forget.

Some Notes of Martin Guildbreaker
on the Simultaneous Advancement
of Four Investigations
(Abridged and translated from the Latin
by Martin themself.—9A)

Cumulative through June 10, 2454
Events of April, May, and June
Written at Alexandria

OVERALL THOUGHTS (written May 9, 2454):

Prioritizing is impossible when one faces two different tasks, each of which has claim to be the most important problem in the world. I face three.

First, no Mason will know rest until we have justice for the violation of the *Sanctum Sanctorum*. As the *Familiaris* customarily tasked with investigating crimes, and as companion to the *Porphyrogene*, I hold the problem to be my personal responsibility. And the exposure of my own name as *vicarius* of the IMPERIUM MASONICUM, should *dominus* Jehovah delay their ascension, makes the problem more irrevocably mine. Never again will I be able to stroll through empty alleys without a wall of guards between myself and my fellow human beings; nor meet another's eyes and not read in their thoughts: "Martin may someday be Emperor." I support the ancient custom that the throne should generally not pass to a *porphyrogene*, and the wise law which prohibits discussion of the *Imperator Destinatus*. Public knowledge of the succession leads to envy, plots, defamation, sycophancy, murder, and, most dangerous, to the successor knowing they are the successor. As Machiavelli observed, Rome showed, tyrant after tyrant, how those reared in palatine luxury, expecting to be master of the world, basely abused the godlike authority that fell to them unearned, while those promoted through merit—Hadrian, Antoninus Pius, Marcus Aurelius—made judicious use of the *Imperium* of which they considered themselves, not owners, but custodians.

It is not power that corrupts, but the belief that it is yours. I *think* I will never believe that any privilege I enjoy—whether Caesar's trust or the Throne—is *mine*—yet, when I face a mirror now, I see the shadows of Caligula and Commodus, and doubt myself. Do I, tasting IMPERIUM before me, have the strength to still commit myself to making *dominus* Jehovah to take the Throne from me? Or will I forget the purpose which Cornel MASON laid upon me those many years ago, commanding that, while my bas'sibs might pursue the Guildbreakers' customary paths in the Senate and high politics, I would instead dedicate myself to a single more important task: "Make my son a Mason," which I now understand as "Make my son a MASON." I must not fail, but if I do fail, it must not be because I let myself desire the power which never should be mine, more so now that the corrupting knowledge that I might receive it throws my fitness in doubt. I do not doubt *dominus* Jehovah's fitness. They are incorruptible. I know therefore that MASON is right to suspend custom and pass the IMPERIUM to this *Porphyrogene.* But if I did not know *dominus* Jehovah so personally, I too would likely doubt, and in my heart of hearts think hard on the words of Ojiro Cardigan Sniper. This doubt of the successor's fitness, sown in our Empire by these vandals, is food for chaos. And the *Sanctum's* violators have not only harmed the present generation. The past suffers as well, for MASON's vaults contained codices, papyri, tablets in stone and clay, preserved since the births of writing and the Empire; the flammable are ashes now, the enduring scarred. And the future suffers too, for with the *Sanctum's* fall, henceforth, until a stronger age devises one, there is now no safe place in this world. I must bring justice.

But I must find Ojiro Sniper. We sit on a steaming volcano as we trust to Lesley Saneer's impersonations, text announcements, and the excuse that the two-time silver medalist intends to minimize public activity while training for the gold. Any hour someone could pierce the deception, so no hour holds peace. Human Saneer, Senator Quarriman, and Hiveless Mardi Mojave are working on strategies to break the news gently to the public if we despair of recovering Sniper, but even should the public accept it, that would solve only half the problem. *Dominus* Jehovah is only recently reconciled with the cosmic pattern they refer to as their Peer, and to have that pattern snatch Sniper away, and so thwart this great test of human dignity, has sown doubt where doubt must not be.

And a third task presses too. The Universal Free Court at Romanova requests my industry in the investigation of O.S., whose history remains still half opaque. The case must, in a matter of days, be presented to the High Court Tribunal as we enter *terra ignota*. This mandate from a power outside the Empire may seem of least import, but I do not hold it so. What I have read of war suggests that the most devastating mistakes are often made either in war's inception, when the front lines take their shapes, or after the surrender. In the latter case, exaltation and vendetta often have clouded victors' judgments as they laid the architecture of their postwar worlds. When this war ends, all Hives, except perhaps the Cousins, Utopians, or Gordian, will have taken many lives, and we will have no precedent to establish the rights of Hives to kill except the bitter memory of nation-states, and this *terra ignota* of Human Ockham Prospero Saneer, which will naturally discuss the Hive leader whose tool Saneer was, former Humanist President Duke Ganymede Jean-Louis de La Trémoïlle. MASON's Capital Powers derive from Mandate and IMPERIUM far older than Thomas Carlyle and their Hives, but, since the Empire has so long consented to be treated as a Hive by the Alliance, I sympathize with those who argue that the Emperor must either submit to the same rules which bind other Hives' sovereigns, or else surrender the pretense of the Empire being part of the Alliance. If the questions I help the Court ask of La Trémoïlle may, after the war, be asked of my Emperor, then I consider this as weighty a task as I may ever receive.

Yet it is on a fourth mystery that my mind dwells. Who stabbed Mycroft Canner the second time? Instinct and intuition are mere nicknames for conclusions one cannot yet consciously justify, and something in me has concluded that whoever stabbed Mycroft the second time is at the heart of all.

Progress of Investigation:

April 17: The Medical report on Mycroft's injuries confirms a right-handed assailant. The wound was clumsily inflicted, without medical or professional training. The knife was a single-bladed kitchen knife, recently in contact with olive oil and used to cut onions, potatoes, orange bell peppers, and parsley (DNA traceable to a Broadland Model GG700 kitchen tree), as well as sausage. The great boon of a complex meat product, produced, not in a home vat, but by a professional kitchen with limited production, indicates that the user of the knife shopped at one of only three hundred and thirty-six shops, all located in Europe.

April 22: I have found the room where Mycroft was stabbed (in Debrecen, which has eight shops supplying the aforementioned sausage). It still contains the chair Mycroft was tied to, and the residue of Mycroft's blood, with Sniper's footprints in it, along with the footprints of three others identified as close Sniper followers—they will be interviewed but their arrest delayed until after the Olympics. Dominic left no detectable trace in the room, nor did any other.

April 24: I had Mycroft tied in the same way to the same chair in the same room where they received their injuries, and had a series of people of varied heights and builds approach them from behind and bend as if to stab. Mycroft's memory of footsteps and the angle of breath and blade verify that the assailant was between 165 and 174 cm in height and weighed between 90 and 105 kg, though a somewhat smaller person might feign this weight with bulky clothes.

ANALYSIS *(April 28)*: My most valuable clue is the fact that the assailant did not say anything to Mycroft, nor pause to "savor the moment." A killer has no reason to hide their identity from a victim whom death will shortly silence. Many thousands of people want to kill Mycroft Canner out of revenge or hatred, but any of these would want to let the "monster" see the face of the avenger, and watch and lecture as the final moment came. This was, in contrast, a passionless execution, an attacker who wished to delete Mycroft as a [resource/factor], but did not care about the fact that this was the most hated criminal in the world. This rules out Hiveless Mardi Mojave, friends of the Mardi bash' or of Apollo Mojave, the many persons morally agitated by Mycroft's crimes, and any members and supporters of O.S. who might begrudge Mycroft's part in its exposure. It also rules out Dominic, who might have stabbed Mycroft, changed their boots, put on a heavy overcoat, and returned to stab Mycroft again, intending that they survive and pass on a misleading story, but Dominic, who harbors such passionate envy of Mycroft's privileged access to *dominus* Jehovah, would certainly have paused to enjoy the second stab as they enjoyed the first. Even a professional killer would, I expect, pause for reflection while executing Earth's most famous amateur, and the possibility of a hired assassin is more thoroughly eliminated by the knife. A professional might choose such a clumsy and traceable tool in order to seem an amateur, but said professional would never, knowing the handicap presented by a single-bladed weapon, use the knife so clumsily as to inflict the comparatively minor injury which accounts for Mycroft's survival.

The attacker, then, is an amateur at homicide. They do not care about what Mycroft has done (which eliminates a large slice of the human race), but about what they will do, either the history they are writing, or their work for *dominus* Jehovah, the Emperor, etc. The attacker also reached Mycroft faster than Sniper could, whose followers Dominic had intentionally tipped off. Thus the assailant must either have been spying on Mycroft, or on Dominic, or must have had access to Sniper's contacts, and been in a position to arrive faster than Sniper themself. Finally, the assailant was with Mycroft minutes before Mycroft's contact with Sniper, on the same day Sniper disappeared. The assailant may well have continued to spy on Mycroft when Mycroft was with Sniper and Tully Mardi. It is therefore possible, though far from certain, that this assailant either authored, or at least witnessed, Sniper's fate.

I will therefore set a series of traps.

Mycroft is my bait—having lured the attacker once, they may again. Since Mycroft's degenerating mental condition necessitates intervals of enforced rest, I can easily arrange for said rest to take place in seemingly vulnerable situations, for example letting Mycroft roam through a fenced section of olive groves without visible guards, or taking them to a beach house where I can arrange a power outage. This bait may flush out my attacker.

May 10: First trap. Isolated Mycroft on a farm. Informed no one. No sign of any attempt to kill or kidnap.

May 11: Second trap. Released Mycroft in chaotic Alexandrian shopping district. Informed no one. No sign of any attempt to kill or kidnap.

May 12: Third trap. Released Mycroft in Alba Longa gardens, where they grew up. Informed no one. False positive when Mycroft dropped off surveillance, but it turned out to be a resurgence of Mycroft's 'younger self' or 'beast' aspect. Recapture was comparatively smooth, and a good opportunity to test the remote tranquilizer robot. No sign of any attempt to kill or kidnap.

ANALYSIS *(May 12):* I conclude that our assailant is probably not spying directly on Mycroft. This had seemed unlikely anyway, since, when the original attack took place, Dominic had taken Mycroft beyond the reach of the Emperor and the Commissioner General, so anyone who might still have been tracking Mycroft must have had access to unknown technology, or magic.

Magic is opened as a possibility by Mycroft's reference to a 'crystal ball' employed by Bridger in the rescue of Lt. Patroclus Aimer. This artifact, if it exists, must be in the possession either of Achilles Mojave or the Utopians—not reasonable suspects. [I have asked Achilles whether the artifact exists and, if so, whether I might use it in my investigation. They have not yet answered.]

My next traps will be for anyone who might be spying on Dominic (we may posit a traitor among Dominic's subordinates from Madame's, among their associates at the Sensayers' Conclave, or among the Mitsubishi). But this step must wait, since tomorrow is the day mandated by the Romanovan Senate for the Cousins, Mitsubishi, Humanists, and European Union to present their proposals for self-reform. Neither Dominic nor anyone spying upon them can be expected to pay attention to anything else for the next days.

*　*　*

This is Mycroft, reader. I must interrupt Martin to present May the thirteenth, that dawn of bated breath when a strangely quiet Senate watched the delegations come, much as the crew of a stranded ship, spotting white sails on the horizon, peers and prays as they wait for the stranger-vessel to inch close enough for the flag to show whether she brings salvation or death. Few mobs assembled, thanks to Papa's diligence in what Censor Su-Hyeon still pretended was not martial law. Bash'es watched this crisis in their hushed living rooms, students in their dorms. Students felt the fear most, as the campuses, which should be—must be, for pity's sake!—unspotted oases of self-creation were suddenly pierced by the elder generation's failure. Can you hear it, reader? The tenuous thunder of their heartbeats? As the colleges and craft-schools which cluster on each campus stand empty, and cafeterias, which should be lively with talk of sport, flirting, and fiction, lie fear-locked and mute? In common rooms, clutches of friends and roommates, just congealing into nascent bash'es, watch the Senate vid-feed, and learn to fear the Adulthood Competency Exam. Why fear? Because, reader, when this bright new generation earns the right to shed their minor's sashes, they should have ten paths before them: seven Hives, three Laws. But, after today, which options will remain of that palette of brave, alluring paths that you, our elders, promised us—a palette you now change?

The Cousins' draft did not disband the CFB. Instead it garlanded it with compromise. In their proposal, the Transitional Congress created by Jehovah's interim constitution would become a permanent Parliament, letting the Cousins join Europe and the Humanists in aping the geographic nations' old faith in the tyranny of voters. Kosala and Jehovah had managed to preserve the Cousins' infinite suggestion box, but it would henceforth be processed by topical committees specializing in different issues: education, sanitation, entertainment, whose recommendations would be passed on to the Parliament as well as to the Board. This left the whole Hive much more a generic government, and much less like itself. One could smell political parties forming too, as Lorelei Cook strided beside Bryar Kosala across the Senate floor, receiving approving applause from the sixteen out of the thirty-nine Cousin Senators who wore the brightly colored mismatched socks which symbolize the unstructured childhood Cook's "Nurturists" paint as the antithesis of the set-set process. Cook's proud, predatory stride made she and Kosala seem dangerously like co-Chairs. Heloïse was Kosala's antidote, Heloïse who trotted behind the Chair, angelic in a wrap of baby blue, and such the darling of the media that, these days, she almost fills the gap left by Sniper and fallen Ganymede. Kosala used her perfectly. Nurturist ringleader Lorelei Cook had traded much to get Kosala to agree to let it be Cookie, not Kosala, who set the reform draft in Speaker Jin Im-Jin's hands, but few noticed the gesture, since what eye or camera would linger on Kosala's rival when we had a real princess to feast upon?

With Apollo as my witness, I swear that acting Chief Director Dominic Seneschal wore, as he marched down the aisle, a full Mitsubishi suit, black with a motif of summer maple leaves in white and red, and not a hint of his usual French finery. The bloated crate of papers which passed for the Mitsubishi reform draft addressed such tangled minutiae of their corporate bylaws that a full day with Censor Su-Hyeon and Kohaku Mardi has not helped me unravel their import. Each Member, or 'shareholder' as Mitsubishi documents term them, will, as before, receive one 'share' (vote) for existing and another for each unit of property, small properties providing a single vote and vast estates vast power. As before, minor shareholders will commit their votes to Managers (who must receive minimum of 1,000 votes to qualify), who in turn commit theirs to Electors (minimum 100,000 votes), who commit theirs to Executives (10,000,000 votes). Among these last, the nine who command the most votes (over a billion each) become Executive Directors, with the Chief Director's throne (desk) passing to that supreme powerbroker who manages the most. What are the changes, then, if all this stays the same? The draft affects, among other things, the ratio of property to votes, the relative vote-value of different kinds of property, and the standardized exams which qualify Mitsubishi members for the Manager, Elector, and Executive tracks. Such changes to the minutest texture of the Hive might, like a field transformed from clay to black earth, yield wondrous new crops, or it might produce the same thorned weeds that birthed the Canner Device. I do not know how to predict which, nor does a nervous Romanova.

The ancient European Union is as accustomed to self-reform as a maple to dropping its leaves, but this was different. This named an Emperor, modeled on the MASONS, to "approve but not appoint" the popularly elected Prime Minister, and to "stand above" the European Parliament, Council, and Commission "as their guide, governor, and conscience." All the old institutions would continue: the European Council composed of the heads of member nation-strats, the European Commission elected one from each member nation-strat, the Members of Parliament elected proportionally from European Members, and the Prime Minister shepherding the cats. Even Europe's signature idiosyncrasy survived, the policy that all nation-strat Members may vote for their Commissioner and MPs, even non-Europeans, so Blacklaw Chagatai can have her say in who should represent Mongolia, Achilles in our dear Greece, and France receives votes from Humans Ganymede and Ancelet, Mitsubishi Danaë, Utopian Voltaire, even the Blacklaws at Madame's. The creation of a European Emperor was the only real change, proof that, when burned, human habit still trusts the legends of Augustus and Charlemagne over democracy. To this new throne, a more modest proposal might have nominated Isabel Carlos de Borbón, and some modern method for selecting his successor. Instead the draft named "the Bourbon Royal House of Spain," one line, unlimited, forever. Those who remembered the Spanish dynasty's generations of ceaseless and heroic public service cheered. Those who, like Martin, thought of Caligula and Commodus shuddered. Those who thought of not-yet-officially Crown Prince J.E.D.D. Mason armed for war.

Humanist President Vivien Ancelet braved the Senate floor last and alone. "This is not a reform proposal," he declared as he placed on the Speaker's desk a sleek white packet, with the Humanist flag bright upon it, the six Olympic rings each paired with one flying V. "It is a defense of the current Humanist Constitution, which I and my fellows on the reform committee believe to be the best and soundest form of government ever created by the human species. As this report makes plain, there is no unsoundness at the heart of the Humanists. Rather an unsoundness in the times drove my predecessors to respond. If O.S. was an extreme means, it was not chosen selfishly. Those who used O.S. used it to preserve this age of peace and prosperity. I agree that O.S. and those who used it must now answer to Romanova's law, but the Hive itself is not flawed for electing leaders who were so faithful to their mandate that they were willing to take painful steps to preserve World Peace. We all hope to move beyond depending on O.S., but, as we strive to do so, we should not throw away the proven stability and flexibility of the Humanist Constitution, we should instead fall back on it. This is not the moment to rashly reject the one institution which has done the most to protect the best age yet forged by humankind. It is the moment to use that institution as we forge a better one."

Screams across the House demanded that the Humanists be expelled from the Alliance at once for defying the Senate's order to reform, and that Ancelet stand trial with Prospero and Ganymede for "murders they condoned." Speaker Jin Im-Jin, in his authority as Grandpa, made everyone shut up. "A proposal of no change is still a proposal. We will consider it as seriously as the others, and thank Human Ancelet for presenting it so articulately." Jin then browbeat the Senate into voting to cool its heels a while, while experts evaluated the four proposals' viability. If the Senate judges the changes sufficient to make these four unstable Hives stable again then all is well; if any proposal is rejected, then we will learn what happens when the Alliance declares a member Hive a danger to the human race, Nature, and the Produce of Civilization.

And what about our students on their fear-hushed campuses, still facing their choice? The Cousins now feel much less unique. The Humanist refusal to reform feels like a heretic's last refusal to recant before sentence is passed. The Mitsubishi too may evaporate, since there is no guarantee Romanova will accept their boggling and opaque proposal. Europe's bulwark has been heritage, and the comfort of self-identity, which its nation-strats provide: "I am Irish," "I am Canadian," "I am Greek, and love the special sense of homecoming when I sit down to a meal with those who speak my tongue, and bake the bread my ba'pas baked. I want my nation-strat, my people, to have a voice in my Hive, and its laws which bind me." Yet now the young Greek or Canadian hears that the European Council, and his Strat President within it, suddenly want to answer to the King of Spain? Uncomfortable. They are all uncomfortable now, these greater hives: the Cousins, Mitsubishi, Humanists, Europe, even the Masons with wrathful Death now at their helm. As for the minor Hives, Gordian, though safe and stable, is intimidating to those not raised Brillist. Utopia? One does not, when all paths seem steep, plunge lightly into thorny wilds. All Hives have oaths of allegiance, reader, but only one names such a frightening sacrifice:

> I hereby renounce the right to complacency, and vow lifelong to take only what minimum of leisure is necessary to my productivity, viewing health, happiness, rest, and play as means, not ends, and that, while Utopia provides my needs, I will commit the full produce of my labors to our collective effort to redirect the path of human life away from death and toward the stars.

Even if Utopia defines its project so broadly that anything from a thrift shop to a life-affirming romance novel is considered a contribution to the human engine, and even if it recognizes the mind's need for rest and play and lets its members carve out ample leisure hours, still, those who do not feel the true vocation wisely shy away from that yoke of self-directed servitude which follows the pledge: my days do not belong to me, but to the future. All seven, then, are fearsome paths. I tell you this, reader: across the Earth on a thousand campuses that day, the students learned at last why, at seventeen, raised in a bash' that saw this crisis looming, I chose to face my rampage and my execution rather than choose a Hive.

* * *

May 18: Fourth trap. Moved Mycroft in a defective car which made a planned emergency landing in an isolated spot outside Esbjerg. Let Dominic's Mitsubishi secretaries hear me discuss the emergency over my tracker. No sign of any attempt to kill or kidnap.

May 22: Fifth trap. Arranged a power outage to strand Mycroft in office while they were interviewing Masami Mitsubishi. Can confirm that Masami covertly informed Toshi Mitsubishi and Yuki Ōoka (former personal assistant to Chief Director Hotaka Andō Mitsubishi). [Must remember to investigate Andō's lines of communication while they are in custody.] No sign of any attempt to kill or kidnap.

May 23: Evidence that Sniper is alive. On April 23rd (nine days after Sniper's disappearance but well before we knew of it), Mycroft Canner sent a written request to O.S. specifying details for the chapter Sniper was to write for their history, which was supposed to describe what happened to Sniper during the hours they went missing on March 27th. Now, one month later, the requested chapter has appeared. It was sent to Lesley Saneer through what they described as "one of several secure channels used by O.S."

The chapter details a rather bizarre encounter involving Sniper being kidnapped by Dominic and Conclave Head Julia Doria-Pamphili. Doria-Pamphili denies all knowledge of the incident, but Dominic has, in confidence, hinted that the narrative is approximately accurate. Sniper's chapter contains no hint of cypher or secret messages. Linguistic analysis suggests that much of the prose is likely Sniper's, though key paragraphs have been heavily edited by another party. Unfortunately, the writing samples are not long enough to identify said interfering party from syntax alone.

ANALYSIS *(May 24)*: If Sniper's chapter is real, the fact that it was edited suggests that Sniper is being held prisoner by some party or parties who permitted them to write the chapter, but censored it to remove hints about Sniper's present circumstances. This makes kidnapping definitively more likely than the other possibilities, i.e. that Sniper is dead, has been injured and trapped somewhere, or has vanished for their own reasons. If such a captor exists, the fact that they received Mycroft's request that Sniper write the chapter implies privileged access, either to O.S., to Papadelias's office which transmitted Mycroft's message, or to Mycroft. I am completely unable to guess the motives of a captor who respects the human species enough to release Sniper's chapter, and thus facilitate *dominus* Jehovah's attempts to disseminate the truth, yet who still holds Sniper prisoner despite the threat of global catastrophe. Similarly, it seems wildly irrational that anyone would try to kill Mycroft, but then facilitate the completion of their book by releasing Sniper's chapter. I must face the growing probability that Mycroft's assailant is not the person holding Sniper, though the assailant may still have witnessed something.

ANALYSIS *(May 25)*: I can now eliminate the possibility that Dominic and Julia Doria-Pamphili have kidnapped Sniper a second time. I had to consider it, even though, if they were involved, they would be unlikely to release a chapter incriminating themselves in the earlier kidnapping. But all possibilities are worth considering, so I approached Dominic. It is clear from Dominic's passionate reaction that, if they did have Sniper, they would have killed Sniper and brought the corpse as an offering to *dominus* Jehovah. They would certainly not have left Sniper in a fit state to write a chapter. In fact, Dominic was so enraged by the suggestion that Julia might have caught Sniper and not delivered the "blasphemer" to Dominic for punishment that they immediately joined my investigation, contributing their usual efficacious vigor. Papadelias has been tracking Doria-Pamphili meticulously since their release on bail, and has uninterrupted surveillance sufficient to account for every minute of Doria-Pamphili's activities throughout the period in question. Papadelias also facilitated a fresh search of all Doria-Pamphili's residences and offices, which confirmed that Doria-Pamphili is a Sniper fan and Lifedoll collector, but uncovered nothing else of relevance. As an additional test, I asked Dominic about the paralysis technique used for Julia and Sniper's earlier liaison. It was developed at Madame's, and apparently Madame had several clients who enjoyed its use. In order to maintain a monopoly, Madame trained only four "Dollmakers" to implement it, and watched all carefully (Madame punishes breaches of professional secrecy as only Blacklaws may). I interviewed all four, then Dominic interviewed them rather more rigorously, and both Madame and Papadelias can account for their activities.

May 27: Sixth trap. Sent Mycroft to wrong address for sensayer appointment. Complained to Conclave members and staff. No sign of any attempt to kill or kidnap.

May 29: Seventh trap. Let Mycroft go see the Olympic Torch pass in Munich. Let plan slip to Chevalier. Dominic called to inform MASON that whoever was in charge of Mycroft's security had made several recent lapses, and we should "keep the stray on a better leash."

ANALYSIS *(May 30):* If there are any spies around Dominic, they are spying for Dominic, not on them. This comes as no surprise. The Mitsubishi would have sent a professional killer, and anyone else likely to spy on Dominic would know Dominic well enough to realize they will brutally murder anyone who interferes with Mycroft, or their pursuit of Sniper. The hand that stabbed Mycroft the second time had neither unsteadiness nor hyper-resolution, the two characteristics of someone who knows they are condemning themselves to a painful death. The only associate of Dominic's who is currently in the right emotional state to accept such a painful death without either confidence or trepidation is Blacklaw Carlyle Foster. Though a little small for our physical profile, Foster had their tracker switched off during the incident (and often does, common for Dominic's associates). Foster was, as I understand, trained in spy-work by both Commissioner General Papadelias and Julia Doria-Pamphili, and is certainly an amateur at murder and timid enough to strike so impotent a blow, but lacks motive, both for killing Mycroft and for holding Sniper.

June 1: For lack of a more direct test, I suggested the possibility of Foster's guilt to Headmaster Faust. Faust laughed. Note: Faust believes Sniper's chapter is mostly genuine.

ANALYSIS *(June 1):* The failure of all these tests, along with the release of Sniper's chapter, has convinced me of the probability of a traitor-spy (or more than one?) within O.S., or at least within the ranks of Sniper's trusted supporters. When Dominic originally kidnapped Mycroft, they informed Sniper by tipping off several fans and doll factory staff in different parts of the world. Word of this might easily have reached Sniper's subordinates before it reached Sniper themself, giving a traitor the opportunity to reach Mycroft first. A traitor in the inner circle of Sniper's faction might well desire Sniper's removal. Such a traitor might also desire Mycroft's death, because Mycroft is a resource for our side, or because the completion of Mycroft's history could threaten the traitor's agenda. How a traitor might benefit from releasing Sniper's chapter I cannot yet say. I would like to set traps for this traitor as I did for other kinds of spies, but it is not easy to plausibly release Mycroft's location to the enemy. Confident that Lesley Saneer is clearly not working against Sniper, and is too physically small to be Mycroft's assailant, I eliminated them as a suspect, and informed them of my suspicions on June 3rd:

Saneer: "And, so you can hunt this theoretical traitor, you want me to give you access to the inner workings of my side? My closest allies?"
Guildbreaker: "Want, yes; expect, no. Your caution is justified."
Saneer: "Then what do you expect?"
Guildbreaker: "Just tell me if there is anyone in your inner circle who doesn't care very much, one way or the other, about Mycroft Canner."
Saneer: "About Mycroft?"
Guildbreaker: "Most people in the world feel strongly about Mycroft Canner. Is there anyone who doesn't? Your Typer twin? Your set-set? Someone new you've brought into your circle? Someone Tully Mardi brought in?"
Saneer: "Not that I can . . . think of. No. Everyone has an opinion of Mycroft."

I will note that Saneer paused. They paused before responding, and in the middle, and afterwards bit their lower lip. There is someone new in Sniper's inner circle. Possibly several people. Definitely someone specific whom Lesley Saneer distrusts enough to fear betrayal. I will devise a [test/trap] for this suspect. Meanwhile, I have sown doubt in Lesley Saneer's mind. If I am right, Saneer will perhaps expose the traitor on their own, and liberate Sniper. If I am wrong, then at least the distrust I have instilled will weaken the enemy. I have no reservations about using such tactics. The Empire is in danger.

As for my investigation of the violation of our *Sanctum Sanctorum* . . .

SECTION DELETED
DICTUM ABSOLUTUM——MMCDLIV: lxiii
DAMNATIO MEMORIAE

. . . I made progress. I focused on the detail that the attack took place when not only *dominus* Jehovah but the Emperor and their intimates, including Mycroft Canner and myself, were safely absent from the tower. All else is condemned to silence.

ANALYSIS (*June 10*): Sniper has now been missing fifty-seven days. Despite the hope offered by the appearance of their chapter, I grow pessimistic about the chances that, if I do find them, they will be in a fit state (psychological or physical) to control their faction. My next move must be to identify this untrustworthy new ally of O.S. who may be the culprit. Since Lesley Saneer will not reveal the names of their collaborators, I will use other means to identify those likely to have entered Sniper's circle. But this must wait. In five days begins the *terra ignota* of Ockham Prospero Saneer. Even Sniper, on whose fate hang both this Olympic truce and *dominus* Jehovah's Great Conversation, must wait while I shape the precedent by which humanity will someday judge my Emperor, their *Imperator Destinatus*, and myself.

—*Mycroft "Martin" Guildbreaker*, Vicarius Familiarisque

The Witch

Written August 16, 2454
Event of June 14
Herstedvester Compound

Thisbe: "Finally! You're nearly late enough to make me lose my bet."
I: "Hello, Thisbe. Are they treating you well?"
Thisbe: "You're not. Six weeks without a visit? Unforgivable."
I: "I haven't needed—"
Thisbe: "At least tell me you've brought me a change of clothes. I'm not going out in these."

Thisbe Saneer stretched back in her seat, and lifted her slippered foot so I could see it over the waist-high frame of the visiting window. Prison might have stolen her silky suits and preferred shampoos, but it had no power over the curve of her calf, or the elusive slice of ankle, usually hidden by her boots. The interrogation room's harsh lighting showed the emptiness of her side of the glass dividing wall, a sterile room, a chair, a table, a paper cup of tea, while my side—my side was crowded with smoke-and-cancer prison specters, which pooled behind me, using my flesh as cover as they swarmed to flee the witch.

"Going out?" I repeated.

Her sharp glance made the specters cringe. "Don't tell me we're not leaving yet. The wait has been beyond intolerable. I know you could've sprung me before this, and I'm not interested in excuses, I'm interested in getting back to work."

"Sprung you?" I repeated.

"I hear you sprang Ganymede ages ago. I'd have enjoyed a month in a royal resort in Spain too."

"I'm not—"

"I know you're the agent, not the architect. It's been fun guessing who it would be, really, there are so many options: Madame, the old president, the new president, the Emperor, the Major. I've been in as much suspense as boredom."

"Suspense?" I asked. "As to . . . ?"

"As to who would recruit me first. So many must be tempted. I'm sure you and Papadelias have shown everyone my portfolio by now."

"Portfolio," I whispered back.

She smirked. "But it's rude making me wait this long. I know you have Sidney and the captured Typer twin already beavering away, and Ockham's doing such fine work with Ancelet, but I've been bored out of my wits waiting. Who sent you, then? Don't string out the suspense."

"Thisbe, I'm only here to ask you to read over these chapters I've written describing how you first met Carlyle, and how you went to Chagatai's, and then Madame's."

A stark stare. "Are we being listened to?" she mouthed.

"Possibly," I replied aloud, "but not by any enemy that I know of."

"Come, Mycroft. We both know I'm too delicious a resource for selfish powers to leave alone this long. Well? Don't just sit staring. What really brought you here?"

"I'm writing this history, of the week of transformation when . . ."

She shook her head. "I know lies, Mycroft. And I know you."

"I . . . actually I did want to ask your advice on something. We have a . . . very large problem, actually. I assume you know about any allies your bash'mates might have or make, and the truth is that Sniper is . . ."

"Oooh, Cardie . . . Cardie is a fun little challenge."

I didn't like her tone. I didn't like her smile, how her fingers twitched within the folds of her black hair, as toes might among controls concealed in boots. There was an edge of murder in her fidgeting, as when a braggart thug plays with his knife, or Saladin with a bone. "No, never mind," I said. "I don't think you'd actually help."

"You want to fight O.S.?" she asked, leaning forward. "Or help O.S.? Or catch Cardie? Or save Cardie? Or break Cardie? You know what I can do. I'm eager to do it again." Her eyes narrowed.

I felt mine narrow too. "Yes, I know," I answered. "Everyone knows how you work now, what you enjoy. That's why you're still here."

"Too many of them, fighting over which gets to have my arts?"

I shook my head.

"Then what?"

"No one's talking about you. Until I thought you might help with this

Sniper business, no one had brought up your name in . . . I haven't bothered to keep track."

She gave a blood-warm smile. "Mycroft, if you're trying to scare me, and make me desperate, to better your boss's bargaining position by making me think that no one's coming for me, it won't work. The attempt demeans us both."

"No one's coming for you," I said flatly.

"They've already gone to the trouble of arranging for Ockham to go to trial alone, so I can stay out of the public eye, and slip into the shadows when it's time to return to my . . . vocation. But I won't do it for just anyone. I'm not going to be a patriotic stickler like Cardie and say I'm only working for Humanists, but I really am the best assassin in the world, so I get to be choosy."

"The best in the world!" I heard affront in my own voice as I said it, but was not quite sure on whose behalf I took offense. Sniper's? Prospero's? Saladin's? My own? She did not know me at all, did she, this self-important witch? I was the reawakened beast, freed by Jehovah's discovery that Gods' universes do not die if They do, freed to prowl and prey again as she had never seen in our decade-long feigned friendship. Can't she tell? The prison spirits that feeding on my ankles grow fat with lust and malice, yet the witch, who should drink and breathe malice, she can't even tell that I have changed?

"Well, I'm certainly in the top three." She thought she was giving real ground there, didn't she? Vile, hubristic thing! "You must grant me that," she continued. "But I've no patience with those who make it obvious that murder has been done, and I'm very disappointed in Cardie for joining you in that category."

What is that noise? A rhythmic shift of air somewhere close by. Am I laughing? "No one's coming for you, Thisbe."

"Very funny."

"No one's coming for you ever. No one wants you."

"This is childish."

"No one wants you, Thisbe. They want Ockham Prospero Saneer. The trial starts tomorrow but there've been crowds camped around the courthouse for days. They want Sniper, the world's turned upside down for Sniper, because Sniper's a noble creature, and Prospero's a noble creature. They're all noble creatures, Thisbe, except you, you're a . . ."

Her eyes dared me to finish.

"You're a tick."

She snorted. "A tick? That's the best you have?"

"You're a tick, Thisbe," I spat it this time, spat it like a curse. "A tick, and you feed, and you bloat, and you crawl, and you think it makes you something poetic and exciting, like a vampire, and you're so wrong."

She threw her head back into laughter. "Says the cannibal."

"You can't see, can you? How wrong you are?"

Again her warm, slow smile. "Are you going to make me see? Come on, then? Make me, Mycroft Canner. Make meeeeEEEEEEAAAAAAA!"

There she screams, the proud witch. I can see her through the newborn darkness as the savaged lamp-wires above me bleed their white-hot sparks. Do you see her, reader? Frozen like a rabbit on the floor, where she fell in her terror. I see her. She knows it. Shall I let her see me, through the dark I made? There, witch. Have a glimpse of my arm, and the javelin in it, with the entrails of the ceiling light still knotted 'round. Will you realize my weapon was, moments ago, a chair leg? Or will you think I sprout blades when I will them, or that I keep them hidden in my flesh and draw them from under old scars when the hunt is ripe? Oh, you fumble with your own chair now, as the spark-shower wanes and the blackness that surrounds us both becomes perfect. Do you want a weapon? Do you fear I might pierce that glass and reach your side of our divided cage? Useless. These prison chairs are welded metal; you need to know just where the weak points are, and how to twist, to snap a sharp leg free. The darkness is complete now, the spark shower gone, but I still hear you panting on the far side of the glass. I know you're listening, but I let you hear nothing. Ask yourself, as your breath speeds, which one of us is hunter in the dark, and which is prey? One tardy spark lets me see you again. There. Those are eyes that realize this is my domain. If you only knew how much. I know this compound, Thisbe. I studied every wall and wire. This is the facility where they would have held me, if I'd been captured early with my work undone, stray Mardis still at large. I had to be ready to escape. And the interrogator's side of these rooms is so much more vulnerable. Here! Let this crunch and echo thrill you, one stab in the wall two hand spans left of the window to take out the junction box, then I count one, two, three, four, five hands down and stab again—*crunch*—*echo*. Three more stabs, Thisbe, is all I'll need to rip the belly from this wall and be in there with you. Your portfolio? How dare you think yourself an artist? How dare you place your idle hobby on a nobler level than works of heroes? Loyal Prospero, brave Sniper, and Mycroft Canner! You dare compare yourself to Mycroft Canner? *Stab*—*crunch*—*echo*. Do you smell me now, through the wall's wounds? I smell you. I don't smell urine yet, or vomit, but I smell your fear sweat, Thisbe, reeking sour salt, and I smell you. How well I know your smell, that was so often near the Major and his men, near Bridger. Bridger.

Bridger's gone.

Martin and Papadelias with four Utopians escorted me with some haste back to Alexandria. It was judged best that I not visit Thisbe anymore.

The Witch Again

Written August 16, 2454
Event of June 14
Herstedvester Compound

Thisbe: "Are you so official now that you have clearance to visit prisons? How times change."

Achilles: "You used it on Mycroft Canner!"

Thisbe: "No 'Hello'?"

Achilles: "You manage to smuggle in one capsule of your psycho perfume and you use it on Mycroft Canner?"

Thisbe: "No one else came by. And you must admit it was a glorious audition."

Achilles: "Audition?"

Thisbe: "It took you, what, three hours to get here? And I'm sure you're the first of many. Everyone in the world worth working for will have heard by now."

Achilles: "You did it to get attention?"

Thisbe: "I've been here nearly three months, and haven't seen a soul apart from crawling little interrogators. I hadn't figured Guildbreaker and Papadelias for such cowards, and you can tell them from me that, if they want my services, they have a lot to make up for."

Achilles: "Consequences, Thisbe. Actions have consequences. How could you do that to Mycroft of all people? You know he's hallucinating half the time already. This could snap the thread!"

Thisbe: "Making me wait has consequences."

Achilles: "Too hard for you, is it? Tasting the bitter grind of patience? You're asking the wrong man, Thisbe, if you want pity. Come to me when you've waited years, when you've had to watch your comrades drop and die!"

Thisbe: "That isn't funny. Come on, who sent you?"

Achilles: "Rage."

Thisbe: "Is that a hint? Should I be guessing?"

Achilles: "No one sent me. I came on my own, to face you, to give you a chance to answer, just in case there was some justification for what you did to Mycroft."

Thisbe: "I told you, I've been neglected. I had no better way to get attention."

Achilles: "I respected you, when I heard you'd stayed and let them catch you so you could help Papadelias protect Bridger. I thought you did a brave thing, sacrificing O.S. and liberty, but you didn't think you were sacrificing anything, did you? You thought some power would snatch you up, since you're so valuable."

Thisbe: "I presume you know by now what I can do."

Achilles: "I know."

Thisbe: "I won't be unreasonable about sides. I realize at this point I have to give up helping O.S., but I'm willing. I'm not as stubborn as Ockham and Cardie. I recognize things need to change. O.S. can't work anymore, not as it was. A new order is shaping up. I'm prepared to help lubricate the transition, for whoever is far-seeing enough to realize what my special arts can do to a riot, or a battlefield."

Achilles: "No one's coming for you, ever. You know why?"

Thisbe: "Pray tell."

Achilles: "You're evil."

Thisbe: "You must be kidding."

Achilles: "Murder has consequences, Thisbe, the unnatural betrayal and murder of your lover, of three lovers!"

Thisbe: "Unnat—"

Achilles: "No semantics. I know what terrible acts are forced on men by desperation and the will of Fate, and what terrible acts we bring into the world ourselves. You kill people because you enjoy killing people."

Thisbe: "And Mycroft doesn't? You don't?"

Achilles: "Not in cold blood. You risked exposing O.S., and blackmailed your own bash' into letting you get away with murder, because you enjoy pushing people to suicide, just for selfish fun. No one wants that, Thisbe. No one wants you. No one will ever want you. The trial starts tomorrow, Prospero's trial, the great trial that will test the mettle of all these leaders and Hives and peoples, and you won't be there because you're not worthy of it. I've talked to Papadelias. You're not going to be tried for being part of O.S. You're going to be tried for the murders of Luca Cormor, Quinn Prichard, and Alex Limner—your lovers, Thisbe, whom you drove to their deaths for nothing!"

Thisbe: "My portfolio. I'm the only one in the bash' who has one of my own. Even Ockham just has their government commissions, but I took the initiative."

Achilles: "Would you have tried it on me? If I weren't immune since I never watch movies. Did it bother you, having someone in your life you couldn't play like a puppet? Or did you comfort yourself thinking that you could crush me between finger and thumb, like the bug you seem to think all other human beings are?"

Thisbe: "I've hurt you. It wasn't like that, Major, not between us. What we had was—"

Achilles: "You are nothing to me, Thisbe! You love nothing and you honor nothing."

Thisbe: "You won't get better terms by throwing a tantrum. I know from your face you're thinking about what my craft could do on a riot field. Do you want me to fix Mycroft? Consider it done. Shall I fix Carlyle Foster? Fix the Senate? Anyone? Mycroft started to ask me for help with something involving Cardigan. I can do it. I don't know what it was, but I can do it."

Achilles: "Sniper . . ."

Thisbe: "Yes?"

Achilles: "Nothing. I want nothing from you, and neither does Sniper or anyone. You're a traitor, Thisbe. You betrayed O.S., and human dignity, and all of us, this whole, beautiful world that you apparently don't care about, you've treated it like garbage, and now you think we'll invite you back to gloat in your comfy armchair like some leisure-bloated queen, spraying your potions while the rest of us sweat and fight it out with honest arms? Well, now you reap the consequences. Now Fate's going to grind on without you, and if this war makes a thousand names immortal, yours won't be one of them. Even if you could help, I'll never beg you. I'd rather face a man bare-handed than with some coward's poison knife, and so would Sniper!"

Chapter the EIGHTEENTH

Terra Ignota

Written August 17–18, 2454
Events of June 15–July 15
Written at Alexandria

"HUMAN OCKHAM PROSPERO SANEER, YOU MAY NOW CHOOSE THE Hive membership of two of the three judges who will oversee your case, or, if you prefer, you may request Hiveless judges. Be advised that, because of the coindictment of all Humanists in the Wish List conspiracy, you cannot choose a Humanist, nor can the Prosecution when they select the third judge."

This was the first of the many crises which burst from the trial like Zeus's lightning from a churning storm. It was impossible to say whether any given blast would scar only a small patch of Earth, or spark a wildfire to ravage the tender slopes of peace. My madness, worsened by Thisbe's 'audition,' kept me tethered in MASON's custody through these weeks, where I worked to finish my history. When I could, I watched the newsfeed, but most of the trial I experienced in jolts, bald summaries as each fresh shock reached Alexandria.

Prospero was beautiful that first day, that first week, the second week, the third, as balanced and statue-steady as when he had stood master in his own house. "I request a Mason and a Graylaw Hiveless. Let my trial begin."

"Perfect." Apollo's voice was gentle, his awe-hushed syllables vanishing into the soft walls of my cell as shadows fade into an overcast day. He lay some moments more in silence, stretched on his back with his feet against the floor-length window, so the Masonic capital spread sideways at his feet like a metropolis dreamed by those gulls that nest on cliff walls. "Perfect."

It was not the common reaction. By then the words 'He chose a Mason!' were ricocheting like shrapnel through the streets outside, and within minutes media speculators would weave conspiracy out of it: Was Ockham threatened? Blackmailed? Bribed? No one could believe O.S.—or any defendant!—would willingly choose the Hive that always handed down the harshest sentences. Offered any member of the family, would you choose severe Father over a manipulable sibling or doting uncle, or the kindly fall-back Mom? So famous is the Cousins' tendency to sympathize with all, and to think of sentences as rehabilitation more than retribution, that it is a rare day when any defendant chooses anything but a Hivefellow and a Cousin. But a Mason? The mob outside reels, baffled. Are you baffled, reader?

Reader: *"Insult me not, Mycroft. It is easy enough to see why the former O.S. would choose the Hive that already believes its leader has the authority to kill."*
Hobbes: "Quite so. Your Empire will commit hypocrisy, Mycroft, if this Mason dares argue that President Ganymede had not Capital Powers when he defended his Leviathan in Time of . . ."
Reader: *"It was not wartime, Thomas. Not in the years O.S. was working."*
Hobbes: "Friend reader, Leviathans are wild humans made macrocosmic, so all Leviathans live in a state of constant War: the war for resources, for land, for subjects. President Ganymede did not trust Civilization's pledge to keep the Peace between Leviathans, no more than does MASON, or any who has sat beneath the sword of Damocles."

Apologies. I had forgotten that the reader now has so expert a companion. Apollo too knows Hobbes well, but most in my era never learned to think so bloodily, so could not see how Prospero's choice here put the Empire on trial too.

"Don't relax yet, Mycroft," keen Apollo warned. "The prosecutor could still choose Utopia."

"Never," I told him, and myself. "Over so many berserking Cousins and Brillists?"

"It would make the trial much more just. Three Hives on trial for killing members of another three. With six compromised, the seventh should be a judge."

"Utopia must keep its hands clean."

"They aren't clean." Apollo said it so serenely, without passion, without emphasis even on the fact that there was no emphasis, a turning point so far behind him that he no longer wasted time remembering the sting.

"But they must seem clean!"

He rolled over so he could face me on his elbows, the coat turning his outline into a hole in MASON's palace, smoking rubble. "Mycroft, I know what chapter you—"

"They're announcing it! The third judge!"

We both held our breath as the feed relayed the prosecution's choice: Gordian. The word warmed me like winter tea. "Providence wants you out of the limelight."

Apollo blinked, his eyes resetting to their calm blue keenness—or was it the vizor that reset them? "I know what chapter you're avoiding."

Guilt drove my gaze as far from my writing desk as possible. "I should see who the judges are."

"Mycroft . . ."

"Did you see Heloïse's report? Cook threw everything behind trying to get a Nurturist in the Cousin judging slot, and now it'll come to nothing."

"Mycroft . . ."

"MASON must have planned carefully too, so—Xiaoliu Guildbreaker!"

It was Xiaoliu who mounted the bench first, his jaw set, cheeks afire with passion, resolution, pride, the opposite of the leeching lifelessness that illness brings. When the athletes take the field in Esperanza, they will flush so.

What? No. Surely even thy incestuous government must acknowledge bias here. A judge who is married to the primary investigator, on whose word so much evidence relies?

Ah, but we need that bias, reader. This Masonic judge must face *the* Mycroft "Martin" Guildbreaker, *Familiaris, Nepos,* bearer of *Imperium Vicarii,* he who will be Emperor should the Addressee refuse. No *Familiaris*—indeed, no Mason—is better prepared to doubt Martin Guildbreaker's word than the spouse who knows Martin's weakness in the face of cauliflower, and watches his sleep-dazed shuffle as he hunts for his shoes in the morning. Besides, by this appointment clever MASON has snuck a child of the Chinese nation-strat onto the bench, doing what he can to give the three accused Hives some voice.

"Mycroft." Apollo's voice was gentle in my ear, like summer wind. Was he behind me now? "You have to tell the truth about me."

I didn't turn. "I don't know this Graylaw. Sithembile Creswell-Stead. No famous cases. A merit appointment, then. How marvelously uncorrupt."

"I know what you're thinking. You want your history to tell the truth about the Mardi bash' without telling anyone I set out to start my own war."

"I should listen to the judges' opening remarks."

"You're willing to hurt the Alien by telling the whole world that they think they are a God, but you're not willing to tell the truth about me?"

What else could Apollo call Him, reader? Utopia's title, the truest, noblest title any power ever gave: the Alien.

There was a taste in my mouth, a meat taste. "Apollo . . ."

"You think the truth will make people fear Utopia?"

"Xiaoliu's talking about precedent, I want to listen."

"You think it'll make them blame Utopia?"

"This is important. The tone of the trial—"

Digital eyes caught mine, so kind and unkind. "You don't have the power to determine who gets blamed, Mycroft. This war won't be about what you say in your book. It won't be about how others twist what you say. It won't even be about O.S. It'll be about a hundred different things for different people, and a month into the fighting it'll be about different things yet. The one power you do have is to let those few who will find comfort in it know that, whoever wins, the destruction is protecting something better."

Apollo waited, let me think now, and we listened together to the judges' admonitions to the chamber. The best was Xiaoliu Guildbreaker, as stonefaced as his Emperor, who talked of geographic nations. "There are acres of precedent if we dig into the laws and cases of the old nation-states. There are international treaties, charters and conventions, codes of conduct, honor and chivalry, manuals of statecraft, ancient trials. These have no place in this courtroom. We are Hives, our ever-changing members voluntarily united by shared ideology. This is not the place for such geographic concepts as homeland, foreignness, citizen, subject, nation, patrimony, birthright, birth-debt, or territory, nor is it the place for language or thought which privileges those Hives which do have geographic nations as part of their background. You will not find one case from the geographic era which treats the justness of government-ordered assassination without relying on several of these concepts. We are Hives. We will not import to this true *terra ignota* the junk we left behind in making this more perfect age."

How long had I been shaking? "This world is so good, Apollo. It's far from perfect but it's so good. How can you expect them to forgive you for—"

"Worlds," his instant answer. "Maybe they won't be better. Maybe no time in human history will be as comfortable as this one. Or maybe they'll be better someday, but for a long time they'll be hard, scraped out with plow and sweat and stuffy rockets. But there will be more than one. There will be Mars, Europa, Titan, more and more, safeguarded by this war. You must let those who are about to die know that, have that. You must tell them what I did, and tried to do."

He waited now, patient Apollo, returning to the window to survey the sprawling world with his distant, digital eyes. He knew it would make me work. I would keep myself locked on task, just to spare myself the sight of Alexandria's martial glory as his coat turned every passing Mason into either a soldier, or ghostly nothing. Days blurred as I wrote, and nights thanks to a tube of anti-sleeping meds a good servicer friend had helped me steal. Martin testified about his visits to the Saneer-Weeksbooth bash'house, while I wrote about how he had arrested Prospero, and how Thisbe had showed Croucher to Papadelias, and might have saved Bridger. A broken Carlyle testified about the characters of his parishioners, while I wrote of how he came again to Avignon and learned What our Jehovah truly Is. Papa testified about deaths stretching back for centuries, while I wrote of when Caesar found me, on my knees before the statue of Apollo, and I had to tell him . . . had to tell him . . .

Had to tell me, you mean?

Yes, reader, you too. I had to tell you that Apollo tried to start this war. But you I trust. It wasn't you I feared, it was the mob. The present. My history was due to be released as soon as it was done, a week, two. The trial would still be going, Prospero on the stand, and suddenly so much truth? I doubted then Jehovah's choice to reveal all. I doubted that humanity was as good as He believes. What would they do?

Prospero refused to answer questions on the stand, even when ordered to by President Ancelet. Duty forbade it, he said, since even his president could not predict whether his answers would endanger Hive security. He consented to be brought a list of questions, and to answer each in the presence of President Ancelet, then have the transcript reviewed by the president, the Humanist Hive Security Chief, and the Romanovan Security Chief, so each could censor anything they thought was dangerous, and Prospero had each of them initial every paragraph to certify that they supported its release. Even his enemies could not make the public see this as anything but loyalty perfected.

They let Prospero read the transcript aloud, so the judges and public could hear his answers in his own proud voice. They had asked him whether he had thought the killings were criminal when he committed them. He answered that he chose his Hive and answered to its laws and to the Black Laws, and no others. They asked whether he thought culpability for an illegal order rested with the one who gave the order, the one who carried it out, or both. He answered that he was happy that Hives had no answer to this question, since it showed how much better they are than geographic nations. They asked whether he had ever been asked to kill, not for peace, but to strengthen one Hive or weaken another. He answered that, as he understood it, the issues were not separate, since the relative strengths of Hives determined the likelihood of peace or war. They asked whether he would take one life to save ten. He answered that each of the sixty-six lives he had personally taken had, he believed, saved millions; if there were a vaccine that would save tens of millions of lives, but sixty-six people would die from allergic complications, then Romanova, any Hive, any power that had authority to say yes would say yes.

"Why did you only target Masons, Cousins, and Brillists?"

"Utopians were too likely to detect us. There was a standing order not to target Mitsubishi or Europeans, by request of their leaders."

"And Humanists?"

"There was no standing order not to target Humanists."

"Then why did you never kill a Humanist?"

"For a target to be acceptable, our predictions had to indicate, both that the death would have a powerful positive impact, and that the target was unpromising and showed no sign of making a substantial contribution to human achievement. We never found a Humanist who met the latter requirement."

You can imagine the outcry at this claim, reader, and the roars of Humanist pride.

"Would you honestly have killed one of your fellow Humanists if they had met that requirement?"

"I believe so, but cannot confirm. I was not involved in choosing targets."

"Did you ever kill without orders from the Hive leaders?"

Here Prospero revealed how this generation of O.S. murdered the last— 'executed' was his word—when they caught their ba'pas discussing wielding O.S.'s power independently.

He also revealed that Thisbe had murdered for fun. Three times. The first time, he said, he had not suspected anything. The second time he did suspect, but it was hard to call a sister 'murderer' so he failed (his words) to take action. The third time, brother informed sister that, if she tried anything like that again, he would execute her without hesitation. He also informed his president, who consented to spare Thisbe, because the O.S. bash' was already dangerously small. Reactions to this were . . . mixed, but no one doubted Ockham would have carried out his threat to kill a sister, not after his calm admission of ba'parricide.

The next eruption came when set-sets hit the stand, Sidney Koons and the other poor Cartesian set-set Martin and Papa had hired to track down O.S. It came out that the hired set-set had only glanced at the transit computer data and instantly been tempted, even compelled, to cause a crash. The Nurturists erupted. This was proof the set-set process made kids into monsters! Stripped them of true sentience! Reduced them to machines! For days Earth talked of nothing else. Someone (we all know it was you, Lorelei Cook!) chose this moment to circulate photographs of Ganymede in prison, wasted and fragile against the sheets' white like a crocus against snow. Ganymede himself was a poor lab rat, reared by an unscrupulous ex-Brillist, just like those who had first twisted Brill's methods to create the set-set process! The terms "gender set-set" and "O.S. set-set" surfaced on the surge, and "experimental rearing" or "clinical rearing" struck ears as hotly as profanity. Even Jehovah, reader, a "D'Arouet set-set," was twisted by his enemies into evidence for the set-set ban. And, of course, Utopians were set-sets, Utopians with their cult names and their blinding vizors, who, like the young Eureka, never saw the Sun. For a terrifying day the Censor's numbers indicated that, if the Senate voted then on Cookie's Black Law, it might pass.

This was when the choice of a Brillist judge bit the prosecutor in the ass. The Brillist declared that a set-set is a set-set, and anyone calling anything else a set-set in the courtroom would be held in contempt. Suddenly Brillists weren't anti-set-set enough. Cousins turned on Brillists; Cookie's Nurturists were split. Danaë surfaced in the media, golden Danaë in mourning black, with diamond tears sparkling on golden lashes, talking of the persecution of her family, her poor husband held unjustly without bail, her brother shockingly abused, and now her children targeted, those not-quite-set-sets, called monsters in the street because of the unfinished training which they themselves wished so desperately had been completed. They would have been so happy! And it was all cruel Cookie's doing, the scheming Minister of Education whose 'thugs' had been secretly hunting set-set training bash'es for decades! Danaë's tears turned support for the Black Law into rage at everything, and peacekeepers came home with black eyes.

"Release the book now." Many agreed, Ancelet, Kosala, MASON, the Interlocutor Himself. "Give the public this greatest of distractions."

"As you command, good masters."

Apollo: "Mycroft, did you rewrite that scene, as I asked? Did you tell them honestly what I tried to do?"

I: "I . . . mostly, but I . . . What if they turn on you?"

Apollo: "We're ready for what comes. Look out that window, Mycroft. You can see a dozen streets from here, dozens of coats, and none alone. Never one Utopian, always moving in groups, two, four, squads, not vulnerable individuals. You haven't seen a Utopian on the streets alone, not in weeks. Not in thirteen years."

I: "I didn't mean turn on Utopia, Apollo. What if they turn on you?"

Apollo: "Don't worry about me, Mycroft. No one can hurt me anymore."

Apollo was right. Mercy of mercies, it turned out that I had feared too much. My book was glue. Groups that had wanted to be allies but were splitting over smaller differences like land or set-sets found in my history facts or outrages to reunite them, and that refocused everything onto the two true sides: Sniper and Jehovah. Somehow Bridger saved us all again. Whenever anyone suggested that it might be true, what I said of Apollo or the Mardi bash', someone cited my ravings about Bridger's miracles, proof positive again that I was mad. Each Hive even managed to read my history as proof that Jehovah was still theirs: still the Mitsubishi's trusted Tenth Director, still the loyal *Porphyrogene*, still a Brillist at heart, still as noble as His royal line, still sensitive and kind and Cousinly, still brave and bold and human; all Hives saw in Him what they wanted, never a God, or a madman who thought himself a God. Oh, some believed the truth about Him—What He Is—a few thousand perhaps among the billions, but those who believe a madman are easy to call mad.

My book was released June twenty-eighth. For nearly a week, the trial was mainly about the fact that the trial could not be about my book. Then, on July tenth, the messages went out, thousands of them, each one unique, and personal, and true:

> "On [January 3, 2387] O.S. killed [Indus Pygmalion Reaper], and thereby prevented [massive gang violence across Portugal] which would have killed your [grandmother], so you would never have been born."

Three-fifths of the world received notes like this, each customized, the particular way O.S. had saved *your* life. Reality hit home. The lives bought by O.S.'s sin were no longer abstract, they were ours. Suddenly the media chatter was muffled and measured. Opponents of O.S. asked for change rather than retribution. Voices that had been screams the day before admitted that the question was not black and white. Bull's-eye sigils multiplied. When the court opened that morning, and Ganymede Jean-Louis de la Trémoïlle, Duc de Thouars, Prince de Talmond, former President of the Humanists

*   *   *

That was a strange place to end a sentence, Mycroft. What did Ganymede do?

Reader? Are you here?

Of course. I am always here, even when thou strayest.

Oh. Still here, then. I . . . they interrupted me, as I was writing. Caesar and Ἄναξ Jehovah. They took me to visit Romanova. I just got back, I just . . . The sky is falling. Disaster, reader, irreparable, absolute. This is the wrong war. No way out now. No solution. Ashes. Ashes. All fall down.

Calm, Mycroft. Each thing in its turn. Explain. Is it the outcome of the trial that shocks thee so?

The trial? We survived it. Now we'll survive this, too. Why couldn't this have been the war I thought it was? Why did they have to be so kind? Too kind.

Who was too kind? The judges?

There is no solution. Mobs chant, torches kindle. No one could stop this now, only He, He, our callous Architect, our Author. Hear me, Providence! I beg You in the name of He Who is Your Guest, Your Peer, Your Friend if ever Friend You had, my Good Master Jehovah! If You have any Love for Him in Your unknowable Heart, then bring my prayer to pass! Do not make it this war! Change once again the course You have already changed so many times! Will us a kinder war!

Mycroft, thy pain is moving, but I cannot understand thee if thou strayest so from the order of thy chronicle. Concentrate on me now, on thy task. What happened next? What of the trial? Of Ganymede? Answer quickly, so thou canst then explain what dark event has so broken thee and thy narrative.

What of Ganymede? They love him. They always loved him. The Humanists could have voted for anyone, for Aesop Quarriman, for heroes. They chose him. He staggered up the aisle martyr-frail, with French silks in Olympic colors and a bull's-eye on his heart, but he was the marksman, irresistible Eros, and they remembered why they always loved him.

What did he do?

He showed Earth what nobility should be. He said he had no greater pride in life than the knowledge that, as President of the Humanists, he had done such great good with O.S. The majority of people living owed their lives to Ockham Prospero Saneer or to his bash'parents. If a Hive had not the right to defend the world by taking lives, then doctors had no right to quarantine a plague, nor did the guards of the Olmek Virus Lab or *Sanctum Sanctorum* have the right to defend their wards with deadly force. Numbers, he declared, did not lie. Since 2441, before the duke became president or young Ockham O.S., the set-sets' data proved Earth was past the tipping point at which only O.S. could stave off war. To have abandoned O.S. would have caused extensive loss of life and suffering, breaking the First Law. This trumped all Hive Law, and if Romanova's Alliance demanded that a Hive renounce the right to safeguard World Peace by a means which cost so little and preserved so much, such an Alliance could command neither the duke's respect nor his obedience. The next day there were twice as many bull's-eyes on the streets, and I hear Ganymede's name now as often as Ancelet's.

A means which cost so little and preserved so much . . . Today's means preserved all, reader: lives and trees and Bach and baby elephants, and took not a single life, yet now they scream vendetta in the streets. Such cost.

Stay with me, Mycroft. You may describe that next, but, quickly, first, the trial.

Oh, the trial. Ockham goes free.

FINDINGS OF THE COURT IN THE *TERRA IGNOTA* EXAMINATION OF OCKHAM PROSPERO SANEER
[July 15th, 2454]:

OPINION: *Hives can command lethal force,* since they can kill their own Members if their laws allow, as Masonic law does. [All three judges agree.]

OPINION: *Hives can command lethal force against Members of other Hives and Hiveless in some circumstances,* since it is established that Hive agents can kill other Hives' Members to protect priority targets, and to save lives in emergency situations. [All three judges agree.]

OPINION: *Current Alliance law specifies no clear limit to Hives' rights to wield lethal force against Members of other Hives and Hiveless.* [All three judges agree.]

COURT ORDER: *This Court hereby orders the Seven Hive Council to draft legislation* acceptable to all Hives defining of the limits of Hives' rights to wield lethal force against Members of other Hives, and to submit this legislation to the Alliance Senate. [Minority opinion Mason: The right of Sovereign Powers to exercise lethal force is well established and requires no clarification.]

OPINION: *The homicides committed by O.S. did violate a notorious and transparent Hive law.* Homicides committed in order to prevent a war might be construed as equivalent to a police officer's right to exercise unavoidable lethal force in order to protect others from harm, but, while some Hives' law codes have variable and opaque requirements in such cases, Gordian's requirement that the threat be provably immediate is notorious and transparent, making the use of lethal force by O.S. against Gordian Members indisputably criminal. [Minority opinion Mason: The right of Sovereign Powers to exercise lethal force is well established and requires no clarification.]

OPINION: *The homicides committed by O.S. after the year 2441 were mandated by the Universal Laws,* because to have abandoned O.S. after this point would have triggered war, a violation through negligence of the First and Second Laws. [Minority opinion Gordian: O.S. merely delayed the war, so its actions were not justified by the First or Second Law.]

OPINION: *The Universal Laws give license to violate a Hive's law only when there is no other way to obey the Universal Laws.* Since the use of O.S. violated Hive Law, those who used O.S. were obligated to try to develop an alternative which could satisfy the Universal Laws without violating Hive law. This obligation fell on the Hive leaders, i.e. the Humanist, Mitsubishi, and European leadership, who had resources they could have used to try to create a better system, rather than on their agents, i.e. the members of the Saneer-Weeksbooth bash'. [Minority opinion Mason: The right of Sovereign Powers to exercise lethal force is well established and requires no clarification.]

RECOMMENDATION: *No charges should be brought against Ockham Prospero Saneer for homicides carried out in their office as O.S.,* since they acted as an agent of a Sovereign Power, and all their homicides were committed after 2441, and were thus mandated by the Universal Laws. [Minority opinion Gordian: After 2441 O.S. merely delayed the war, so Ockham Saneer's actions were not mandated by the Universal Laws.]

RECOMMENDATION: *Charges of homicide should be brought against the Mitsubishi and European Hive leaders who distorted the mandate of O.S.,* since their requirement that O.S. never target their own Hive Members demonstrates that they used O.S. to pursue selfish interests rather than universal peace. [Minority opinion Mason: The right of Sovereign Powers to exercise lethal force is well established and requires no clarification.]

NO RECOMMENDATION: *This tribunal has no recommendation about criminal charges to be brought against the Humanist leaders responsible for commanding O.S.* The question should be examined by a separate *terra ignota,* by the Senate, or by a Tribunal of Ten with representatives of all Laws on the Bench.

First Minority Opinion Graylaw Hiveless: The Humanist leaders who commanded O.S. before 2441 should be charged with homicide. Those who commanded O.S. after 2441 were mandated to do so by the Universal Laws, but must demonstrate that they sought alternatives to O.S., or else be charged with homicide on the grounds that they did not seek to avoid committing these homicides.

Second minority opinion Mason: No charges may be brought. Creating a better means than O.S. was the morally and practically correct course, but the right of Sovereign Powers to exercise lethal force is well established and requires no clarification. Other Sovereign Powers have the right to retaliate in kind.

Third minority opinion Gordian: All Humanist leaders who commanded O.S. should face charges of homicide. After 2441, O.S. merely delayed the war, so its actions were not mandated by the Universal Laws.

We have our answer. Those who agree trade hate-glares with those who scream, but all remember the Olympics, turn passion into patient malevolence, and wait. Except Papa; Papa must keep Prospero from rejoining Sniper:

"Ockham Prospero Saneer, I hereby arrest you as an accessory to the murder of Alex Limner by Thisbe Saneer, whom you aided in concealing the earlier murders of Luca Cormor and Quinn Prichard." That buys time.

Time. What have we bought now? Earth. And what have we paid?

Angry, the Leviathans

Written August 18, 2454
Event of August 18
Romanova

WERE YOU STILL THIRSTY, PROVIDENCE? YOU COULD HAVE told me You required more sacrifice. I serve Another, but I can still be Your blade. If Apollo and the Mardi were not blood enough, bid me take whom You will. Take MASON. Smash the dream that Alexander dreamed of grand and lasting empire. Take Spain and his virtue. Take Papa and his justice. Take the Blacklaws, and make all humankind the slaves of law again. Will that not sate You? Take Saladin, then! My beautiful Saladin, just . . . those who guard the baby step we have taken outside this world, who plan the next step, why must You take aim at them? Have mercy, pray, not on me but on Gagarin, and Galileo, and Odysseus, and Jason and his Argonauts, and on Your Guest, Who will suffer so if He must see them fall! Have mercy, Maker! Erase this past hour from Your Great Scroll! Return the billion arrows of complacent Earth to their quiver, and make a different war.

Jehovah and MASON took me with them, a fast car's flash from Alexandria to Romanova. The Hive Council Building stands in the Forum where the Temple of Concord did in true Rome, but that upper chamber with its monumental statues of Hive founders is nothing, merely the wound through which you enter lower halls which spread beneath the Forum and Capitoline like the foundation of a pyramid. Sunlight followed us down, through science's ingenuity, so the Hive Council Chamber was day-bright, and kitchen trees choked the outer walls with every fruit in Nature's palette. The bench that ringed the center of the hall was built to seat a hundred, a relic of the days after the Church War, when Thomas Carlyle had imagined that the multiplying Hives would multiply still more, a law for every dream that had a million dreamers. Now a little ring of chairs stands in the center, eleven, the seats of the last few dead Hives kept on hand for the convenience of guests, and Guest. I was heartened to see Chair Kosala in her Cousin's Wrap and President Ancelet in his Olympic Committee jacket sitting side by side as couples should. Faust fidgeted with excitement, and Dominic in Mitsubishi raiment twitched in his chair, uncomfortable sitting in a company he was used to waiting upon as a servant. The King of Spain rose to greet his Son as we arrived, then warmly greeted Caesar, and Achilles, who entered with us, plucking an apricot from a branch but shooting the underground sun a distrustful stare. Oh, the wonders Jehovah's Utopian guards made of those fruits, reader: eyes, books, egg sacks, ore crusting an asteroid, while their U-beasts played among the branches, a blue-scaled horse grazing on grapes while a dwarf wyrm, a microceratops, and a coyote chased each other among the trunks. Dominic fell from his seat as his Lord God entered, and kind Jehovah walked quickly to him, so he would not have to dishonor his Mitsubishi colors by crawling. Caesar made for his customary seat, Achilles following, but had no chance to sit.

"Cornel Semaphoros MASON!" Faust's shriek and the long-discarded name of the Emperor's birth bash' made us all spin and stare at the Headmaster, who shook his head like a disappointed parent. "I know my sister broke your heart, and a rebound is natural, but Achilles? Really? There is such a thing as asking for it!"

Death in the guise of MASON blushed.

Just as you cannot see a mantis spring, or as an arrow seems less to fly than to vanish from the archer's bow and reappear quivering in its target, so no eye could trace the speed with which Achilles was—I cannot say ran or leapt—he *was* across the room, with blood spattered across his knuckles, and Faust flat at his feet. Achilles didn't speak, just flexed his shoulder and enjoyed a couple practice clenches of his fist as he strode back, smiling, to stand at wide-eyed MASON's side. Faust tried to hoist himself onto his elbows but slumped with a moan, and rolled onto his side. It was his cheek that bled. The hero had avoided the nose, probably to make sure the old man lived, but I have little doubt he cracked Faust's cheekbone. Not even Kosala rose to help, and the Headmaster soothed his own bodyguards with gentle Brillist German. The King of Spain ordered some ice.

"If we're all here, let's start." Bryar Kosala had the least qualm about showing her impatience. "Unless Joyce is intending to burst in and surprise us all, but this summons had better not be Joyce's doing. With the Olympics in four days, none of us can waste time on frills and tea cakes."

"I made very certain my fiancée is ignorant of this meeting," Spain re-assured her—reassured us all. "As I was asked to."

"Asked to?" Ancelet took a fast breath, fearful, which made me fearful. "You didn't call us, then? Who did?" The Humanist President looked from seat to seat, to Kosala, Dominic, still-crimson MASON, back to Spain.

"No one!" Headmaster Faust pronounced with glee. "You didn't . . . you didn't . . ."—he pointed to each in turn, peering at telltale faces—"you didn't . . . I didn't . . ."

Softness brushed me from behind, and warmth, and pressed me gently to the floor. It was the black lion, playful, not like a kitten's play but like a mature beast's that knows the force behind its claws and chooses not to use them. It forced me to the ground and sat upon me, pinned me, its legs on either side of me so it could keep just enough of its weight off to spare me pain, while its heavy belly trapped me gently, like an overflowing blan-ket filled with lead.

"We summoned you." A Utopian stepped forward.

They all stepped forward, a ring of strange worlds orbiting the ring of chairs. Had there always been so many of them? Five, six, I counted, seven, craning my neck as the lion held me pinned.

"Why?" Faust asked fastest.

MASON's face as he took his seat showed that he too did not know.

The Utopians reached into their coats and drew out tablets, a strange design, bulky and sharp-cornered. All but the speaker, who stayed still as the others each approached one Hive leader and handed over the tablets with a simultaneity which must have been intentional.

"Each of you is receiving a list of resources officially gifted from our Hive to yours as of . . ."—a pause, a held breath, something through the vizor—". . . now. These are henceforth yours, without condition or any hid-den reservation, bond, or geas. Many are patents or copyrights, and for these, as for all treasures whose market value is challenging to assess, you will find three independent esti—"

"Your Space Elevators!" Every leader had gone slack-jawed reading through the lists, but Kosala cried aloud. "Why would you give . . . ?"

"We're keeping the Maldive Ridge Elevator. You get Ecuador, Gabon, and Borneo."

"Twenty-one billion . . . twenty-seven . . ." Ancelet muttered.

"Why are you doing this?" Spain asked, light. "Why help us all?"

I knew this Utopian, didn't I? The speaker in a coat of smoky storm.

This was the Delian who guarded me in the Sensayers' Conclave, and carried me from Hobbestown Hall on the gentle lion's back. The lion's partner. "You will receive emergency signals from your Hive governments shortly. Please give me your attention, since I am explaining what is happening more efficiently than they can. The second item on each of your tablets is a list of properties owned by your Hive Members or governments which contain facilities or materials which, by our estimates, are harbingers, or capable of producing harbingers within six to twelve months"—digital brows tensed—"harbingers being technologies capable of hatching uncontrollably destructive weapons, nuclear or worse. Weapons whose very existence threatens to break the First and Second Laws. As of when we handed you your tablets, these facilities have been destroyed."

Gasps rose, and I saw fingers twitch and lenses glimmer with arriving reports.

"There has been no loss of human life," the Delian continued. "Our peacebonding forces evacuated everyone, including intelligent animals, from the properties."

"You blew up Geraldton Station!" Kosala cried. "Kolkata University Hospital!"

Ancelet now, "The Olenek Virus Lab! Half of Utarutu Campus!"

"The properties gifted to you are of equivalent value to what has been destroyed, plus an additional sum to cover the criminal fine for one Hive's Member destroying another Hive's Member's property—we calculated appropriate fines using the average result of comparable property destruction trials, though obviously there has been nothing on this scale before."

It was Ancelet from whom the names kept flowing: "Lægerneset, the Liland Energy Institute, Iğdır Tissue Archive, the Archdale Array, three buildings in Chislehurst, a bash'house in Bogotá, a Compressions Lab in Riga, complexes in Copenhagen, Manchester, Caxias do Sul, Montreal, Strasbourg, Tongcheng, the Pierce-Long Crater, the Great Wellington Microwave . . ."

Dominic released a long, soft whistle. "Even museum pieces."

Smoke rose in my lenses, news networks' images of thread-fine black smoke columns rising over city after city, like so many signal fires.

"We are coordinating proclamations, so the public won't think this is another Brussels."

A twitch from Spain.

"And how exactly is this not another Brussels?" Dominic tested, leaning forward, smiling. "How is this not a hundred Brusselses?"

The Delian remained recital-cold. "There are several more items on your tablets."

MASON rose, and took a limping half step forward. "Why did you do this?" His voice trembled. "Why didn't you talk to me first?"

"This is an act of war." Dominic said it first. No, that can't have been the first time. It must have been said a hundred times by then, by angry voices in Kolkata, Utarutu campus, Bogotá, Copenhagen, and Tongcheng. So many fires.

I saw no doubt in the Utopians' digital eyes as they watched us, but there were glances, one nowhere to another, and those who had delivered the tablets backed away toward one side of the chamber, farther from the leaders, farther from the leaders' bodyguards.

As the other Utopians retreated, the lion's dark partner joined the leaders' circle, standing between two empty seats opposite where MASON stood, with Achilles by his side. "This will be seen as an act of war by many. But I think not by you?" Lightning crackled through the coat's storm-world as the Delian turned to Jehovah. "Not in the sense that would fail your Great Test?"

The Addressee too held a tablet in His Hand, Hiveless properties to be handled by the Tribune as their representative. "Your motive?" He asked.

"We held a vote." My Delian hesitated before answering this time. *Your Delian, Mycroft?* Yes, reader, I began to realize then how many times—in Romanova, Hobbestown, Crete—I had been touched and guarded by this same stormy nowhere. A dozen Delians to guard Micromegas, and one for me. "Utopia is unwilling to let this war begin with harbingers in play. We struck before the Games, since it seemed likely someone would try to use a harbinger before or at the Opening or Closing Ceremony."

A vote. Did I recall Utopia ever voting before? Not some vague consult of constellations, intricate as neural networks, but a plain vote?

"You do not trust humans to preserve themselves," the God pronounced.

Utopia faced Him. "Not enough to gamble with the Earth. We decided, as a Hive, not to let the feuding parties start this war with arms capable of ending life on this world."

"But you have another!" Caesar limped another pace forward. "You have two!" Wait. This was not Caesar's limp. This was different, a stagger, bodily, and he clutched his side with his gray-sleeved right hand. I feared a heart attack, but realized it was the spot where Apollo had stabbed young Cornel with his pocketknife, the day after a Utopian first turned down Mars. Honest Apollo. He knew Caesar could never see him as an enemy unless he shed first blood with his own hand. Cornel MASON didn't understand then. Does he now? "You were—"

"Hsht." I cannot call the sound Achilles made a word, but from his glance, and his hand on Caesar's one gray shoulder, I understood as clearly as if he had spoken: Whether they're breaking our secret alliance or not, don't make it worse by revealing that secret alliance in front of everyone.

Utopia turned to the Alien. "Have we failed Your Great Test?"

"You emptied the arsenal," Jehovah pronounced, "but no thinking thing has been unmade. This is still peace."

You might think Dominic would curse seeing his hope for God tears crushed, but all Jehovah's words are miracles to him, new Truth revealed, precious as Scripture. As the beast's body sits silent, the mind within is re-defining war and peace to reflect this Revelation.

"We are glad You agree," the Delian answered. "We do not expect the world to." Not a glance, not even for Caesar. "Third item on the tablets, each of you will find twenty-three different scrying techniques for seeking evidence that others are brewing harbingers. This way you can watch each other, and know when the threat returns. Each of your lists contains sev-eral techniques we have shared with all of you, and several which are unique to your own list, so the others can't craft counterspells."

"But you know all of them." The frown settled most darkly on Presi-dent Ancelet, although Kosala too fixed narrowed eyes upon the Delian.

"Yes," Utopia answered. "Even if we vowed to purge our knowledge of these arts, we have no means to make you believe that we have purged it."

"And you still have harbingers yourselves."

"We cannot prove we don't."

Ancelet crossed his arms. "And you expect us to see you as what? Neu-tral referees?"

The Delian remained recital-cold. "The next three items you will find are lists of names."

"You haven't answered my question."

"You still haven't heard our most objectionable act." Utopia waited.

No one would break this silence.

"Thank you for letting me continue. These next three lists contain the names of all known harbinger adepts, that is, people with mastery of techni-cal knowledge which we believe could hatch new harbingers within the next year. The first file lists those adepts who yielded themselves to us freely, whom we now hold cloistered in an occult, where we are certain none of you can touch them. The second lists adepts who did not yield; these we abducted, and now hold by force in an equally shrouded occult. The third lists adepts we were not able to access, who remain dangers to the Earth and life upon it. Our criers have proclaimed these lists in all alpha fora, so the public knows what we have done, and what safety it has bought."

A hush. "You are . . ." It was the King of Spain who framed it first. "You are holding people against their will?"

The former Censor did fast math. "More than a thousand people?"

"I am empowered to offer wergild for the Members we have taken from you, but we expect few of you will accept."

"Money?" I have rarely seen Bryar Kosala make fists. "You would bribe us to condone kidnapping?"

Delian: "It is not a bribe. Most of you have forms of wergild in your laws. We offer only what precedent dictates we should."

Cousin: "You're holding more than a thousand people against their will!"

Delian: "None of those taken has been injured," to Jehovah, "no thinking thing unmade. They have been peacebonded." The grim crispness of those syllables 'peacebonded' made us all shudder, Achilles most of all, our battle-starved Achilles. He loves war, reader, needs it, every bit as much as he hates it.

Cousin: "Just to stop them from—"

Delian: "Endangering all life on Earth."

Cousin: "There's a difference between having an ability and being willing to use it. No Cousin would—"

Delian: "Succumb to torture? Or to receiving a ba'kid's fingers in the mail?"

Cousin: "You know we're neutral, just working for peace."

Delian: "We hope you remain so. If you use the Space Elevators to transport aid and never arms, they may not become a military target, and may survive this. Their loss would be a great setback to all human achievement."

A sound from MASON's throat. Was that a sob?

Kosala herself was not unmoved as the image rose in her mind of the destruction of those great ladders to the heavens, from which all children first see proof that Earth is round and blue. Her mind's eye saw those cables snap, the anchor-stations moan and split like fruit clawed open by some selfish monster, but she is stronger before such fears than Caesar is, and did not sob. "And you just expect us all to trust you? Leaving all this in your hands? A superweapons monopoly? And a thousand innocent people held against their will?"

"No," the Delian answered. "We expect you to turn on us, and distrust us, throughout this war and ever after. But you will have an ever after, now."

Hush edged out rage, leaders silenced by the imagined futures that flowed one to another down the logic chains in all their minds. Achilles was silent too. Calm. Was he too calm? What had they talked about, he and Utopia, when I was forbidden to hear? Had he known? Had he chosen not to stop this? Peacebonding the harbingers like this had not been in Apollo's *Iliad*, but the Delians shared more with Achilles than they shared with me. Had Achilles known about this? Known they planned to bring down all Earth's wrath upon them, and consented? No. I know Achilles, reader. I've known him longer than anyone. His was not the face of one facing something he expected. His was the face of one who had warned his friend, again and again, against some reckless course, and thought the friend had yielded, but now comes the unwelcome messenger to say the friend has done it after all. He knew they were going to hold a vote. He did not expect them to choose Earth.

"Did Madame approve this? Or have you broken the terms of your surrender?" Dominic asked it, his dark creatrix ever on his mind.

"We have betrayed Madame."

"Don't worry, MASON." A different voice now from Utopia, gentle, a gentle hand on Caesar's shoulder. "We got out safe."

"Voltaire!" A ghost of joy awoke in the Emperor's face as he spun and grasped the shoulders of the nearest nowhere. The hood fell back; it was indeed Voltaire Seldon, Madame's hostage, disguised with a coat of real and robot fish instead of ruins. "And Mushi? Aldrin?"

"Safe." Voltaire at least, in all this, had a smile. "We were ready for this. All our people are well bulwarked right now. Mobs will find no prey. We voted on this, as a whole Hive. We won't abandon the present to Madame, not when the present is World War." A more personal smile. "We won't abandon you."

I wish you had—those were the silent words I read in Caesar's eyes.

So did Voltaire. His smile dimmed. "We are not ready to abandon Earth."

Not ready? What did that mean? I strained against the gentle lion, tried to read digital eyes. Not ready? Are their preparations incomplete? There had been plenty of time. I knew Apollo's plan. Stock Luna City with everything life requires: samples, soils, fuel. The Moon will be the backup world, a second home, ready if human folly destroys the first. This world may burn, but on the safe and distant Moon Utopia will wait for Earth to cool and Mars to warm, and there will still be humans. Luna City can't hold all of Utopia, not a tenth, not a hundredth of its current Membership, but it can hold a precious few, enough. The rest would stay on Earth, lie low, the smallest Power doing its best to be invisible as the great Leviathans make war. If Earth survives, Utopia survives; if not, Utopia survives still on the Moon, and guards our Second Chance. But instead you attack the Leviathans? You have pulled out their deadliest fangs, but now the remaining fangs will seek your throat. They can destroy you! Rip you down, so there will be no exodus! No seeds to fly! No vanguard of the Great Project! Utopia could die! Why do this? Did the lunar preparations take longer than expected? Has our cruel Maker made the fledgling not quite strong enough to fly yet, as He sets the nest afire? No. There was time. The Moon is ready. The failure is Utopia itself, kind, weak Utopia. You have a conscience. You are ready, but not *willing*, to abandon Earth.

Apollo: "I want to drink with you, and live with Seine, and stand on Mars, and breathe the air we made, but I'd go mad, I know it, I'd go mad living on, knowing I left them to go through this alone."

You failed first, Apollo. You know you failed, I hear it in your breathing as you crouch behind that gutter waiting for our attack. Your heart broke the first time a Utopian turned down Mars, but you have done the same. You could have escaped, taken the waiting shuttle to the Moon where Saladin and I could never touch you. But you knew Seine Mardi was in danger, and you have a conscience, and you think you could not live with yourself if you abandoned her. You were never strong enough to destroy this world to save your better one. You bound your fate to hers, and once my Saladin and I have steeled ourselves with a last kiss, we will burst out from behind this dumpster and face you two in battle. You and your earthbound lover must either slay us and survive together or die here, on Earth, failure Apollo, and never touch the stars. And now it turns out they are all as weak as you are. Grounded by conscience, the Utopians are not brave enough to let billions die while they hide away to safeguard everything. They won't abandon this world to destruction, not even to protect all better ones. They bind their fate to Earth's. No second chance. Utopia will join the war.

"Do-on't," my voice cracked. Are you surprised I stayed silent so long, reader? I was not silent. I was screaming through all this, screaming beyond what breath and blistered throat could sustain, but the Delian's black lion had muffled my screams with its kind paw, until exhaustion weakened grief enough to grant me words. "Don't be Troy."

Somebody has to be.

Not them. Not them! They could have been distant Phaeacia, guarded by the black and airless sea that lies between them and the bloody fields of Troy. Or like Olympus! They began this conflict, hold the heavens, but have no need to fight in it. Let them descend from time to time to aid some side, or mourn some passing hero, but suffer nothing worse than fleeting wounds and sorrow. You know, my master, what story was in the mind that conceived this war, whether you blame Bridger or Apollo. The side that gives the first offense, the one that breaks trust and hospitality, that steals Helen and all her treasures, that side unites all the Greek forces against it. That is Troy. That side will fall. We cannot afford for it to be their towers that topple when their towers touch the stars. Don't be Troy. Someone, I beg you, make them not be Troy.

Fear not, Mycroft. They gave those towers away.

"Achilles . . ." I choked out. That was the someone to pray to, not our distant Maker; He had already given us the key. Achilles can stop this. He can choose them. The side that has Achilles can't be Troy.

Achilles met my eyes, and showed me the tears in his, for the Great Soldier finds no shame in tears when Fate gives cause. Then he turned away, and placed his hand on MASON's arm.

"I imagine," the Delian continued, "that most of you now need to go denounce us. I recommend that you make it very clear that the payment you have accepted from us was in return for the property destroyed, and that it in no way means you condone the kidnappings. Unless you happen to condone the kidnappings."

"Your motive yes, your methods absolutely not," Kosala answered, clear and calm.

Spain nodded agreement.

Spain and Kosala looked to Ancelet, expecting agreement from him too, I think, but he was hushed, a Censor's instincts warring with a president's inside him, as the casualty predictions, multiplying in his calculator-mind, muddled his duty.

Kosala's was not muddled. "If you thought disarmament was an issue, you should have started a dialogue."

"Even had all Hives agreed to cloister all harbingers and adepts in neutral custody, we do not believe all would have acted on that compact in good faith. Several Hives have proved themselves willing to both conceal and use abominable means. But you are right that, by striking alone, we have violated the compact between the Hives. You must go denounce us."

I read respect in Kosala's pursed lips. "Yes, you . . ." Confusion exiled it. "Jed? What are you doing?"

He was stripping. He stripped off the black coat with its pleats and cording, and as He did so it withered somehow, wilted, the black pigment draining from it as it left His body, as if it could not exist without a Maker to sustain it. My eyes could not explain it until the coat blipped static for a moment, then died away into the dull green-gold of inactive Griffincloth. I should have realized. It had always been Griffincloth. All Hives had let Him wear their sigils: Mason, Mitsubishi, Europe, Cousin; all who thought Him one of them had marked Him so. Even Utopia. This Visitor has worn His nowhere all this time, an eighteenth-century cut but Griffincloth, showing a world with nothing in it that can be understood by our senses, so we see only his Peer's opposite, pure black. That must have been the shimmer, I realized. During His resurrection, that shimmer on the video that some call proof of fakery, others of miracle: it was His coat rebooting after Sniper's Weeksbooth Counterbombs fried all the electronics on the Rostra. Just Griffincloth, no miracle, no fakery. Just truth.

Utopia: "What are You doing?"
Jehovah: "I return this to you." He held out His coat.
Utopia: "No need. We've broken with your mother, not with You, we still—"
Jehovah: "I shall not accept the terms you gave My mother."
Utopia: "What?"
Jehovah: "You gave My mother only your conditional surrender."
Utopia: "I . . . we . . ." Digital glances flew.
Jehovah: "I will have your unconditional surrender."
Utopia: "It would be wiser to negotiate this in private."
Jehovah: "I shall not negotiate. I shall remake this world. For that I must have the absolute freedom granted by universal absolute surrender."
Voltaire: "Mike, we know You want a future with us in it." Vizored eyes may be false, but not the kind smile on Voltaire's bare cheeks. "We know You love what we love."
Jehovah: "I love many things. What if My new world has no room for you?"

The Visitor still held out His coat. "I return this to you, and thank you for it, and for your hospitality. Give both to Me again when you give Me your unconditional surrender."

Voltaire: "We'll give You everything you want. We won't set any maximum on what You can ask of us during the war, or during the reconstruction, so long as we have enough to keep our terraforming schedule. The only things we'll keep from You are harbingers, Mars, and the far distant future."

Jehovah: "What if I want Mars, and the far distant future?"

Voltaire: "You want a world that doesn't need O.S. or death. So do we."

Jehovah: "I do not know what I will do to this world if war makes it Mine. What if I banish Utopia forever from the Earth? What if I chase you, homeless and unwelcome, from every corner of human dominion—My dominion—until you flee into the black of Space? And what if even there I follow you, and take from you the Moon, and next take Mars, and next Europa? What if I drive you from every rock and hiding place technology can touch, home after home, as I exile you to the dark exhaustion of forever?"

Even Caesar caught his breath.

Voltaire: "You wouldn't do that."

Jehovah: "I do not know what I would and would not do; no more do you. Mycroft has indeed taught Me to love you, and to love what you love. In the name of that love, I will not deceive you into thinking you are safe from Me. What if I do not choose you to be the architects of My future? What if I choose them?" His steady finger pointed to the silent, wide-eyed form of Felix Faust.

Voltaire: "I know You, Mike." The hostage who had watched this Boy grow up still smiled. "I've known You almost since First Contact. I know what You wish this world was like."

Jehovah: "Do not mistake Me for a human thing."

Voltaire: "I never have. I never would. I recognize You are an Alien. I welcome that. I will never stop trying to help You communicate, and—"

Static flashed, the coats displaying harsh white mourning blankness. Caesar paled. How good were your preparations for today's mobs, frail Utopia?

"Natural causes," Voltaire announced. "We haven't failed the Great Test, not yet." A breath. "You're not going to make me fear You, Micromegas. I know you are omnibenevolent."

Jehovah: "I Am the same Species as My Peer your Maker, Who created plague, and death, and earthquakes, and forgetting, and hid from you the nature of your souls, and, for the sake of Our Conversation, We—not He alone—*We* drive you now to war and your destruction. If I say I do not know what I will do, that I may hunt you like beasts through every corner of My empire, believe Me." He turned to Chair Kosala now: "Believe Me." To Ancelet: « Believe Me. » To Spain His father: "¡Believe Me!" Dominic: « Believe Me. » Caesar: "*Crede Mi.*" His uncle Faust: "You already believe Me."

Faust: "Yes, my Boy, I do." The old Headmaster inclined his head, a gesture I was not quite able to interpret. Respect?

Hobbes: "Do you, friend reader?"

Reader: "*What? Do I believe that this Guest of Mycroft's is so dangerous?*"

Voltaire: "I don't."

Hobbes: "You don't?"

Jehovah: "Why not?"

Voltaire: "Because I babysat our Visitor, so I was there when, once upon a time, little Micromegas saw an insect, as small as the jot of an *i*, crawling on a windowpane. They wanted to know if it was outside or inside, so They reached to feel, but crushed it, accidentally, nothing left but a splot of color, not enough to call a drop. They refused to move for hours after discovering that, in this strange Universe, so innocent an action could unmake a living thing. In the end I think young Micromegas would have starved in place, had we not convinced Them that even breathing kills invisible creatures, so even doing nothing wouldn't spare all life. The Alien still mourns that insect, and wears black for it, and is a much, much kinder Being than a human."

Hobbes: "A worthy fable. But I have to say, it makes me fear Him more."

Reader: "*More, Thomas? Why?*"

Jehovah: "In the end I moved."

Hobbes: "Precisely."

Jehovah: "I am reconciled now to killing."

Hobbes: "See? You taught Him to step on insects long ago, your Visitor. And now that statecraft makes Him such a vast thing, He will step on men, and soon forget the little splots of color left behind."

Voltaire: "But you care. You care the way that humans care, more. You are not yourself the Author of earthquakes. You know sorrow, and ignorance, and woe, and hope. You want to guard the garden we have worked so hard to cultivate. You even want to cultivate it more Yourself. Put

the coat back on, Micromegas. It may take some time to work out details, but that coat's still Yours, and we're still friends, and we still welcome this First Contact, even if it's difficult."
Jehovah: "I—"

"Epicuro," Spain interrupted with a firmness that made us all turn, "you don't want humanity to fail your Great Test because the lot of us, who should be out there shepherding, were stuck here, riveted, listening to you arguing theodicy with Voltaire."

Jehovah nodded slow assent, and donned His otherworld of black again.

That pierced the bubble. Kosala rose, Spain, Ancelet, and crawling Dominic, commanded by a gesture to quit his Master's blessed company and do his Mitsubishi duty. The rising leaders' bodyguards bunched dense around them, and I saw the Utopians draw farther back, and hold their hands, not up, but out, where suspicious bodyguards could see they held no . . . wands? runes? lasers? warheads? books?

Faust lingered. "Why didn't I get a Space Elevator?" His whine was playful, but play left when the storm-cloaked Delian approached the old Headmaster, and held out a hand.

"War?" Utopia offered.

Had I ever before seen Felix Faust's face grow truly serious? He accepted the handshake. "War." A glint of smile returned. "I thought you might squirm out of it."

The stormy Delian did not smile. "We expected the same of you."

"Oh, I fully intend to squirm out of it." Faust squeezed the proffered hand. "You won't see Brillists involved in anything. Lie low, that's the only sensible strategy for we teeny-weeny Hives. But you know that, don't you?" He leaned in close, peering at the vizor's surface. For a few breaths Faust studied the Delian's face, and I saw Faust's shape through the coat of storm and lightning, his body outlined in spiral ropes of rain like twisted waterspouts. "You voted against," Brill's successor pronounced. "You personally voted to abandon Earth. But you lost the vote, and they made you the ambassador today anyway, not Mushi as usual, you. Interesting. And you never introduced yourself. That's interesting too."

Some learn with practice that it is more comfortable for the other party if we break off a handshake before we speak our names: "Huxley Mojave."

"Gorgeous." The Headmaster positively glowed. "Gorgeous. Now!" He clapped his hands. "Cornel, Achilles, Donatien, and . . . Huxley . . . you'll be wanting me to leave, so you can get on with patching up the . . . bruising that today's surprise and Donatien's tantrum have inflicted on the alliance you're still pretending you don't have. I'll leave you to it. Just kiss and make up fast. Don't want you missing the race!"

Achilles squinted. "We have four days until the Games."

"Not your foot race," Faust laughed. "Tonight's race. The list with one name."

Caesar and Achilles traded frowns. "What are you talking about?"

"Did you not read through the lists, Cornel?"

Death in the guise of Caesar had recovered enough to make fists. "Explain or leave."

"The weapons-makers," Faust answered flatly. "The 'harbinger adepts.' There were three lists. The first list is people who surrendered, the second people they kidnapped, and the third list is those Utopia couldn't get their hands on, who are still at large, and capable of weaving massive, massive death. Everyone has that list now: you, me, O.S., the pretty public. There's only one name on it, Cornel, one person still not in Utopia's control who could make superweapons, the most dangerous and valuable person in the world. Everyone who's anyone will be in the race now, to snatch that fruit. Everyone but me, of course. I shall remain voyeur."

"Who is it?"

"Cato Weeksbooth."

The Race for Cato Weeksbooth

Written August 19–20, 2454
Event of August 18
Klamath Marsh

As, IN A FAMINE, A WISE MAN DOES NOT CLUTCH HIS LAST biscuit to the end, but chooses carefully the hour it will serve him best, so my many masters judged this the right day to use the bloodhound that is Mycroft Canner.

The first alarm which went off at the Klamath Marsh Secure Hospital was not the perimeter alarm, but an internal security system on one of the pharmaceutical storage lockers. Possibly someone tried to access the locker, but more probably the alarm box was jostled when one employee body slammed another against the door. It took eleven minutes from the publication of the Utopian lists for reports of trouble at the hospital to reach Papadelias, and twelve further minutes for Klamath Marsh Secure Hospital to fall silent. By then we were already en route—myself, Achilles, Martin, and a mix of guards—but it was sixty-five minutes from Romanova to Oregon, whose mountains offer Nature's therapy to those minds Science can't yet heal, and there were many already moving on Cato's side of the Atlantic. Individual tracker calls leaked from the hospital, but these were few and calculated, most calling their own Hives or personal contacts rather than general emergency lines. The six Masons employed at the hospital could describe only being trapped in some wing far from the prisoner. Papadelias and Spain forwarded us fragments which were not much better. Silence from Kosala, Ancelet, and Dominic confirmed they too were in this race.

Huxley Mojave supplied our first real view of things, a bird's-eye view (or dragon's-eye, or pterosaur's, or robot's, or ariel's) offered on the car's screen. The mountainside hospital-prison had been quickly fortressed. Someone had severed a pipe, whose foaming spray made the lower slopes to the south and east an impassable cascade of white water and crumbling mud. At the main northern gate of the complex, two heavy construction cranes lashed their long necks like frightened brachiosaurs, and the lynch (or anti-lynch?) mobs stayed well clear. The only remaining approach was the forested crest above the hospital, which, in the predawn blackness, sparkled with the tiny lights of moving figures winking in and out of visibility among the trees. For a mob to reach the mountain so quickly it must have consisted of people who had clearance to land cars in this secure zone, so a mix of cops and the administrators who had already known Cato's secret location, plus allies they tipped off. The hospital itself was a showpiece of spectacle architecture: curving folds of warm wood, like a tangle of ribbon candy, forming the core structure of walls, halls, balconies, and levels, while all remaining surfaces were glass, which glittered in the clarity of night. Achilles read some patterns in the movement on the slopes, a large group blocking several smaller ones, a parley in progress among some of them, but I concentrated on memorizing the hospital's blueprints: the gauntlet I was about to run.

Kill or kidnap, that was the real question. I would not be the first to reach him. If whoever beat me to him just wanted to make the world safe, then a quick snap of the neck might have ended things already. But, while all the Powers on Earth were racing to seize Cato, the first to reach him would be nurses, doctors, orderlies, and guards. The power is theirs. Imagine them as the news breaks, night shifters laughing in the snack room, guiding restocking robots, checking beds, when the news crosses their lenses and death's hush falls. Breath catches, eyes avoid each other, muscles tense. Suddenly it matters which staff members wear boots and which a wrap, who cheered at Prospero's acquittal and who cursed, and on whose breast the bull's-eye sits. They know the first of them to act will . . . what? Will win? Will save the world? Will live? Each guesses what the others might try: Kill Cato? Guard him? Offer him to one side? Which side? Those far from Cato's cell might think of the hospital's other inmates first, protect (against) them by jamming doors and locking down what can be locked down. Others will go for the prize. Barricades will rise, to trap enemy colleagues in a break room, in the staff wing, in their beds. A trail of brawls will trace a path to him, unconscious doctors, others grappling, screaming, forcing doors. I do not know which cell holds Cato, but they know inside, every one of them, and, when I see them, tension and guilty glances will tell me which door they fear. Their fear will be my map.

We landed at the southwest edge of the complex, where a group of twenty had built a fort of upturned benches and safety foam. Our volley of stun fire sent most of them to Hypnos's kind kingdom before I recognized the uniforms of forest rangers. This was Greenpeace Mitsubishi land, and its defenders were well prepared for a wolf's rush or a cougar's stealth, but not for us. Achilles took most of our force north to make himself master of the crowds outside, while Martin with eight Masonic guards and Delian Huxley followed me up tree trunks, then a quick rope's swing to the nearest layer of roof. I did not look back. Those who could keep up would guard my back. Those who could not would fade.

The first high window offered reading couches and a clump of wide-eyed figures silhouetted against a full-wall screen on which howling pundits alternated with the smoking rubble Utopia had made of so many seats of science. Haste could not tempt me to enter here. I would choose my entrance as an epicure chooses the fig whose navel, just starting to part and leak a drop of sweetness, proves the flesh within will be crimson and perfect. I climbed the outside of the hospital, level to level, freezing whenever the curve of a turret or a security bot came into view, waiting for a shot from one of Martin's Masons to make them still. Rooms with closed doors were nothing to me, whether empty or full of staring faces. I sought damage, and found it, a door smashed open, and the carcass of a table whose sharp steel legs had been harvested for a more primal purpose than standing.

The security glass sang as we cut through it, and a smell of cleanliness and chemistry welcomed us to the first room in our maze. I snatched a shard of window, since I had not had time to kit myself with a periscope. The ghost of the hallway reflected in the glass showed upturned carts and stillness, and, beyond, the branching hallways which the blueprints told me led, one to the recreation wing, the other to the hospital's secure heart. I charged. Quiet hallway, turn, quiet hallway, turn. That must be Martin panting behind me, not quite equal to this speed. And what is this, a sense of fullness flanking me, like the barely perceived caress of an air vent but a breath too warm? Delian Huxley and the lion, one on either side of me, invisible—such was their synchrony and softness that I could not tell which was which.

A stock-still startled stare was the first face I found, a skinny figure in pajamas standing in a hallway opposite a door which was jammed shut with boxes and hastily angled chairs. She spun and aimed an apparatus at me, a chemical extinguisher perhaps or safety foam, but the tautness in her shoulders promised defense, not offense, and the swirl of her leg as she turned spoke of habituation to a Cousin's wrap. "We're extraction, not a hit squad," I barked at once, as gently as my racing breath would let me. "Is there anyone in Security HQ?"

Her neck straightened with the sudden realization that she held power. "Who sent you?"

"Romanova," I half lied.

She looked us over, but we wore nothing recognizable, not here. "There were noises from that way recently," she said. "I didn't look."

I nodded thanks, moving forward until I could see through the window in the door she guarded, and spot the enemies she held caged, hard to identify by pajamas and physique alone. I did not care who they were—I only wished her to believe I cared. "Backup is close. Do you think you can hold things here for . . . twelve minutes or so?" Encouraging tone, make her feel brave, make her feel coequal.

A timid nod grew firmer. "Things have been quiet up here."

"Good. It'll be over soon. Once we get Cato safely out it'll all calm."

She flinched again, glancing left, head tilted slightly upward, thinking of the left fork and the ramp beyond: Cato was up that way, then, but not too close, southwest . . .

I smile. "Cell 605, right?"

She bites her lip, draws back, aims the apparatus at me, tucks in her right elbow, thinking of her tracker. I've made a mistake. I'll get nothing more here. I charge ahead, left turn, up the ramp, aware of some last words of calm spoken to the Cousin by panting Martin. I summon the blueprints before me: only six cells on that end of each floor, numbered #02 to #07. Was Cato on the seventh floor, not sixth? No, the Cousin's stiffness spoke of some more glaring error. Something I should have known. Was he not in a normal cell, then?

A barricade at the top of the ramp: tables and sofas and a sideways exercise grid with defenders cowering behind. I fly. I grasp the chair leg brandished at me as I soar over their heads, and now it is a weapon in my hand as well as theirs, and my hand is the stronger. A foe's yelp spurs me as an arm crumples, a bulky arm, well trained, but only against weights and robots that do not strike back. I land among my adversaries, five, four Humanists and a Greenpeace Mitsubishi. I kick one in the temple, and block a chair leg with the one I carry, the aluminum rods singing like swords, but chair legs have no crosspiece to guard clenched knuckles. I slam my opponent's knuckles and the weapon falls, the throat forgets language and syllable as it gurgles in pain. I leave that one for Saladin to finish off and body-rush another, half burying my face in the salty, soap-scented looseness of shirt. I can feel, with my embracing grip, how the ribs jolt inward like a closing turtle as I slam this body against the floor and banish breath.

An ally's tap on my hip reminds me I should use the stun gun Martin gave me. I draw it, test the grip, and now feel something at my back, the dumpster's corrugated coldness as I count the breaths before I charge out onto this first battlefield with Saladin beside me. Will I kill you, Apollo? Will I stop your war? No, this is not a dumpster at my back. It is a coat of storm.

"Mycroft Canner!" One recognizes me, the least winded of these fallen partners of my exercise. Good Humanist. He will not answer questions, not without pain, and pain takes time, but he might answer with his eyes. I throw him to the floor, loom over him. His teeth are chattering. I loom left: no greater terror. Right, then, the hallway toward the northern wing. No change in his face. What is he staring at? Not me. Over my shoulder. Huxley? I press Huxley back. Not Huxley. The lion? Yes, the black lion, which shows itself now, sitting on another prisoner, its soft weight removing the painful duty to attempt escape. He fears the sight of a U-beast? Of course. I whisper: "Room 600, Ráðsviðr's cell." My foe's eyes tell me I have hit the mark. Never let me think myself clever, reader, when it took me so long to realize. This is Klamath Marsh. This place will have the right to call itself a Prince of Prisons to the world's end, for here, in our hour of horror, mankind confined Ráðsviðr, "Plan-wise," the first and only A.I. U-beast that used the intelligence we gifted it to plan murder. Utopia stopped it in time, and delivered the beast at once to Romanova's Minors' Law, which had been prepared for this in theory for half a century, and had precedents among high primates. The judge's call was easy. It was a separate challenge designing a cell that could humanely confine an amphibious arctic shapeshifter which could disassemble into hundreds of swimming shards. Since parts of Ráðsviðr were biological enough for age to claim it, its cell has been repurposed since its death: storage, sauna, swimming pool; but the design remains, armored still against technology and genius. Where better to imprison Cato Weeksbooth, a fake mad scientist but a true murder adept, who must know as well as I do how to exploit door locks, ventilation grilles, and slivers of sharp toenail?

"Mycroft, look at this." Martin pointed to a dark spot on the carpet near the wall. Poor, panting Martin, slowed by his vocation which left less time for exercise than we have who train each day for MASON's safety, or, in my case, for my coming battle with Apollo rouser-of-armies. I crouched. A tremor through my fingers told me that I smelled blood before I registered the salt scent. I crouched over it, a spatter on the floor, no more than a broken nose might dribble in a fist fight. Then Martin shot me in the back.

"August eighteenth," he dictated to his tracker as he leaned over my paralyzed form. "Eighteenth trap. Incapacitated Mycroft in Klamath Marsh Secure Hospital while many forces, including Sniper's, are in progress infiltrating in search of Cato Weeksbooth. Arranging plausible defeat scenario." He turned my head to let me see him and the hallway, then nodded to the Masonic guards around him, who slumped to the ground in feigned stunned postures. Next he adjusted his tracker. "Achilles? Weeksbooth is in cell six hundred . . . Yes . . . I have Mycroft in position now. Can you confirm Sniper's forces are inside? . . . Good." Another shift of tracker. "Guildbreaker in position . . . Target is in cell six hundred. Are you ready to reactivate the surveillance system? . . . Thirty seconds is enough."

Martin leaned over me, and I heard the subtle shift of Griffincloth, then one more shot, and Martin slumped across me, the stiffness of true incapacitation adding verisimilitude to his sprawl. In a fitter state my trained eyes might have spotted Huxley Mohave hiding away the stun gun that had added this last bait to Martin's trap. Someone invisible threw something over me and Martin, stuffy, clinging like a blanket, invisible but buzzing with electric life. I heard Huxley casting similar invisible blanket-shields over the faking Masons, but Martin's stun blast had been a strong one, and my thoughts quickly decayed into the fragmentation of half dream. My tasks. What was today? Tuesday. Must check the trash-mine bots for clogs tomorrow, and have my session with Julia. What else? My chronicle, I skipped some weeks, must go back, tell how Achilles's Myrmidons saw their first action. And Bridger, yes, Bridger has homework due to Cato's Junior Scientist Club tomorrow. What's this week's topic? Hadrons? Hubble? Hobbes?

The whoosh of something fast as a whirlwind made me feel the terror of paralysis, as my mind woke keenly but my flesh would not obey. Something had plunged across me, shrieking down the hallway. It halted at the end to consider its next turn, left or right, and at my angle I could just make out the profile of a motorbike, and, on its seat, a Typer twin. A rush of bodies followed the rider, clambering over the barricade and us too hurriedly to check what bodies these were that they stepped between. I could see only their backs as they advanced past us: assorted jackets, some Olympic patterns, Humanist Blue Team, Green Team, Black, others all six colors. One vigorous, petite figure might have been Lesley Saneer. Their Spanish was too soft and hasty for me to parse, their passage swift, around the corner, silence.

Twenty seconds, thirty seconds.

Then a blast, as someone peeked back around the corner where the enemy had just passed, and fired off a scatter pattern. Silent and dim, the blast struck the invisible net across myself and Martin, the faking Masons, and the original unconscious makers of the barricade. Whatever lay across us drank up the blast, but its crackle made my ears ring and my pacemaker bleep.

The single figure approached us, quiet, neither fast nor slow, a dark athletic jacket with the hood up taut. The size was right: not short, not tall, a little heavy; my second stabber? They braced their scattergun and fired a second shot, a third, a fourth—wise caution. A Mason lying near us faked a twitch at the first blast, a slighter twitch at the second, and after that leaked drool. The stranger drew close, and my eyes could just focus enough to see them sheathe the scattergun and draw another gun, dark and heavy, with a thick, round barrel as in olden days, whose black mouth promised lead. They aimed at me.

"I want to watch." It was the tiniest of voices, too soft to be the enemy's—a tracker call?

The figure crouched and pressed the barrel to my head.

"I want to watch!" the voice repeated. "You know how long I've been waiting."

The enemy gave a cough of hushed contempt as their free hand reached into a pocket and drew out a tiny man. I could not make out the face beneath the army helmet, or the ugly, ugly smile upon it, but I did not have to. Private Croucher. Coward, traitor, deserter, Croucher.

"Ooh! Guildbreaker, too!" the deserter crooned, his head and slouching shoulders peeking between the enemy's fingers. "Do Guildbreaker first. Let him watch. Let him know."

The other did not argue, too practical, too aware that one shot takes less time than one objection.

Croucher's tiny figure leaned as close to me as he dared. "Martin first, then you—and Achilles will be next." His words were thick and bitter. "You think the world wants this to be your war? You selfish coward heroes? Your MASON bawling over Alexandria getting scratched up, and you and Achilles fawning over him like smitten girls. And you're what we're supposed to die for?"

"Gloat later," the gunman whispered. It was a man. The invisible tarp across us crinkled as he pressed the barrel to Martin's temple.

Lions really roar. Did you know that reader? And a lion's real roar, inches from his head, makes the calmest killer wet himself. Warm heaviness leapt over me, but, in that shadowed hallway, not even an owl's eye could have tracked the charge of a half-invisible black lion. Blood happened, and a shot, a second shot, almost inaudible over the roar. Huxley leapt in too, a living wall between us and the fray, and I heard and saw the flash of weapons unknown to me, for all my studies of Apollo's coat. The lion slumped, bleeding, sizzling, beeping softly as its internal systems improvised, but the Masons were on their feet now, holding well-trained guns. The attacker stagger-ran desperate retreat.

"We have your blood now." Huxley Mojave's words could not be called a shout, just clear and planned command. "We'll have your identity in minutes. Tell us what happened to Sniper and we won't expose you to the rest of O.S."

My pacemaker bleeped satisfaction as I calmed. This too, then, was good Martin's plan. Why pull this thorn from the heart of O.S. when he could leave it in place, and use it?

The enemy halted, just out of fire-range around the corner. "I don't hop when strings are pulled." It was a mature voice, low. "Tell them if you like. They won't believe you. When you run that DNA, *you* won't believe you."

"You've betrayed O.S. If you tell us what you want we—"

"Threats to bribes in six seconds? You are desperate."

Huxley rushed forward, fluid motion like the flapping of a swan, but a spray of scatterfire from the corner forced retreat. "Tell me what happened to Sniper or—"

"Thirty-three million."

"What?"

"I was paid thirty-three million for delivering Sniper. Black market auction, anonymous at every stage. Even I couldn't track the buyer if I tried. Things got heated toward the end, I understand, two very determined final bidders. Either that or I fed Sniper through a meat grinder and fed the slop to my piranhas. Which do you believe?"

"Wha—"

Heat and force and poison wind, like rot and vinegar, blasted us back. It was half explosion, half hiss, like the bursting of champagne, and in less than a second the end of the hall was a wall of pinkish foam. I could hear the gunman's limping retreat on the far side, coupled with shouts for help to the O.S. comrades who could not be far ahead.

"Circle around!" Half the Masons raced at once back down the ramp, while the others stayed, guarding Martin and myself as one knelt to administer a revitalizer. Huxley returned and knelt over the slowly breathing lion, stroking its muzzle and checking its wounds: reparable.

"Can you I.D. them?" Martin gasped as soon as he was strong enough to speak.

Digital eyes were wide.

"You have the blood. Can you run it?" Martin rose carefully.

"I've run it, but . . . I saw their face just now, I'm sure I've never seen that face before."

"Who is it?"

"According to this sample, genetically, that's Casimir Perry."

A wait for reinforcements let me think. Could Perry have survived? The man had changed his face before, the quick and promising young German M.P. Merion Kraye shedding his skin when Madame exiled him from politics and boudoir, to become the industrious Polish bulldog Casimir Perry. He had planned the Brussels attack so carefully, arranged that every stray member of Parliament and Cabinet be hunted down, no matter how estranged. Had he arranged a trapdoor under the podium too, so he could fake his death? Flee laughing into Brussels's underbelly as the flames rose high? It seemed mad, but he was a madman, and it did make sense of how dispassionate the hand had been that had plunged the second knife into my wound. The man who burned the world down to avenge himself upon Madame and Andō, the man whose love for Danaë turned poison, who did not care one jot about Carlyle even upon discovering she was his real child, such a man does not have hate left over for Mycroft Canner. To all the Earth I am a horror, but to him I am an asset of his enemy, to be extinguished, nothing more. And he did love sausages. But if Perry-Kraye wanted revenge, his work was done. Madame's had been destroyed, O.S. exposed, Ganymede and Andō shamed and arrested. I remembered feeling done when I had finished my two weeks. Death was all I wanted. Perry-Kraye was as haunted and monstrous and tired a thing as I had been, so why choose life? And why infiltrate O.S.? Was he not done, then? Were there more steps to his revenge? This maniac commanded a vast, world-snaring network of Madame's exiles and bitter enemies, a force which had no side in this war, no sigil, only hate for her and hers. Another power hiding in the dark. I felt like I had spent months planning an assault on some grim but well-studied fortress, only to be told mid-battle that the castle had an underground.

«Weeksbooth's gone.»

The news and tired Papadelias waited for us when we finally reached Cell 600. The condition of the hall outside confirmed that many had fought here: sweat, smashed walls, shattered chairs, dents and scratches on the doorframe, and, down the hallway, medics bearing wounded away.

«No fatalities,» Papa confirmed, the Great Test on his mind as much as ours.

«Achilles?» I asked.

«Got here faster than I did, but not fast enough. They're chasing O.S.'s people now.»

«Then O.S. got Cato?»

Papa shook his head. «They weren't first either. There's a note. Come.»

Breath left me as I peered from the cell entrance down to the distant floor of what had once been a cylinder of artificial ocean. I had not imagined there could be a throne room in this world that I had not yet seen, but here it stood. A throne of paper. That was all they would give Cato in their caution after his many suicide attempts: paper and soft wax pencil, but paper rolled into a tight tube becomes a stick, and sticks arranged in careful triangles become strength, strength architecture. So, within this soft-walled chamber, patient Cato had made himself a table, tools, racks to store them, machines to rip and roll the paper tighter, building blocks, a bicycle, models: a plane, a space shuttle, a jointed arm, a helmet, a city, a racetrack to test fantastic vehicles which may never have names. The walls were papered too, sheets covered with sketches and calculations layered like feathers all the way from floor to ceiling, and tall comblike structures on rollers standing against the walls, so their tines could pass across and flip the papers over to expose their undersides, wasting no surface. Against the far wall, commanding a view of all, Cato had built his seat, high and contoured, perfectly proportioned, with mass upon mass of papers, used and virgin, flanking it in high, attendant piles. Every instinct in me knew that mass of spit and paper was a throne.

One page lay upon the seat: "We would have left Cato if you were willing to keep them safe and untapped, but none of you are. And they were ours to begin with.—CMSIJSS."

"Papa! Look at this!" An aide found Cato's Humanist boots lying among the papers at the throne's feet, their soles slashed with deep, intentional X-es and their Griffincloth surfaces dead. "Cato didn't have these in hospital. How'd they get here?"

"I got the video up!"

"Surveillance?"

Papa raised it for us on a screen. There sat Cato Weeksbooth on his paper throne, at work on some device. His hands trembled, rolling the paper with precise but frantic speed, leaning low in the dim lights of emergency power. Suddenly he flinched, eyes flicking up to the door, as some sound from outside warned that enemies were about to pierce his sanctum. After a few seconds, he returned to his work, assembling . . . I think it was a blowpipe designed to shoot capsules of complexly folded paper. Another warning sound, keep working, keep working, his fingers flying with the steady desperation of a diver repairing her broken air tank, who hears the submarine crunching around her, and cannot know how many seconds she has left. Then, in an instant, light too pure and sudden to be fire ruptured the empty air, as if some rift in space had birthed suns out of nothing. A cluster of suns ringed Cato, and after some seconds the bodies showed themselves. I saw a coat of chrome and steel, a coat of ice, a coat of farmland, coats that made the walls of paper into dragonscales, into hydroponic rows, into the rib cage of some robot colossus, and two coats that showed seawater and the black shards of ghostly Ráðsviðr schooling in different patterns. Delians. He ran into their arms. Tears of fear and desperation turned to joy. They embraced him, soothed his shoulders with kind hands and his mind with words, though Papa's techs had not restored sound yet. Some plans and gestures were exchanged, and four Delians set to gathering papers and creations, carefully selected from among the mass. The others faced Cato solemnly, and one produced his boots, still active, their Griffincloth showing the bones and muscles of the hands which held them. A second offered Cato a knife, and a third a data tablet, sleek and gold-plated like the entrails of a satellite. Tears of joy gave way to tears of something stronger. Trembling Cato took the knife and slashed the boots with a fierce intentionality, as when a man signs the contract he knows will forever guide his life. I did not need sound to know what words he spoke when he placed his hand upon the golden tablet through which all accumulated human knowledge raced as fast as thought:

"I hereby renounce the right to complacency, and vow lifelong to take only what minimum of leisure is necessary to my productivity, viewing health, happiness, rest, and play as means, not ends, and that, while Utopia provides my needs, I will commit the full produce of my labors to our collective effort to redirect the path of human life away from death and toward the stars."

They threw the coat about his shoulders, and were gone.

We were silent. What could we have said, witnesses to something so hasty, so illegal, and so right.

"What's CMSIJSS?"

Papa and I answered that one together: "The Chicago Museum of

Science and Industry Junior Scientists Squad." I smiled, and caught Papa smiling too, despite his knitted brows. "The kids grew up."

The Moon. I didn't say it; that was my complicity. They'd given away Ecuador, Gabon, and Borneo, so they must be taking Cato to the farthest elevator, Maldive Ridge, almost two hours' flight from Klamath Marsh. Papadelias or anyone could still catch Cato if they too realized there was only one right path for him now. How long had it been since he last set foot in Luna City? Ockham had forbidden it, fearing defection. Ockham even sent bash'mates as watchdogs when he let Cato go as far as orbit, once or twice a year for a field trip. Cato let me watch by video when it was Bridger's turn, a club trip up to watch weather patterns, play a game of tag in zero-g, and launch their little handmade satellites. They built them in teams, their own designs but with grown-up guidance, like a kid's first cake baked from scratch. Bridger's, I remember, had many little claws like a crustacean, and was designed to gather bits of debris too small for most cleaner satellites, and sort them into useful sacks to deliver to a host station to be reused, "so the old dead satellites can keep helping. They'd want that." The boy's face glowed when he and his friends watched the work of their own hands take flight, and something in his eyes brought back my childhood: the first time I cast off in a little boat from the rocky shores of home, and watched the sharp prow carve my ripples into the sea. Cato had never asked me where Bridger came from, or why I was his guardian, or why his club dues were always paid by random donors, and his registration at the museum was obviously fake. Cato didn't care. If we were bending the law, we served the higher law that kids deserve to learn. I was complicit back then too, wasn't I? Just like I was here in Cato's cell. I sent Bridger to Cato. I didn't send him to Alexandria, or Paris, or Hobbestown, or Tōgenkyō. I didn't send him to the 2450 Olympics, to play sports, to any of the fun camps offered by Cousins and Brillists, or even to meet the Minor Senators in Romanova. I sent him to Cato. I never chose a Hive for myself, but I chose one for Bridger. I think, reader, that I might be a traitor. I should want Jehovah to have Cato, to have everything that could add to that political prosthesis which substitutes for His rightful omnipotence. Here in His Peer's realm, my Master is a blind, deaf Paralytic, and I took something which might have been His new thumb, His new eye, and let the ants carry it away. I even gave Achilles over to Jehovah for His war and slaughter, but I wouldn't take Cato from Utopia, even for Him. I am a traitor. Or is it that I am not enough of a traitor? Am I weaker than Carlyle and Dominic, too weak to commit absolute filial impiety? I tried to turn my back on my Maker's Plan, to stop thinking of myself as a sailor on His sea, but I still love Apollo's stars so much that I forget Jehovah is bigger. My dreams are still within this universe, so infinite, so small, so near. I want to smell Mars dust. If I can't then I want somebody to: Apollo, Cato, you. Don't tell Achilles, reader. I think I let Utopia take Cato Weeksbooth. I think I might have let them become Troy.

Greek profanity streamed from Papadelias like blood from a severed artery.

«What?» I asked.

He tapped his tracker. «While we were all here chasing Cato, someone sprung Thisbe Saneer.»

Chapter TWENTY-ONE

༺༺༺༺༺༺༺༺༺༺༺༺༺༺༺༺༺༺

Written September 12–14, 2454
Events of August 22–September 6
Esperanza City, Romanova

IT IS WITH A HEAVY HEART THAT I TAKE UP THIS CHRONICLE.
Mycroft Canner—long your guide and my beloved teacher—was killed in
action six days ago, on Sunday the sixth of September, 2454.

No one knows how to mourn. Almost everyone in the world thought
Mycroft deserved death, except those who knew life was a harsher punishment. We're not allowed to call this feeling 'sadness.' MASON, Vivien, none
of them can look me in the face now, because I remind them too much of
how dirty they feel for missing Mycroft Canner. We have no ritual for this,
no stock phrase. If we had a funeral, they might at least get some closure
from pointedly refusing to attend. As for the Prince, J.E.D.D. Mason, when
humans mourn we need the words and hugs of friends and equals, but, in
the Godly language spoken by Them and Their Peer, World War seems to
be the word for 'Hello.' I shudder to imagine how They would ask Their
Peer, "Why did You kill My angel?" 'Angel' is the right word. Others would
say pet, or slave, or friend, or monster, but I know what Mycroft was. The
Prince came here alone, so Their Host lent Them what all Gods need. And
what They lend They take away again. I should not wish Mycroft rest; they
would not want it, both because they left so much undone, and because
they believed a universe would be unjust which granted Mycroft Canner
mercy. But I must wish them something. I know what they wanted. It's impossible, but the impossible doesn't tend to stay impossible when humans
are involved. Times change because we change them, and therein there is
hope, even for Mycroft. I cannot reach them, but perhaps somehow, someday, someone will read this who can. If progress continues, time must someday stop being a barrier. Perhaps science will crack Bridger's legacy and
replicate the resurrection potion, or make a time machine, or a portal to

the underworld. Perhaps Utopia will finally finish disarming Death, or we will pierce the veil enough to get a message through, if not into the after-life, then at least through time, beamed back into a long-dead person's fi-nal living thoughts. I believe we will achieve this someday, and if this chronicle survives, and you, who are reading it, have these arts, perhaps you can reach back and grant the one prayer Mycroft Canner dared pray for themself. Tell them the seeds have flown. Tell them the Great Project continued, that the destruction of this world did save a better one. Tell them that this war, that Utopia's sacrifice, did not turn humanity back toward Earth's safe, complacent harbors. Tell them that you have walked on worlds which make Mars seem a stepping stone. Tell them that, who-ever won this war, the human race did not stop here. If you are out there, distant, distant reader, reach back, for pity's sake—you are the only one who can—reach back and tell Mycroft: "The seeds have flown." Tell them, and tell me, too.

*　*　*

I apologize for interrupting my successor, reader, but I should tell you: I am not actually dead. This universe is not so unjust as to grant Mycroft Canner rest. When I read this eulogy, I did not have the heart to erase words of such kindness, but neither am I so cruel as to leave you, my good mas-ter, deceived. I was missing for some months, and surely should have died amid such dangers, but our Maker is a good Host, and cares for the needs of His Guest. He took me from Jehovah as the war began, I think in order to talk to Him about loss, but then He restored me, lest His Guest's Grief become too great. I entrust you, therefore, for these next months, to my successor, a worthier guide than I, but I assure you that I shall return to serve again at your command, good reader, when my Maker wills.

> NOTE: The paragraph above was inserted into this chronicle several weeks after I wrote this chapter, but several weeks before we discovered Mycroft was alive. I have no explanation as of yet.—9A.

*　*　*

Now I am to continue Mycroft's chronicle. To start with, I shall do pre-cisely what Mycroft didn't. The weird period customs Mycroft introduced in their first history require that I, in their words, "introduce myself, my background and qualifications, and tell you by what chance or Providence it is that the answers you seek are in my hands." After setting up this expectation, Mycroft flagrantly did none of it except to give their name. I shall do the opposite, and tell you everything about myself, except my name.

Believe it or not, you know me already, at least as well as you know Prospero Saneer, or Felix Faust. I have already appeared six times in Mycroft's history, but Mycroft never named me, or let you realize I was the same person. You first met me when I held back the other Servicers who would have defended Mycroft from being carried off by Vivien, the first time Mycroft showed you Romanova. I also sat with them in the Pantheon on Renunciation Day. I was with Mycroft when we first stumbled on their Enemy, Tully Mojave, on their soapbox, and, in the moments before the dragons quelled the mob, I dove to place myself between my mentor and the crowd, a moment which verified empirically that I am indeed ready to give my life for Mycroft Canner. I also oversaw the relocation of Bridger's toy collection after Dominic discovered it. It was I who saved Carlyle Foster-Kraye from curious Humanists, and then failed to stop Foster-Kraye from flying into Dominic's trap at Madame's. I set up Bridger's safe house, and kept the kid company there, so to me too goes some of the blame for failing to keep Bridger away from Sniper at the end. More recently, Mycroft described the Servicers who watched the Senate chaos with Achilles, when Achilles told me my uniform designs were stupid. For that scene, while Mycroft gave the others the names of Myrmidon captains from the *Iliad*, they gave me the playful title *Outis*, 'No-one' in our native Greek; in other words, Anonymous. I am the Ninth Anonymous, Mycroft's successor. It was my name sealed in the *Sanctum Sanctorum*, though happily those who stole the MASONS' Oath don't seem to care about exposing me. Still, I have no intention of redoubling their violation by revealing my name to you. I will answer to Anonymous, to Ninth or 9A, at Madame's to the Compte Déguisé, and even to *chiot* (puppy, or *Hundchen* from Faust), but I will not answer, as my predecessor did, to slave, or wretch, or monster. You know my voice because I have been Mycroft's editor, in the last books and this. I patched together their fragments, made bearable what was too passionate, and in the history I used to edit out the signs of Mycroft's madness, though I've decided to leave them in this more recent chronicle. It is some consolation to me to remember how broken Mycroft was toward the end, how ready for release. Perhaps it will console you, too.

My background? I am a Greek, and a Servicer. I was a Humanist, raised in a mixed Humanist-European bash' with one Brillist member, all Greek save two. I excelled at sprinting, sailing, biology, debate, and logic puzzles, enjoyed helping my ba'pas train Cretan Hounds, and loved strategic board games, though I never specialized enough in one to place in competition. I passed the Adulthood Competency Exam at fifteen, and immediately became a Humanist. I studied logic, literature, and law, first in Athens, then at the South London Campus, then at Romanova's Quirinal Campus, and my first job, while I was still studying, was as a speechwriter's assistant in the office of Senator Alexis Cosmatos. When I was twenty-two, and still deciding which of two newly forming bash'es to join, three fellow Humanists abducted my youngest bas'sib, abused, tortured, and murdered them, for sport. A hiccup in the law acquitted them. Shortly thereafter, I lured them into a warehouse and beat the three of them to death with a steel bar very, very slowly. I did not attempt to hide my crime, and psychologists confirmed I was unlikely to repeat it. One of the three guilty parties was a vocateur physician, and another an architect, so, since my own career path was promising but not promising enough to make it probable that I could pay for their estimated lost production even with a lifetime's work, Humanist law made me a Servicer. That was just over three years ago.

The Eleventh Hive, as Servicers sometimes jokingly call ourselves, is strangely familial and fulfilling. We travel the world, forage for work, make and fix things with our own hands, and labor's exercise makes us sleep well in dorms full of equals. We aren't fully real in the eyes of free people, like how two large birds fighting over a feeder barely register the little ones that hop around gathering seeds they drop. I quickly came to enjoy the simplicity of it, especially how it let me alternate between the catharsis of physical labor and signing up for brain work, impressing the snot out of whoever hadn't realized what they were getting. I heard whispers that there was a "Beggar King" among us, but had no further clue before I realized I was being watched by several very veteran Servicers, the unofficial elders of our unofficial tribe. I couldn't guess why; I hadn't requested help, and hadn't stepped out of line enough to risk bringing public wrath down on Servicerkind. I cornered one elder in a bathroom and demanded what gives. They said that I was smart, Greek, reliable, knew politics, and that they had a job for me. I was afraid they meant criminal work, one of these situations where one of us has unfinished business in the outside that we all agree can't be ignored, even if trouble follows. Instead they showed me Mycroft.

It took more than a glance but less than an evening with Mycroft to realize they were something special. It was like a myth, a pool where village maidens go to skinny dip, and one day we realize a nymph has joined us, glowing like the Moon and not quite real. No one says anything, and we treat the nymph like one of us, for fear any acknowledgment might scare this marvel off forever. And if one day the nymph follows us back into the village to take a turn at weaving, we don't dare refuse, we just take constant extra care with this visitor who lends the town a little touch of magic. That constant extra care became my job. "Did you eat today, Mycroft? How long since you last slept? How many hours?" Mycroft was a master of lies of omission, but not so good at direct lies, not to a friend. We were friends instantly, the instant Mycroft realized they could pour out all the mad convolutions of high politics to me, and in our native Greek, and I would understand. Even better, I was a junior Servicer, younger and newer to our ranks, the only type of person in the world who was not, by crazy Mycroft logic, their superior. Mycroft hadn't realized how desperately they needed that, but the elders did. So I became Mycroft's apprentice, and babysitter to the Beggar King. Mycroft was never really a ruler to the Servicers, not like Achilles is now. They were more a teacher and adviser, like a quiet, deposed king who labored modestly alongside us and solved our problems with masterful statecraft when we asked for aid, but had no heart for the bloody road back to the throne. No, king isn't otherworldly enough. Nymph is still better, and when our little guest nymph disappeared on strange jobs, it didn't take me long to discover it was Olympian gods who carried them away. So soon enough I met MASON, the King of Spain, President Ganymede, Bryar, and Vivien. I entered the netherworld that was Madame's, and sometimes helped clean up a little cave under a bridge in Cielo de Pájaros, though I never knew for whom. And one day, I realized: "Mycroft, there's no way you don't know who the Anonymous is. In fact, I bet you weren't secretly informed like Papa was, but you figured it out on your own. In fact, you're the next Anonymous, aren't you?" Of course they were, in line to be Eighth, so figuring that out made me the Ninth. Vivien glowed with joy like a new grandba'pa when Mycroft presented me, a successor to carry the precious title past the instability that was Mycroft Canner. That was when I started spending more nights than was strictly legal stretched on sofas in the Ancelet-Kosala bash'house, enjoying midnight chess and Bryar's curry, training for my accession. It came soon. Mycroft was too overworked and broken to actually serve as Anonymous, and they wanted their history to expose their identity anyway, so I succeeded to the title of Ninth Anonymous the day the first book was released, June the twenty-eighth, 2454— ten weeks to the day before we lost them.

Mycroft had no time to write during the Olympics, so that's where I'll begin.

Sniper did come. They rode into the Opening Ceremony on a white horse that sparkled like diamond in the stage light, and the torch they lit blazed so brilliantly across the ice that they say you could see it from orbit. But even more important, Sniper turned up three days before that, the morning after Thisbe and Cato disappeared, and Sniper's return let us all stop panicking. Lesley called us first to say Sniper was back. A couple hours later Sniper did an interview, a stirring speech about how proud they were that we had kept the peace so long, and an apology to fans for being so out of the limelight during their training for the Games. But Sniper wouldn't say what had happened to them, not even to Lesley. I saw them the second day after they got back. On the training field they were lively, if a little out of practice, but exertion can block thought like clouds block sun. It was in the breaks between training that frightening new habits surfaced. Sniper lapsed into long quiet patches, speaking or moving only when prompted, and sometimes it took two or three repetitions to get any reaction. They flinched at bright light, fidgeted intensively for short periods, and sometimes got up suddenly and ran around and around whatever space we were in, sprinting until they couldn't run anymore, which for a pentathlete is a very long time. They were still perfect, lively Sniper in front of fans or cameras, but it was all performance. Once I caught them on the floor curled up in Lesley's arms, sobbing. They were missing four months. Sniper has a billion champions ready to beat the crap out of whoever did this to such a hero, but in me they have one more. That is assuming it was a person, and not a fall down a cave followed by a long fight out through a thousand savage mole-men or something, who knows. (Personally, I don't think Perry-Kraye really knows where Sniper was, I think Perry-Kraye was just taunting Martin and Huxley.) But we had Sniper back in time, and Sniper had their family: the Humanist Black Team, all the teams. Every pentathlete and everyone from every relevant sport dropped everything to help Sniper get back into shape those last three days. Even Achilles.

If those Opening Ceremonies are the last pure thing our civilization ever does, they were worthy. The Milky Way turned out to watch, its long line of hypercrowded lights, more like city fog than stars, staring down at us through the black of the long Antarctic night. The stadium roof was open to the sky and darkness, and the spectators were darkness too, tens of thousands of silhouettes, since the stadium itself was the light source, glowing from beneath, now azure, now fire, now sunny white, to suit the evolving spectacle. It was all built of ice gels: soft and fluffy for the seat cushions, springy for the walkways, steel-strong for the base, and even the veins of light which branched like lightning through the clear blocks were some conductive form of ice that leaflets bragged about. Mycroft and I got to sit right behind Vivien, personal guests of an Olympic Committee member, so we had even better seats than MASON.

The spectacle portion started with ships, real creaking wood, which braved the choppy currents of a pool that filled the arena. Then the pool rose, a transparent cylinder of water as high as the highest seats. Swimmers danced through it in costumes of fantastic colors, inspired by the ancient microbes that were first to inhabit Antarctica, or anywhere. They trailed structures as they swam, lines of what seemed like glitter but hardened in their wakes into permanent trails, like jet smoke, or the shapes that ribbon dancers weave, but solid. It was ice. The water they swam through was far below freezing, kept liquid by some science, but at the top of the tank was a layer of some other water, warmer and quick to freeze, which the swimmers would splash in and then veer down, so it froze as they sucked it down with them through the sub-zero currents below. They wove the ice streams together like maypole dancers, constructing dive by dive a shape, which seemed a fan at first, then a flower, then the chalice-shaped cauldron which we realized must soon hold the flame. A parade arrived to ring the water column, people and creatures, and we gasped as the swimmers joined it by exiting through the sides of the pool, forcing their bodies through what was not solid glass but gel, which resealed around them, letting only the faintest glittering drips escape. Kipgel I think it's called, and Mycroft gushed at me about how it can make a space suit that you can reach through to eat and scratch your nose. Horses came next, riders with long lances, who slashed the gel tank and released streams of water, which froze mid-air to form arches and stalagmites. Dancers climbed them and waved colorful things around, and there were huge sheets of cloth which they got wet and flapped so they snap-froze into stiff curved sheets, and they built structures out of them, and climbed up those and built other structures, and sliced up the now-empty tank, and used the gel pieces to build trampolines, and jumped everywhere, and flung colorful water which froze in the air, and then it all lit up and suddenly it looked exactly like a city, and we cheered and cheered and cheered.

They didn't let us forget the war, but they did let us feel ready for it. Earth's top musicians played old battle-marches, and they projected war art on the walls, and brought in great actors to read quotations: Homer, Shakespeare, Tennyson, Korn, Faulkner, Gerribloom, Siegfried Sassoon, Osamu Tezuka, Euripides, Sun-tzu, and Victor Hugo. As they read, dancers in historical military costumes ripped down the ice-and-fabric city piece by piece. Then, just as it was too much to take, the whole stadium turned from blood red to pure white in a flash as they passed out two hundred thousand Peacedoves. These, they announced, were newly commissioned from a U-beast designer, programmed to seek out humans, and had a compartment inside for emergency supplies. It would take them a few months to fly from Antarctica to the cities where they would be needed. We were each given one dove to fill with the supplies they handed out, and were asked to write a message to put inside, addressed to someone a few months in the future. We couldn't know who our doves would find: Humanist or Mason; Hive-guard or Remaker; friend or foe. They gave us the whole Parade of Nations to think about what to write, and we needed it.

We also needed cheering up, and we got it with the parade of flags, and colors, and amazing ethnic hats. The Greek team marched first, the tiny figure of Achilles with them, but the hero wouldn't take the honor of Flag Bearer away from Krathis Piteras, the first biological female to ever take gold in the open division javelin throw. The French team wore gold to de-clare support for Ganymede, and the Spanish team received a particularly enthusiastic roar of welcome, while in the stands the king and queen-to-be waved their support. The Hive teams either felt or faked high spirits. There were uncomfortably many Masons, and I couldn't believe how many ath-letes marched stratless and unaligned, not just under the three Hiveless flags, but a big mass of them marching under the naked Olympic flag; I am used to two or three athletes going without a team due to some protest or tran-sition, but forty-six stank of chaos.

Each of the six Humanist teams chose its Flag Bearer as brilliantly as ever: for the Gold Team's dedication to the parallel honing of mind and body, poet-calligrapher-boxer Wence Courrier; for the Blue Team's focus on record-breaking through advances in knowledge and science, Takeshi Dubois, whose research on joint structure had revolutionized racewalking; for the Red Team's commitment to bringing each unique body's strengths to peak perfection we saw a new face, Dara Hiketrail, the most promising young gymnast of the Games; for Red's rival, Sniper's Black Team with its obsession with all-body training and maintaining top form over a long career, six-Olympiad veteran sailor Claude Langlais; for the Green Team's teaching-focused ethic, three-time debate medalist Ohlanga Coder; and for the Gray Team's focus on team training, if it could not be Quarriman them-self, it must be water beltball captains Tigris and Euphrates Webguard. It was strange having the host team be, not a nation-strat, but the Humanists' own Gray Team, but Antarctica had more than earned it, and, as the Olympic Oaths were taken and Aesop Quarriman declared the Games of the One Hundred and Fortieth Olympiad officially open, their speech hammered home that we were all sitting outside in Antarctica in August. The fireworks that crowned the ceremony drowned out the Milky Way, and screens showed that at the same instant they set off matching fireworks in Olympia where the Games were born, in Athens where they were reborn, in the first city on each other continent that held the Games, and in Kanpur, which would host them next. As the thunder climaxed I saw Achilles twitch and curl up, and the other Greeks leaned over them to see what was wrong. I don't think veterans can enjoy fireworks. I wonder how many of us will still be able to enjoy them in 2458.

It went dark then, the stadium dimming to leave just a hint of ocean-blue light deep within the frozen ground. A gaggle of children entered, and Kagera Marbank with a single lantern, who told the history of the Olympics with their famous hand shadow puppets. But suddenly the shadow puppet runner they projected on the wall was a real runner, and the instant they said 'torch' there it blazed in the hands of Avon McKenzie the wrestler, who represented the ancient Games by wearing nothing but a faux-classical loincloth. As Marbank's hand shadows provided opponents to race against, McKenzie passed the torch to Robin Tapolin the cyclist, who was costumed like the 1894 revival Games, and cycled a stunningly fast loop of the stadium with the torch. Then, stopping before the box where the Olympic Committee had made their opening speech, Tapolin ignited a faceted ball of what the program insists is flammable ice (how?), which soared up on a wire until it dangled above the ice chalice. Ting Ting Foster came out and sang a song, but by then we were all a sea of craned necks, looking for Sniper.

We were looking in the wrong place. Sniper broke above us like the Moon, up on the top lip of the stadium, so their diamond-white horse was barely a point of light. They show jumped down, a spiral path on horseback, run and jump and run and jump, down the structure of the stadium. They stopped on a platform level with the flaming ball, and fired up the crowd with a wave of their perfect arms and their signature pistol-shot hand gesture. Then they raised a very real rifle. They took aim at the cable which held the flame above the waiting cauldron, and we all braced: Can they really do it? Can they hit that tiny cable from clear across the arena, and light the Olympic Cauldron with a single perfect shot?

A second platform lit up suddenly, level with Sniper's on the opposite side of the arena. There stood the Prince, J.E.D.D. Mason. All through the opening They'd worn their six-colored Olympic Committee jacket (which looks absolutely wrong on Them), but now They wore Their customary black, with the new military cording, gold and gray and purple, that still makes Mycroft cringe. Made Mycroft cringe. Sniper looked up from their scope and nodded across at the Prince, and then the whole crowd cried out as we realized it was a clear shot, Sniper's gun to the Prince, and that the angles were so close that, as Sniper leaned over the scope, it was impossible to tell whether they were aiming at the cable, or at their Opponent's skull. Then the Prince raised something over Their head, the size of a small melon, and triggered it.

A flash. Crackling exploded around the device in the Prince's hand, sparks raining down and skittering across the clear ice of the platform. The air darkened as a swarm of defensive robots lost their cloaking, then their motors, and tumbled to the floor around the Prince like apples. The lights in that half of the arena failed next, and we spent a few breaths in darkness, cut only by the firelight and the Milky Way above, which spanned the skyscape like a long scar. My seat was close enough to the Prince that my tracker rebooted, and I heard Mycroft's pacemaker bleep beside me. That made me realize what it was: a Weeksbooth Counterbomb, like what Sniper used at the Forum to short out the Prince's security and give themself a clear shot. This time the Prince had fired it Themself, on purpose, and now They were just standing there, calm and exposed among the twitching wreckage of Their defenses. Since I knew what I was looking for, I spotted the moment that Their suit flashed static, the rebooting of the Griffincloth: complex programs like Mushi's and Huxley's took a while to restart, but it took mere moments for "make everything black" to come online again. This wasn't planned. I could tell it wasn't when I heard guards racing, and Vivien murmuring predictions: "Not here, Sniper, think, stampede, backlash, it would be an even worse war..." I remember Sniper's black hair sparkling as they bent over the rifle's silver shaft. They fired. The cable snapped. The fireball plunged into the icy cauldron. The torch erupted, a cone of fire blazing through the translucent body of the chalice, so healthy that its snap cut through the crowd's cries. Sniper and the Prince locked eyes again, and Mycroft squeezed my hand: "We pass the Test."

If anyone in the world could take the podium and pretend not to be rattled right then, it was Aesop Quarriman. Then Hugo Sputnik joined them, *the* Hugo Sputnik! In the flesh! And in the coat which made everything into Hugo Sputnik worlds, and just this once the art team cheated and let Sputnik share their coat program with the spectators' lenses, so you could turn it on and everybody was a Hugo Sputnik creature, and you could see yourself and which Clutch you were, and which your friends were, and the arena looked like the Gilderfield at Optimapolis, and even Spain and Andō Mitsubishi squealed like little kids. Fear faded, and Hugo Sputnik could make even the squirmiest crowd sit through another lecture about Antarctic tech, and how so much of it was developed on the Moon, though that part was mercifully short. We knew the gifts the Utopians had already given to Esperanza City and the Games. Sputnik was here to introduce a new one. A screen unfolded across the sky above us and showed more fireworks, not a tenth as lavish as the first round, but artful in their modesty, so each blast streaked its own lines of blue or red or glitter across the field of stars.

A voice: "Greetings! This is Bradbury Crick speaking from the Mars Odyssey Base. What you are seeing are the first fireworks ever set off on the planet Mars. We launched these fireworks at the same moment that you launched yours in Esperanza City, but it has taken almost eighteen minutes for the images to reach you on Earth. We created these fireworks with native chemicals harvested from the Martian surface, in order to celebrate the technology exchange between Esperanza and Odyssey that made these Olympics possible. On behalf of my fellow Martian residents, I am delighted to help initiate the Games of the One Hundred and Fortieth Olympiad, and to welcome Antarctica to the ever-expanding range of habitat where the human species can live and prosper."

I cannot say Mycroft wept, since Mycroft's eyes had not been dry since the pageantry began, but now they collapsed into weeping. I held them, let them sob, glad to see them so transported by a force other than grief. Then Mycroft caught their breath enough to murmur "Oxygen," and I sobbed too. Fireworks devour oxygen. The chemicals may have been Martian, but precious breaths they fed on were Mars oxygen, crafted over two centuries of agonizing patience by the incremental growth of plants and microorganisms, fed on nutrients extracted from the bodies of Utopian dead. And now they burned it, undid that work, those lives, for this, these Games, to remind wrathful Earth of their solidarity, and salve the public's bitterness about the Harbinger Peacebonding Strike. Their bid to not be Troy. I didn't know enough about terraforming, or fireworks, to guess how much wasting this oxygen would really set things back: a week, a year, a minute; but even if it was only a minute, the thought of it felt hot inside me.

"And now, on behalf of the Utopian Mars Terraforming Project, and following proudly in the footsteps of the organizers of these Esperanza City Games, Hugo Sputnik will present to the Olympic Committee our bid for Odyssey to host the Games of the Two Hundred and Eighteenth Olympiad in the year 2766, three hundred and twelve Earth years from now."

A fresh round of live fireworks joined the Mars broadcast, so we saw them through the screen, and three circles fired on Mars lined up with three fired here to form the six Olympic rings. I hoped the cheers were genuine, not just automatic in the noise and colored lights and the climax of soundtrack and smelltrack. Mycroft believed the crowd was truly moved, but, as people clumped out, blocks of Hiveguard with their bull's-eyes avoiding the Remakers with their V of Vs, it was my task to doubt.

The Games themselves were not spectacular. In fact, the 2454 Olympics set a record for setting the fewest records of any Olympic Games. The flyweight tae kwon do finals were extraordinary, as were the last few rounds of debate. People who know more about the trampoline than I do were excited by some developments there, and the ice sculptures made the distance, boat, and equestrian events spectacular. But on the whole, there was a shadow over the athletes. I don't think it was just the war. People were nervous, knowing that, on the far side of a millimeter's barrier, the air they breathed was deadly cold, and the water they swam in colder than ice. That niggle was enough to make a stretch a hair shorter, a breath a hair shallower, a heartbeat a hair slower, and the whole species just that much further from our best. Our technology was ready to brave Antarctica, but we were not. The seemingly endless stretches of Antarctic night were dispiriting too. Spectator attendance was low all around, record low, except for showstopper events like the pentathlon.

Sniper placed seventeenth. Everyone was shocked except we who knew. It was a wonder they placed that well, with only three days' rehabilitation after months of . . . something. But they took gold in two pistol events. Well we recall the embarrassment at the 2450 Games, when Sniper came second in the pentathlon again, after making such a great fuss about giving up the shooting-only events to concentrate on pentathlon gold. After the rapid-fire pistol gold went to a rather pathetic show from Red Team favorite Yuli Durban, a quiet but infuriated Black Team Captain hauled Sniper down to the pistol range and demanded that they fire a demo round, and Sniper broke the world record right there, where it couldn't count. This time it counted, and when Sniper finally heard their own team anthem play over the winner's platform, I think even they managed to forget the war. It wasn't easy. When the shooters turned up for the match, someone had pasted pictures of the Prince on all the targets. Sniper didn't shout, or redden, just declared they would withdraw from the Games right then if the responsible party didn't confess, remove the pictures, and resign. It was over in eleven minutes.

Best by far were Achilles's exhibition matches. The Olympic Committee didn't let Achilles compete for medals, but let them choose any event they wanted, modern or ancient, and have separate exhibition matches in which any competitor from any discipline could volunteer to participate. Achilles chose a full regimen: boxing, wrestling, the decathlon and all its subsections, long jump, javelin, discus, even the pole vault, which Achilles hated but did anyway, plus hurdles, relay, seven different foot races, one in armor, and the full ancient pentathlon, though the committee had to hunt hard to find drivers who would brave the chariot race. Achilles is something from another world. One glimpse of them in motion is enough to convince anyone, not that Mycroft's tales of Bridger are true, but that there is less difference between the brawniest weightlifter and the sleekest diver than there is between everyone on Earth and this Greek stranger. The doctors who examined Achilles made excited noises about bones which had not grown on our diet, muscles and lungs which had not trained on our air, but seeing is believing. There is nothing extra in Achilles's motion, or their body, just pure, streamlined purpose. If the other athletes were vigorous lions, Achilles was a cheetah, anatomy stripped of everything that wasn't necessary for the perfection of a single goal. For cheetahs it is speed; for Achilles it is clearly war.

Achilles didn't win most of the matches—how could they when they measure barely 150 cm and 41 kg—but they came so impossibly close, this child-sized figure facing giants. Javelin they actually won, the cleanest, most perfect flight of anything I've ever seen a human throw, and they had a completely different starting technique, with a sort of half spin before the final step, so I'm told the sport will never be the same again. They won the run in armor, too, the chariot race, and their pentathlon, and, oddly, the 400-meter and 5,000-meter runs, which somehow were the two where Achilles's tiny stride length was sufficiently compensated for by their incredible sprinting dash and impossible endurance. These exhibition matches were open to anyone, so they were adjudicated like the open divisions, but for the sports that are usually segregated they sized the obstacles to the light/women's class, since Achilles was tinier than all but the slimmest gymnasts. That suited Sniper perfectly, who signed up for half the exhibition matches, and was even on Achilles's relay team. There is a photograph of the handoff,

Achilles's dry, dark fingers almost touching Sniper's, sleek and pale, and other photos of them side by side at starting lines, the ghosts of smiles softening their faces. The 3K run was suspense itself, the pentathlete's native length, which Sniper knows so well. We all forgot the lanky frontrunners as we watched the two small heroes running neck-and-neck the whole way, now Sniper ahead by three paces, now Achilles. It was Sniper's best time ever for the run, and if the camera claims Achilles beat them by some fraction of a meter, our hearts know when to call a tie a tie. Achilles also ran as a pacemaker with the official marathon, where Quarriman took bronze. Whispers wondered why the Committee didn't let Achilles actually compete, but it wasn't the Committee's decision, it was a quiet and apologetic Mycroft who had reminded the eager runner of the truth: "Achilles, you're not human."

I've gone on too long, haven't I? I'm sorry, I'll try to edit better here on out. It's hard to face up to the Closing Ceremony. My mind keeps straying, refusing to focus on what hurts so much. It came on us quickly, as if the Games themselves passed in an hour. Everyone was working throughout, preparing, MASON's industrial machine no less than every corner bash'house stockpiling food and water. By halfway through the Games everything had that trancelike feeling of hyperfocus, more real than real, which comes from binging anti-sleeping meds; it was reckless but we all did it. If there is a Kingdom of Dreams, I bet its gods spent that week wondering where everybody'd gone. But who could sleep when every sofa a neighbor carried in or out might be preparation for a barricade, and every tourist who strayed into an athletes' area might be a more reckless assassin than Sniper? Everyone watched the Games at home, but only out of the corner of the eye, while they practiced first aid drills and self-defense. Then suddenly it was Sunday.

Romanova was overcast, I remember, the kind of glaring white overcast which is painfully bright even if you haven't just come from two weeks of Antarctic night. I arrived with Mycroft and J.E.D.D. Mason; no one would deny Mycroft's right to stand by their Prince in this hour of peril, nor mine to stand by Mycroft. The Forum is no stadium, so the pageantry and parade were still in Esperanza City. Only the opening of the Temple of Janus would take place here. The crowd's colors were garish, Olympic jackets and Nurturist Cousins' wraps, and the Mitsubishi in their summer landscapes. The Hive leaders weren't there, they'd flown to the security of their capitals, and even Vivien had to make a show of Hive patriotism by going to

Buenos Aires. Vivien had hugged me so tight as we said goodbye, and urged me over and over to keep Mycroft safe, and to keep myself safe. I managed the last, at least.

Papa stationed me and Mycroft under the laurel trees between the Senate house and the little temple. Mycroft was tense, but in a healthy way, their stooping cringe gone, so they were all lightness and energy, like a greyhound. Achilles was even more energized, like a hound that's scented blood, and they used the invisibility setting of their Utopian coat to range all over, coordinating the Myrmidons we'd snuck in as a precaution. J.E.D.D. Mason was, as ever, dead as wax. There were no bull's-eyes in the crowd, but there were a lot of black looks. No surprise. The footage from the Opening Ceremony had made everyone realize at last that the faint glow you could see around the Prince on the video of the assassination was Their suit's Griffincloth rebooting. Suddenly what had seemed to be evidence of something supernatural was instead evidence that They conspired with Utopia. If Griffincloth could fake Hugo Sputnik creatures, it could certainly fake a brain getting spattered across the Rostra. There was plenty of proof that one Griffincloth suit jacket had no power to trick many cameras from many angles, or to produce the stains science had verified as Their cerebral-spinal fluid on the stones, but people wanted to doubt, so they seized this thread and ran.

The Temple of Janus looks like someone's overdecorated shed, barely tall enough to be called a proper building, with the edges of the peaked roof so low that visitors can take rubbings of the embossed roof tiles. The sculptures of garlands that sealed it shut were not designed to be removed, but workmen had weakened them the night before, to make the ceremony go smoothly. The temple is modeled exactly on what we think the ancient one was like, with two gates on opposite ends, so the winds of change can blow clear through the temple of the god of beginnings, changes, ends, and end-times. It felt like end-times. We were sure apocalypse would come, we just didn't know from where. Would some assassin—imitating Sniper—shoot the Prince the instant the gates were open? Would the mob charge in? Would fire rain down, like it had on Brussels? Sniper and Bryar had made endless speeches about how everyone should be allowed to leave the Games safely before the war began, but a game of hide-and-seek without a fixed amount of time you have to wait before pursuit becomes a game of tag. We had every safeguard imaginable: people, robots, devices, and Utopia had enough invisible monsters in the area that I smelled zoo. But I had every war film ever boogeymanning my imagination. At least we didn't have to fear the mushroom cloud. If we died here today, it would be a reasonable number of us, a portion of the city, not an eternal scar upon Nature and human conscience. Thank Utopia.

The Prince was to open one set of temple gates. Morally, Sniper should have opened the other, but it was too tricky working out how far to let them flee before Papa could pursue, and there was no way we could have kept Dominic from trying something. So it fell to the Censor, Jung Su-Hyeon Ancelet Kosala, the last neutral figurehead Earth has, to pry open the second set of doors. (Here I edited out a long ramble about my friendship with Su-Hyeon, which I realize was just my mind avoiding what comes next; I am the Anonymous, successor to Voltaire and Custodian of the Age of Reason, but even I cannot pretend the mind is tame.)

No one would call J.E.D.D. Mason a sensualist, but They do use the senses in ways most of us forget to. They ran Their hands over the doors, the touch of bronze, of stone, of dust, They smelled it, tapped it, listened. My introduction to Plato said they thought disembodied souls were like flying eyeballs that could see 360 degrees, but got trapped in bodies that could only see 120, so were always unhappy, like if you have one eye taped shut. That never hit home for me until the first time I saw how desperately the Prince uses the crutches of Their senses. I thought I heard Them whisper: "With this We make war?"

Su-Hyeon just stood clutching the prybar like a teddy bear.

Murmur became silence.

It was time.

Mycroft returned to stand beside me, and I politely looked away as they faced a laurel tree, and closed their eyes, and pretended not to be praying. I remember a shard of sun that raked their hat, how the fibers had little auras of fire. Su-Hyeon and the Prince put their bars to the garlands, and we, who had just witnessed the human perfection of Achilles racing Sniper, watched the un-perfection of two human bodies trained for desks and data pulling on crowbars with all their clumsy might. Su-Hyeon's gave first, the garland falling with a clatter, and they jumped back, as if they'd dropped a knife while chopping in the kitchen. The Prince's clattered second, and then the two grasped the rings of the bronze doors and pulled. The groan of metal against rock made me think of tanks and armor and exploding shells. Mycroft's right about how pictures of history hit us harder than we know. Just like how images of skirts and corsets taught us enough gender to let Joyce Faust sink their claws into the world, so images of gore and weapons had us all pretraumatized, ready to flinch at sounds we imagined should remind us of battle noises no one has really heard since the Church War.

I held my breath. Leaves stirred in the dust as the wind blew through the open temple. I let one breath out and took another as the seconds of hush ticked by. The world hadn't ended yet. Mycroft looked at me. We were all ready to react, not to act. Whispers started, and craning of necks. Somehow it didn't occur to me until then to wonder what was *in* the temple. The ancient one would've had a statue of Janus with their double face looking both ways. I couldn't see from where I stood, but Su-Hyeon was clearly peering in at something. Except now there was a murmur, and a voice which pierced the murmur.

"Mordred?" It was a cutting voice, worried.

A second voice: "Curie? Curiosity, can you hear me? Hello?"

Third: "Oz? Come in, Oz?"

"Poe? What's going on? Poe? Answer me! Poe!"

Now all in a torrent, different voices all around the Forum screamed out names: "Kepler! Milton! Caspian! Quark! Avalon! Watson! Kirk! Adamant! Euclid! Svalinn! Joyeuse! Kili! Pix! Mallory! Fermi! Phoenix! Delany! Olivant! Polo! Clarke! Dragon! Shenzhou! Venture! Franken! Tianlong! Hal! Gulliver! Leto! Freeport! Bochica! Hadaly! Elric! Zamyatin! Quasar! Vimana! Galileo! Talaria! Shadow! Earheart! Pluto! Arcadia! Jules! Vinndálf! Kelvin! Sherwood! Mercury! Helicon! Bard! Zuse! Aegis! Wukong! Cabal! Chaucer! Galaxi! Kusanagi! Leif! Coyote! Bletchley! Ijiraq! Starbuck! Thule! Mina! Hyperion! Mulan! Atom! Yuri! Pan! Spaceway! Capricorn! Storm! Grimm! Kamalu! Perrin! Condor! Asphodel! Nig! Sirius! Kennedy! Appleseed! Enkidu! Han! Stardust! Abbas! Lyra! Altair! Deimos! Grendel! Char! Langley! Faun! Tesla! Carnwennan! Mab! Ovid! Gandiva! Akatsuki! Argo! Sampo! Turing! Jinn!" and finally, "Atlantis! They've attacked Atlantis!"

A rush of wing wind overflowed the Forum, tossing leaves, clothes, hair. Creatures lifted off all around us. We could only see them as they rose to go, abandoning invisibility for speed: rocs, hippogriffs, giant ravens, pterosaurs, dragonflies as long as horses, the twining flight-slither of Asian dragons, the hot, leathery flap of European dragons, and the rustle of coats as the U-beasts' Utopian partners swung into their saddles, the Delian sun sigil blazing on every back. Bright fluttering things swarmed up too fast to name, joined by robots whose designers loved metal too much to feign biology, and above my head something between a kite and a stingray undulated on the wind in folds of turquoise and copper. The sky was color. Animals appeared too, and spread translucent rainbow wing films, so I saw a jaguar take to the air, a golden stag, a python, wolves, and unicorns, and hounds, and antelope. Every rider whose beast could hold two helped another rider on, so the sky lit up with overlapping coats that turned the clouds into cities and those cities into stars. Then all at once the sky's glare seemed to turn harsh, but it was the coats, a hundred in the sky, two hundred, more, which all together turned to mourning static, blank save for the crisp lines of Delian suns.

A rolling thunderboom reached us from the north now, muffled and too deep, so I felt the vibration in my bones more than I heard it. That made it real. Sardinia is small; it was less than ten kilometers northwest from the Forum to the north coast of the island, then another twenty kilometers of sea to where New Atlantis nestled on the seafloor between the encircling coasts of Sardinia and Corsica, like a chick cupped by kindly hands. I had visited Utopia's underwater city myself, seen the crystal bubble-domes framed by struts whose surfaces teemed with barnacles and weedy life. I had schooled there with wrasse and damselfish along arched shopping galleries, swim-raced friends from spire to spire, played fetch with octopus, and watched patrolling hippocampus herd young sharks away to safer waters. I spent a week there once, long enough to half forget the pack that breathed for me, to stop craving the air-filled sections, and to almost shake the terror of the warning videos about how, if I returned to the surface world too fast, my blood would bubble and bring pain, paralysis, and death. Someone had attacked Atlantis. The blast had been big, big enough to feel thirty kilometers away, but how big? Small enough to crush some structures, flood the airy sections, but leave the swimmers safe? Big enough to end all life in the ocean city in an instant? Or was it cruelly in between, so helpless thousands were now being dragged up by the currents toward the sunny surface, screaming like Icarus?

Now I realized Mycroft wasn't next to me. I panicked, spun, searched, saw. Mycroft always said that they could fly. This run was flight, a run across the crowd, leaping from shoulder to shoulder like a mantis, taking off again when each startled human foothold toppled. True it was Earth and leg muscle that lifted Mycroft then, not air and wing, but what is flight if not soaring above those who let gravity confine them? Mycroft leapt, and seized the leg of a whirring robot with both arms, and, after a moment's indecision, the Delian rider helped Mycroft swing up to ride behind them. I heard Huxley beside me mutter as they mounted their own black lion to join the exodus. A whole layer of life lifted away from the Forum, taking with it color, texture, animal breath, and a hundred brilliant suns, leaving the Forum gray.

It took Papadelias's curses over my tracker to make me remember it was my job to make sure Mycroft didn't run away. I ran three useless paces. What could I do? There lay Mycroft's hat in the dust beside me. Could I call Huxley? Make them bring Mycroft back? Huxley's parting mutter had been a curse, I realized; Mycroft had evaded them, too. Martin, Papa, and I had debated whether to handcuff Mycroft to one of us as usual, but decided for the ceremony, just this once, that it was safer to keep Mycroft mobile, ready to dodge, and help. And there they went to help. I should help too. That was the solution: catch up with Mycroft at the shore. There would be a rescue mission, nurses, decompression tanks, boats, blankets, and I would find Mycroft again. I babbled the situation to the Prince, Who digested it in masklike silence, which somehow awoke dread's first traces in me, like the first scent of some deadly gas.

The Prince called a special car to take me to the coast as quickly as was safe with the airspace full of wonders. I was to meet Achilles there, who had hitched a giant bat, and was shouting commands to all Myrmidons to follow as we could. I thought about it more now. Atlantis was defenseless. At MASON's order every aquatic U-beast had been on the far side of the sea chasing the *Sanctum Sanctorum* violators, every hippocampus and seahound and panoctopus and plasma-ray and kraken, absent in this moment that the billion arrows of complacent Earth flew, just as Mycroft feared. That was the thought in my mind when my tracker bleeped the tsunami alert.

It feels like a cruel joke calling it a small tsunami. I've been told it wasn't a nuclear device that collapsed the city, just many smaller blasts, plus the implosion of the city structure. The safety systems in my car refused to go within four kilometers of the coast with the tsunami warning; I had to land and run the rest of the way. Images flowed in of the water receding from the beach, of the crest, at first just a band of different blue across the sea's horizon, which only an expert could read as danger. Satellite photos showed the blast zone as bull's-eye ripples around a heart of bubbling froth, but only as they neared the coast did the crests swell into monsters. Mycroft was airborne, I told myself. Utopia's soaring rescue force is safe from even the ocean's longest claws. Still, I ran harder. Footage from the coast showed colorful wings and coats of static hovering high among the gulls as the tsunami hurled sailboats and shards of dock against the walks and shops of Romanova's famous northern beachfront. I ran even harder. A camera bot zoomed in on flotsam and bodies bobbing on the sea. I ran harder yet, or was it that the running grew more difficult? When I reached the coast, it was all hospital floats and volunteers. The fantastic vanguard had moved on, flying across the waves to the blast's heart, leaving on shore only common human chaos. Spotting my uniform, everyone was quick to offer me work, but a ride out to sea was a long time begging.

Neverland rushed to Atlantis to save Utopia. The brightness of the wild fleet felt like hope itself when my tracker showed them approaching the froth-white epicenter. We on the coast were trapped, but they came from the west, where the tsunami crests were but one more ripple on the belly of the sea. The Seaborn nation-strat loved Atlanteans like bas'sibs, and knew every current of the Mediterranean, and the dangers of the human blood-stream, too, which was the survivors' true enemy as eddies bore them surfaceward. Houseboats, racing yachts, schooners, ferries, silverjacks, spitting hydrofoils, and tiny runabouts all knew their parts as the voice of Graylaw Tribune Jay Sparhawk and the salt-white sails of the *Ahab's Folly* led the rescue. Dragons and griffins flocked to them, and robots sparkling against the broad jewel of the sea. Utopia's static-bright vanguard alighted on the boats and deferred to the instructions of those who know waves as we know sidewalks. People were hauled from the sea, the drowning given breath, the dying dignity. Then explosions ricocheted across the seascape, white and savage. I still don't know what they were: mines, time bombs, leftovers, some accident of pressure as further infrastructure burst below, but I saw one explosion claim a brave water taxi, another a shimmering milliwing, another a schooner whose planks shattered in the blast, and then the medical alert told me that Mycroft was unconscious, then that their blood oxygen was dropping, dropping, and the pressure rising, rising, and then the heartbeat stopped. I shrieked, begged, attacked a nurse and stole their hoverbed and started out, and Achilles marshaled a ship, and Papa barked orders from HQ, and MASON sent a special force, and Huxley let the Sea Knights know, and the Nemo Watch, and O.C.E.A.N.U.S., and all that time the heartless tracker kept on making us watch a green line fall as Mycroft's blood grew stiller and more toxic, and the pressure gauge ticked off meter by meter the sinking of the corpse.

It wasn't real as long as I was still working, helping Neverland haul bodies from the sea. It wasn't real as long as my arms burned, and fresh tasks made time blur. It wasn't real at sunset. It wasn't real when strong arms dragged me to a bed, and made me realize I was too exhausted to rise again. It wasn't real when I was carried back to Romanova, and laid on sofa plush, and commanded to eat soup. Mycroft couldn't drown, Mycroft was Mycroft. It was another trick, a plan. We didn't have a body. They would turn up again, bruised and salty, or O.S. would call to say they had them, or Madame. But the tracker kept transmitting. Maybe they slipped their tracker? No, they couldn't anymore. Not even Papadelias has the authority to make prisoner attach a tracker nonremovably, but MASON could have a *Familiaris*'s head grafted onto a zebra if they wanted, and had granted with vindictive enthusiasm Papa's request have a surgeon make Mycroft's tracker permanent. Now that tracker counted out the stages of decomposition. We would've sent a diving team after the signal, but there were so many corpses, and so many survivors waiting injured in the depths, we couldn't waste resources hunting for one body. After seven hours the signal started moving, the flesh still with it, and the tracker registered the belly acid of some fatted sea beast. A few hours later even the flesh was gone.

It still didn't feel real. If I had seen them die, if we had had a body, a photograph, blood in the water, then maybe, but we had nothing, and nothing felt like nothing. Missing in action. Lost at sea. Mycroft could have walked in through my door anytime, full of excuses. And there were injured to treat, and actions to plan, and I was still working from the sofa when J.E.D.D. Mason came in, with Their suit set to white mourning static like the coats, and walked up to me, and stood there staring with Their black eyes, and said in Their gentle monotone: "Mycroft was." That was all. They came all that way just to say it to me. They knew I needed to hear it. I needed to hear it. And then I said it to myself inside, and it was real.

My nose itched, and my cheeks were wet, and my eyes were hot. I got up and ran. I didn't know where I was running, but there was Papa's office—no one stopped me—into Papa's office, and there was Papa, and their cheeks were wet, and their eyes were red, and we hugged each other so tight, and we screamed. I'd never screamed crying before, but it came. There was no difference between the sounds: screams, sobs, gasps, mine, Papa's, together. Mycroft always said no one should mourn them. Well, shut up, Mycroft, we're going to make you eat your lunch, and take your pills, and sleep your hours, and rest your rest, and we're going to mourn you, and there's nothing you can do to stop us.

And we're going to make sure your damned seeds fly.

Except it's so, so kind that Mycroft doesn't have to see this stupid war. See people praising the Atlantis strike. Oh, at some point someone announced that Atlantis was where the Utopians had hidden the harbinger adepts, the willing ones who consented to go with them and give Utopia a monopoly on Armageddon. Now most of them are gone, and no one (or fewer people anyway) can end the world. We're all supposed to feel safer. And a lot of people do feel safer. Except who knows if it's true. And even if it is true, they—we! Human beings!—we built a dream city under the sea, and then we blew it up. "To keep the world safe!" Maybe. I do like the world. But I loved that city, and they killed thousands of people, and while they weren't all innocent, they were all dedicated to the quest to conquer death, age, and the stars. I suppose Atlantis will become one of those city names that means 'atrocity' forever now, like Hiroshima. But there's no room left in me for that to sink in. Mycroft is dead. I want to say "the best and wisest person I've ever known is dead" but saying that of Mycroft Canner feels wrong, even though it also feels so right. What am I supposed to do now? Write an obituary? I'm the Anonymous, I have to write an obituary for civilization as we know it, not just Mycroft Canner. Then someone said I'd better take over Mycroft's chronicle and—strange, I just finished crying, I didn't expect this sentence to make me start again. Someone said I'd better take over Mycroft's chronicle. So here I am.

That was the first day of the war.

HERE ENDS
The Will to Battle
Mycroft Canner's Chronicle
of how Humanity learned to make War again

HERE BEGINS THE WAR ITSELF
whose Chronicle I name
for Mycroft's hope and mine
Perhaps the Stars